Michael F. Russell grew up on the Isle of Barra before leaving to study Social Sciences at the University of Glasgow, followed by a postgraduate diploma in Journalism Studies at the University of Strathclyde. He is deputy editor at the *West Highland Free Press* and writes occasionally for the *Sunday Herald*. His writing has appeared in *Gutter, Northwords Now and Fractured West*. His debut novel, *Lie of the Land*, was shortlisted for the Saltire Awards 'First Book of the Year' (2015). Michael lives on Skye with his partner and two children.

Lie of the Land

MICHAEL F. RUSSELL

First published in hardback in Great Britain in 2015 by
Polygon, an imprint of Birlinn Ltd.
This paperback edition published in 2016 by Polygon.

West Newington House
10 Newington Road
Edinburgh
EH9 1QS

www.polygonbooks.co.uk

ISBN 978 1 84697 360 4
eBook ISBN 978 0 85790 840 7

British Library Cataloguing in Publication Data
A catalogue record for this book is available on request
from the British Library.

The publishers acknowledge investment from Creative Scotland
towards the publication of this volume.

Typeset by 3btype.com

For Helena, Danny and Joe

October

1

Carl closed the graveyard's rusty metal gate, breathing hard, lungs aching from the effort of walking. What was it – about half a mile from the hotel? Too fast, he'd gone far too fast for a body that had spent most of a month lying flat and then a week shuffling between rooms.

Crows rasped in the trees as the wind freshened from off the sea. The place reeked of wet earth and rotting leaves. He felt light-headed, dizzy, the fresh air knifing his lungs. He coughed, hawking a gobbet onto the gravel path that skirted the graveyard.

He soon found Howard's grave, a fresh mound next to those of the two German tourists. Carl stood for a while, then dropped to his haunches and scooped a handful of earth from Howard's grave.

An oystercatcher alarm-called as it flew, arrowing level with the dark-rock shoreline. He had come to know the sound of the bird. The soil was cold and sticky in his hand.

'Sorry,' he whispered, throwing the handful back onto the pile. His throat tightened. 'Why did I fucking listen to you? Why did I let you do it?' He gasped for breath. 'Where is everything? What am I doing here?'

Now that the fever had left him, realising where he was and what had happened threatened to blot out every other thought and feeling. Consciousness without purpose was now the dominant state. Never waking up at all would have been better.

Mistakes: to the nth power.

The world was dead, and he had helped kill it, in his own little way. Call it a sin of omission. Carl could add his only friend to the list of the dead while he was at it. There was guilt enough to gorge on, with extra guilt to go. It entered his bloodstream with every breath, all washed down with a cold glass of grief.

He stood for a moment, staring down at the grave. Insects crawled on the rectangular mound of earth. They had a job to do, above and below the ground. Wind stirred the trees again, making them sway and creak. Everything had an appointed function, except him.

There was an obvious destination: somewhere he had to go. As he looked around the bay, judging distances, Carl wondered if he could make it. Going back to where Howard died meant taking one of two routes: he could cross to the south headland, on the main road, before heading inland and into the hills. But that meant going through the main part of the village. Which meant people, and the gauntlet of shock and sympathy. Or he could continue the way he had come, up the back road over the north headland. That way he'd avoid people, but it also took him away from where he needed to go, behind the village, over rough ground, circling around Inverlair and to the south. Call it nine miles of trudging through heather and bogs. That would take him hours, if he managed it at all. With no real conviction, he set off for the hard way.

On the back road up and out of Inverlair Bay, past the church and the community hall and the start of the forestry track, he made it as far as the roadblock, a line of shin-high boulders splashed with red paint. Never mind being at the edge of the world, he couldn't have gone much further anyway.

He sat on the stones, gasping for breath. To his right, over a rusty barbed-wire fence, fields of rushes and thistles sloped down towards the grey sea. He scanned the horizon for a white boat, for salvation, but saw nothing except the fusing of cloud and water.

Some way off the road was a derelict old house, windowless,

with a ragged corrugated-iron roof. To his left, the hills rose to the fissured rocky summit of Ben Bronach, and beyond, to the deer forest. After a few minutes Carl got up and, standing at the roadblock with his hands in his coat pockets, considered the road ahead. He stepped over the painted boulders.

Maybe today was the day when the world would open up again. He could drive away from Inverlair. He could leave Room 14 and Simone and the baby, today, the eighty-second day of his confinement. This would be the last day he'd have to spend here, in this prison refuge. The redzone would open. Its signal would fail.

He took Howard's deltameter out of his pocket and watched the EMF waveform on the screen, spiking at 85 microtesla today, close to the active neural level. Another hundred metres or so and, he knew, the buzzing sound would start in his head. Another two hundred after that and the pain would skewer through his head, from temple to temple. Any further and sleep was death.

Today was not the day. But he'd known that anyway. There would be no escape. Even before he took his dead friend's gadget out of his pocket to check the signal he knew what it would tell him.

•

The next day, he stood in Room 14's en suite, in front of the mirror. Pits of ash where his eyes had been, thick phlegm-flecked beard and limp coils of oily hair.

With a pair of borrowed scissors he cut his beard to a point where shaving could finish the job. Without hot water it stung and he nicked the skin a few times as he went, hair filling the sink, red drops on the thin scum of soap and grease. Even though the razor was blunt he managed to shave off half his beard, stopping to touch the hairless side of his face, the fever-scooped hollows where his cheeks had been. Two months ago his face had been full and he hadn't felt like a decrepit wreck of a man.

Death had looked in on him, given his lungs a squeeze, then let him go. *I'll be back later for you, pal. Take care of yourself – until I take care of you.*

Neck next, and he was done; now to complete the transformation, from stinking caveman to heroin chic all in a few snips. Reaching above his ear he gathered a handful of greasy, matted hair, and started cutting until he was right down to the scalp. Getting rid of his hair made the scab on his forehead stand out. He tried to forget how it had happened, and continued cutting. The person he'd been must be somewhere underneath this feral disguise. He must be.

That night, Carl stood on the hotel's first-floor landing. Above the dark stairwell there was a stained-glass window, red roses and green petals on a blue background, the full moon blazing the colours alive. He heard an owl hooting. This is Tuesday, he said to himself, as he gazed, open-mouthed, at the moon-bright glass. Nearly a week since the fever had left his bleached bones washed up in a single bed.

He was hungry again. Appetite had been reborn. And that was a good thing, on balance. Resurrection. Coming back from the brink. Five days he'd been up and about, and now it was time to visit the ground floor. Maybe even rejoin what was left of the human race. He was in the grip of life now. He took a deep breath and, as planned, his lungs cracked a volley of phlegm, which he spat into a hankie. In the soundless night, it wouldn't do to cough in an inconvenient place and alert anyone to his presence.

On his seventh step down, the stairs creaked. Carl held his breath, gaping up at the stained-glass roses shining in the moonlight. What did he expect to happen? Simone's dad come stomping through from the annexe, dressing gown flying, shotgun at the ready? The only sound was the clock ticking in the lobby; moon glinting on the brass pendulum as it measured the night.

It was even darker on the ground floor as Carl made his way

along the lobby past reception, through the fire door and into the annexe, cupping the candle, which he'd stuck onto a saucer. He waited a few seconds, listening out for signs of life, letting the fire door swing gently back into place. But there was nothing except his own breathing as he crept into the kitchen. It was still warm; he could feel heat radiating from the stove. There wasn't much to eat: the remains of a mushroom omelette in the fridge along with milk and some butter, still chilled, even though the generator was off for the night. And fish, of course. At least there was no question of an Omega 3 deficiency. No danger of that in this place. Insanity maybe, but at least his heart wouldn't pack in.

He set the candle and saucer down on the worktop, next to a kid's storybook. Simone kept things as normal as she could for her boy. Fair play to her.

Carl ate.

Scoffing the greasy slab of omelette with his fingers, he saw an open black bin bag on the wicker kitchen chair. He reached into it.

His jaw stopped working.

The bag was full of baby clothes, sleepsuits and tiny vests. He lowered the candle to read the handwritten label taped to the bag: Under Three Months.

He laid a sleepsuit out flat on the table, adjusting the position of the candle so he could get a better look. The suit was pink with little smiling teddies on it. The bag of clothes certainly answered The Burning Question. Carl imagined the pink suit filled with a screaming, red-faced baby.

Without warning the candle fell over and went out, the air heavy with smoke.

Darkness.

Fuck. He hadn't melted enough wax on to the saucer.

He wondered if he could negotiate his way back upstairs, in darkness, without knocking anything over. As he visualised the obstacles, his eyes grew accustomed to the lack of light. Gathering candle and saucer, he crept into the hallway. There were no windows in the corridor between the annexe and the actual hotel, and it was darker there, but he could still make out all the important shapes to avoid, the edge of the reception desk. And the big brass bell, on its stand by the front door, a touch of baronial charm for the tourists. Better not knock that bugger over.

He was near the annexe fire door when he heard a sound from upstairs. It was Simone's dad, George, sobbing, groaning and calling out in his sleep. Carl froze. There came another, quieter moan. Then silence.

Bad dream, probably. Everyone had them. Dreams of death, playing on a loop. Anyway, there was now food in his belly, and he felt like he needed something to wash it down.

Making his way through to the public bar he nudged a table, low to his left, and set something rocking on top of it. The ornament, or whatever it was, shook, but stayed upright, thank Christ.

And breathe again. Take it slow through another fire door, between the chairs and tables. Past the pool table, baize under his fingertips. He mustn't rush it. There was always the unexpected obstacle.

He reached the storeroom door. There were no windows here, so the moon couldn't light his way. Easy does it now, one slow foot-sliding step at a time. He edged to the back of the storeroom, knew which forgotten cardboard box to find, felt the edge of the cold metal filing cabinet, then down and along to the box. Flipping the flaps open he took out four bottles, one at a time, careful not to let them clink together. Carl put a bottle into each pocket of his dressing gown, carried the other two in one hand, by their necks, candle and saucer in the other hand. He was fully laden now, and there was no room for mistakes. Watch that table in the corridor. Mind the big brass bell. Ease open the fire door, hook it with a foot. Let it sink back nice and quiet. And whatever happens, don't bloody cough.

For the second night in a row Carl sat in Room 14, on the edge of his bed, four bottles of lime-green alcofizz inside him. He watched his palmpod's on-screen clock count the seconds, considered – then rejected – the idea of watching a certain personal video file.

Tomorrow he would have to endure real-time interaction with George and Simone. He'd put that off for long enough.

The booze he had just guzzled equated to less than two pints, but he was pissed nonetheless. Weight loss and illness had reduced his tolerance for alcohol. It was 2.37 a.m. He lurched over to the windowsill, unsteady on his feet. The fat bluebottle that only this morning had bounced and buzzed against the room's dormer window, in thrall to the light, was dead, stiff legs in the air. He had watched the fly pound the glass, unable to stop what it was doing. If only the fly had known the impossibility of breaking through the glass it might have stopped. It might have accepted imprisonment and fate, making no fuss about its situation and inevitable end in Room 14 of Inverlair Hotel. That would be the sensible thing to do.

Rolling into bed, he pulled the duvet around him and closed his eyes. He dreamed of a giant baby that cried all night and would never go to sleep. Being so big, the screaming kid was dangerous. It might roll over and crush the life he'd only just regained back out of him.

2

Brittle brown leaves swirled around the garden. Staring into space George stood, rake in hand. Wind ruffled his grey hair. It was cold today. Dry. His jacket was on but wasn't zipped up against the morning chill. George tried not to look at the carved oak bench nestling beneath the ivy-covered trellis at the bottom of the garden. Maybe he should store it in the shed now. The bench could do with a coat of wood stain anyway, and that's something he could never face doing.

It had been their bench; the two of them used to sit on it. In future there would be only him. Maybe he should stick the bench in the shed after all. No luck with the leaves today, too windy to rake them up.

He stood there, clutching the rake, as the dead leaves flew where the wind took them. Part of him wanted to smash the bench into pieces.

Unless George kept tight control, it would start in his stomach, the spasm of awareness, and from there it would engulf him. Pain and sadness would sweep him away, and he would crumble again. But remembering was so sweet, even as it made ashes of his heart. That was the thing he couldn't get right in his head: the sweetness of letting memory swim in his blood, and the nausea of grief that came with remembering her. He was frightened of remembering his wife, and just as frightened of forgetting her.

He examined the rake he held in his hands, looked towards the pine trees and the hills as if someone was there, in the distance, waiting for him.

What had he been doing? No luck with the leaves. Too windy to bother with them.

'Dad!' Simone stood on the back step of the annexe, a cardboard box in her hands. George thought he heard a voice. He found himself staring at his daughter, and remembering laughter from long ago.

'Come and see what I've found in the loft.'

Let the leaves swirl and leave the rubbish in the loft, girl. Nothing up there but dust.

George straightened his back. 'What is it?' He put the rake back in the garden shed, in its proper place.

Simone came over, took a small paper sachet out of the box for her father to sniff; in the box there were many more: coffee, sugar, tiny cartons of milk and — holy of holies — about twenty cellophane mini-packs of biscuits, two in each. Shortbread, mainly, but there were a few custard creams.

George's face fell. 'We ordered too much stock. Then the bookings dried up. It was before you came back.' He sniffed the coffee again. 'We stopped putting them in the rooms after that.'

He dropped the sachet back in the box, bit hard on the memory. Can't keep that kind of pain in the fucking shed. 'This should really be handed in to the committee,' he said, wiping his hands on his trousers.

'It will,' said Simone, trying to catch her father's eye. 'But I thought we could sit down and have a cup of coffee and a biscuit first. One each, that's all.'

She smiled. George nodded, touched his daughter's arm, and they went inside.

Stale. He figured the biscuit would be, but it was still satisfyingly sweet. George sipped his coffee, fingering crumbs on the tabletop. He thought about how he could broach the subject of the father-to-be who was lurking upstairs.

The oak bench would not be moved from its place.

•

That evening, Carl crept along the annexe hallway. The kitchen door was open and he could see the table laid for dinner, pots bubbling away on the stove; George was fussing over the food as Simone sat at the table, her son on her lap.

'I can't fix the games visor, darling. I don't know why it's broken.'

But Isaac wasn't entirely convinced by his mother's lack of expertise. She had to fix it. The visor had to be fixed so he could play the game. Why couldn't she see that?

Carl coughed in the kitchen doorway, rubbing the stubble on his head self-consciously. The kid looked at him, open-mouthed, eyes wide.

Clothes too big. Shirt like a sack. Trousers belted on a skewered hole. Carl felt like shit and probably looked it too. Can't blame the kid for staring.

Standing at the kitchen door, he wasn't quite sure what to do. He shifted from foot to foot. 'Smells good.'

Startled at first, George said hello and went back to his pots, ladling stew into bowls. Carl sat down at the table.

As he ate, he became conscious of the watchers and the silence. Maybe he shouldn't have made the effort to smarten himself up. He glanced round the table, carried on eating. 'I'm still alive,' he stated. 'I'm not the ghost at the feast, I hope.'

George sniffed. 'I wouldn't call it a feast.'

Carl smiled. 'Thanks.' He caught Simone's eye. 'For everything.' She nodded.

The boy had lost interest in his food. Isaac was silent, eyeing the skeletal stranger from upstairs who had appeared like magic, like the first time. Only back then lots of bad things had happened. Maybe he was going to make more bad things happen this time.

Carl slurped his stew, though he had no appreciation of what he was eating, only a studied lifting of the spoon. He began to sweat, food and silent awkwardness going to work on him.

'The *Aurora* was out the other day and came across a yacht, a big one,' said George, trying to ease the tension.

'Yeah,' said Carl, the food dry in his mouth. 'Simone said.' He took a sip of water.

George offered another forkful of food to Isaac, but the boy squirmed in his seat, lips clamped shut and eyes on Carl. George shook his head, exasperated. 'You're far too old for this nonsense. Do we have any of those biscuits left?'

'I don't know,' she said. 'But I do know there is something sweet for boys who eat their dinner.'

George pressed the fork up to the boy's mouth. It could have been a shit-covered slug Isaac was being asked to eat, but, after a prolonged show of disgust, he accepted the piece of boiled carrot.

'It's a pity about the yacht,' said Carl.

Isaac chewed another mouthful. Every time Carl spoke he felt pinned back by the boy's stare. Maybe the kid knows the truth.

'A lot of gear on a boat that size,' agreed George. 'She wasn't in sail, probably broke her moorings down the coast in the storm last week. But the tide took her into the redzone.'

The only two questions that mattered to Carl had been answered: the redzone was still there and Simone was still pregnant. Nothing else really mattered.

'Too bad,' he said.

His mind blank, Carl ate quickly, desperate to leave the table. Isaac's unyielding scrutiny hastened his exit.

Stop staring at me, you little fucker, or I'll stick that fork in your fucking eye.

After dinner he made for the hotel's residents' lounge, where a fire burned beneath a grand hardwood mantelpiece. There was a massive portrait above the fireplace, of some bewigged gentleman of yore gleaming with brocade and buckles, a sword hanging by his side. The guy had more or less founded Inverlair, back when war meant Napoleon. Captain Theodore Melkins looked very satisfied with himself, his military colours and stern smugness glowing above the mantelpiece. It's amazing how something as simple as processing potash from seaweed could make a man important enough to be preserved in oils.

Carl went over to the bookshelves. He pulled out a book on geology, and sat down by the fire.

He read: 'The Moine Thrust is a linear geological feature in the Scottish Highlands which runs . . . extensive landscape of rolling hills over a metamorphic . . . Ben More Assynt (pictured) in the centre of the belt, is a typical example that rises from a glen of limestone caves . . .'

He recognised the picture in the book straight away. There was no mistaking it. Now he had a name to go with the unmistakable image of the mountain. Suddenly, as if a switch had been thrown, a hail shower machine-gunned against the high casement windows. Carl jumped at the sound of ice clattering on glass.

Fetching a dog-eared road atlas, he traced a path all the way up from Glasgow, along the edge of the Moine Thrust, until he found Ben More Assynt on the map. He recognised it from the drive up, a million years before, looming like something out of legend. Now he knew the mountain's name; maybe he'd climb it one day. Everything has an identity: a name and a purpose. Even hills. That was the rule. Surely there were still rules to obey.

Tectonics and the Moine Thrust were the reason for Ben More Assynt's existence. Shifts and faults and time: a combination that could produce innumerable consequences.

He pulled another book from the shelf: *Highland Animals*. Flicking though the pages he learned that adders are Britain's only poisonous snakes and are found throughout the Highlands. *Vipera berus* was sure to sink its fangs into him at some point. Perhaps its bite would prove fatal.

3

Thick cord rattled against the metal flagpole. Maybe another electrical storm was on its way.

Carl looked up at the gathering clouds, and wondered what would happen if lightning struck the viewpoint flagpole. Would an arc of current reach out and fry him?

No flag flew above Inverlair. Maybe the pole had never been used. But there were wooden picnic benches, flaking apart, below on the crumbling concrete platforms, and the concrete stairway that led to the viewpoint was overgrown with a gnarled prickly plant. It had yellow flowers: dollops of sunlight on stunted branches. Honeysuckle was yellow – he knew that, so maybe that's what the plant was. Surrounding the flagpole, at the highest point of the picnic site, was a waist-high concrete wall. Carl picked his way up the steps, his jeans snagging on inch-long thorns.

He was now facing inland and had a clear view of the whole village, the steel-grey length of Inverlair Bay, and the tops of the mountains beyond, to the south and east. The hills in the distance could be five miles away, or they could be fifty. It was impossible to tell. There was an interpretative weatherproofed plaque, angled like a lectern, set into the viewpoint's wall. Each mountain peak on the inland horizon was named, and the area's geology described. The plaque told him he was exactly 190 metres above sea level.

The wind whipped the flagpole's cord again. Carl turned up his collar against the cold breeze, read the rest of what was written on the plaque, then took the steps back down to the path that eventually came out near the hotel's moss-covered car park. One old car – tyres flat, packed with junk – lay abandoned in a corner.

Almost a thousand metres of ice. That's what the plaque had said. Ten thousand years ago there would only have been the tops of the highest hills poking through, nothing but rock and scree and the grinding ice advance.

The path down to the hotel branched off and took him onto the north road, beyond the last house, where he could relax, the pressure of curious others falling away. He turned up the forestry track and headed inland, between blocks of tightly packed pine trees, up the boulder-strewn slopes of Ben Bronach. Two hundred metres up from the road, beyond the greying swarf of felled timber, an excavator-type digger stood, hydraulic arm poised. Yesterday he had seen it working, roaring, buzz-sawing, stripping and sectioning trunks into manageable lengths, each one processed in less than a minute. He walked the wide access track into the scented forest, climbing, then along a narrow trail, teasing out the contours of Ben Bronach, on a walk he knew too well.

On the hill's shoulder he looked down on the village. Inverlair was definitely a rosier prospect from here than seeing it up close. He felt his mind wander, growing less focused. Up here on the hillside there was nothing but wind and open sky to bother him. Even in the middle of Glasgow he hadn't felt so suffocated, even with CivCon snoopers breathing down his neck 24/7. It was good to get out, to get better, good to walk out of the hotel and away from the village. He was stronger now; a week of generous portions had fattened him.

He walked.

There was only one destination that mattered. No point in pretending otherwise. Now that he was well enough he could get there easy enough, following the sheep track through Ben Bronach's gullies, along the hill's northern ridge.

He made the edge of the inland moors in less than an hour,

through heather and rushes and bracken, past wind-shivering pools; a bird, some kind of raptor, vigilant, gliding away over the village and the arms of the bay. He walked on, heading downhill off the ridge this time, to where the River Lair rose, oozing from the blanket bog through numberless pores and streams and capillaries.

Dr Morgan had told him not to overdo things for at least two weeks. A stroll around the village was okay, she said, until he got his strength back. Perhaps she would take a dim view of a nine-mile hike up into the squelching hills on a chilly October day. But he was stronger now, and anyway, he had to go to a certain place. There was unfinished business to finish. And he had to walk. If he stopped he would go crazy.

Skirting an outlying house at the head of the bay, he started climbing the southern hills, moving away from the sea all the time, but still able to make out the river, sunk deep into the fathoms of peat, before it plunged through Inverlair at the head of the bay. Further on and he crested the hill's swelling moorland summit, where he could no longer see the sea or the bay.

Here he was.

Below him, in a deep glen, was the same farmhouse, the door still wide open, the Range Rover still with one wheel in a stream, and the driver, or what was left of him, scattered between the vehicle and his idyllic downsized cottage-industry-cum-bolthole. The recording in Carl's head raced to its screaming climax.

This is the edge of the Inverlair notspot. This is the end. This is where it happened.

Heart pounding, Carl spun from what he saw and remembered, and half-ran back towards the village. After a while he stopped, turned around.

No point in running away. Better to let it in, to face it. That was the way it had to be done.

A while later he was sitting on the ground, looking down at the farmhouse and Range Rover, waterproof trousers keeping out the wet but not the cold on his arse. He took Howard's deltameter out of his pocket; there were spikes right across the waveform. This was almost as far as he could go before the redzone started to bite. He coughed, pain in his chest. Perhaps he'd pushed himself too hard.

This pilgrimage, this penance, hadn't turned out the way he thought it would. Here was the place where the knife had been twisted, where Howard had died. There should be a reckoning, or at least a revelation of some sort. But, after the shock of remembering that day had subsided, there was nothing, just the impassive context of land and sky.

From his pocket he took out a bottle of water and a plastic bag containing four slices of venison and two waxy cubes of polycarb. Without taking his eyes from the farmhouse, he ate and drank. It might rain; in borrowed clothing he'd be safe and dry.

He just wouldn't mention it. That was the way to handle things with Simone. Keep ignoring it and it'll go away. It: growing inside her, not yet a bump. A lump? Embryo or foetus? There was no accelerated hormonal flood to swell her like a balloon, give her all sorts of cravings and mood swings. She would be an invalid in a few months' time. Isn't that what happened? He would end up doing everything for her. She would expect that, and so would everyone else.

He shook his head. It was hard to believe. The more he thought about it, the more unjust and unfair it seemed. It was almost funny. By next spring, it would come along, and the non-stop crying and shitting would start. Isn't that what happens? And what would Isaac think — the kid who already thought the Grim Reaper stayed upstairs?

Man appears. Granny vanishes. Everyone gets sad and starts crying. Now man reappears, and Mum's talking about a baby. Man is the baby's daddy, but he is not my daddy. The man from upstairs was the angel of life and death. But maybe kids didn't think like that, didn't mull over all the ins and outs of a situation. He didn't know how they thought.

It couldn't be ignored, though. Not a hope in hell. Younger guys might carry on as before until reality kicked them in their dog-blind bollocks. But he couldn't push it away, could he? There was no bump yet. Nothing obvious. But it was coming. He could wriggle and struggle and ignore it all he liked. She could miscarry. There was still time.

From the north a gunshot cracked, breaking Carl's febrile cascade of thoughts. The sound bounced around the bay, fading into a scatter of echoes. He cocked an ear, looked towards Ben Bronach and the ridge, but the gun was not fired again.

Must be the stalker.

Should really go and say thanks to the guy. But Carl didn't even know what he looked like. He'd get round to it. Soon.

It was no small thing what the man had done.

A crescent moon came out from behind the clouds. Birds flew towards the forest for the night, and the wind picked up.

Better get used to it. Better forget about what once had been out there, including himself. Everything is here. There's no point trying to deny the truth of that. But it wasn't easy, and just thinking about it made him want to tear his hair out, hurt himself, do something crazy. How could the world just cease to exist? How could it all be unreachable, a shadowy realm of the past? What kind of arrangement was that to come smacking out of clear blue nothing? The whole thing was deranged. Rotten. But the world had been pretty deranged and rotten before the redzone threw a curtain of delta wave sleep around Inverlair. It was no change of state, really, just an end to all the familiar derangement he had known.

Carl pulled his hat down over his ears and shivered. It was getting dark, and the first nameless stars had come out. At the far end of the glen, pools of still water, like spilt mercury, reflected the half-light in the soundless, windless evening.

People were watching him, judging him.

From somewhere below – in the farmhouse glen, but from precisely where he couldn't say – an animal noise boomed, a deep bellowing that rolled around the slopes. He stood still, listened.

A cow? It certainly wasn't a sheep or a dog; hell of a racket whatever it was, as if someone was retching into a toilet bowl. A deer?

He strained to hear.

Not a sound came from the glen, its electricity pylons carrying their dead wires to the silent south.

Wind gusted from the east.

In an instant it started blowing, with force, picking up bits of dry grass. A few seconds later and the first crackle of electricity fizzed across the upper atmosphere, then another flash, and another, until the ionosphere blazed with a tracery of angry voltage.

It was just like Howard had said.

The electrical storm crackled across the eastern sky, lighting up the dark hills. He felt small and exposed under the storm.

Carl hurried down the rocky slope to the main road, the Atlantic horizon still aglow, sky flashing and sparking behind him in the east. For a split second, he was relieved to be going back to the hotel. He almost formed the word home. There were four walls, a bed and a regular supply of calories given to him by other people. But there was nothing and no one he had known from the life before. Now there was just hunger and the redzone and the consequences of action and inaction.

As the wind dropped a little, the animal noise came again from the glen below, a roar that rang around the regimented forest. From deep in its throat the cow-dog-bear called, a moaning bass note that swelled and echoed.

Carl quickened his pace down the gloomy track, between the gorse, and into the dark trees that loomed along the back of isolated houses, stumbling in the fading light. The old fear was behind him, on the hunt. After every few strides he cast a wild glance back through the wind-tossed trees, as if he were being followed, as if he were being watched and there was no escape, and nowhere to find rest.

July

4

The 11 p.m. surveillance drone, tail-light blinking red, banked at 600 metres over the city centre, heading north towards Bishopbriggs. There was something comforting in the regularity of the machine's routine, beyond his window, as it flew past, on the hour every hour, by day and by night. No matter what was going on in the rest of the world, the CivCon drone turned at the scheduled time, banking left over Glasgow, scanning for ID defaulters and clocking up their zonal debits for the council. Everything was as it had become.

Carl sat at the window of his third-floor flat. He wasn't really paying much attention to the drone's tail-light as he thought about the following day. Pollokshaws Road was dry and quiet.

Reports and photos and witness testimony covered his desk. It all added up to a great story, and one his boss would undoubtedly spike. It wasn't really Eric's fault though; he didn't make the rules; he just knew what would happen if they weren't followed. The newspaper had run out of last-chance saloons. It had called the Emergency Authority's bluff once too often.

Carl got up from his desk and made himself a fruit tea. As he flopped onto the sofa, the wall screen bleeped again, for the third time that day.

He let it ring until his ansa clicked on, watched Sarah's moon-face in the inset as she left her message. She was still playful, sarcastic, even though it was her fourth unreturned call of the day. Her blonde hair was more ruffled than earlier, her lipstick smudged.

'Hello, my darling,' she crooned. He reckoned she was stoned; her voice was hoarse. 'Are you there?' She waited. 'Are you trying to tell me you've really and truly had enough?' She smiled, seemed to look right into him. Even though she couldn't see him, Carl turned away towards the window as she left her message. 'Sorry I'm making a show of myself,' Sarah continued. 'Sorry I over-stepped the mark the other day. I mean, this is as good as it gets, right? Me here and you there, but that's okay because . . .'

Carl sighed. 'Mute ansa,' he ordered, and Sarah was left to plead with her mascara-lined blue eyes alone. After a minute or so she hung up. Call and message logged.

He couldn't figure her out. First of all she seemed not to care about anything expect having fun and sharing her new lenses with him. It was a turn-on; the lenses she'd sent him were amazing. An imitation of life, every pore and hair, reproduced in high-res perfection and beamed right onto his retinas. Like she was actually in the room with him. But it was still just self-stimulation, for all the cleverness embedded in the biogel lenses. With spraysuits they could have crossed over into the promised land of personalised virtual togetherness. Without them, it was literally wanking 500 miles apart. The company promised a secure connection, but Carl had his doubts about that. There was always a chance that CivCon were listening in, although they had more to worry about than a largely neutered journalist at a failing newspaper.

It had been Sarah's plan, her idea, to try out the lenses. Now she was getting heavy, and the fun was over. When he'd suggested spraysuits, he thought she'd jump at the chance, but she had resisted the idea, before suggesting a meeting, somehow, of the meatspace sort. Transit endorsements and endless biosecurity bureaucracy would make the 500 miles to Bristol unbridgeable; CivCon could make the separation permanent, and probably would, given Carl's probable status on one of their watch lists. Surely Sarah knew all that, but still she banged on about meeting up.

If only she'd shown some sign of this honest yearning before he'd become too involved.

No. All things considered it would have been better to keep their relationship a netspace one. Women always want more from you, thought Carl; they're never content with being content. And when you become the kind of person they want you to be, they crap on you from a great height, from out of the blue. Well, he wasn't going there again. No chance. He hoped Sarah would leave him alone and not become one of those saddos who couldn't let go, who keep trying to wheedle their way back in. No point in doing that. Once it's finished it's finished: pleading and emotional blackmail just pushes the other person further away, makes them more convinced that they were right to chuck you. It was like some kind of Newtonian law: for every action there is an equal and opposite repulsion. Life would be less complicated without Sarah. It was already complicated enough.

Carl sipped his fruit tea, studying his reflection in the dark window, flicking through the papers and photos that littered his desk. There wasn't much he could do about any of it. All the ingredients were there, but he couldn't do any cooking.

Back at the bay window he caught sight of lights ascending from the helipad on top of the Hilton. The spires of the uni were black shards against the western sky.

The wall screen resumed its scan of his crowdmap, drip-feeding the chatter from 457 individuals and organisations, picking out key words and logging the information. Some of it mattered, but Carl wasn't sure if he could be bothered processing what his wall had to tell him any more. It was like some mythic jug he could never empty, no matter how deeply he drank from it.

•

The following morning, sunlight and birdsong awakened the notion of actually going in to the office. He could sit in the flat tweaking press releases and fluffing official announcements. He could lose himself in lensed-up exploration masquerading as research. Or he could leave the flat, walk through the hot dusty streets, and join the bedside vigil for a dying newspaper.

Today, he wanted to get his hands dirty, see those happy few helping speak truth to power. And it would be better if he spoke to Eric face to face about his latest article, give him the righteous spiel, for old time's sake. The online contributors were invisible, compliant, but Carl knew Eric was better persuaded in person if there was a hard sell to be sold. He would pick his moment to pounce for a result.

As if.

Walking to the bus stop he saw a mini-drone hovering over Queen's Park, the morning sun glinting from its rotors. There was loud popping and seconds later a large group of ragged men, women and children emerged from the trees, panicked and angry. The mini-drone barked a command, in several languages including English, about no unauthorised settlements and warned that a mobile unit had been despatched and was en route. Carl doubted the mobile unit would turn up within the hour, but if they did there would be more than loud bangs to worry about.

The bus came and he rode it into town.

Besides Eric, Caroline was the only other person in the office when Carl arrived, just after nine. She was yawning over supplier invoices. She took her glasses off and rubbed her eyes.

'Too many late nights, my girl.'

'More like far too many jobs,' Caroline replied. 'For one person. And this heat's making me sleepy.'

'It's only another week till the volunteer accountant starts,' said Carl. 'Then you'll have more time to spend on important stuff, like making me coffee.'

'You'd better be careful, or I might get round to installing that new payroll software,' said Caroline, smiling. 'A mistake with someone's salary could easily happen.' She returned to her printouts. 'Don't you have some pretend work to be getting on with?'

Carl gave a little bow. 'But of course, Liebling.' He straightened. 'Ajay and Val out and about?'

Caroline nodded. 'Yeah. Eric's in.'

Of course Eric's in, Carl felt like saying. Eric hardly ever left his cave.

An hour later, and Carl had pounced with his story and, amazingly, managed to persuade Eric to phone the Press Liaison Committee. The subject matter made approval unlikely.

The active denial shield was a crowd control weapon – a tightly focused microwave pain stick wielded from 400 metres that caused intense pain by exciting the water molecules in the epidermis, but did not actually damage the skin. At least, that was the manufacturer's pledge, picked up and parroted by the Emergency Authority. But it wasn't true. Carl sat at his desk, trying not to listen to his news editor in convo with the Press Liaison Committee.

There was a photo of a young Asian girl on Carl's desk screen. If he put his hand over one side of the twelve-year-old girl's image, she was pretty, but the look in her eye said something was very wrong. That something was the other side of her face, the bubble-blistered, angry red and black-crusted vitrified side, where the active denial shield had been a touch heavy on the dermal excitation. He had another dozen or so photos from the food riot at the Kelvingrove centre, of young and old, male and female. None of the images would see the light of day if the Press Liaison Committee slapped on a Section 4 interdict. Sentinel protocols would have locked down every mobile device in the neighbourhood while the riot was in progress, so that nothing would leak out. But there was always a leak, somewhere in the pipework, and this kind of damage was hard to hide.

He had the evidence and the testimony and, a fact he knew full well, zero chance of a publishable article.

The door of Eric's office opened and Carl knew straight away there was no deal. Eric would have been dancing if Nigel Fuckface at the PLC had agreed to a page two down-pager, voicing concern but nothing too strong. Hints of errant behaviour by the crowd at Kelvingrove. The manufacturer's spotless safety record. Immediate inquiry. A caring Emergency Authority in action.

At least the story would have been a start, something to build on. Carl looked at the photo of the disfigured girl on his computer. Tough luck, love.

'Mr Nigel Flitch-Pace,' said Eric, as he had a weary habit of doing, 'has the manufacturer's assurances that the aforementioned product's "calibration issues" have been resolved and that, as an added safeguard, efforts will be made to explore the inclusion of governors, fitted as standard, on the next generation of active denial devices. Mr Nigel Fuckface regrets resorting to Emergency Order Section 4 but ABC, XYZ, goodnight and fuck off.'

He studied the crease in his trousers.

A few workspaces away, Caroline looked up from her invoices.

'Guy's a prick,' she called.

Carl smiled, chewing his lip.

'Efforts to explore,' he muttered, drumming his fingers on the desk. He looked up at Eric, 'And what did the board say when you told them?'

Eric stiffened. 'I haven't told the trustees yet.'

'Hang on,' said Carl. 'How will the Emergency Authority know if the calibration issues on CivCon's new toy have been sorted?'

Eric shrugged, lowered his voice. 'Nigel . . . um, we didn't go into that kind of detail.'

'Nice one,' said Carl. He could see Eric trying not to look at the screen, at the image of a twelve-year-old girl with cheese on toast where the right side of her face should be.

'I'll tell the family,' Carl said, looking at the photo. 'They didn't really want the exposure anyway.'

'Piss off,' Eric grumbled, with no real venom. He glanced over at Caroline, lowering his voice. 'Do you fancy dinner tonight? Lesley's cooking, she got hold of a real roast.'

Carl raised his eyebrows. 'Should I be worried? The last time you invited me round for dinner we sacked everyone and moved into this leaky shithole.'

'Nothing to worry about this time.' Eric looked away. 'Just thought you might fancy some decent food, that's all.'

'What time?'

'Lesley said seven. That okay?'

'Fine by me. I'll try and get hold of something drinkable.'

Eric nodded and closed his office door. The need for privacy always meant a heated discussion with the board or the Press Liaison Committee was in the offing. Eric was up to something.

Carl studied the week's food briefing from the Emergency Authority. He'd introduce some coded ambiguity to leaven the official bullshit. There would be a place within the text where a mote of truth in heavy disguise could be inserted.

His screen flashed. Carl opened the mail.

It was Jeff from ScotNet, a low-level mole.

The email read: 'Hows trix? That gizmo you sent ovr ystrdy the custmr is a real screamr. Meet?'

Time-check. The word 'screamer' meant a same-day meeting, 4 p.m. at the usual place. It also meant something big. He had two hours before he saw Jeff – the stupid prick. 'That gizmo you sent over yesterday.' Carl shook his head. Why even write that? Why give Sentinel anything to work with? Keep the exchange to a minimum, the bare bones, and don't use any key words or phrases that might alert the system.

Gizmo. For fuck's sake. It was time to tell Eric.

Carl opened a drawer and took out a postcard of a smiling cartoon Loch Ness Monster wearing a tartan hat. He rapped on Eric's door and went in.

'I got this,' Carl said, and handed the postcard to Eric.

SCOPE

Inverlair Hotel

IV54

Thursday

There was no name or address.

Eric handed back the postcard. 'This a joke?'

Carl shook his head. 'The card came in an envelope with some kind of chipset. I'm meeting someone from ScotNet at four – an IT guy. He's gonna give me the lowdown on it, thinks it's something big, something that might be part of an upgraded version of SCOPE. He couldn't tell me much more on the phone, but we have this code word. Anyway, there's a new hydroelectricity scheme being opened in the area – it's in the Highlands – so I could kill two birds – an on-the-spot colour piece, lots of crunchy figures and a good news story for the Emergency Authority.' Carl smiled. 'They'll like that. Then I'll swing by Inverlair Hotel and have a word with Deep Throat, or whoever the contact is. And on the way back down to Glasgow I'll swing by and have a look at the Ardmonie Yard – KBS are the new tenants there ...'

Eric folded his arms and sat back. 'That's a lot of swinging by you've got planned.' He pursed his lips. 'What kind of "big" did this IT guy say the chipset was?'

Carl shrugged. 'No idea. He'll tell me at four.'

Eric sighed. 'No story is going to come out of this, got that? You'll end up under a control order, at this rate. I'm not having another run-in with Nigel, or his prick of a boss, about SCOPE. Not again.'

Carl nodded. 'A simple reconnaissance mission.' He put his hand over his heart. 'Word of honour.'

Eric shook his head. 'Where is IV54? Inverness?'

'Yes,' lied Carl. 'Just outside.'

'Hmm,' Eric frowned. 'Transit clearance will be difficult.'

'No, it won't,' said Carl. 'The car hasn't been on the road for six months, and I'm heading north within Area 1 on work-related business, not on a jolly. The nearest white rust infection is in North Yorkshire wheat crops. It ticks all the biosec boxes. If you ask Nigel Fuckface nicely I'm sure he could expedite my transit application, just for the new hydro plant.'

Eric tried not to laugh. 'You've got it all figured out, eh?' His face fell and he leant forward. 'If you cause any trouble at all – if you chase the story – I will let you go, this time. I will. Got that? The board will be delighted if I find some more fat to trim, and you'll be queuing for polycarb rations at Kelvingrove with the rest of them. *Capisce*?'

As one of only three staffers, Carl felt he could push his luck with Eric, not that it had done him much good story-wise, of late. This time, though, he figured the guy was in no mood for further aggravation. The Emergency Authority could intervene at any time and put its own press people in charge. They could turn the paper into a mouthpiece, if it wasn't that already.

'If this chipset proves to be significant, I'll meet the contact, see what he or she has to say, then leave and do a nice piece up north,' said Carl, meaning every word. 'No more than two nights. Straight up and back.'

There was no sign on his face that Carl was being disingenuous. With a bit of blagging – once up there – he could make it three or even four nights away.

Eric nodded. 'Good,' he said. Grinning, he added, 'By the way, our friend Nigel says we can refer to injuries sustained by rioters at Kelvingrove, but we can't go into any details. The phrase "microwave pain stick" is definitely off-limits. Think you can do something with that?'

'Yeah,' said Carl. 'I'll work up some carefully nuanced truth. Between the lines is where the action is.'

5

The cellar bar was quiet, lights on low, all comfy booths and jazz-funk fusion. Carl let Jeff buy the drinks. They sat in one of the booths at the back.

'How's the dynamic world of cochlear implants?'

Jeff giggled into his half lager and lime. 'Barely enough. How's the grubby world of journalism?'

Carl girned at his orange juice. 'A lot grubbier than you could possibly imagine, young man.'

Jeff asked about the new polycarb factory at Hamilton and the latest on the white rust fungus. The guy was looking for fresh insight, for solid news. Instead, scraps of reliable information were sewn together with educated guesswork, and Carl passed it off, adroitly, as incontrovertible truth. Jeff was impressed. The Emergency Authority would tell Carl the real story, and expect it to be published as they had given it, just as soon as they had decided what the real story was to be. One thing he did know about for certain was the arrival of an aerostat that was to hover over the Central Belt, bristling with all sorts of total awareness kit. It would be the seventh such blimp deployed in the UK. Jeff was suitably impressed, but unconcerned.

Carl sipped his drink and cut to the chase. 'So what's the score with the chipset?'

'Well,' began Jeff, pushing his glasses up his nose. 'This is a plasmoid board, the smallest I've ever seen. Something special all right – a high-temperature superconducting microwave filter. Or at least part of an HTS filter.' He drooled over the tiny rectangle in his hand. 'Superb architecture. Doing a bit of reverse engineering, I would say that the whole thing can provide enhanced tunability right into the terahertz wavebands . . .'

'Interesting,' said Carl, glancing at the few punters sharing the gloomy bar. 'What does all that mean?'

'Well, HTS filters are used in base stations and repeaters to filter out noise and give high front-end sensitivity . . .'

Attention wandering, Carl's eye was caught by the barmaid, in jeans and a cut-off T-shirt, a spiral tattoo around her belly button, a stud in her eyebrow. She was bending over to pick a cloth up off the floor. She moved to another table and wiped down the dark wood surface, her breasts swaying as she cleaned. He turned back to Jeff's noise.

'. . . the RF channel time delay on this is configured to some extremely low frequencies.' Jeff nodded, held the thin sheet of plasmoid in his hands, like it was alive. 'Yeah,' he murmured, smiling in awe. 'It's a beauty.'

The barmaid moved away.

'So it's comms?' said Carl.

Jeff looked up, open-mouthed. 'Yeah, a small part of it, but the HTS filter has an unusual crystalline component that . . .'

'Is it part of something really new and advanced that's designed to cover a large area, like Wimax?'

Jeff nodded. 'Yeah, but . . .'

Carl held out his hand. 'Thanks.'

With obvious reluctance, Jeff handed the chipset back to Carl like a kid being forced to hand over sweets to the teacher.

'Thanks for that, Jeff. Much appreciated.'

Jeff fiddled with his glass. 'Am I going to get paid this time?' He watched Carl sink the last of his orange juice.

'You know, Jeff, that's what I like about you. You're very direct. It's a rare quality these days.' Carl put the chipset in his inside pocket and stood up.

'Thanks for the drink.' He tossed two unopened packets of tobacco onto the table, four ounces in total. 'Don't say I'm not good to you.'

Jeff stared at the packets. 'You're having a fucking laugh – I don't even smoke.'

'Then it's money in the pocket for you,' said Carl. 'It's just a question of finding a buyer.'

Groaning, Jeff pocketed the tobacco.

They climbed the narrow staircase back to street level. It was pissing down, but Jeff didn't seem to mind; he just turned his collar up and strode off through the downpour along Sauchiehall Street, hands jammed in his trouser pockets. Carl wasn't so sure about getting soaked, so he stood in the doorway, under the tiny awning, looking up at the grey sky. Summer in fucking Glasgow. There were jobs he could have taken, years ago when travel was easy. Jobs in hot places like Cyprus or the Costa Brava; plenty of expats there, enough to warrant a newspaper or two; local drama clubs and breast cancer fundraisers. That would do him now. Away from CivCon and the pissing rain, to settle down near the beach with some hot young Spanish nymph, or Greek, or Navajo, who'd ride him all day and then make him dinner. It really didn't matter what race she was. The only girl he didn't really want to do it with was Sarah. Why did they always make things difficult? What do women want? The answer is a million things, every day. And it's a man's job to guess the right one at the right time. That's all any man had to do.

So, he said to himself, SCOPE is a communications system, and an extremely sophisticated one at that. There was no telling what it might be capable of.

A police van splashed past the pub. The coppers were still okay, not like CivCon. In fact, the coppers he knew hated CivCon. Maybe they were jealous of the perks as well as the power. They got decent booze, for starters, not the Government pish.

Carl looked at his watch. He had twenty minutes before the Central Business District checkpoints timed out and he'd have to chase up some digs for the night, another zonal default disappearing from his account. His account couldn't take another hit. Plunging into the rain, he ran to Central Station for the last shuttle train to Queen's Cross.

•

Standing in front of his wardrobe Carl wondered how much of an effort he should make for Eric and Lesley. News preferences were updating over his bedroom speakers: two guys shot while trying to break through the white rust biosec cordon around wheatfields in Wiltshire; the latest Citizen Vote results were narrowly in favour of neutrality on the Middle East; another big blackout in Eastern Europe.

A bandwidth capacity warning flashed on his crowdmap. All his categories were nearly full and he would need to go through the feeds and delete the unwanted. Let them fill. Let the warnings flash.

Carl picked up a shirt and sniffed it. He decided against wearing a tie or anything too formal. When in doubt, clean and neat was the best bet, and he always felt better after a shave. He swigged a cold beer and pulled another shirt from the pile on the chair. One night off the wagon wouldn't do him any harm. Now where had he left the iron?

'Music,' he said out loud. 'Favourites 17 to 21. Shuffle.'

Carl shaved, showered, and put on the cleanest clothes he could find. Was he dressing to impress? Eric, for want of anyone else to fit the bill, was his best friend, as well as, technically, his employer. But Carl couldn't shake the idea that Lesley was bored and looking for something, someone. Maybe she had a yearning for disorder, because disorder belongs to the young, and to be young is to be vigorous and passionate. Isn't that right? Maybe she wanted to break out of the life that was fossilising around her. Having an affair would mean risk and freshness and discovery and stolen sex. Having an affair would also mean exploding the people you love into thousands of dagger-sharp fragments. And that meant Eric.

But she was up for it, Carl could tell; the last time they'd met it had been obvious. He saw that this could go one of two ways: either he'd shag his boss's wife or he wouldn't. That is, essentially, what the situation boiled down to. As he showered, he felt himself harden. Best not to think of Lesley in that way. Much too complicated. Messy. And there had been too much of that.

Eric was obsessed with his job. He was stressed and in his fifties, and stress could have that effect on a man of his age. It had consequences in all sorts of departments.

6

Sitting across from Carl, Lesley smoked a post-prandial fag. She had her bare feet up on the chair, curled under her, black skirt tight over her thighs, smoking and listening to the music, smiling to herself, three glasses of Cab Sauv down and sipping at a fourth. Carl sat on the L-shaped leather sofa, legs stretched out in front on the hard oak floor.

Eric came back into the living room waving a single sheet of paper.

'Here comes salvation,' he breezed. He moved empties and an ashtray on to the floor and laid the sheet of paper out on the glass coffee table. It was a front-page mock-up: the splash was an exposé of CivCon brutality and the main photo was of a gesticulating Adolf Hitler. The headline read: 'Brownshirts Batter Britain!'

In the bottom corners of the page were two arrows, one pointing left and the other pointing right.

'We're saved, lad, I tell thee,' smiled Eric, reaching out to touch the right-hand button. The text and photos on the front page immediately shimmered and turned to a perfect page two, even making a rustling sound as it did so. Hitler and his Brownshirts disappeared, and were replaced by some half-pissed celebrity getting out of a limo.

'Wow,' breathed Carl, sitting up, his head clearing of wine and whisky. Eric riffled forward a few pages using the right-hand arrow, then turned back to the front page.

'Wow,' said Carl again. He laid his hand on the page, felt it. 'It's not like newsprint. So this is what all the secrecy is about?'

Eric glanced at Lesley, then tapped the sheet. 'People keep this page and the next edition is downloaded the minute we send it. And look . . .' He handed the page to Carl. 'Try tearing it.' After a fair effort, Carl made an inch-long rip along one edge. It wasn't indestructible, but it was tough, durable, and it handled like ordinary paper.

Eric smiled: the proud father. 'Nanotube construction. Microtransducers – actually embedded in the paper itself. The upshot: we can practically give it away. A one-page 42-page newspaper, downloaded fresh every morning.' He let Carl handle the page. 'So, what do you think?'

'Well,' began Carl, 'so far as distribution and raw material are concerned, we'd save a packet. The content's another matter.'

'That depends on what you want to write about. Do you want to tell the truth for a change?'

Before Carl could answer, Eric said, 'Oil hit 300 euros a barrel today, and it barely registered a blip. Why? Because the media have been told to play it down. Sentinel can block everything negative online, except DeepNet where the geeks and criminals live. It's the usual spin – pipeline shutdown or attack on a refinery. Supply chain pinchpoint. Whatever. But we can't make a big deal of it any more. That's the level of control the PLC is trying to squeeze us with.'

He smoothed out the paper on the table. 'With the new palmpods Eddie can get his hands on, you guys could file straight into the paper.' He prodded the paper. 'This paper – from anywhere. And the paper puts itself together, using preset protocols.' He glanced at Lesley and then back at Carl. 'No editing required. You see, if we carry on like this, there won't be a paper any more. We both know that. Either that or you won't have a job and it'll be press officers from the Emergency Authority who take over.' Eric laughed. 'Some of the guys we had to sack the last time now work for them. Imagine them coming back as the ones in charge.'

Carl snorted. 'Maybe I'll apply there myself.'

Eric shook his head. 'Come on, man. This is all you've known, this is what you are. What else are you going to do? Keep shelving real news?'

Carl considered his empty glass. Eric poured a couple of fingers of whisky into it.

'Countermeasures is big business, Carl, if you have the money or the contacts,' he said. 'We don't have a huge amount of one, but we do have a very well-positioned other – Eddie.'

Now the purpose of the evening became clear. It was a proposition, made all the more palpable after real meat and some lubrication.

'The main man,' said Eric. 'Always one step ahead. This time it's uncrackable quantum encryption, so he tells me.'

'Except that nothing's uncrackable.'

'Correct. But he said it was good for six months.'

'Then what?'

Eric smiled. 'Then Eddie and his ... partners produce another set of encryption algorithms for the paying customers, for those who like their anonymity.'

Carl considered the paper on the table. He realised Lesley was looking at him, and her skirt was now riding a little higher up her nyloned leg. Eric was watching him too.

'So,' said Carl, 'what exactly are you asking me?'

Sipping his whisky, Eric squinted across the coffee table. 'I think you have a good idea about that.' He took a deep breath. 'Call it guerrilla journalism. Filing on the hoof.' He rapped his knuckles on the mock-up. 'Eddie says that half the cameras on the South Side aren't even working. The contractor hasn't been paid for over a year to fix them. There's a map of the broken ones, apparently, networked safehouses, new zombie uploading of ...'

'Whoa,' said Carl, getting to his feet. 'Safehouses? Cameras?' He shook his head, pacing the room. 'What the fuck are you talking about? They'll close us down as soon as we publish. And what about you? Where will you be when all this is going on – directing operations from a CivCon black site?'

Eric sighed and put down his empty glass. 'One more negative story and the helpful Mr Flitch-Pace hinted, pretty much said it really, that the Emergency Authority will step in and put their own people in charge.' He looked up at Carl. 'We'll be finished as a newspaper, and so will all the noble stuff about speaking truth to power.' He glanced at Lesley. 'But the paper isn't the only reason why I asked you to dinner.'

For the first time in several minutes Lesley spoke. 'We're getting out.'

Carl frowned. 'Out?' He tried the word one more time. 'What do you mean *out*? Where?'

'My sister,' said Eric. 'She works for the Ministry of Agriculture, in Brazil. There's no white rust down there – not yet anyway.' He tried a smile. 'Travel is a bit easier for the diplomatic class. There's this house by the sea and a job for me, one that doesn't really exist. My sister's arranged it all.' He toyed with his glass, got up for a refill, taking Carl's empty from his limp, compliant hand. A weight had been lifted from Eric's shoulders. It was out in the open, and he felt better for saying it.

Lesley held her glass up behind her head. 'Thanks, darling, you're so very kind.'

'Oh,' said Eric, taking her empty. 'Sorry, love.'

Carl got up and sat down across the room, on an uncomfortable cane chair that Lesley had insisted on bringing back from a holiday in Egypt, before the biosec shutdown. Apart from a single 'fuck' he was speechless. They left him to sit, digesting the shock news.

After a minute or so he said, 'When?'

Lesley answered. 'We applied four months ago. Transit clearance should come through in another six weeks or so, and our new passports. We were more or less given the green light this week by the Security Ministry. Just procedure to go through, that's all. I think they're glad to get rid of us.'

Half an hour later, Carl was more or less over the initial surprise. He could see the sense in their leaving, and he wondered about Lesley, skirt riding high, and the looks, the suggestions, over the last couple of weeks. Was it a final fling she was after? He watched Eric dancing in his socks. Grown-up kids and a second marriage, and he can't perform when and where it counts. Do animals suffer from impotence? Of course they don't; there's nothing to interfere with their programming so long as the stimuli are right. Psychopathology doesn't come into it.

'... the Emergency Authority know fine well what's going on,' bellowed Eric above the music, 'no point pretending otherwise. CivCon aren't gonna let go when all this is over, if it ever is over. Like fucking Pit Bulls they are. They've got their teeth into this thing and they're not going to let go of us, not while there's money to be made, and even when there isn't they'll probably do it for pleasure and just because they can. Isn't that the way of it?'

Lesley got up and went through to the kitchen. 'Time for bed, tiger. Grab the bottle will you, Carl, before he sees the bottom of it.'

She could be a cold bitch. But it must be hard for her, Carl thought, watching Eric trying to keep the paper afloat single-handed, encased in his own space, his own struggle. A caveman trapped in ice. Anyone who still believed in the power of the press was a primitive, clinging on to some outmoded animist belief.

Lesley stacked the dinner dishes in the washer. 'Use the spare room if you want,' she said. 'It's pretty late.'

There was no denying that. At this time of night there was always the chance that if a CivCon patrol saw who they were dealing with they would put him through a full biometric, just to piss him off. That would take the best part of the night. But it was nothing too serious: not like in some places. People seldom disappeared never to be heard from again. Of all people, Carl had to stay ID- and zone-legal or they could pull him in and keep him. He watched Lesley wash the good wine glasses in the sink. He grabbed a dishtowel to help. A little potbelly at forty-seven didn't constitute horrible deformity. Her perfume mingled with lemon fresh washing-up liquid.

'Thanks for the offer,' he said to her, drying a plate, 'but I'll take my chances on the street with the Brownshirts tonight.'

Lesley was just about to speak when, from the sitting room, came the sound of Johnny Marr's chiming guitar. Grinning and swaying on the spot, Eric was sloshing whisky onto the floor. He raised his glass, not quite in time to the music. One side of his shirt had come out of his trousers. Carl watched him for a spell while Lesley clattered dishes in the kitchen. She was pissed off. That's what women do when they're pissed off, they take it out on the dishes, or the bathroom floor, or . . .

'People didn't give a fuck in the old days,' shouted Eric, the daft grin fading. He rambled some more about a pristine past that never existed.

He stopped, stood still for a moment, then dropped his empty glass onto the dining table, glass on glass knocking hard together but nothing breaking, and collapsed onto the sofa.

Carl went over to the sofa and stood, watching. He picked up Eric's legs by the ankles and hoisted them onto the sofa.

'The enemy within is the outsider, and we are all suspects,' said Eric woozily. He smiled, his eyes closing. 'Stay on the outside, eh?'

'Yes, Eric,' said Carl. 'Whatever you say.'

Within a minute Eric was snoring, mouth slack and sucking for air, flat on his back, one foot on the floor.

'I'll get a blanket,' said Lesley. It probably wasn't the first time that her man had ended up sleeping on the couch, pissed. It was now almost 11.30. Carl downed the last of his whisky and picked up his jacket, as Lesley came back down the stairs with the blanket.

'You sure you won't change your mind? The spare room's there, if you want it.'

He shook his head, afraid to catch Lesley's eye. Sex gripped him by the guts, made his voice thick and uncertain. 'It's fine. My zonal credit is good until one. I'll just head home, if that's okay.'

Why say that? She was standing next to her unconscious husband, waiting for something to happen, willing it.

'Thanks for the meal,' he said, pulling on his jacket in the lobby. 'Best bit of flesh I've had in a long time.'

Light-hearted. Easygoing. Saying goodnight to a friend. That's all. Simple. Why the fuck use the word 'flesh'?

'Goodnight then.' He stepped out into the warm summer night. The earlier rain had all but dried up; Byres Road was ten minutes away and he could grab a cab there. A quick peck on her cheek and he was gone, relief and desire churning within him. Usually, he would have given her a squeeze. But not tonight.

'Yeah,' Lesley said, watching the retreating figure. 'Take care.'

7

Most of the office space in the St Vincent Street complex had not been let since it was built. The gleaming glass had lost its shine over the last twenty years and some of the upper floors on the east side had not been fully weatherproofed. It was watertight at the other end of the building, but lately the lights had begun to flicker every time the wind rose, and there was now a drip from the ceiling near the lift.

Today, there were two large vans parked outside, half on the pavement. Eric had said Nigel at the PLC had arranged some building repairs, without any thought of a quid pro quo, of course. How nice of the man to think of the struggling newspaper without any thought of what he could get in return.

The sudden thought of driving – no, zooming – along by Loch Lomond occurred to him, then he killed the image. Best not to get carried away. There were the biosec checkpoints to get through first. Once CivCon saw who was trying to leave the city they might get antsy, focus on a minor irregularity just to frustrate him. Carl might have to spend all day waiting at their Clydebank compound for nothing, and end up back at the office without ever getting to enjoy the twists and turns of Loch Lomondside. They might just do that, the bastards, and enjoy every minute of it. He made his way down to the basement car park. The one and only company car, one tyre flat, hadn't moved for months and no one had seen fit to throw a dust sheet over it. Carl ran his finger down the windscreen and drew a clear line through the dust. He blew his finger and wiped it on his jeans. Beeped the lock, chucked his rucksack on the back seat, and got into the driver's seat. It still had that clean car smell, but the air was a little fusty.

Sitting there, his hands on the wheel, all the functions of the car still to be awoken, it was hard not to think of the long road north, music blaring and the miles blurring past. Almost a year since he'd driven a car. The smell of the interior and the smooth curves, the seat adjustable to the perfect driving position; it was all there to command and enjoy.

The stair door clanged shut and someone came walking across the car park's bare concrete, clip-clopping a scatter of echoes. A stocky man in black biker's leather, a man that wasn't Eric.

Carl got out of the car. 'Christ,' he said, smiling. 'It's Santa Claus himself.'

'How's it going, big man?'

'Fine, Eddie. Yourself?'

'Not bad. Still fighting the good fight.'

Carl smiled. 'Yeah, if the price is right.'

Eddie grinned, a gold tooth glinting. 'Eric tells me you're after a bit of anonymity.' He took a slender black case, no more than seven inches long, from his inside pocket, the leather jacket creaking over his bulk. 'Pop the bonnet, will you?'

Carl did as he was told.

Eddie put on a pair of rubber gloves, then set to work. From the open case he unwound two thin black wires that ended in crocodile clips. Under the bonnet he grunted and footled about in the guts of the engine.

'So how's life treating you, Eddie?'

'Could be worse. Countermeasures is the place to be.'

'So I gather.'

With a bit of effort, Eddie found the contacts and attached the clips. 'It puts food on the table.'

'How's the family?'

'Still giving me grief, but I wouldn't change them for the world.'

'That true?'

'I'm always open to offers.' Eddie grinned. 'But so far none have come in.' He touched the screen in the little black case, some kind of meter, and watched the results. 'Good,' he said. 'Now. I've inserted an impedance circuit into the RF tracker, to create a feedback current. Wait until you're past the emergency perimeter and out near Loch Lomond. Keep an eye on your bars and when you hit a notspot keep above forty and switch the engine off for a couple of seconds, then back on. You might smell a bit of burning, but don't worry. It's only the RF tracker circuit shorting. If you get stopped by CivCon, which is highly unlikely outside the cities, it's just a burned-out circuit and you had nothing to do with it.'

'Nice one,' said Carl. 'Thanks.'

'Thank Eric, he paid for it. He must have friends on the board.'

'Yeah, well, I suppose he must . . . if only you could give me a new ID.'

'There're guys that can do that for you, no bother. But I doubt if the paper's budget will stretch to it. CivCon are sharp, but not as sharp as they think. There're ways round most things, even who you are. So what's the scoop, scoop?'

'Not sure. A tip-off. It might be nothing.'

Eddie handed over the ignition key. 'The usual, then. This should get you up north and back. There's a full month's quota of carbon credits on there as well.'

Carl got into the car, inserted the key, and opened the window. Over the internal speakers an expressionless female voice said: 'Autodriver engaged. Smart screen display on. Fuel quota at maximum. Tyre reflation in progress. Pressure now optimal. EMS at 95.6 per cent efficiency. Have a safe journey.'

Thumbs up to Eddie. Let's burn rubber.

'Not today, honey,' said Carl, switching off the autodriver. It was easy enough to feel powerless without a car doing all the driving into the bargain.

'Autodriver disengaged. Smart screen display off,' the female voice told him in a disapproving tone. He slipped into first gear, and the car went lurching forward. The engine stalled. Carl looked rueful and started the car again.

Smoother, and for the first time in a very long time, Carl drove out of the car park and onto the streets of Glasgow. His hangover, not the worst he'd ever suffered, made him jittery.

But there was driving. Music. Control. Purpose.

They're not as clever as they think.

As he drove along Waterloo Street and onto the Kingston Bridge, he couldn't help smiling. The warm weather had brought the people out onto the streets. People, patrols, CivCon, coppers, pigeons, bouncing tits in small tops, council workers, assorted city centre misfits, and the few who still had cash to spend. Everything more or less normal, in an abnormal kind of way.

•

There weren't many other cars. Electric cabs, but not many. Lamppost scanners would already have clocked his car; maybe the drones would keep an eye on him, the city beneath laid out for their inspection. Next month they were launching the aerostat, bristling with sensors, to do the job even better than the fleet of hover-drones.

By now, the first CivCon perimeter would have been alerted; Sentinel's multivariable analysis would have produced a response. Maybe it had already allocated the appropriate resources to deal with him.

The machinery of control would swing into operation, unless it was broken, like the cameras on the South Side. In the old days he would have headed up Woodlands Road, but that now took him too close to Kelvingrove Park and the rationing centre. No chance was he going near there, not at this time of day; the road would be packed, queues out the park gate; maybe trouble, answered by microwave pain sticks with calibration issues. At least he'd written the story, albeit missing most of what he would like to have said. But there was something out there, a blip on the flatline of controlled reality.

Today he was going to leave it all behind. Today he only had one thing in mind and it was going to happen, surely it was, just like he prayed it would. As he approached the sliproad for the Kingston Bridge he saw the sign: CIVIL CONTINGENCIES ENFORCEMENT. CHECKPOINT AHEAD (INNER RING) BY ORDER OF THE EMERGENCY AUTHORITY. A few years ago CivCon had been known as the Civil Contingencies Rapid Reaction Force. Now rapid reaction had morphed into a permanent presence. This subtle descriptive shift always made him smile. By degrees was the screw tightened, turning always, by those in the background, who now took silence and compliance for granted.

Halfway over the Clyde, there were seven other cars in front of him, a few pedestrians on foot, being body-scanned in and out of the Inner Ring. He licked his lips and strained to see ahead, nervous. CivCon could put the kibosh on his drive before it even started.

The cars in front went through okay, each one sprayed in the biosec booth, and the barrier came down again. Darth Vader's Stormtroopers waved and barked, no helmets today because of the baking heat. He slid the window down and held out his ID, took off his sunglasses and waited for the iris scan. The CivCon grunt, Scottish regimental tattoo on his bare forearm, smiled when his hand-held scanner revealed the next driver to be a 'fucking journalist'.

Carl smiled right back. Without a hint of reaction, he said, 'Yes. I'm off to cover the opening of the new hydroelectric scheme in the Highlands. An on-the-spot interview with the Minister.'

His goofy smile broadened. This bull-necked prick could pull him in for no reason, find a way to block his progress. The merest suspicion would be enough. Playing it sullen never worked. They loved to pull up people who tried to ignore them. This one looked at his terminal, saw the letters SIP – Surveillance In Progress – and followed his training to the letter. He looked at Carl, checked inside the car, then stood up to look at his scanner again.

The smile was there, the sly smile around the eyes. I know about you, Mr Carl Shewan, right down to when and where you bought your last pair of socks, every preference and perversion.

'Transit clearance in order,' said the grunt, glancing up at the sky and handing Carl his ID. 'Follow the instructions in the biosecurity booth. Have a safe day.'

An awareness passed between them. Carl knew what was going on in the background, and so did the guard. He pocketed his ID and slipped the car into gear. If he'd been heading south, towards white rust instead of away, he'd have to allow himself to be disinfected as well as the car in case of white rust. Doing three miles an hour he followed the green light into biosec, stopped when the red showed, and drove off when the spray had finished, a trail of disinfectant glistening on the road behind him.

He was over the first hurdle and onto the M8; the beginning of the great arterial arc that didn't really stop; that just went on into the Highlands until there was no more road.

He knew CivCon hated a good summer because it brought people out onto the streets, and that was a very bad thing. Being outside was unsafe, as any risk management manual could tell you. Better for order and security if the unemployed stayed in their pits and played the Lottery.

At every major exit there were CivCon Humvees parked up, the new J7 models, unless Carl was mistaken, fresh from the Solihull factory. The guys inside gave him the eye as he passed. He was part way out of the shithole, though he had a nagging doubt about the Outer Ring checkpoint on the Erskine Bridge. Making it through the Inner Ring didn't mean he had escaped altogether.

Maybe this was part of their game: let him through the Inner Ring, turn him back at the Outer.

After eight years controlling the streets, CivCon knew their turf by now, knew where and how to squeeze, always tighter, like a bully not satisfied until he heard a cry of pain. They were here for the long haul and their grip would not easily be loosened. But clearance is clearance, so play the game, you fuckers. Play by your own rules.

Past the airport the buildings thinned out, more land than concrete. Almost there. Fingers and toes crossed. To feel a little freer, to breathe a little easier.

From the Inchinnan industrial estate a column of black smoke rose. Two helicopters hovered on either side of it.

None of it mattered.

Another few minutes and the road started to climb into being the Erskine Bridge. The Clyde estuary shimmered and the northern hills were massing. Right now, he was the only vehicle breaching the biosec cordon at Checkpoint 24.

There were supposed to be a minimum of twenty CivCons at each of the twenty-eight exit points in the city's Outer Ring. Most of them were arseholes: ex-army, Special Forces, the best coppers, private security from overseas; all on decent pay and food. There were meant to be twenty, but today he could only see five. Maybe there was trouble somewhere, and they were overstretched.

Same as before, he told himself. Hand the thing over. Don't get smart. Give him the spiel and the smile.

Thrash metal was blasting from the sentry booth, the singer screaming over white noise feedback. The five CivCons had their helmets off; tunics open in the warmth. An older one, South African by the sound of it, moaned about the shit music.

A black guy, English, did the honours.

Pulse quickening, Carl held out his ID card for scanning. He tried to look impassive, bored even, for his retinal scan. This time the guy didn't spit the word 'journalist'. Maybe the surveillance drone had watched him since the city centre, seen that he hadn't stopped near any known subversives. Maybe nothing had watched him at all, and he was just imagining it. He drummed his fingers lightly on the steering wheel. ID's fine, man. Transit clearance has been given. Pull a fast one or let me out.

The CivCon didn't say a word, just nodded, handed back the ID, with the same sly smile as the first. He walked away and, after what seemed like an age, the barrier floated upwards. Stop had become an invitation to go. Just the disinfectant spray-booth, and he was away. Carl followed the arrows, stopped in the booth, and waited. The nozzles started spraying, and then they stopped.

The light was red.

Red. That meant stop. No go.

Shit.

He looked up, hands trembling, at the figure striding towards him.

The CivCon bent down. 'Have you had a shower this morning, sir?'

Carl felt panic rising. 'Eh ... what? I don't unders—'

Please. Let me go. Let me get out.

The guard bent down, grinning, and looked Carl straight in the eye. 'Close your fucking window. The spray won't work if it's open.'

And he walked away.

Relief made Carl feel like laughing. He understood, did as he was told, felt tension draining from his body.

The spray-booth went to work, and the light turned green. He put the car in gear and drove away from the checkpoint, the road ahead straight and empty. For a while, he kept checking the rear-view mirror, casting anxious glances behind. There was no sign of activity at the checkpoint, nothing to indicate a change of mood, no sudden alert; only the dayshift, hot and listless.

The checkpoint disappeared behind him and he was back on the north side of the River Clyde.

Carl took a deep breath. Then he screamed at the top of his voice until it hurt, thumping the steering wheel. He cranked the music up loud. For the first time since the Glasgow Emergency Order had been imposed, he was outside the city. An exit had been engineered. Ordinary coppers and the old laws were the worst that he would encounter unless he went near Aberdeen, Edinburgh, Stirling or Inverness, and he had no reason to go to any of those places.

8

The sun was shining. For a few days he could relax. CivCon had enough trouble in the cities to contend with to go chasing after him, though Sentinel would doubtless keep a locus on him, just in case. In any event, outside the urban emergency zones CivCon were supposed to leave everything to the police, stretched and under-resourced though they were. As he sped towards Luss and Loch Lomond, Carl kept reminding himself of that. Older laws were now in operation.

Speeding past the Luss turn-off, trees drooped their lush branches over the road, and he had to swerve every so often to avoid them. Every few minutes there was a grey patch, like mould, on a far hillside where the conifers had been harvested for wood-chip fuel. He drove, loving the feel of the car, unbelieving. There were only a few other vehicles on the road, and the occasional truck from one of the few haulage firms still in existence. A bus came towards him: folk going to Glasgow to see friends and relatives, after waiting weeks for a three-day entry permit.

The car in front of Carl turned off the main road. He was on his own now, nothing in front or behind, taking the tight curves by Loch Lomond like a rally driver, dodging the potholes. On and up towards Tyndrum he went, cloud-shadows passing across hills that reared on either side; gates and fences, old cars by the side of the road; long grass and signs for closed hotels. Then the hills relaxed, settling down for a spell, stretching out, and the sky broadened. On a straight he made sure he was above forty, then followed Eddie's instructions.

After restarting the engine, he caught the whiff of burning plastic as the circuit in the engine burned out. Maybe some blip of light on a screen back in Glasgow or Edinburgh or London had gone out. Maybe someone in Command and Control had looked away as it happened, and was now scratching his or her head at the amazing vanishing car. Maybe they were alerting the rural police right now.

'Fuck them,' Carl shouted over his music. Second-guessing what the authorities had in mind for him was a pointless, stress-inducing exercise. The people who would make life unpleasant were there, watching and waiting. If they were going to pull him in for a Category 1 offence, keep him in a black site for as long as they pleased, then that's what they were going to do. No point in worrying about it.

Easier said than done.

At Tyndrum there was an automated biofuel station. The sign was missing a few letters. Most of the other buildings that looked like they might once have housed a business were boarded up and in the same condition. He sped past.

After another half an hour he pulled over into a lay-by. The last time he'd been to Glen Coe, many years before, the weather had been foul and the cloud low. But now the sky was higher and, miles ahead, the towering land was dark under cloud, spears of sun being doused as the steel sky rolled in over Rannoch Moor. The place was a gateway to somewhere else, the jaws of the earth waiting to swallow you whole. He sat for a few minutes, watching the change of light and shade, each movement of cloud casting a shifting intensity over hill and moor.

'Engage autodriver,' he said. With autodriver on, the safety parameters governing the smart screen were switched off, and the windscreen lit up with object-tags and insets, a brief history of Glen Coe, its geology, and a tag for the one hotel. Still trading, but there was no information on a menu. He switched settings and the smart screen flipped into weather mode, displaying cloud types, atmospheric pressure, humidity and the chances of the rain continuing. There was a 64 per cent likelihood that a shower would fall within the next hour.

He started the car and drove on. Within the chasm of Glen Coe itself, just twelve minutes later, the rain hit, like a hose being turned against the windscreen. It lashed down, turning the road into a river, potholes invisible, drowned. Water hammering and scorching and furious, wipers barely able to clear the windscreen. Then, as quickly as it started, the rain stopped; the tap turned tight in the off position. The smart screen was bang on the money.

'Fuck's sake,' Carl breathed, glad to be through the downpour. He could look up at scree-strewn slopes now. He stopped the car again, getting out this time. Fresh air, damp and earthy; he could hear the river now, down below, gushing and rushing through the rocks.

Where he was headed, the blue-grey hills faded by degrees into the blue-grey sky until it was hard to say where the hills ended and where the sky began. He was hungry. Sitting on a stone, he scoffed his sandwiches, gazing up at the high tops, the ragged drops. When had the massacre been? What were the causes? He couldn't quite remember. He tried to imagine women and children being stabbed to death in the snow.

He finished his lunch and drove on. The smart screen told him about rock types and a brief sanitised version of what had happened in 1692.

•

He passed scarred hillsides where conifer plantations had been levelled for biofuel and which now resembled First World War battlefields. He passed shuttered hotels, overgrown verges and, deep into the north, empty glens and the gaping ruins of old stone houses.

Wind turbines turned on a summit or two and some stretches of road were so bad with potholes that he had to slow to walking speed to weave through them. Two buses and four cars had passed him, heading south; one big Jag had overtaken him, going north. He had not seen a single police car north of Fort William.

And everywhere, he would spot a mast on some hilltop, skeletal metal and antennae against the sky. Nothing tagged with RFID moved without being monitored, and most of the under-18s had theirs implanted for 'safety' reasons. Sentinel sensed everything and everyone, except those who had the means to avoid it.

He drove through Fort William without stopping. SCOPE was just another tool in the state's outsourced security toolbox, another supply chain driver. No single journalist, he knew, could ever hope to slow that juggernaut as it moved up through the gears. The masts and the miles and the silent villages came and went. Afternoon eased into drowsy evening. He'd long passed Ullapool, still plenty of north left.

'Tourist coastal route' said a faded road-sign. Now there was a laugh.

•

An hour later Carl pulled into a lay-by. To the west the evening sun cut through the clouds. He had not seen another vehicle for eighteen miles. Rubbing his eyes and the small of his back, the thrill of being behind the wheel had soured. He stretched and took a lungful of warm air. Around him there was nothing except slopes of rock and heather, up-thrusts of naked rock. He took out his palmpod; it barely registered a signal.

The sun's rays were playing on the distant hills, shadows scooped from the hunched massifs. A bird of prey hovered, lasering its target, then dropped like a dead weight. He took it all in, the spectacle.

Satnav said thirty-four miles to Inverlair. From the glove compartment he pulled out an old frayed map, spread it out on the bonnet of the car, and traced his journey. Some ninety miles south-east was the new hydroelectric dam that he was meant to swing by. It was a bugger that he had to drive there the day after tomorrow. Anyway, here he was, wherever it was. What do people do up here? Nothing. Nothing around him as far as he could see, just the vast opening north, swallowing the line of the road.

He stretched his back again, smelling summer in the grass and on the wind, easy sun over a glimpse of sea between the hills. The surrounding summits were scraped bare of vegetation, crags fissured and scrubbed like this rhino he'd seen up close once, in Edinburgh Zoo, its skin cracked and weathered and out of the reptilian past. His sandwiches were gone, and there was no more water left in the bottle. His legs were aching. Glasgow felt a long way away.

Away from the road – he had no idea of distance – was a bare fist of mountain that burst through the thin covering of green. Somewhere in his mind, the outline of the dark shape rang a bell. He had seen this photo, he was sure of it. And now here he was, looking, open-mouthed, at the real thing. He stopped the car again and got out. After a while, he became aware of another sensation – absolute silence. Only the breeze in the grass registered in his ears, birds calling in the distance. By the side of the road, in the long grass of the verge, a bee, droning and moving from flower to flower sounded like a chainsaw. The pure air filled his lungs. There was nothing to do but look and listen, but he found himself unable to do either for very long.

He drove on.

•

At a derelict filling station he stopped again to check the map. Weeds were poking up here and there through the concrete forecourt and the station's high metal roof was missing. There were no fuel pumps on the two concrete stands. Plastic electricity cables, sheared at the root, stuck out of the ragged holes in the concrete where the pumps had stood. The booth's livery was fading under the scrub of Atlantic weathers, windows intact and covered in dust. Carl cleaned a spot with his fist and looked inside. Most of the shelves were still in place; the metal shell of a coffee machine; a chewing-gum display stand on the counter; empty plastic water bottles; a glass-fronted fridge, for sandwiches and soft drinks. He could murder a coffee. Not far now to Inverlair.

•

A few miles on, the dark scarp of a sea-cliff appeared in the distance, and the road veered abruptly down, following the curve of the bay. A road sign said 'Inverlair'. Carl pulled over to the roadside and reached into the glove compartment. Taking out a pair of binoculars he scanned the village, most of which lined the other side of an inlet – more a fjord – bordered on three sides by steep forested hills and a few dozen houses, about half of them clustered around a pier that was jutting out into the bay. Outlying houses were spread across the green and brown hillside, with fenced fields between them and the sea. A river split the rounded uplands at the head of the bay, a rocky summit rising to the north. Carl could see what he figured was some kind of boatyard, a large grey corrugated-iron building with a high doorway. Inside, he could see a shower of sparks. Probably welding gear. On the pier there were guys hauling plastic boxes, streaming seawater, up from a waiting boat. There was nothing out of place, no CivCon, and no cops that he could see. And no telecomms mast, though most houses had a satellite dish.

In the centre of the village, halfway up the opposite headland, Carl could see 'Inverlair Hotel' above the doorway of a solid two-storey stone building. Smoke was billowing from one of the chimneys. There was a church at one end, a small shop and post office in the middle, and what Carl took to be a schoolhouse at the other end.

He got back in the car and drove the last mile or so down and around the bay towards the hotel, followed the sign into the car park, parked, and made his way round to the front door. Inside, he waited in the reception lobby, all dark wood panelling and claret carpet. There was no one around. A button on the counter told him to 'Ring For Attention'. He did, heard distant bleeps within. He waited, and was just about to press again, when a man in his sixties, wearing a navy-blue fleece with the RNLI logo in red, came through a fire door.

'Yes?'

'Hi. I'd like a room, please. A single, if you have one.'

'A room?'

'If you have one, yes. I should've phoned, but I assumed . . .'

For a second the man, who spoke with the faint trace of an American accent, seemed unsure of what was taking place.

'Sure,' he said at last, narrowing his eyes at Carl. He went behind the reception desk. 'The ID machine's broken, I'm afraid. We've been trying to get a technician out for weeks.' He smiled and slid a ledger across the counter. 'You'll have to do it the old-fashioned way.'

Carl signed his name, scanning the rest of the entries as he did so. The previous signature was dated two months before.

'Did you drive here?'

'Yes.'

There was a glint in the man's eye. When Carl looked up from the ledger he saw it fade. There was a stag's head mounted over the reception desk. That's enough information for you, you nosey old bugger.

'You don't get many tourists here then?'

The man raised his bushy eyebrows, amused. 'Not by car, no.

We still get the odd busload and even a few by boat, but the last tourists to arrive here under their own steam was nearly a month ago, a party of Canadians in the bunkhouse, backpackers, and a German couple staying in one of the holiday homes.' His mouth drooped. 'That's been more or less our season.'

He looked at the name in the book. 'Mr Shewan,' he said. 'I'm George Cutler, the owner.' He handed Carl the key to Room 14. 'Come on and I'll show you up.'

The hallway of the hotel had a musty smell. Paintings of old soldiers – the braid-and-wig brigade – hung on the walls. A fat fish mounted in a glass case. A shiny brass handbell stood on a dark-wood side table. A stained-glass panel lit the staircase to the first-floor landing.

Cutler opened the door of Room 14. 'Coffee over there,' he said, pointing to a kettle and basket of sachets. 'It's old stuff but it should be okay.' He pointed at the TV. 'We've got satellite, broadband that works, just about. Would you like breakfast?'

Carl nodded, inspecting a tatty brochure that listed local attractions: walks, heritage centres and archaeological sites. Half-eight was the time agreed for breakfast.

'You can have something to eat now, if you want?'

'Sounds good. What is there?'

Cutler smiled, his soft colourless face cracking. 'Plenty of fish. Potatoes and veg. I think there's some venison pie left as well. It's good stuff.'

Not exactly the seaweed gruel that Carl had been expecting.

'Venison pie it is. I'll be down in ten minutes, if that's okay?'

Cutler said that was fine. As he made his way out, he stopped, reached into the pocket of his fleece.

'Oh, this was left for you at reception yesterday.' He handed over an envelope which had CARL SHEWAN printed on the front, nothing else. Carl turned it over a few times. There was something inside.

'Thanks,' he said absently.

Cutler closed the door and Carl ripped open the envelope to see what was inside. It was a memory stick, and nothing else.

He unzipped his bag and took out his palmpod, and inserted the stick. At the password prompt he thought for a second.

He typed 'SCOPE'.

Bingo. There were two video files. He played the first one.

On his palmpod screen, inside what looked like a tent, a bald man in his fifties sat cross-legged, his tightly muscled face sombre, downcast. He cleared his throat, adjusted the camera.

'Hello, Mr Shewan. If you've come this far, then I thank you for that. I hope to Christ I'm wrong, but . . . anyway, my name is Howard Brindley and I am – was – senior head of research at GeoByte Support Services. You probably haven't heard of us, we did some work on SCOPE, just the GPS telemetry.'

Howard Brindley shifted position. He clearly wasn't used to sitting cross-legged on the ground inside a tent. He rubbed his stubbled face, clearly exhausted.

'You had some financial concerns about SCOPE, Mr Shewan,' Brindley said, looking away. 'My concerns are more . . . technical. We were only the subcontractor, but I got hold of the full spec for the SCOPE transmitters, and ran some harmonic modelling on the crystalline microwave filters, the new ones . . .' He stopped, sat up, straight-backed. 'Sorry for talking shop. The second file on this memory stick will tell you the rest . . . in plainer language. It is time-locked until twelve noon on Thursday, seventeenth of July.' Brindley pursed his lips, looked intently at the camera. He then leaned over and switched it off.

The video file stopped. The seventeenth was tomorrow.

Carl tried the other file. Time-locked. Why would he put a time-lock on the rest of his story?

The guy better not be another crank. But there was the plasmoid chipset to consider – no crank would have sent him that. Carl checked the time. He was hungry and thirsty. Brindley wasn't in the hotel – he could be anywhere in the area – and there were sixteen hours until the time-lock on the second file expired. Nothing to do except relax.

9

The pool ball smacked off the baize and clacked along the bar room's tiled floor. It thumped against the counter. A scruffy collie darted over, picked the ball up in its mouth, and spat it back out onto the floor where it bounced into a metal bowl. The dog looked expectantly at the drinkers, who chuckled and clapped at the trick. Cute Collie Dog picked the cue ball up and did it again. This time, a louder cheer went up and the dog was patted and praised by its owner. All the customers were middle-aged men, the dedicated early-evening crowd, happy enough with their price-capped product and a big screen showcasing some Reformed League football. Bellies and flushed faces in the bar, a dozen or so, and the only woman in the place was pulling the pints.

Carl told her he would take his food in the dining area.

It was a big enough room, breakfast bar and French windows. He reckoned it could sit about seventy; there was only him. Peak season and here he was, the one and only cover. What did people do around here? Maybe the Canadians or the Germans would come in, give the chef a real thrill-ride of a night.

Half the dining room was a tip, with chairs and tables stacked any old how. Boxes of crockery, piles of bed linen and curtains, garden parasols standing in the corner – a bike half-buried under it all. The place was more storeroom than eating place. He supped his flat lager. It was hardly worth a second day off the wagon.

The barmaid had become a waitress. She came through with Carl's plate of food, and set it down in front of him. She was early thirties, bobbed black hair, pretty, but not exactly a customer service expert. There was no warm Highland welcome here.

'Do you want another drink?'

'Yeah, I might get lucky this time. Is it spot the bubble and win a prize?'

The waitress/barmaid eyed him, not even attempting to see the humour in the remark. 'That's what we're given up here, Mr Shewan. It's take it or leave it, I'm afraid.'

'It's the same in Glasgow. We don't get special treatment – well, most places don't.' He took a long pull on the glass to show his acceptance. She nodded curtly, cracked the faintest smile, and left him to eat.

Three hours later Carl was well on the way to being completely relaxed. In the hotel's public bar he was being harangued by a pissed old local with a scruffy white beard. A jukebox thumped out some techno and a few lads were larking around at the pool table. The pissed local persisted with tales of the good old days at the oil fabrication yard down the coast. Most of the older men had worked there, including George Cutler as a backpacking young tourist, so the barfly had slurred. The good old days, so far as Carl could tell, lasted only a few years until production was moved to the east coast, and the yard closed. But that was several drinks ago, when the man had made sense; now he was firing off in all directions. 'Glasgow's best fuggin siddy in gundree. Always fuggin welcome there.' He shook his head. 'Can't put a price on that.' He paused, succumbed once more to thoughts that made sense only to him. 'Fuggers,' he spat. 'Not a penny from them cunts after the accident, y'know?'

He was oblivious to the white pool ball smacking onto the hard floor at his feet. Some of the pool-players roared their laughter. Flying pool balls seemed to be a habit around here. One guy shouted over, 'Hey, Frankie, you've laid another fucking egg!'

While Frankie tried to look menacing, Carl downed his drink. Time for some fresh air.

A piss first. The toilet wall told Carl that LORNA GIVES GOOD

GOBLES. Where the fuck was Brindley? He didn't want to ask Cutler about him. A direct question could arouse suspicions, and other people might be informed about these suspicions, and so on. Even up here that could still happen. Sidling in at an angle was the best way, nicey nice, terrible fucking weather, winkle a wee bit out of them, pull back, talk about footie or food but keep it behind your ear, then come back for another wee slice, and so bit by bit he could get what he wanted. If only that strategy had worked in other areas of his life.

He headed outside.

Jesus.

Under the clear sky the bay was quiet and dark, and in the east were stars. But to the west was a pink and red fugue under shreds of high cloud, each shade of colour luminous, unpolluted, diffusing from the red sun's vanishing core. Carl headed down towards the pier and away from the streetlights to get a better look.

Absolutely amazing. Dark arms of the narrow bay and the quiet breath of the night, with just the waves lapping and a late bird calling. Warm salt reek at the end of the pier. He stood for a while watching the world turn and the stars come out, stuff that was invisible in the city. No midges so far, maybe the breeze kept them away. George Cutler said to watch out for midges if he went for a walk, the buggers'll eat you alive on a quiet night. The fizz in Carl's mind came off the boil. There was nothing to do except absorb the slow ending of the day. He breathed deep at the end of the pier.

After about ten minutes he headed back to the hotel, none too steadily. Sea legs not what they never were. Was the pier moving? He hiccupped. Better not start with those fuckers. Pain in the arse when you think they've stopped and they start again. This place would do him for a couple of days, maybe try stretching it to three or four. Maybe he'd move here and never go back. No way. He'd go nuts within a week.

Brindley. Brindley and his state-of-the-art chipset . . . Carl cleared a shadow from his mind. Better not go there. Stick to the facts and not the fears. As he walked back towards the hotel, the streetlights went out, their filaments glowing and dying; little suns fading.

'Ho!'

Power cut?

But no. The houselights were still on, the sign over the hotel's public bar, and even in the few houses on the other side of the bay. A minute later, his eyes had adjusted and he could see the tarmac at his feet, the fading light in the west sharper, the church a dark silhouette, and the stars overhead. Who had killed the streetlights? His watch said 11.32 p.m. Just over twelve hours until the time lock on the second video file expired. Maybe Brindley would show up at the same time. The edge of the pavement caught Carl by surprise, and he stumbled, crossed the road to the hotel path. Guys were yammering away. He heard a North American accent, a young woman, part of a group who were smoking outside a guesthouse. Six months it had taken her to get travel clearance from London, apparently. A month for each emergency zone. She said it was her birthright, this trip, part of her emigrant heritage – so she deserved it. Carl passed them by and followed the path up to the hotel.

The waitress was in the lobby. He grinned, nodded, his brain lagging behind the desire to say something. She bustled past him and locked the outside door. 'It's chucking-out time from the bar. I wasn't sure if I could lock the door on you or not.'

'No bother. What's with the streetlights going off and everything else staying on?'

'It's the council, they're saving money.'

'I suppose it causes a few accidents, not being able to see in the dark.'

The way she looked at him, straight in the eye, as if to say here's another smart-arse trying out his patter.

'Breakfast is between eight and half-nine. There are enough eggs and toast and porridge. Night.'

'I thought you didn't lock the doors up here?'

She snorted at him. 'We do when there's strange men around.'

And away she went, through the fire door.

'I just wanted to talk,' he said after her. 'That's all.'

She stopped at the doors, half turned towards him.

'It's just my cack-handed way of starting a conversation.' He looked mournfully at the floor, hands in the pockets of his jeans. 'I'm not trying to be funny . . .' He grinned. 'Well, I was trying to be funny, if you know what I mean.'

A woman laughing at your jokes was a good first step. You were on your way if you could get them to laugh, not overdoing it, but just breaking the ice, then weighing in with some well-considered remark that, depending on the woman, would prove there was depth to the man as well as a reasonably inoffensive surface. Then maybe a follow-up funny, a listening ear, a question or two. Repeat and vary until she's eating out of your trousers. That was the theory, anyway. Did the evidence back it up? His field research was ongoing, but this one didn't take the bait, he could see that straight away. She had this way of looking at him, weighing him up. He started climbing the stairs to his room.

'The guy who dropped that package off for you must be camping up at the forest,' she said, softening. 'You told my dad that you were meeting up with an old friend.' Her raised eyebrows said it all: what kind of an old friend hides in the forest?

Thankfully, Carl wasn't so drunk that he'd lost control of his tongue. There was an abridged version of the truth that could be used on those who asked awkward questions. He pointed to the glass cabinet that lined one wall of the lobby.

'Are these bottles full of whisky or cold tea?'

'I don't know,' she said. 'They've been on display for years, most of them. For as long as I can remember.'

Carl considered the lines of bottles. 'And how long has that been?'

'Since I was seven.'

Uncertain, Carl peered at the waitress. 'Bit young to start working, isn't it?'

'That's when my dad bought the place.'

'Who – George ...'

'Cutler. I'm Simone.'

Carl processed this information. He turned back to the cabinet full of whisky bottles. 'Well, Simone, if you uncork one of these to find out whether or not it's tea inside, I'll tell you my dark secret.'

'What happens if it's cold tea?'

'Then it's name, rank and serial number, and nothing else.'

•

He threw the room key on the dresser of Room 14 and sat down heavily on the edge of his bed, tugging at his laces. He kicked off his shoes.

Struggling into bed, he lay a while with the lamp on. Simone was a funny woman. Music student then single mum, her defences too ready to come up.

There was a funny feeling in his guts, and he assumed it was to do with the booze. Eventually, he fell asleep.

10

His alarm went off at 8 a.m., the tone knifing into his head. Once
he was over the shock, something like consciousness seeped into
him. It hurt. Off the booze was an altogether gentler place to be.
As he lay there, getting used to being awake and in pain, he
wondered whether Inverlair Hotel could stretch to a full fry-up.
Furred arteries and high cholesterol were best avoided, but a
hangover demands such damage. Only saturated fat and sugar
can make the morning-after body shock better. He lay there for a
while, thinking about Simone. Sensitive subject, her son's dad.
As soon as he'd touched on it, Carl had seen the shutters come
down. She was happy enough to talk about playing the flute and
being a session musician and living in Bristol, content to hear
about his journalism and life in Glasgow. But the personal stuff
was off-limits. Her dad might be American, but Simone had not
inherited any propensity to gush at complete strangers, be it on
the subject of medical complaints or familial tensions or any
other stuff that Brits deemed too private to talk about. And thank
God she hadn't.

He got up to piss, groaning as he splashed into the bowl. In the
bathroom, beside the wash-hand basin, there was no mini-soap
and no towel, so he splashed his face with water a few times. He
made a coffee, swallowed two painkillers, pulled on yesterday's
clothes, and crept downstairs. He heard Cutler complaining about
how the weekly minibus from Inverness was late, and there was
no answer from the brewery. Carl accepted the offer of two fried
eggs and tomato on toast.

'You couldn't spare a towel as well, could you, and some of those wee soaps?'

Cutler said he would bring them up.

It was just after ten. Less than two hours until the time lock on the video file expired. Carl wasn't sure if it was the fact that he was hungover, but he was beginning to feel a bit unsettled. There was no wireless signal in Inverlair; he couldn't check his texts or his feeds. Brindley's cloak-and-dagger act was a pain in the arse. He must be on the run, to camp out like that.

Fried food was the second part of the remedy for his hangover. Showering had been the first part. Now that he was out walking in the fresh air, the fuzz of seven pints and an after-hours whisky had all but lifted. Salt on the breeze. Sun on the water, oily rainbow diesel-sheen lapping against the pier's legs. He felt better for being outside. Carl leant on a railing, looked out across the bay at the open horizon, and behind to the rising land, the dark hollow of Inverlair Bay. What the fuck went on here? How could people live?

If Brindley was on the run then he wouldn't stay anywhere official, like a hotel or guesthouse. Had he come by sea? Carl walked back through the village, along the shingle shorefront, stopping at some old boat sheds, his mind wandering. He had to tell the waitress, Simone, something. Yes, he was a journalist, and, yes, he was working on a story, but it was nothing to do with Inverlair or any of the locals. Doubtless she had her own story to tell if he could be bothered to probe for it. Everyone has a key, well hidden usually, even from themselves. He turned back along the shingle beach towards the concrete slipway.

It was 12.04 p.m.

In Room 14, Carl played the second file on the memory stick for the third time. Nothing but the inside of Brindley's tent. No sign of him. He played the first file again. Brindley looked tired, kept rubbing his bald head, massaging his eyes. He hadn't shaved for a few days. But his words were definite: 'The second file is time-locked until noon on the seventeenth – tomorrow if you made it in time. It'll explain everything.'

Yet the evidence on the screen said the opposite. File two was empty.

Okay. There was no other option: he'd have to find Brindley, wherever he was hiding. Carl grabbed his jacket and shoulder bag and headed down the stairs. At the reception desk a German couple were asking for directions to a prehistoric cave in the hills. Simone nodded to Carl as he walked past and out the main door.

Standing on the steps of the hotel, Carl let the door bang behind him. What the fuck was Brindley playing at? He could be anywhere in the forest – if he was up there at all. Nothing for it, he'd have to get his trainers wet. So intently was he looking across at the conifer plantation at the head of the bay that it took him a few seconds to register who was walking towards him along the rhododendron-lined track. Unlike the video file, this Brindley was clean-shaven and didn't look quite so tired.

It was Brindley who spoke first. 'Your picture in the paper makes you look older.' He forced a smile. 'You've tried the second video file and now you're on your way to track me down.' It was a statement.

Carl nodded. 'Yes.' He looked about, at hills and water, and wondered who might be lurking close by. 'Look, do you want to talk out here, or shall we go inside?'

Brindley's faced darkened. 'Do you have a car?'

Carl nodded.

A flood of emotions crossed Brindley's face in an instant, before settling on anxiety. He could only stare at the ground. 'Let's go then. Rather than talk, I'll show you what SCOPE has done.'

•

Two hours later, Carl came into the hotel's public bar, ashen-faced. He stood for a while at the door, watching the few regulars, Simone pulling pints.

'I'll tell them,' he said to Brindley, who sat down at a corner table.

Behind the bar, George Cutler was complaining that the bus was almost four hours late and the satellite TV was still down. 'We're nearly out of draught lager,' he murmured to his daughter. 'And the bloody power is still off.' He quietened when he saw Carl in the doorway. 'Enjoy your walk, Mr Shewan?'

Without answering, Carl pointed at the optics. Simone gave him the glimmer of a smile, but it didn't register. None of this was real any more, he thought. It was finished. There was a wrecking ball on its way. Any minute now it would shatter everything.

George shook his head and took silence for an answer. 'Feeling rough, eh?'

They don't know, Carl thought. They don't know, and he would have to show them, like Brindley had shown him. That was the only way to convince them. George went into the office and Simone eyed Carl from down the bar.

'Are you all right?'

He threw back his whisky in one gulp as George stamped through from the office.

'They're still not answering the phone,' he said to his daughter. 'I can't even get online. The shop's expecting a delivery as well.'

Another whisky went smartly down Carl's throat, firing his stomach and clearing his head. But he didn't want a clear head. He wanted a head that was unable to form coherent thoughts, so he smacked the empty glass back down on the bar and demanded another shot. The only real thing left was to get pissed.

Brindley appeared by his side.

'Who are you waiting for?' he asked George.

It was a direct question, spoken loudly and without any hesitation.

'The brewery,' began George. 'Every two weeks they arrange for a deliv—'

'They're not coming.'

George looked puzzled.

'Are there any police in Inverlair?' It was another direct question from Brindley.

'Yes,' said George slowly. 'P.C. Gibbs.' He glanced at Carl. 'Is there any ... trouble?'

But Brindley kept firing the questions. No time to waste on politeness.

'Do you have a local councillor, community leaders?'

'Look, what's this about?'

'Do you have a local councillor, Mr Cutler? Yes or no.'

Flustered, George said: 'Yes, but ...'

'It is vital that you get a group of people together immediately.'

'Look, whoever you ... what the hell's all this about?'

Brindley considered an answer, then gave up. He looked at Carl, who was now well into his third double. Carl knocked back what remained of his measure.

'Come with us and we'll show you.'

•

George sat in the back of Brindley's car along with the moustachioed P.C. Gibbs. As they drove away, a woman came out of the tiny shop and wondered where they were all going in the same car.

Just over two miles into the drive they all began to hear it. George touched his temple as Carl stopped the car and turned the engine off. He glanced in the rear-view mirror at Brindley.

'What's that noise?' said George. 'Something's clicking.'

'Microwave hearing,' said Brindley. 'The sound isn't actually hitting your eardrums – it's being generated in your brain's auditory centres.'

'Where's it coming from?'

Carl started the engine again, and they drove on.

The noise changed to a continuous high-pitched intensity, growing louder and louder. They drove on, south and east, away from the bay, their headaches growing worse, until the shrieking noise cut right into them. Carl stopped the car, wrenched the gear stick into reverse, his eyes streaming, and turned back the way they'd come, the passengers shouting and grabbing at him to stop. He fought them off. 'Don't get out,' he shouted, racing the car back towards Inverlair and down into the bay. The high-pitched tone vanished, and their headaches eased.

•

They all sat in the lounge bar. It reeked of stale beer and sweat. They listened, or at least appeared to listen.

'The system is named SCOPE,' said Howard. 'That stands for Secure Communications Open Emergency. It's a system of transmitters using pulsed microwaves designed to give complete asset management and communications coverage in the event of a national emergency or crisis. Most base stations have SCOPE now, site-sharing with commercial operators.' He looked at his watch. 'SCOPE was networked, across most of Europe and North America at 09.28 GMT, just over three hours ago. An imperfection in tiny diarite crystals that are used in the microwave filters has caused a standing harmonic, a signal, that has propagated throughout the entire system. This harmonic resonates at 2.14 hertz, the same frequency as deep sleep. Everyone outside a notspot – an area without signal coverage – is now asleep, and will remain that way until they die, within a few days, a week, however long it takes, unless SCOPE, somehow, shuts down. The pain and noise you felt and heard were simply interference patterns at the very edge of the electromagnetic field.'

Councillor Diane Matheson gave a nervous laugh. She turned

to George Cutler. 'What's he talking about, George? Stupid bloody nonsense . . .'

Cutler could only stare at Brindley. The councillor waited for an answer.

'We can't leave,' said Carl, helping himself to another whisky. 'And everybody who's within range of this fucking delta signal, which is a big chunk of the developed world, is as good as dead.' He looked out the window while slugging his drink. 'I think that just about covers it.'

There was silence in the room.

'Mum,' said Simone. She looked at her dad. George knew, and Brindley wouldn't meet his eye. 'My wife is in Edinburgh,' he said, pleading.

Brindley took a deep breath. He looked from the councillor, to George Cutler, to Gibbs. 'You have to start planning, because there is a chance that nothing is going to come in from the outside world for a long time.'

'For how long?' said Gibbs, tears in his eyes.

'Well,' said Brindley, 'the delta signal in rural areas is coming from hundreds of base stations, but in the cities there are thousands of smaller nodes in the grid. They all use high-temperature superconductors so they only need a tiny amount of power. The system is designed to scavenge the national grid. Solar and tidal will give it what it needs . . . for years . . . for power.'

'No,' said Simone firmly. She stormed though the fire door and into the annexe.

Gibbs stood and buttoned up his uniform jacket. 'You seem to know an awful lot about this SCOPE system, Mr Brindley.'

'Our company worked on systems integration, telemetry, for CivCon's main contractor.'

Councillor Matheson slammed her hand down on the table with such force that it made everyone jump. 'Constable Gibbs, what absolute bloody nonsense is this man talking about?'

The policeman glanced at Cutler.

'I'll take her,' said George.

'Take me? Take me where? What're you on about, George?'

Carl slid his car key down the bar.

George picked it up and walked out, the councillor on his heels.

Gibbs went behind the bar and poured himself a brandy. He put some money in a shot glass and contemplated his drink.

'For the first time in thirteen years, I'm about to drink while on duty.' He took a gulp of brandy, grimaced. 'You're a journalist, Mr Shewan,' he asked. 'Is that correct?'

'Yes.'

Gibbs nodded, paused. 'And you wrote some newspaper articles on this ... SCOPE system?'

Carl had the feeling that that he was being probed. 'A few years ago now, yes. But the articles covered how SCOPE and its budget were being hidden from Parliament. They were political, not scientific.'

Gibbs nodded again. 'Uh-uh. And you have both managed to find your way to one of the few *notspots* left in the country, if not the whole of northern Europe.'

Carl stiffened.

'That's very convenient,' continued Gibbs. He nodded to himself. 'Quite remarkable, really.'

There was silence.

Brindley sighed. 'I managed to get hold of a partial map of where the main transmitters were. I figured Inverlair Bay would be one of the biggest notspots, judging by where the nearest masts were. As for Mr Shewan, I thought he could help me stop it. I should have gone to him earlier.'

Carl rapped his empty glass down onto the bar. 'We didn't do this, Gibbs. Surely to Christ you can see that? You heard what Brindley said. You guys had better get folk together. Set up a roadblock. Go house to house. Do something.'

Gibbs agreed, and Brindley went with him.

Carl sat at the end of the bar, staring into space.

There were distractions on which to focus the mind, blot out the impossible horror. Sun showing up the streaks of polish on the dark-veneered tabletop, or glinting on the pool table's coin slot; the movement of the clouds across the bay; stains on the carpet; swirling dust motes in the sunbeams. He sat and watched the sun and the dust and the high clouds crossing the windows.

After a few minutes, Carl got up, went behind the bar and took a bottle of single malt off the shelf and headed upstairs. Maybe it was absolute rubbish. SCOPE would stop working tomorrow and everyone would wake up. Yes, there would be deaths, but nothing exceptional, nothing that couldn't be boxed off and forgotten about. There would be an official inquiry, held in private of course, and some contracts would be reviewed. Normality would be restored.

11

He stirred after 10 a.m. the next morning, head pounding, stomach lurching. It wasn't just the hangover that hit him in the stomach. He stood up, shuffled around the room, wished he hadn't stopped smoking. There were a few sachets of coffee left, so he boiled the kettle, shut the window, made a coffee, had a shower, opened the window again, and paced the room. Birds were chirping away. Summer sun was warming the bay. The stirrings of perfection were there, all happening around him. But the view was poisoned. The prospect was desolation.

Eric. Lesley. Eddie. The girl from the Kelvingrove riot. Sarah. Jeff from ScotNet and most of the people he had ever known. His dad in a nursing home in Stirling. His sister: Brighton was bound to have it too.

No. He shook his head.

'No,' he said out loud.

There was a soft knock on the door. It was Brindley. He had to be bringing good news.

'Is it down? Can we leave?'

Brindley shook his head. 'No. We, um, we held a meeting, last night. Not many turned up. A lot of family and friends, a lot of .. . I don't think they believe it. I don't think they're up to planning anything.' He leant against the bureau, clasped his hands together, and took a deep breath. 'I was thinking we should map the delta signal, for fluctuations. Get a few readings over . . . however long it lasts. See exactly how big this notspot is. You could help me.' He shrugged. 'If you feel up to it.'

Carl sat on the edge of the bed, hangover and fear making his voice and hands shake. 'They will stop transmitting, the masts, the nodes. They might pack in tomorrow, right?'

'They might,' said Brindley. 'But SCOPE was designed with resilience in mind. It's robust. And the two-hertz harmonic is a standing wave, with a strong magnetic component. Impossible to shield against.'

Sitting on the bed, Carl considered the whisky bottle on the bedside table. Enough for a hair of the dog remained.

'I heard someone crying. Or maybe I dreamed it,' he said, taking a slug from the bottle. 'Maybe it was me. I'm not sure. But there was crying, somewhere. Everywhere. There's always someone crying somewhere.'

Brindley shifted his stance, pursed his lips. He sighed, standing awkwardly, breathing in the silence and sweat and alcohol fumes in Room 14.

'I'll leave you to it then.' He opened the door to leave. 'I'm in Room 22 now. It's down at the end of the corridor. Let me know what you think about mapping the area.'

The door closed. Carl sat there for a while, then went to splash his face in the bathroom. Another slug of whisky made him feel almost human again. He grabbed his jacket and the ignition key for the car.

It seemed like most of the villagers were out of doors, and they stared at him as he drove through the fine morning. Fair enough if they thought he was nuts. He would just drive on, drive on, drive on ...

He went around the bay and up onto the southern headland. After turning inland for a short distance, he stopped. There were four cars up on the grass verge, and about thirty people standing at a line of traffic cones, a police roadblock sign lying flat on its back. Someone kicked one of the cones into the ditch.

Carl joined the crowd. Getting out of the car and walking

towards the cones he felt a sharp twinge of pain in his temple, and a faint clicking noise. A bit further and the faint clicking would become a sonic skewer that would make his nose bleed. Day 2 and SCOPE still hadn't packed in. How long can people live when they can't wake up, lying where they fell?

He laughed. One or two from the crowd glared at him. Just ahead of the roadblock was the road sign for the national speed limit, a fading black slash across white. 60mph had been enjoyed by the few of late, an unreachable pleasure. Now the sign may as well have been in a different universe.

Down the road. Where sleep ruled the airwaves.

A crow flew across his field of vision. The bird was already in the delta field when it veered further, deeper, where humans could no longer set foot. Animals seemed unaffected; Brindley said they had different brains. Or maybe it was just crows that had different brains. They could feast now, and the rats too.

'They'll survive,' he said to the sky and hills. 'Rats always fucking survive.'

He jumped the ditch and started walking at a right angle to the road, ignored by the crowd, up the green slopes that rose towards the heather and hilltops of bare rock. He left the crying and silence behind.

Late in the afternoon he returned, exhausted, to the hotel, his feet soaking, clothes and hands filthy, knuckle grazed from a fall. George was right about the conifer forest though: you couldn't really go through it because the trees were so densely packed. He was tired, worn out, limbs aching as he flopped onto the couch in the residents' lounge. Burned it off, he had. But the terror would be back. Even now he could feel it around his stomach, coils tightening. He lay there, dozed, imagined; tried to feel lucky. A car pulled up outside. Who was driving? He heard the hotel door open.

Footsteps. Silence.

Still lying on the couch, Carl opened his eyes, aware he was being watched. It was Brindley.

'I've been looking for you,' he said, sitting down in a leather chair.

Carl turned away, faced the back of the couch. He just wanted to go to sleep, but his curiosity got the better of him.

'How did you get here, Mr Brindley? To Inverlair, I mean.' His voice was level, expressionless.

The leather chair creaked.

'With great difficulty. Friends of mine, they tried to get me to go with them, on their boat.'

'Friends?' Carl sat up. Sleep could wait.

'Yes.'

'So where are they now?'

Brindley sighed. 'West coast of Ireland, I hope. That's where they were headed. SCOPE was being trialled in Dublin – they had their own Civil Contingencies Secretariat – and down the east coast, and in the north, but parts of the west coast should be okay, I think.'

Carl turned to face Brindley. 'So you did manage to persuade at least some people that SCOPE was a danger?'

'Yes, close friends, my sister and . . .'

'That all?'

Brindley narrowed his eyes. 'Yes.'

'So why didn't you go with them, these friends of yours?' Carl sat up on the sofa. 'And why exactly did you choose to bring me up here?'

'To save you, I suppose.'

'Save me?'

'Yes. Who else would follow a lead connected to SCOPE all the way up here? It was your job.'

That was something Carl didn't want to think about. Instead of thinking he could sleep, or walk. Being hungover didn't help matters, made it harder for him to judge the truth of what he was being told. It had been his job to sniff around ugly secrets such as SCOPE. Exposing that kind of crap was supposed to be a calling, a vocation; at least that's what he'd believed. Maybe he'd failed to do his job properly. If there had been any saving to be done, he should have been the one doing it, in banner headlines over an exposé. But nothing like that had been possible.

'Why didn't you try to stop it?'

Brindley folded his arms, his eyes flashing. 'What the fuck are you talking about? You don't think I tried to stop this?' He jabbed a finger at Carl. 'You must have known that SCOPE was more than a communications system. You knew that. You must have. You said you had the full spec – you mentioned bioactive frequencies for Christ's sake in one of your pieces. You must have known, at least suspected . . . you must have talked to Cobhill or Haarland or one of these guys.'

Carl heaved himself off the couch, anger rising in him. 'I couldn't have stopped this any more than you.'

Silence.

The hint of a smile played around Brindley's thin lips. 'You think I was any less impotent than you?'

Carl didn't answer. He headed upstairs without looking back.

•

Shadow marked the deepening evening, sun sinking behind the northern headland. Carl got up to sit by the window and look out across the sun-bright bay.

In the quiet, he could hear the sea stir against the bay, a background rush of water lapping on rock. The day moved into early evening and it was warm, and the smell of the sea was strong. He leant on the sill of the open window. There was crying somewhere, though he wasn't sure where, and a steady stream of people coming back from the edge of the delta field. He reached for the cigarette he had been given by one of the locals. There was a big NO SMOKING sign on the back of the door, but he guessed that George Cutler would have other things on his mind apart from the smell of smoke in one of his rooms. The death of his wife would be fairly high on that list.

A knock at the door. He listened. It came again, louder. He heard a woman's voice, out in the corridor.

'Are you there?'

He sat up, his lips parched, wearing a T-shirt and boxer shorts.

'Come in,' he rasped, rising from the bed.

The door creaked open and Simone Cutler looked in, her face pale, eyes red. Sleepless. Just like him.

'We were wondering if you'd like anything to eat?'

She came into the room. Instead of her waitress whites, she wore a dressing gown. Her hair was loose.

'No,' Carl said. 'Thanks. I'm not hungry. How . . .' He stopped, unable to finish the question. There was no need to ask.

Simone started to shake. She was next to him now, and Carl could smell traces of perfume and, deeper, her true scent. She raised a trembling hand to her eyes. The next thing Carl knew they were holding each other, a full-on hug, in the summer stillness as the birds sang in the sun.

He stroked Simone's unbrushed hair, pressed her closer. They sat on the bed and, as her dressing gown parted Carl automatically slid his hand between her thighs. He felt himself harden, and he gave himself to an emotion that blotted out fear.

November

12

Autumn was on the move, flinging storms in a fusillade from the Atlantic. On the main road south Carl stopped in his tracks, sucking deep for air. He was pushing himself too hard, full recovery still some way off, evidently. How long would it take?

This is how it is and how it would be. Pneumonia had given him a glimpse of the future and he now existed as a weaker, older man. He'd never felt so tired and worn out. Was this to be his new peak fitness? Maybe he'd never fully recover.

Bed had suited him too well; it was as if he belonged in the hollow his dead weight had pressed into the mattress in Room 14. Try as he might, he couldn't make himself as strong as once he'd been, couldn't shake the disease. A deeper resting-place than his bed would have been no bad thing, one next to Howard and the German couple. But he wasn't going to die any time soon. There was here and now to consider; pressing concerns that demanded a response, even if it was jumping off a cliff or slitting his wrists. That was always an option.

Perhaps he'd pushed himself too hard, walking into the hills, following the invisible bars of his cage from one side of the bay to the other.

They were watching him, the villagers. Through binoculars they were scrutinising him as he plodded and puffed along the southern headland, on the road that curved up and out of the bay. He knew they were watching him because he was watching them. There were two pairs searching for him, he could see through his binoculars: the old woman in Bayview Cottage, standing at her living-room window, and one of Cutler's boatyard crew down on the pier. Well, he'd give them a good show. He put one foot in front of the other, a feat of dexterity that was bound to amaze the observers.

He walked out from behind the trees, adjusted his headphones and headed south in time to the music throbbing in his ears. Thank Christ for solar power.

•

On the main road out of Inverlair where there was an opening in a line of rowan trees, a gravel track led to a rusty metal gate that was wide enough to let a lorry through. Hidden by low branches Carl saw a washed-out sign for Levanche Aggregates, Inverlair Quarry. The metal gates were chained together and a wheelless windowless old car was taking root among the bushes. Carl climbed over the chest-high gate and continued down the rough track and into the quarry. Warning placards atop wooden posts, all flattened by the wind, urged site visitors to WEAR PERSONAL PROTECTION EQUIPMENT and DON'T TAKE UNNECESSARY RISKS. As far as the pregnancy was concerned, it was a bit late for any of that. He crunched on down the stony track, into the great gouged pit.

The main part of the quarry must have been over 300 metres wide and at least 50 deep, one side open, leading down towards a sagging ballast-filled pier where the cargo ships had loaded up with gravel sand and aggregate. Long gone now, everything rust and rot: prefab site office with broken windows; corrugated-iron works shed rattling and squeaking in the wind; corroded tank and concrete bund for waste oil; lorry trailers with flat tyres; a long conveyor-belt machine, angling into the air, a dead dinosaur like Eric. Like himself.

At the far end of the quarry another dirt track ploughed up and through banks of peat, until it opened out again into a steep-sided lagoon. Signs warned of deep water. Young pine trees had taken hold on the lagoon's stony slopes, along with gorse and tufts of heather. Wind ghosted in gusts across the dark water.

Nobody was watching him here.

On a stone track overlooking the lagoon, Carl picked up a fist-sized stone and hurled it underarm down towards the deep water. The splash echoed round the pit, setting birds to flight. Some of them sped from the quarry's floor, twittering in fright, flashing towards the safety of holes in the sand cliffs, at the far end of the lagoon. When the sun was out it was warm, but the cool breeze sped the clouds, and it was cold in the shadows, spines of winter needling into autumn.

Carl made his way down the side of the quarry towards the lagoon. The wind dropped away and, sitting next to a pile of huge boulders, he felt some heat in the sun in the rocks and on the ground. He unzipped his jacket and pulled out his water bottle.

There was sand on the quarry floor, around the lagoon. The plaque at the village viewpoint said the sea level had fluctuated since the last Ice Age. Maybe that explained why he had his own private inland beach.

Tenacious buggers, those young pine trees, half-submerged on the slopes of the lagoon, green shoots bursting through the gravel, some of them saplings barely knee-high. The earth was reclaiming this man-made scar in the landscape, creeping down the sides of the quarry, covering the pit and the tracks, the mounds of till and rusting machinery. Healing over. Carl sat with eyes closed and out of the wind until the next cloud, a big one, came and blocked the sun. Shadow lowered the temperature and sitting there became uncomfortable after a spell. He got to his feet. The book in the hotel said there was a prehistoric structure, and some caves, up in the hill. There was nothing else to do but walk and hide and think. Despite what George had said, people probably blamed him for everything that had happened; when they found out about

Simone they'd blame him for that as well. Fair enough. Rather than question their own lack of awareness, their blindness, they could pin SCOPE on him and Howard. Simone's brother seemed to have Little Man Syndrome. Carl doubted whether being an uncle again would cause him unbridled delight.

•

Two hours later he was 300 metres up on the opposite headland, at the remains of a Bronze Age broch, trying to envisage what this pile of stones had looked like, standing twelve metres high and with two-metre thick walls. There was tightness in his chest and weakness in his legs. But he'd managed the climb, all the way, whereas the week before he hadn't.

People had looked out from here once, he thought, across the same hills and bay, out to where sun and cloud danced on the same leaden Atlantic. Hungry people, perhaps, watching from this spot. How healthy had the prehistoric diet been? It seemed to consist mainly of nuts, berries and fish. How could you square a healthy diet with dying young? Simple: death had more than one trick up its sleeve. It could seep into your bones with the drizzle, or it could strangle you with your own umbilical cord. A harsh winter. The point of a sword. These were the ways before Alzheimer's and cancer and the industrialised race to extinction. Erase the main road from the picture, the forest plantation too, and you could be looking at a million years ago.

The broch was anywhere between 2,000 and 4,000 years old, according to the book in the hotel, but there wasn't much left now. The thing had collapsed in on itself, or been knocked down. A defensive structure, built to keep watch over a wide area with one face towards the sea and the other inland. Inverlair was an ideal spot: a river at the head of a sheltered bay. But something, someone, would have come along to break the peace. Did the invaders export their desperation, taking by force what Inverlair had?

SCOPE would fail – everything man-made did, sooner or later. SCOPE would retreat, mast by mast, and those who were left could take over again, could . . . what? Scavenge over relics? Worship the fucking masts like some death cult?

Looking down the hill towards the village Carl could see the spill of big stones from the collapsed broch, some of them completely grown over. He walked down the slope and knelt, touched one of the buried stones. Within this grass swelling, this bump, was a missing piece of the past, and it would stay there unless he freed it. Perhaps he should help the rock get reborn.

Stamping with the heel of his boot, he struck a solid edge under the grass, worked around in this way until he had the outline, then with his hands he pulled the sods and black soil from the broch stone. After a few minutes of effort, sweat running into his eyes and down the small of his back, lungs straining, he'd worked the boulder loose, like a molar in its socket.

Straining every sinew, he extracted, a heave at a time, a hundredweight of rectangular stone, dragging it free of the centuries and onto the grass. Many stones were buried further down the slope.

Gasping for breath, Carl sank down next to the slab, dark earth reeking from the hole. After a few minutes, he sat up. Already the soil was drying on his hands; cold sweat on his face, nails topped with a line of dirt. There were dozens more stones to dig out. Big ones on the outside, smaller ones forming the inner wall of the broch; the whole thing tapering upwards for seven metres, just like the book said. His arms were shaking with the effort and his lungs were sore. Maybe he could dig more out, maybe all of them, in time.

He lifted his binoculars and scanned the village. If he could see them clearly, then they could see him. He searched the backs of houses, upstairs bedrooms and kitchen windows. Did he see a movement in one, someone ducking behind a curtain?

Carl patted the stone he had just dug up, the first of many. He could do it. He could resurrect the dead.

That would give them something to talk about. The nutter on the hill. The guy who knew about SCOPE and who didn't try to stop it. The guy who killed his friend.

After a while he stood up, drank some water from his bottle. It was too early to go back yet; too early for the awkward silences and the hints and the looks. Simone wanted a conversation, but he doubted if anything he had to say would improve the situation, although, now that he thought about it, he wasn't sure if he could find any words of significance at all. Sometimes it felt like a dream, and at other times everything came sharply into focus; a reality he had no idea how to handle.

Best not to think about it. It was easier to push it away. He had to push it away.

13

Sitting on the roadblock on the north road out of the bay, Carl pulled Howard's deltameter out of his pocket. Howard must have had it in his own pocket, his body wet and cold from six days lying on the hill. Carl sniffed the phone, expecting the lingering scent of putrefaction, but it just smelled of plastic. One day he would be able to leave the redzone; the deltameter would tell him when it was safe. It would point the way to when he could get back into his car and drive.

Better park Howard's car somewhere. Garage it. Top it up with biodiesel every now and again. Run the engine. Keep the tyres inflated, ready for when he could take off. To where?

Somewhere. The road would open. The masts would fail and the delta field would open, and he could drive on to where he wouldn't feel like someone in a cage. But that was for the future; just now he was an inmate who would have to do his time.

There was an old stone cottage a short distance away from the road, chimney at either end, and no windows or door. It stank of animals and shit. Two rooms, the corroded hulk of a stove in one, and no floorboards or furniture in either. No internal walls as such but there were beams standing, holding up most of the ceiling. The bottom three steps of the wooden staircase were missing. Carl looked up. The roof was intact, apart from over one gable-end.

He tried the staircase and it held, so he tried a foot on the first step, let it take his full weight. The wood protested, and he thought the whole lot would come crashing down. But it didn't. He climbed and poked his head up, level with the upper floor to see what was what. A metal bed frame in one of two rooms, and nothing else. Musty smell of decay and the sheepshit stink on the ground floor.

The staircase held him. The bare floorboards in the bedroom held him. Carl edged towards the bed, testing every step, pressuring the wood, listening, waiting to plummet. The skylight in the bedroom was still unbroken. The cobwebbed stalk of a light fitting, minus bulb and shade, hung in the middle of the ceiling. He sat, gently, on the bare metal springs of the old bedstead. It squeaked. Ribbons of wallpaper had peeled and drooped; most of the paint that had once been on the ceiling lay in flakes on the bare floor.

Carl lay back and waited, his feet still on the floor, ready to rise at the first sign of trouble. But bed and floor held his weight. He lifted his legs onto the springs; they still had their bounce, and it wasn't too uncomfortable, no, not at all . . .

He closed his eyes.

Eric. Lesley. Sarah. Eddie. All now populating a dream world. Were they real, or had he dreamed his previous life? This life involved Simone, and the dreaded by-product of real sex. It wasn't even that; it hadn't been sex, not really. What had it been? Comfort. A gift from terror. She hadn't been wearing underwear. Didn't say anything to him, afterwards, just left the room. Spunk on the carpet. He blanked the details, the pressure, and the urge.

At least with CivCon and food riots he knew what he was dealing with – all that stuff had origins that could be understood, oppression that could be traced and plotted. Even an ugly world moulds itself around a person, and they become the impression it makes of them.

After a while he found closing his eyes easier than keeping them open.

He was grateful for extinction.

•

It was dark when Carl came back to the hotel. As he reached the back garden he heard a stag's bellowing moan echo round the dark hills, sounding his power. George had told him they'd be shagged out in a few weeks after the rut was finished. Carl let himself in quietly and listened for activity. The clock, ticking in the lobby, was the only sound.

His eyes grew accustomed to the dark. There was always light, he just had to give himself the chance to see it, to stand and look until the black released the objects it was holding. Carl made his way to the kitchen, found the lamp on the table, and the box of matches. He opened the door of the stove to warm up. Lighting the lamp, he sat at the kitchen table.

Outside, the wind was picking up. In the silence he could hear dry leaves scraping against the back door. Fried fish and potatoes were warming in the oven, enough to take the edge off his appetite. As he chewed the food, he thought of the sleeping village, and him creeping back to it, stealing into this house, like a burglar breaking in. Was it a foetus or an embryo? He knew there was a difference. It was all a matter of time. Maybe it was awake, percolating its mother's nutrients, more thing than person, inside the sleeping Simone; maybe he and it were the only two entities awake in the village.

He heard a noise in the corridor.

The door opened. It was Simone, in her dressing gown, yawning, candle in hand

Carl collected himself. 'I thought I was being quiet when I came in.'

'People are never as quiet coming in as they think,' she said. 'I just wanted to tell you something.'

Carl stiffened.

Simone warmed her hands on the stove. 'Adam told me that they could use someone at the forestry. One of the guys hurt his arm. If you're feeling up to it – I don't know if you are – you could fill in for him.'

'Doing what?'

'I'm not sure. Helping cut more of those probably.' She pointed at the basket of logs by the stove.

Instinctively, he wanted to say no. He didn't want anything to do with Simone's twat of a brother, or anyone else for that matter. He thought for a second.

'I've never used any forestry machinery before. Maybe I'd just get in the way.'

'You don't have to use any machinery. He said he could use you.'

The wind gusted against the kitchen window, moaning in the chimney flue as the rain started.

He told her he would think about it.

•

Hard workers. All of them. Cutting wood. Catching fish. Growing food and fixing things. Everyone mucking in, unless they were too old or too young. Everyone doing their bit. Everyone except him, the parasite feeding off the hard work of others, eating their food, absorbing their heat, shagging their women. Too clever to get his hands dirty like the hard workers. He can hardly hold a hammer. Where does he go during the day? What's he doing mooching around the hills when there's work to be done? Let him get on with it. Get a grip. Get his head down and lend a hand. Do his bit. Muck in.

Well, the hard workers could all piss off. Let them watch him. Let them invent whatever stories they wanted.

It all came down to calories — energy. Young kids got the most, followed by working men and women. It was Howard's first-winter survival system. Carl wasn't young and he wasn't exactly useful. He was now on the bottom rung of the rationing ladder; he may as well have had a yellow U for useless stamped on his forehead. He lay on the bed, lime-green alcopop bubbling in his stomach, and fell asleep. In his dream, a giant adder was coiled and standing, at the foot of his bed, watching, tasting the darkness with its flickering tongue.

14

Being under surveillance, with no escape possible. He was used to that. Emails, texts and calls intercepted. His ID a permanent locus on the CivCon watchlist. Anonymity was a thing of the past for most people. At least he wasn't safety-chipped, like the kids. What he did, where he went, what he said and who he said it to, was of sufficient interest to someone, somewhere, that various procedures were enacted to ensure it was all logged and cross-indexed, put through pattern-recognition filters, and presented as a case file to some CivCon technocrat. Liberty and incarceration were entirely matters of procedure, depending on what Sentinel recommended. After a while, he had learned to live with that. If there is no immediate physical threat, people can learn to live with just about anything. There was nothing he could have done about any of it, so ignoring it as best he could seemed to make sense, otherwise it would have driven him crazy. Same applies now.

After a few days spent mulling it over, Carl finally decided to act on Simone's suggestion. Walking up the track from the north road he could hear the forestry machines before he saw them, smell the strong, sweet scent of freshly cut pine. Splintered branches, their fibrous ends wrenched apart, littered the track up to the conifer plantation; caterpillar chains had gouged a mud-trail over the rough ground. He followed the trail and the noise of the machines until he came to a clearing. There were guys there he recognised, a pick-up truck and a Portakabin. Through the trees, Carl caught glimpses of the felling machine, its claw reaching out to grip a ten-metre trunk, cutting it at the base, turning it as if it weighed no more than a broom handle. Each trunk was stripped of branches and sliced in ten seconds flat, puffs of blue smoke belching from the machine's exhaust. The roar and the wrath of a huge beast, smashing a path through the trees as it harvested low-grade carbon.

Stacks of cut trunks were waiting to be lifted by another machine onto the pick-up truck. George had said there were seven in the forestry work crew. Today, there were only two guys in the Portakabin, one older man, late fifties, wearing thick black-rimmed glasses, dozing in a plastic chair, a cap on his head and booted feet crossed on the tabletop. The other, a thick-necked younger man wore an oily orange boiler suit and was playing a hand-held gaming machine. It took him a few seconds to realise that Carl was standing in the doorway. The game-player looked up, kicked the sleeper's boots to wake him up.

'The gaffer said you might be along. You were with that other guy when he died, the bald guy.'

'Howard,' said Carl. 'Yes, I was. I'm Carl, by the way.'

'I know,' said the nameless gamer. 'And you got pneumonia on the hill.' There was nothing like the direct approach; a smirk on the guy's face, the trace of secret amusement. The CivCon smile.

'Yes, in both lungs,' said Carl, trying the bluff approach. 'That's the kind of double I could do without. Sorry, I didn't get your names.'

Gamer toggled his thumb, first at himself. 'Casper. And this is Shit for Brains.'

Shit for Brains stretched himself from his doze. 'You're a twat, Casper,' he laughed, arms crossed, boots still on the tabletop. 'It's Dennis. So you've come to join our band of merry men have you, Carl?'

Carl said yes and tried to see the funny side of it. He'd once shadowed a fire crew for the night: two call-outs, one a faulty fire alarm and the other a chimney fire. Mainly, there seemed to be a lot of eating, cleaning and playing of pool involved in being a firefighter, but Carl managed to get 1,200 words out of it. These jokers, Dennis and Casper, were different. He would have to get along with them, maybe for a long time. This was work of a different kind.

Almost two hours later he was halfway up the forest track when he stopped what he was doing. Though the day was cold, the exertion had warmed him. After dragging about twenty loads of branches up the hill, something important dawned on him. He hadn't really thought of it when Casper had shown him his job for the day, but now he was starting to wonder what the fuck he was actually doing.

He looked back down the forest track to the Portakabin, where a droning crane-lift grabbed a clawful of man-sized logs and dropped them onto the back of the pick-up. The machine in the forest had stopped felling and stripping; Casper and Dennis were standing around waiting for the driver of the crane to finish loading. A few at a time, the claw-lift picked up the trunks of spruce and placed them expertly in the vehicle, which rocked as each new load was banged down. There are supposed to be seven guys in the wood crew, thought Carl: one's doing the work, two are standing around, and four aren't even here. He looked at the head-high stack of offcuts he'd built up over the last two hours.

Why the fuck was he dragging bundles of useless branches further up the forest track? He dropped the rope and walked back to where the logs were being loaded. The more he thought about what he'd been doing, the more it didn't stack up, so to speak. And Casper giving it the old CivCon look. That bothered him. Something wasn't right, and Carl had a gut feeling that the wrongness of the situation was at his expense.

The pick-up was loaded with twenty or so logs, then it rumbled off towards the village. Someone at the boatyard would chainsaw the wood into smaller logs for the fires of Inverlair. Another guy, blond crew cut and red scar on his cheekbone, got out of the claw-lift; Casper was sitting on the Portakabin's step, playing his game as Carl walked over to him.

'I was just thinking there,' said Carl, pointing back up the track. 'Why do all the offcuts have to be moved up the track?'

In reply came the smirk, the secret smile. Casper shrugged. 'Site management,' he said gruffly, fiddling with his game.

'Eh?'

'See the gaffer if you want an explanation,' Casper said, glancing at his mate. The blond man laughed, turned back to the claw-lift. 'Adam'll fucking batter you for dropping him in it.'

Casper just giggled, glanced up at Carl. 'See the gaffer.'

As he walked back to the village, Carl was sure he heard the words 'site management', followed by more laughter.

At the boatyard, he saw Adam's pick-up, heard a rattling chainsaw make short work of the spruce trunks. It was a cold day. Though the sun was out and there were few clouds, it was breezy, from the east. That usually spelt cold and dry, George had said.

Adam Cutler had plugged an electric chainsaw into a biodiesel generator and was oblivious to Carl standing at the gate. When he finally caught sight of him, Adam eased up on the revs and lifted his goggles. He came over, leaving the chainsaw idling on a bed of fresh sawdust.

'You finished already?'

'Not quite,' said Carl. He rubbed his stubble. 'I'm sort of wondering why I have to move that stuff at all. It doesn't make sense.' His eyes narrowed. 'If you're taking the piss . . . I'm not interested.'

Adam grinned. 'Oh, lighten up for fuck's sake.' He shook his head. 'Can you not take a joke?'

Carl frowned. 'A joke?'

'Yeah, the guys are just messing with you. Of course there's no need to move the fucking branches, they just want to see how you take it, that's all, see who they're dealing with.'

'Right,' Carl said. 'I see. There's plenty to laugh about, I suppose. It's a very ... humorous situation, this.' He gestured at nothing in particular. 'Everything's funny. Hilarious, if you look hard enough.'

Striding back to his chainsaw, Adam waved Carl away. 'Oh, come on, man. People respond to things in their own way. Crying about it won't put food on the table, and that's what's important right now, more than ever.' He picked up the chainsaw. 'The work crew get more food because they work, so thank your lucky stars you're on it.' He revved the chainsaw. 'And thank my sister as well,' he shouted.

Over the next few days, Carl turned up for work, cut kelp for the biofuel processor plant; the extra food, his work rations, slipped down nice and easy. He moved from Room 14 into Room 7, casting off some of the traces of death. Three days later, when there was no need to cut any more logs or kelp, he went down to the pier to help unload the *Aurora* of its catch of mackerel and pollock. Even that task only involved taking a few boxes to the community-centre freezers on a handcart. People were getting fed up of eating fish every day, but alternatives were thin on the ground, apart from venison and the odd rabbit or grouse shot by the old gamekeeper. He learned, as he guessed, that Casper was a nickname and that it was indeed connected with the friendly ghost. They'd never be bosom pals.

After a week, Carl arrived at the clear-felled forest. Today he was supposed to learn how to operate the log-grabber. The guys were in the Portakabin.

'Adam wants to see you,' said Casper, without looking up from his game.

'What for?'

'Dunno. He's at the house.'

Dennis was paring a piece of wood with a penknife. He didn't look up either.

Carl assessed the situation. 'I'll nip down later.'

Shifting in a plastic chair, Dennis coughed. 'I think he wants to see you now.'

'Now? I've just got here.'

'Yep,' chirped Casper, his eyes still glued to the action. 'That's what de man say.'

They wouldn't meet his eye. He turned on his heel and set off.

Adam's house, a massive harled bungalow, was one of eight ranged in a line behind the main part of the village, on the northern headland. Carl walked the main road back from the forest and along the headland until he reached the track that led to Adam's house. Built on top of a double garage and partly buried in the hillside, the house was shielded by a belt of mature willow trees that provided shelter on the seaward side.

He didn't like this; no, not one bit. Something was wrong. He knocked on the heavy varnished back door. A woman in her early twenties opened it. She was small, fair-skinned, with long hair tied in a ponytail, dark rings under her blue eyes. She told Carl that Adam was in his office.

Some people are touchy about their places of origin, especially when they're living somewhere else. The woman was definitely from either America or Canada. Carl recognised her. She'd been too hungover, the day SCOPE had gone live, to go with her friends for a drive. Her friends never came back.

What could Adam want with an office?

It wasn't really an office as such, more a storeroom, though a semi-circular desk had four screens arranged upon it. Three of them still had cellophane wrappers around them, brand new.

Another door was open. Footsteps sounded from below, coming up stairs. It was some kind of cellar, probably down to one of the garages below.

There was no greeting from Adam. 'This was going to be my nerve centre,' he said, pointing to the screens. 'Links with the boatyard and with both fishing boats. A monitoring system for the biofuel plant – we had a CivCon contract to serve their Inverness depot. We even had a contract in place with a seaplane firm; it would have cut through a shitload of biosec red tape. Just think about it: shellfish delivered fresh to European buyers in a few hours.' He pressed the tip of his index finger against one of the screens. He pushed, applied a little more pressure, and the screen fell off the desk, corner first, crashing onto the floor. 'Every litre of diesel and every rivet and every lobster. Every debit and credit with every customer and supplier, logged automatically.' He smiled. 'My accountant would've loved it.'

His face fell. 'You've made my sister pregnant, you fucking tosspot.' He looked at Carl, blank-eyed.

A response was expected. An explanation. 'Yes,' Carl said.

There was silence. Two can play at that game, he thought.

Adam snorted. 'Is that it? Is that all you've got to say? *Yes.*'

'Yeah. You asked me a specific question. I answered it.'

'Okay. Do you mind telling me how it happened?' In response to Carl's raised eyebrows, he added quickly: 'The circumstances, smart-arse. She's nearly three months gone. You arrived here three months ago. So you didn't fucking hang about there, did you?' He came out from behind the desk.

'It wasn't like that,' said Carl. 'Who told you Simone was pregnant?'

'Never mind who told me. Wasn't like what, exactly?'

'It wasn't meant to happen.'

'Is that a fact?'

'Yes. It is.'

'So, what was the scene? Let me see.' Adam clicked his fingers. 'That's it: a vulnerable woman seeking comfort ...'

Carl jerked his thumb at the door. 'What – like yours?'

'Fuck off,' said Adam. 'It wasn't ... like that.'

Carl put his hands in his pockets. Round 1 to him. 'So, is this where the older brother gets all protective? Are you going to make me an offer I can't refuse?'

'Look,' said Adam. 'She's my sister, for fuck's sake. I want to know what your plans are. What are you going to do about it?'

'Something,' said Carl. 'Or nothing. There's not much I can do about it, or so I've been told.'

He turned to go.

'Fine. Excellent.' Adam took a quick step forward. 'Well, don't bother coming anywhere near the pier or the boatyard until you make your fucking mind up, useless prick.'

•

Carl sat on the twenty-fifth broch stone he had managed to unearth and looked down at the bay.

The days were shorter now, and colder. A crow landed nearby, across a gully, on top of an outcrop of lichen-covered rock. He watched it, keeping quite still. This seemed to unnerve the crow.

People threw stones. People took no notice. They didn't just sit, stock-still and staring. The bird hopped from foot to foot, bobbing and blinking, confused.

'*Corvus corone*,' Carl said out loud. 'I know what you are.'

Maybe this was the bird that had pecked Howard's eyes out, the one that had tugged and nipped off bits of lip and ear. Here was another scavenger shitting out digested human. There had been plenty of those. The crow hopped and called, squawked enquiry, coal-eye glistening. Carl spied a stone at his feet. He grabbed it. As he did so the crow snapped from the rock and barked away into the grey sky. Carl threw the stone even though he knew there was no chance of hitting the bird. Just taking aim at it would do, but the crow was too quick and the stone climbed, looped to earth, well short of its target.

The bird had come to taunt him; knew the man's habits and had lain in wait for him. Your friend filled my belly. How do you like that? Why don't you just lie down and do likewise? Turn yourself into meat. Give up your corporeal tribute for the greater good of crowkind. Maybe he should do that; grab whatever pills he could get his hands on; swipe one of George's bottles of malt, swallow the lot. Find a hole to hide in, neck the lot, and fall asleep for the last time. Give the crows and the worms a good feed. Sleep and death would be reliable, this time around.

Out at sea, there was still no white boat. Howard's friends would never come for him. Even if they were able to, they'd stay where they were if they had any sense.

He'd been a journalist, once. You do a job for long enough and that's all you are. He was seeing that now.

Without a job, what are you? People don't like thinking about that, with or without full stomachs. It's easier just to work, without thinking of alternative identities or meanings. He'd been a journalist. But that label no longer meant anything. There were now other labels being written for him to wear.

15

For two days it rained, without let-up, the dry spell well and truly broken. In his room, he considered the calendar on the wall, the months in motion.

The rain didn't stop Carl going up the hill. Three days ago the river through the forest had been a delicate trickle; now it had transformed into a roaring beast, churning peaty froth as it thundered over the falls and out under the road bridge.

He could have hung around the hotel. Easy enough, he could have gone downstairs just to talk to Simone or George, or to pass the time until the rain stopped. Make the effort. Reach out. Somewhere inside him there was an awareness that that was what he had to do. It was stirring – this need to reach out – but it could yet be strangled in his inner darkness, unborn.

He climbed the stile at the back fence, near the stalker's cottage, and headed squelching through the rain up to the ridge towards the broch, spade slung over his shoulder, oilskins keeping him dry and warm. It was true: there was no such thing as bad weather, only bad clothing.

Why sulk in his room? He looked back down the hill at the hotel. It wasn't her fault. It wasn't his fault. Extenuating circumstances. End of the world, and all that. Adam Cutler was a Grade A prick though, he didn't need much clarity of thought to see that.

Not even crows out today. Sheep huddling bedraggled and quiet in any shelter they could find. Cold with it – and getting colder. The steady climb to the broch took about forty-five minutes; a few weeks before it had taken him twice as long, but now his lungs and legs were strong and he didn't need to pause on the climb. At least there was no wind today firing rain into his face.

Sitting on the low wall he had exhumed from the ground, he wondered how many other communities there were like Inverlair. There were probably some, where SCOPE and mobile coverage had been poor. Isolated rural hill villages or natural depressions. Inverlair was both. Carl watched sun and shadow fight it out on the far headlands, the *Aurora* motoring back into the bay.

Maybe Adam Cutler was just looking out for his sister. Just doing his best for everyone in the village. Like hell he was. He was playing the saviour, the man with the big plan, and he relished the part.

Carl took out his binoculars and scanned Inverlair. Walk and climb, climb and walk, pressure easing in his head, rain pattering on his hood. He was walking away from all the crap that had to do with how other people felt and what they expected from him. He could walk as far as the bars of his cage, measure them on the deltameter, and look out at the dead world that had once been alive, or at least not quite so dead. Maybe he couldn't call it living, but at least it had a point and a purpose, however basic: to stay alive.

They'd be watching him now, he reckoned, not with RF trackers or GPS or Sentinel in Glasgow, but from back windows that faced onto the hills of Inverlair. They'd see his yellow oilskins, watch him rebuild the wall of the broch, stone by stone, the nutter.

Carl took a detour, cutting south towards the road instead of north behind the village. His change of routine would be noticed, he surmised.

Down below was the road, winding into the drift-net of low cloud that smothered the southern summits. At least Howard and the German couple had been given a decent burial. They were lying next to others: people threw in their handfuls of dirt; said a few words. SCOPE had done away with all that ritual, preferring instead an open-air smörgåsbord approach. Is that not what the Indian Parsees did? Left their dead exposed on the hillside for the wind and the eagles to devour? Meat going around on the big wheel. A parade of predators to scoff the bodies: foxes, dogs, birds, rats, cats, trillions of maggots pupating in the ripening flesh. Mass human death would have caused a sudden flowering of insect life.

Good eating, all round.

•

The rain eased. Each hole that had held a broch stone was full of water; there were twenty-five holes altogether, twenty-five pieces of a Neolithic puzzle.

It was a sick fucking joke, that's what it was; a new life on the way and he'd put it there. That wasn't right. To say it was a sick joke wasn't doing it justice. What would its future be? Stuck in Inverlair, hungry and clueless about the world. Another mouth gaping for food, a burden that was his doing and his responsibility.

There had been no agenda with Simone when she'd knocked on his door, no ulterior motive. He never meant for anything to happen; he had felt something that wasn't to do with sex or lust. Maybe fear was the basic driver for so much of what people did, even when they were shagging. Even that could be a cry against extinction and terror, the obliteration of self and conscious awareness. Or was it the unmasking of the true self, the revelation of insatiable appetite in its twisted, personalised glory?

All he'd wanted to do was hold her.

The rest of it just happened. That is what he believed to be the truth.

Carl hacked round another broch stone, clearing its outline in the sticky earth. He was keeping watch, but he wasn't really sure on what.

The sea would have been scanned, when the broch was a

broch, for uninvited guests; it would have been Mission Control in the fight against invaders. Where was the threat now?

It wasn't the redzone or the sea that Carl watched. It was Inverlair. With Howard's binoculars he scanned for movement; old women finally able to hang out clothes to dry; fish unloaded at the pier; Isaac playing in his sandpit. All this was perfectly normal for a world he could not penetrate, that held him at bay; so he had to watch it. Stay vigilant.

Carl dug out another stone, heaving it up and onto the grass, purpose being regained and reconfigured. One curving section of wall – almost a half circle – was rising to join the remains of the other. Higher than knee-height would cause him problems, but he'd figure that out when the time came.

Graft? He'd show the fuckers all about that. He would rebuild this thing, stone by buried stone. Fuck it – he would live in it. He would defend the broch against all comers. He would fight.

Fight.

So there was no time to waste.

He worked faster, hacking round a stone, levering it out, muttering to himself.

What's the point in trying to make a difference? Why risk what you have when protesting – the stance you take – means nothing? You're just one man. You're being buried, bit by bit, and you're just about to go under. If only you'd stop struggling, all that weight would lift from your shoulders and you could breathe again, take it all in your stride. So why bother trying to shine a light? The darkness is all around. Let it claim you. Get used to the dark that everyone else is groping around in. He should have let CivCon take him by the hand and show him the right way to behave now that there is no light in the world. Thrashing around in the dark is dangerous. You might hurt yourself, sonny, and those around you. The dark is all around you. Accept it. Let the shit wash over you and don't try to see into it or through it because that's just a headfuck and why bother bringing that on? Just keep your head clear and down and accept what's around you, now and forever. Amen. Accept the darkness. Stop struggling. Stop resisting. Stop trying to make other people see the foul things that are whispering how blessed is the darkness. Let it alone, and keep your mouth shut.

No.

And another stone, his sixth that day, was reclaimed from the earth. Another piece of the puzzle. Another step towards wholeness. It was important. It meant something. The broch was older than SCOPE and white rust and CivCon. Only hunger and death were older.

Sweating and gasping as he spaded up chunks of turf, Carl imagined himself a savage, repelling hordes of invaders from his perch. He would club them aside. Hack them to pieces. Machine-gun the lot of them. A caveman with an M60.

He'd make a difference. He'd make them pay.

'Hello there,' a voice said.

Carl let out a cry, jumped up from his digging, sweat, mud and hair plastered across his face. Wide-eyed, he gawped at the figure standing nearby. The stalker; Carl couldn't remember his name. The man smiled, adjusting his cap.

'The view is nice, but you won't have much in the way of mod cons.'

Carl cocked his head, still brandishing the spade. 'Eh? What the fuck are you on about?'

'The broch,' said the stalker, calm and even. 'A view but no loo. Not what you'd call a des res.'

Carl looked at the guy, sixty if he was a day. He felt the blister sting on his right palm from the digging. The pain wouldn't stop him doing what he had to do. No fucking way.

'Definitely not cosy,' the stalker said quietly.

Carl clutched the spade, and took a deep breath. The wall of the broch was forming; the long dead was rising.

The stalker leant forward on his stick. He wore a dark Gore-Tex jacket and thick brown socks above his heavy boots. Wisps of greying hair stuck out from under a tweed cap.

'You're busy,' he said.

Carl sat down on the mud-plastered stone he had just spent twenty minutes exhuming. The rain had stopped. He wiped his face clear of sweat and hair, nodded, said nothing.

The stalker squinted at the sky, the fog-shrouded bastion of Ben Bronach. The day was clearing, wind swinging to the north, getting colder. A seagull soared, silent over the ridge.

'Do you mind if I ask you what you're doing up here?'

Here we go. Never mind the matey chinwag.

'Why? Are you going to tell me to get off your land?'

'No,' said the stalker, his voice steady. 'This isn't my land. I'm wondering why you're digging these stones out of the ground.' He lowered his eyes from the sky and hills to inspect the foundations of the broch wall.

Of course there was a reason why a man would climb up into the hills to dig large stones out of the ground in the pissing rain. Alec John could remember, as a boy, when stones just as big had been used to build, and rebuild, walls. But this was different. This man was not digging for a practical reason. He was digging because he was compelled to.

For a second, Carl felt like telling the stalker the truth about the stones. He was rebuilding the broch, he felt like saying, because he was sick of living in that goldfish bowl down there, and because he needed something to do with his time. He was sick of the people down there muttering about what he had or hadn't done. They were sly bullies, the lot of them. So much for Highland hospitality.

'I wanted to be an archaeologist, once,' Carl found himself saying. 'I just wanted to see the broch as it was. Not just a pile of stones, but . . .' He faltered. 'Just to preserve it, you know? Before it's too late.' He looked at the ground, eyes roving over the stones.

'That's a fair enough explanation, I suppose,' said the stalker. He cleared his throat. 'But maybe it is too late, for the stones anyway.'

Shouldering his shotgun, he gestured up at the ridge. 'I've got traps where the grouse are,' he said. 'Stoats – they're fucking pests.' He jerked his thumb towards the village. 'They're even worse than that lot down there. And that's saying something, believe you me.'

Carl stopped inspecting his blister and looked up at the stalker, his mouth open.

'I'm Alec John Stoddart,' said the stalker. 'You'll be Carl Shewan. I remember you. I found you, lying half dead with your friend.'

Carl nodded, still staring. 'I know,' he said softly. 'I meant to say thanks for that and . . .'

Before Carl could finish, Alec John set off up the slope towards Ben Bronach, his dark form soon vanishing against the dark flank of the hill.

'Don't worry about it,' he said over his shoulder. 'Sorry about your friend.'

Carl got up and continued to dig, but it took him the whole afternoon to unearth one more stone. He kept stopping to think, looking up the hill to where the stalker's dwindling form had vanished into the dark slopes of rock and heather.

A while later Carl gave up digging. Late afternoon sun appeared, spotlighting the horizon as wads of grey nimbus opened. Carl shouldered the spade and headed in the direction of the north road, down to the old house near the roadblock.

Careful in the gloom, he eased his way up the broken staircase and, almost in darkness, lay on the bare bed frame. Eventually, stars appeared above him, visible through the dusty cracked skylight.

Patterns.

16

Down to the dunes and the waves, past the quarry, behind the southern headland, among the flotsam on the shoreline, sliding in the autumn sunlight among the stink of rotting high-tide seaweed, Carl stood on the glittering shore as the water played, filling the gullies with each surge, slooping and slurping between the cracks in the rocks. The sea kept on, coming in, going out, carrying stuff in, and spiriting it away again. Label-less plastic bottles full of what looked suspiciously like piss; oil drums half buried in the sand; and wooden planks, beams and branches – tossed high up the beach to soften and rot at the foot of the dunes. The sea was patient at its business, coughing up the rubbish, the indigestible. An election placard from Ireland, washed-out blue and white, the bleached grin of some straight-up, honest candidate was lying, half covered, in a slimy mound of kelp. He wondered if a wind had ripped the placard from a lamppost, maybe at the seafront somewhere, and sent it spinning into the Irish Sea. It might have been years in the water, a drifting relic of the old pre-emergency order. All that trust: washed away and beached in a far corner of nowhere.

Carl walked further along the high-tide line; the sea fizzing on the sand as the waves dragged out, feeling the first sting of redzone in his right temple.

The sheen of oil on a stretch of sand, its rainbow iridescence spreading on the water, black gobbets in the tideline froth. The oil had no obvious source. God knows where it had come from, but here it was – the dead world, like a decomposing corpse, leaking putrescence onto the pure sand, still with the power to hurt.

Above a shingle cove, near the main road south, he could see the small cairn of red warning stones that Howard had built and painted to mark the edge of the redzone. Making his way through the soft dunes, through the spiky marram grass, he headed back to the sub-lethal tranquillity of Inverlair.

No matter what happens, the sea comes in and the deer walk their ancient paths and the wind blows, or it doesn't. Nothing else enters the equation or disturbs the equilibrium, not old oil drums or Irish election posters. And certainly not SCOPE. All that stuff wasn't even a nuisance. Arrowhead and atom were all the same to the sea and the wind. Human triumphs had come and gone in a blink, and now the tide was high and the time to move to higher ground, or drown, had arrived.

'You're an arsehole,' Carl muttered to himself as he made his way between the dunes. 'At least talk to the woman. What other choice do you have?'

The stalker: it sounded as if he didn't exactly see eye to eye with the rest of the village. The guy had made a wise choice. Up there in the hills a man could think his own thoughts, be himself. There was no one watching, judging. There was nothing except air and earth.

Carl would keep picking away at the broch, building what he was compelled to reassemble, somehow. The stones were waiting to be fitted back together, and he shouldn't let them down. They could be recast; with effort they could be returned to what they once had been. Order could be restored, a semblance of purpose and pristine machismo.

He walked back up to the main road, grass knee-high on the verges, wanting something hard and level under his feet for a change instead of soft sand and shifting shingle. The road would vanish too, just like the quarry was doing. Creeping vegetation would do for both.

He took the track that led up past the stalker's house and onto the ridge, to where in the summer he would aim for the summit of Ben Bronach, at a shade over 670 metres. In the summer . . .

As he walked the south road that swept down into Inverlair Bay he slowed, looking ahead. There was a guy putting a chain on a bicycle. Before Carl could make a detour, the guy straightened from his upside-down bike, saw him approaching, and waved. With no real conviction, Carl waved back. A bit closer and he recognised the guy from the previous month, up the ladder, cleaning the guttering along with ex-Navy Patrick or Peter.

'Hey, dude,' called the guy, wiping oily hands on his black combats. He was smoking, and Carl didn't have to get too close to realise it wasn't ordinary tobacco. Gusts of weed came to him on the breeze. Carl wished he still smoked, the craving sparked by the sight of someone doing it for real. As he approached, the guy grinned. 'Never try riding a bike when you're stoned.'

'Can't say I've had the pleasure,' said Carl. He glanced at the spliff. There seemed to be writing, tiny script, covering the paper. The guy handed it to Carl with a twinkle in his eye. 'The good book contains the path to enlightenment.'

Carl studied the joint. A page from the Bible, ultra-thin, rolled into a fat cone. He took it and had a suck, the raw weed harsh on his throat. He coughed immediately.

'I'm not a true believer.' There were tears in his eyes as he struggled to catch his breath.

'You the journalist?'

'Was. There's not much call for news-gathering any more.'

'Certainly not in this place,' said the guy. 'Everyone's a journalist in Inverlair.' He grinned. 'They make up what they don't know.'

Shaking his head, Carl declined another puff. 'I must be hot news.'

The guy mounted his bike. 'You're a household name, for sure.' He stuck out his hand. 'I'm Terry Sullivan.' He picked up a can of white paint.

'You decorating? An autumn makeover to banish the blues?'

Terry smiled. His battered leather jacket was covered in sewn-on patches: Greenpeace, Shiva, Yin and Yang. The usual New Age hodgepodge. 'I'm in the Care and Repair Detail,' he said. 'Mrs Mackay is eighty-seven and her windows need doing before the winter.'

Smoke snaked from his nostrils and was carried away on the breeze. He climbed back on his bike and set off down the road. 'Come over for a smoke any time you want,' he shouted over his shoulder. 'I'm in the caravan.'

•

Two days later, Carl considered broch stone number 34. It was the last one before the slope. The harder work was about to start: heaving the stones up the slope, a few inches at a time, would take every ounce of strength he had. And the second layer of wall, lifting one stone onto another, would need a crowbar. Making the broch higher could not be done by brute strength alone. It was stacking up to be a mountainous problem.

Binoculars poised, Carl watched Terry Sullivan's grey static caravan. A couple of hundred metres down from the main road, it sat on the opposite headland where the ground levelled off near the shore. By the look of it, Terry's neighbour was an old hippie: grey hair in a ponytail, glasses and sandals; going in and out of three big polytunnels lined up next to his house, a two-up, two-down with a flat-roof extension out the back.

Carl lowered the binoculars. He could walk round the shore or into the quarry, the forest, anywhere. All the way to 2.26 miles, if the fancy took him, as far as he could go, which was nowhere near far enough. Maybe he could pop over for a visit, and a smoke.

For today at least, stone 34 could stay buried.

•

Out in the corridor Carl heard children's voices.

'The monster will get us up here,' came a whisper. He recognised Isaac. Another kid spoke. 'Is there a monster?'

'Yes,' said Isaac. 'He makes noises, stamps on the floor. I get shaky in my bed, and the walls get shaky too, cos the monster is very strong.'

'Is it a man monster or a lady monster?' his friend asked.

'A man monster, of course.' Isaac scolded. 'You don't get lady monsters.'

There was silence, then a thud on the stairs, and something hitting the walls. Carl heard yelps of delight and the drum of footsteps going down the stairs and coming back up.

'Your go,' said Isaac. 'Why don't we make them crash in the air like planes?'

There was another thud against the wall; whoops of delight and little feet pounding the stairs followed. Carl opened the room door and crept out into the corridor, down to the corner, peered round at the two boys. They were kneeling at the top of the stairs, firing two sleek but scratched metal cars down the steps and onto the landing. They zoomed the cars along the soft carpet and off the edge, metal hitting the wall with a crash.

Carl watched. He could see the scratches from here, the white wood beneath the dark varnished skirting board. Perhaps he shouldn't be watching this. Isaac fired his car again, and it hit the wall, gouging out a big splinter.

Carl stepped round the corner. 'Guys, maybe you shouldn't be doing that. It marks the wood.' He pointed. 'See? Over there.'

At exactly the same time, both boys jumped to their feet, shouted 'The Monster' and ran downstairs, laughing, terrified. They banged through the fire door and into the annexe.

Carl went over to inspect the walls. You couldn't say they intended to cause any damage; sometimes it just happens that damage happens, especially with kids, or so he thought. Anyway, it hardly mattered if the walls were fucking scratched: it wasn't going to put the tourists off or affect the sale price. He looked at his watch. By the time he made the broch it would be getting dark, and he'd have to come down again. There was a glimmer of something that wasn't fear or despair inside him. Something had been planted.

Across the bay, wisps of white smoke curled from the thin metal chimney of Terry Sullivan's caravan.

•

Carl shivered as he washed himself in the bathroom sink. Balls and armpits. The works. Call it a reacquaintance with recent convention.

The water was barely warm; there was nothing but a stream of ice from the shower. He couldn't say he was a picture of health, but in nearly a month he'd filled out a bit. Colour in his cheeks. Other people had made that happen, fed him and looked after him. He sighed, rubbing the short hair on his head. Softer now. Not so bristly. Time for a trim, maybe.

On his way down the stairs he picked up the two metal cars. Isaac and his pal could get them later.

The fire door to the annexe opened. It was George. 'The kids said there was a monster upstairs.'

'Only me.'

George folded his arms and leant against the wall.

'Look,' said Carl. 'Don't start again, George. It's your son you should be having a go at, not me.'

'I wasn't thinking about Adam. I'm sorry I let it slip to him.' George shook his head. 'But he had to find out, sooner or later. No, it was more my daughter I was thinking of.'

'What do you want me to do, George?'

'Talk to her.'

Carl rubbed his forehead. 'I'm having trouble doing that, George – with anyone. Mass death. Being trapped here. Howard. A baby. Stuff like that, you know, bit of a shock to the old system ...'

'It's a shock, yes, but ...'

'It's extremely unfair that you guys expect me to ...'

George started laughing, shaking his head in pity. The humour faded. 'My daughter's friend is right – you are an asshole.' He looked coldly at Carl. 'My wife going to Edinburgh and not coming back – that's not fair. Millions falling asleep and never waking up – that's not very fair. All the work *some* of us are having to put in to staying alive – that's a little bit unfair as well.'

Carl considered picking up the toy cars and hurling them against the wall. But that would only have caused more damage to the varnished woodwork.

George pushed open the fire door, chuckling to himself. 'Unfair: that's a good one. Fucking priceless.' He poked his head back through the fire door, all trace of amusement gone. 'We're here. You're here. And you're going to be a dad. Deal with it, like the rest of us have had to.'

The door swung closed.

Outside, the morning was cold in the fresh onshore breeze. An old guy on a chopper bike pedalled along the shorefront, nice and easy, going slow from A to B. Carl said hello – a proper hello, not a furtive glance and a mumble. It was returned with a wave. Acknowledgement. It wasn't so hard, this greeting lark; the old habits could soon re-establish themselves given half a chance. Anyway, he was going round to someone else's house, and that had to be a good thing. In a world of very fucking bad things smoking grass with someone who seemed reasonably entertaining had to count as progress.

He crossed the stone bridge at the head of the bay, river frothing down to the foreshore; sponge bogs, up in the hills, sluicing out two days of rain. The *Aurora* was chuntering back into the bay, trailing a raucous flurry of seagulls in its wake. The main man was bringing home the bacon. Altruistic Adam.

Carl climbed the southern road to Terry's gate, and walked

down to the caravan. A bike stood against a wall. There were fat, stunted cacti lined up inside the window of Terry's caravan. Carl knocked. Not a sound from within. He knocked again, waited. There was no one home.

Carl looked in the window: a few clothes strewn about, plasma screen propped on a bench sofa, dirty plates on the table; pencil sketches pinned everywhere, a bookmarked Arthur Koestler. Overflowing ashtray. Everyday layabout stuff. Just living: the things you have to take care of, sooner or later, no matter what has happened to a sizeable chunk of humanity.

Carl turned away from the window and started back up the track to the main road.

Down at the hippie's house, he saw Terry, waving and shouting. He walked up the path as Carl started down.

'You said to come over any time.'

'No bother,' said Terry. 'I'm down at Hendrik's. Come and have a drop of some truly foul home-brew.'

'You're kidding. What is it?'

They walked down the track.

'Elderflower wine, but it didn't turn out quite right.' Terry smiled. 'It works, but with a few unpleasant side-effects.'

People were introduced, Hendrik de Vries and his Filipino wife, Maganda. Cloudy, tasteless wine was sampled. The bible was smoked.

Up close Carl could see Hendrik's yellow toenails needed cutting, probably with a bolt cutter. The Dutchman sat, hands on belly, like the brass Buddha on his mantelpiece.

He liked the sound of his own voice, that was for sure. Carl had given the guy enough of a chance, but the conversation hadn't improved. Second hearings were all very well, but after two hours on journalism's failure of democracy, the trials of building an orphanage in Thailand, and plant nutrition, enough was enough. Carl wouldn't be popping in to see Hendrik any time

121

soon. Shame about that. Maybe Terry was a bumptious prick as well.

Maganda was good company though. What she was doing with an old goat who must have been at least twenty years older than her, you had to fucking ask yourself. Her and Terry could share a joke and, if he wasn't much mistaken, Carl had seen a knowing smile from Hendrik at that. Prick was probably dreaming up a threesome. There was something dodgy about the guy, with his laid-back bohemian air and self-aggrandising anecdotes. Something not right about the whole thing: sitting there laughing, having a fucking party.

Through a fifth glass of cloudy elderflower rocket fuel and a few spliffs of home-grown, Carl realised that Hendrik was talking to him, directly, about something important. It was hard to focus on the words at first; the logical train of thought was always a station ahead. But then he caught up with the conversation, jumped aboard, with a little help from Terry.

'Hendrik's got issues with the emergency committee.'

Carl nodded, rubbed his face. 'Issues,' he repeated, focusing on Hendrik's face, the glasses and grey goatee. 'Issues with the committee.'

The big Dutchman nodded, sitting up straight with his hands on his knees. 'People are being greedy,' he said.

'What Hendrik and Maganda mean,' said Terry, smiling, 'is, can you have a word with George Cutler about the whole . . . situation? He's chairman of the committee, although how he got that position isn't quite clear if you come to think about it. A little bit cloudy, like this pish, Hendrik.'

Hendrik passed another joint to Terry. 'You'll drink it all the same.' He turned to Carl. 'It is not good when people think I am dishonest.'

'Absolutely,' said Carl, waving away the offer of a puff. 'That's what you said. But can you be more specific, if you can be specific about the . . .' He was getting edgy, and he felt a little nauseous. He forgot what he'd been talking about.

Hendrik cleared his throat. Maganda stopped giggling. 'I will tell you.' He smoothed his grey goatee. 'Yesterday I had a visit from the policeman, Gibbs. We grow lots of nice things in our polytunnels, you may know that.'

Carl tried to concentrate on the man's words. Policeman? Did he say policeman?

'Anyway,' continued Hendrik. 'Gibbs said he had to check that what we gave to the committee was what we produced.'

There was a shift in the air, a change of frequency. Carl didn't know what to say; his thoughts were confused, unnavigable.

Hendrik seemed agitated. 'I am an honest person, Mr Shewan.'

Terry fixed his eyes on the Escher print hanging over the fireplace. 'Come on, Hen, no one's saying you aren't.'

The Dutchman held up his hands. 'Okay.' He tugged his beard again. 'Ninety per cent goes to the committee. We have four goats, hens, tomatoes and lettuce and so on in the polytunnels – we get biofuel for the generators from Adam Cutler – and a few eggs we keep, not many.' He squinted at Carl, then leant forward. 'We have been here for over twenty years, Mr Shewan. A lot of hard work we have put into this place – our home, you know? Now we are under suspicion. This is not the way it should be. Not here. Not now.'

Carl's mouth was dry. He drank some water. 'I really don't know,' was all he could say. 'I'll have to think about it.'

What was the guy talking about? Just stringing words together. A noise coming out of his bearded hole. What did he say he'd think about? Think about thinking about . . .

'You weren't well for a long time, so maybe this is something you don't know about,' said Terry, sitting up straight on the soft, shapeless couch. 'Adam Cutler and his guys have made the food rationing system work in their favour. Food is divided by age, but also by man-hours worked, by activity levels. Your friend designed the system. See, it's Cutler and his crew who do all the work. No one else is getting a look-in. So, seven guys, plus their families and one or two others, are not exactly as hungry as the rest of the village.' He glanced at Hendrik. 'Some of us don't think that's very fair.'

Fair. There was that word again. Where had he heard it before? Was it now, or yesterday? Carl felt dizzy. 'That's right, that's fine,' he said. He stood up unsteadily, trying to breathe. 'I need some fresh air.'

Hendrik laughed, slapping his knees.

Outside, the wind had dropped. Somewhere in the hills a stag bellowed, his cry carrying round the bay. You go for it, big man, thought Carl; you let the world know you mean business because your very fucking essence is bigger and stronger than anything else is. Not even the galaxy, constellated to infinity in the clear night sky, was a match for the living illusion of perfect projected power. Give it big licks, big man, and fill your boots while you can.

He felt better in the fresh air, in the breathless night. Only the glow from the oil-lamps in Hendrik's living room stained the blackness.

Inverlair was across the bay, invisible. There were no streetlights, no warm glowing windows of welcome. Without electricity or cars on the road the place might not even exist, out there, in the darkness. It would never be home. But where else was there? Even when it became safe to leave, where would he go? Howard had said Spain was clear of SCOPE. Fair enough. Spain. Maybe things were okay there. But how would he get across Europe? He'd keep Howard's car, not let anyone cannibalise it here, pick up fuel along the way; he'd take his chances.

Really?

He felt himself grimace in the darkness, the unreality of escape making him shiver. Get a grip.

'You all right?' It was Terry.

'Yeah,' shouted Carl. 'Felt a bit woozy in there. I haven't smoked that much weed in quite a while.' He said no more, conscious that more was expected.

'Hendrik lays it on a bit thick,' said Terry. 'He can be a bit full of himself. If you can't be arsed walking back to the hotel, feel free to crash in the caravan. The couch folds out.'

That was a tough call. Creeping about the hotel like an intruder was great fun; getting hassled by George and Simone was a hoot.

Standing there looking into the night, Carl felt the stirrings of ordinary discontentment.

17

In the morning the wind picked up; Carl could feel Terry's caravan moving, even with a gable-end of brick to protect it. It had rained in the night, drumrolling on the caravan's flat metal roof.

His guts were churning. Dry mouth and pounding head. It was daylight, so he figured it would have to be at least 8 a.m. His watch was in the pocket of his jeans, and his jeans were on the opposite couch, and it was cold.

He pulled the sleeping bag around his ears, groaning, his bladder fit to burst. Well into November and it was freezing. Maybe he'd end up sleeping in his clothes for the duration of the winter. Pity he couldn't hibernate. If he lived in a caravan he might even not bother to wash. At least in Room 7 he could have a wash in the bath, even if the water was cold. That was important to him. Staying clean. His arse wouldn't be clean, though; a bad case of the squits during the night had seen to that. No bog roll either. Old newspaper had done the job instead.

He tried to close his eyes and go back to sleep, but his guts were still rumbling and he badly needed to piss. He shouldn't have told Terry about a SCOPE prototype that was trialled in Africa, driving villagers to murder each other when it went live. It was just more inexplicable butchery on the Dark Continent, with no suspicion falling on helpful development-minded Western telecomms companies.

Carl lay on the couch, gazing without focus at Terry's charcoal sketches of twisted gorse trunks and brooding headlands.

There were noises-off from the bedroom, which was more like a cupboard just big enough for a bed. Terry was up and about, belt buckle jangling, then a yawn. He came out of the bedroom, rubbing sleep from his eyes, tangle of straw-coloured hair sticking up and out and every way.

'How's it going?' he said, his throat dry.

Carl wasn't sure. 'I've felt better.'

'You get the squits?'

'Oh yeah ...'

Terry smiled, drank some water. 'I thought Hendrik had ironed that problem out, unless maybe he gave you a bottle of the old stuff by mistake.' He sat down on the sofa, moved a pile of clothes aside. 'When you were out of it, when you were ill, there were a few cases of Delhi Belly. Hendrik didn't clean his fermenting gear properly.'

Rain came gusting against the caravan. Terry made sure the windows were closed properly. He tested the soil round his plants, gave a few of them a drink from a three-litre plastic bottle. Carl sat up in his sleeping bag, reached over for his fleece. Maybe Hendrik knew fine well he'd handed over the wrong bottle, containing the stuff that was shat out in the same state as it went in: liquid. You get the sense that he would enjoy that, giving someone the shits, laughing about it the next day.

Terry picked one of the potted cacti off the windowsill. It was squat and sprouted tufts of purple hair. 'Pal of mine was in Mexico and he brought back two of these for me. Peyote. Over a few years two became four. They're hard to grow, so I don't use it very often. Fucking wild though. All that doors-of-perception stuff, surfing the archetypes. You hungry?'

On balance, Carl figured that eating would do him good. He nodded. 'Some muesli and semi-skimmed will do nicely.'

'Only unskimmed cows round here, I'm afraid. How about an omelette with an optional slice of mutton?'

'Even better.'

'Coming right up.'

Terry put his prized peyote plant back on the windowsill and went to a cupboard, took out a camping stove and a Tupperware dish, lit the stove, and scooped some lard out of the dish. 'Alec John gave me this,' said Terry. 'Sheep fat.' He broke three eggs and mixed them in the pan.

'Another day in paradise,' muttered Carl.

From another plastic box, Terry took out four slices of fatty meat.

'What did you do?' said Carl. 'Before the redzone, I mean.'

'You're seeing it,' said Terry. 'I was here about a year – before.' He tore a rubbery cheese slice into pieces, dropped it into the egg, his thin face darkening. 'I was in a bit of trouble in London, took myself off to Glasgow, but the trouble followed me up here. Then I found out my uncle had died and left me his place.' He tried to smile.

'What kind of trouble?'

Terry cleared his throat. 'The wrong sort of chemical habits with the wrong sort of people. Nothing new in that. Anyway, everybody's got to end up somewhere, and we can't all be in the same place, so here I am.'

Breakfast was served.

'Unless you have a pressing engagement we can head down to my uncle's house,' said Terry through a mouthful of meat and egg. 'There's something that might interest you.'

•

Down the lush seaward slope, a two-minute walk along the headland path, stood a solid-looking stone house. Across the bay Adam and the boys were setting off from the boatyard, back to cut more firewood.

From the outside the stone house looked in reasonable

condition; the date 1934 was carved into the stone lintel. Inside, it was more or less unfurnished, with bare floorboards and bare plasterboard walls, watertight apart from a leak in the loft, said Terry. It had two bedrooms. The front room was full of junk, and stacks of black plastic bin bags, each one tightly wrapped with Sellotape, lined the walls. The committee would have taken the clothes and the shoes, but there were books and magazines, knick-knacks, photos, two TVs, a foldaway chess set, and a shitload of other stuff lying around.

'Have a look at these,' said Terry, tearing open one of the black bin bags. He took out a newspaper, handed it to Carl.

He held it reverently in his hand. 'Jesus.'

An old edition, yellow round the edges, dated almost nine years ago. Big pic on the front and HEATWAVE KILLS HUNDREDS along the top. Carl looked at the plastic bundles. He couldn't believe what he held in his hands. He lifted a few more, opened another bundle. The same, going back years.

Turning to page two in one paper he saw his own name under the heading WHITE RUST FUNGUS CONFIRMED IN SPAIN. He read the first paragraph: 'A total ban on all exports from Spain was in place today as the European Emergency Authority confirmed an outbreak of the white rust fungus in wheat fields outside Malaga...'

'Twenty years' worth of newspapers in here,' said Terry. 'Right up till February of last year, three weeks before my uncle died. You could say he was a bit of a hoarder. Thought you might be interested.'

Terry went upstairs to empty the bucket that had filled with rainwater, leaving Carl to browse the bin-bag archive.

There were plenty of leaks in the pages of these newspapers. Insiders. Sources. Once, years before, the information flowed freely from numerous contacts. But then the stream dried to a trickle, a few drops still coming out. The insiders had too much to lose.

Carl checked the date on the front of one paper: four months before Glasgow became the third city under Civil Contingencies Enforcement. He used to go out then, socialise, go to the theatre, plays at the Citizens. He had a life. They tried to ban that play at the time, fuck knows if he could remember the name. It closed after four nights; didn't tour. Funding was cut. Official threats.

Eric. Lesley.

He leafed through some more issues, opened another bundle, stopping as soon as he saw the masthead and the headline's first word. He knew which issue he was holding; his first big scoop, the flats in the East End built on contaminated land. The same front page was hanging, framed, back in Glasgow on his bedroom wall. It may as well have been on the moon now. He unfolded the old newspaper and spread it out tenderly on the floor.

The date was five years before the privatised insanity of CivCon, when targets were plentiful and you could be sure of hitting one if you pointed your nose in the right direction.

For years this front page had hung in his room and he'd barely noticed it. Now he touched the dried-up, yellowing newsprint with his fingertips.

And then he saw it clearly. His old life was no longer invisible; it was present and alive in his longing for something that he couldn't return to. This was all he had been, right here, in 500 exclusive words, part of an award-winning series. How many articles had he written altogether? How many deserving targets had he harried over the years? His words, or rather the paper they'd been printed on, had become a resource of a different kind now. The paper was more important than the words. In fact, the words served no purpose. Truth was now measured in calories, and his investigations were all closed – spiked on thousands of SCOPE transmitters. Maybe the village would use the paper for something. It could still have a vital function to perform, like wiping arses or as bedding for animals. The committee would decide. Truth was now a full stomach and a warm room: the same as it had been before SCOPE, for many. No wonder people never wanted to know the truth he'd been trying to serve up, in steaming piles, on a plate. They had other things to worry about, like eating and paying the bills.

Carl tossed the old newspaper back onto the pile, the layered strata of his fossil life. It hadn't amounted to much. That was that. End of.

He went outside.

And there was the village, houses strewn along the edge of the northern headland; the viewpoint flagpole; guys on the pier; dark clouds brewing over the Atlantic. Out in the distance.

For the first time in a few weeks, he wished the pneumonia had finished the job.

He went round the side of the house to the shed. With a heavy nudge from his shoulder, Carl opened the door.

There was only one small window and the light was poor. The shed smelled of engine oil and creosote. As his eyes got used to the gloom, Carl could see a workbench along one wall and the guts of an outboard motor in pieces on the dirty concrete floor. Rusty saws hung on nails; a grass strimmer; a stack of old paint pots in one corner; oars, rakes and spades standing in another.

In a dark wooden chest he found literature of a different kind, also yellow with age like the newspapers. Internet printouts: women and girls of all ages and races, with their muscular male jockeys and sex toys. The detail was difficult to make out, so faded were the colours. Carl pushed the pile of loose pages out of the way. At the bottom of the chest was a grubby olive-coloured case of some sort, fastened by brown leather straps. As soon as he grabbed the case, he guessed what might be inside it.

It was a rifle — but only an air rifle. And he couldn't find any pellets. He held it in his hands, cold and heavy, took aim through the window at the boatyard across the bay. It felt good to aim at what he'd love to hit.

Brandishing his ammo-less peashooter he went back outside and back into the house to find Terry.

'You got any pellets for this?'

•

His hangover easing, Carl took the track at the head of the bay up towards the stalker's house. It was set apart from other houses, more in the hills than in the village. The noise of the biofuel generator made his brain hurt.

He knocked on the porch door. There was no answer. Peering through the dusty glass in the porch window, he could see walking-sticks in the corner, each one with a carved horn on the end, along with walking-boots, wellies and jackets. A barometer hung on the wall, and the framed photo of a woman. He knocked again.

No response.

Carl slung the air rifle over his shoulder again and headed back down the path. A dog barked behind him.

'Hello there,' said a voice from round the side of the house. A scruffy Border collie trotted round the corner. 'What can I do for you?' Alec John stopped. 'Oh, it's you.'

Carl unslung the air rifle, walked back up the shell path. The dog came trotting towards him, tail wagging. He took a step back.

'Hi. I found this in Cathal Sullivan's shed. Terry said you might have pellets for it.'

As he got closer to Alec John, Carl could see there was blood on his cheek, and on his forearms, and all over the plastic apron he was wearing.

Alec John took the gun and studied it. 'You won't get much with this popgun. Maybe more rats and crows than Cathal did. It's in good enough condition, though.' He walked around the outside of the house. 'I'm sure I'll have a tin somewhere.'

The stalker disappeared into a low-roofed concrete outbuilding. In the middle of the straw-covered floor, on a metal bench, the headless, skinless carcass of what Carl assumed to be a deer was splayed. Chains and hooks hung from a shiny metal runner that curved along the underside of ceiling beams and into a steel-lined cooler; saws and cleavers and knives glinted in the dangling strip light.

Carl tried not to gape at the remains. Pelt and waxy dermis in a pile. Hooves and head, minus the antlers, and a huge rubbery tongue lolling from a blood-crusted mouth. The smell of flesh.

Jess waddled in and stood, panting, near Carl. Alec John opened a few drawers and cupboards until he found three small round tins. He shook them. 'Here we are,' he said, prising the lids off. 'They're still pretty full.' He put the tins down on the trestle table next to the skinless, headless deer. 'Help yourself.'

'Thanks,' said Carl, eyeing the inside of the animal's ribcage. 'Is that an ordinary saw you're using?'

Alec John went back to work on the deer's hind-leg, sawblade rasping through the femur. 'Aye. A joiner's.' He smiled. 'Once upon a time, if we knew the hygiene inspectors were coming we would get a proper butcher's saw out for them to see – they were sticklers for that – but once they left we'd get this out.' He paused, the saw still at work. 'You look much better than the first time I saw you, up close.'

Carl couldn't meet the man's eye. 'Yeah,' he said. 'Getting there.' He picked up the tins of air-rifle pellets. 'Thanks for these.'

The stalker jagged a hook into the carcass, hoisted it up by a chain pulley, and pushed it along the ceiling runner and into the cooler. He shut the heavy metal door with a thud. 'You're welcome.'

Alec John watched Carl walk back down the track. After wrapping cuts of meat in old newspaper, the stalker put the parcels into big plastic boxes and loaded them into the trailer of his six-wheeled argocat.

He went back round to the front of his house, dog trotting at his heels, and opened the front door.

As always, his wife's smiling face met him in the porch – the framed photo an icon of her enduring presence.

18

'What the hell's he doing with that gun?'

George was standing at the kitchen window, watching Carl fire pellets at old tin cans arranged along the fence posts.

'Terry Sullivan gave it to him,' said Simone. She was gutting a pollock in the sink, slitting the soft white belly, pulling out the guts. Tail next, then the head, spine grating under the blade.

'Well,' said George. 'Trust that guy to have a gun.'

Father and daughter stood watching.

In total, Carl had about 300 pellets. After a few pot shots – without hitting a target – Carl did a quick calculation. How many pellets would he have to fire before he became reasonably proficient? How many would fly wide of their mark and be lost in the grass?

He lowered the gun and studied the line of five tins he'd placed on top of five fence posts. Perhaps he should rethink his target practice. If only there was some way to gather the pellets up once he'd fired them, so that he could re-use them. He looked around the garden for a solution and noticed Isaac sitting on the back step.

'Can I have a shot?' the boy asked.

'Maybe,' replied Carl. 'But I've got to rig something up first.'

Isaac wrinkled his nose. 'When can I have a shot?'

Carl ignored the boy and sized up two rowan trees at the bottom of the soggy garden. They were just the right distance apart. He went to the shed, Isaac on his heels, and dug out an old bedsheet covered in crusted splashes of paint. He also found a length of rope and some string.

He rigged up his target range and pellet catcher. The tin cans were now suspended by string from the rope he'd tied to both rowan trees. Behind the line of dangling cans was the old bedsheet, staked into the ground so it wouldn't blow about in the wind. A sheet of plastic, to catch the falling pellets, was staked out on the ground with old tent pegs. His theory was ready to test.

He raised the rifle and fired. There was no satisfying *ping* of projectile on metal. But, he saw the pellet hit the sheet and, on inspection, he noticed there was a spent slug, intact, beneath the line of cans.

Bingo.

Pleased with himself, Carl loosed off a few pellets, then turned to offer Isaac a shot. But there was no sign of the boy.

He looked back at the house, saw Simone and George at the kitchen window, probably wondering what the hell he was doing shooting at tin cans in the garden. Should've asked about his little pellet-catching set-up before raiding the shed.

Simone had been playing her flute earlier, something by Debussy, Aeolian analgesic that must be resisted. Life has to be rougher than that.

He fired another pellet. There's always some fucking committee, or council or cabinet or conclave, he thought, enforcing and reinforcing their own particular worldview. People in authority were always giving you some spiel or other to justify their own positions. Whether it was shaman communing with ancestors or government ministers rhapsodising about fantasy futures, there was always a message to sell.

Ping.

A dangling can jerked on the line.

About fucking time.

'About bloody time,' muttered George at the kitchen window.

Isaac was sitting on the floor, wearing his visor and gloves, his little body jerking around as he played a game. 'Mum, is Carl going to be my new daddy?'

George rolled his eyes at his daughter.

'No, darling,' said Simone, 'he isn't.'

Isaac took off the visor and considered, with relentless logic, his next line of enquiry. Before he could ask his next question, Simone hopped directly to what she knew was the next phase of the conversation.

'Dad's in a place called Bristol, Isaac. You know that. It's very far away. I told you that before. And he's probably dead. I told you that as well. But we're all okay here.'

The brutal facts needed confirming, and reaffirming; repeating them was making the brutal facts stick in the boy's memory. It was easy for her to rattle off the salient points of the situation, even the one that involved her mother. If she just repeated the same phrases to Isaac as soon as he asked her a question, Simone could say the words like a mantra, and not have to think about their meaning. And that was no bad thing.

Soon, she'd have to tell Isaac something new, that he was going to have a little brother or sister.

•

In Room 7, Carl wondered how to disassemble the air rifle. Isn't that what people did, take guns apart to clean and oil them? Kneeling on the floor, he had the parts spread out on old newspaper. He was going to look after it.

At the head of the bay, beneath the bridge, there were rats in the rock embankment, so George had said. He'd also mentioned that he might be able to persuade Adam to take Carl back on the work crew. Carl said he'd think about it.

Well, he'd thought about it: Adam could shove his offer.

There was something satisfying about the feel of the metal and wood in Carl's hand; the snug fit of the rifle stock against his shoulder. And the *ping* of the cans! That made him feel good. Taking aim. Having an effect. When you don't have any real power, even over yourself, you'll take whatever fetishised substitute comes to hand. With a screwdriver and pair of pliers he undid the rifle's mid-point hinge and exposed the spring piston inside. He poked it with the screwdriver.

In a heartbeat, the spring shot out of the stock, whizzed past Carl's face, and cracked off the plaster wall behind him so hard that it also bounced up and hit the ceiling before landing on the bed. Instinctively, Carl dropped the gun and jumped towards the door. He stood for a second, then went to look at the spring, now three times as long as it had been when compressed inside the barrel. An inch-deep hole had been gouged out of the plaster where the spring had hit the wall. Carl picked the spring up, the oily metal spiral flexing in his hand. Better a hole in the wall than his skull.

He looked at the space in the rifle stock from where the spring had rocketed, tried to slide it back in, and realised it wasn't going to fit. There was probably a special tool to do that; a tool he didn't have.

He thought of Simone. So much for the tool he did have.

When would her bump start to show? Everyone else would know the truth when it did. Carl knew that she had seen him looking. She knew the pregnancy, or at least the size of her stomach, was making an impression on him. The information had registered. But what Carl was doing with that awareness he himself hardly knew. The baby was growing inside him as well. It might have been taking all Simone's nutrients and energy, but it was stealing his fucking headspace, the dark shadow of it moving across the sun, blocking out everything else that he needed to think about. In a few months' time the eclipse would reach totality, and there would be no more light.

Getting back up to the broch appealed again, briefly. But it was nonsense, trying to rebuild it. It was insane.

He put the rifle parts back in their soft leather case. Alec John might know how to put the spring into the barrel.

•

There had been something unpleasant in Room 14. New sheets couldn't hide it; illness and the scent of death haunted the room, and he was glad to be out of it. He washed himself in the bathroom, in a few inches of lukewarm water.

At the top of the stairs, a moment passed before he registered exactly what Isaac was doing. The boy was in one of the vacant bedrooms, number 4, boring a hole in the plaster wall with a screwdriver. Carl watched for a spell as Isaac removed a handful of plaster chalk, put it in a cup, and went off to the bathroom, where he added a splash of water to the cup from the bath tap. With a teaspoon Isaac stirred the mixture, looking very pleased with his morning's work.

Carl coughed. For a split second a nervous smile made Isaac cute: he'd been discovered, and it was time to turn on the charm.

'What're you doing?' said Carl, coming over and taking the cup out of the boy's hand. 'What d'you think your mum will say to that, eh?'

With a fair degree of venom, Isaac kicked Carl sharply in the shin and ran for the door. Carl dropped the cup of sticky plaster mix and it smashed on the tiled bathroom floor.

'Fucker,' he growled, clutching his shin.

Isaac bolted from the room, screaming for his mum. There were footsteps drumming up the stairs in response to the commotion.

'What the hell is going on?' Simone shouted from the corridor.

Carl opened his mouth to bellow the truth, then paused. 'I just dropped a cup of water,' he shouted back, his shin stinging. For once, the wee bugger had been wearing his shoes, worse luck. Carl stood blocking the doorway. He smiled at Simone.

'Sorry. I didn't know Isaac was up here and he gave me a bit of a start. I dropped the cup on the floor.'

Isaac was hiding behind his mother.

'Sorry about that, wee man,' said Carl. 'Didn't mean to give you a fright.' He smiled again at Simone. 'And sorry for swearing, eh? Shouldn't use that kind of language around a wee kid.'

'I'm not wee,' said Isaac, peeping round his mother's thigh.

'Of course you're not, darling,' she soothed.

'I'm not wee,' the boy repeated, eyeing Carl.

Carl shrugged, still standing in the doorway. 'Yeah, okay. You're not wee.'

Simone nodded, none too convinced by the explanation of what had happened. She looked at Isaac, then back at Carl. 'Pavel's coming round to play in a while,' she said to her son. 'Come on.'

'Oh,' said Carl. 'Don't bother cooking any food for me tonight, I'm going over to Terry's.'

For a second, Simone allowed her face to fall, then pinned it back into a position of fixed blankness. 'Thanks for telling me,' she said, shooing Isaac downstairs. 'You're a very polite and thoughtful man, I'm sure.'

Isaac was a cute kid – Carl could see that. He had all the right attributes for cuteness, which he used to good effect: cherubic smile, big brown eyes, tousled mop of sandy hair. But when he didn't get his own way, the kid could also be a temperamental little shit. Angel and devil. Or maybe Carl couldn't see the good, just the bad. People never really pay much attention to a kid that's sitting nicely or playing quietly.

George, as granddad, did his best to jolly the boy along, but there were limits to the guy's patience. Sometimes his temper would go and he would just snap, usually over something trivial. At other times George could tolerate the worst tantrums in the kid. The man was doing his best to deal with his own stuff, and he had bad days when he had no patience. It must make it easier for George, having his daughter and grandson to fill the void.

He set off for Terry's.

It was all fucked up. Right to the very edge of the redzone was 2.26 miles. Maybe he could live in a tent, high in the hills where no one except Alec John ever went. He could live there until the nearest SCOPE mast failed. That's what he would do. Then, when the masts started to stop working he would . . . What?

Walk another ten or twenty miles until he came to a dead village? There was bound to be another Inverlair out there, another prison shelter. There would be lots of empty houses, for sure. Desiccated corpses in their beds or slumped at the kitchen table. He could make his way south – a wanderer in the silence, following the masts as they packed in, until he got to the Channel; then he'd find a boat, or a magic fucking carpet to take him to the land of milk and honey.

For the first time since before his illness, he'd walked around the bay, and through the village, entirely by road. When he reached Terry's, and without really knowing why, Carl blurted out the truth about Simone.

'Christ, you didn't hang about there.'

Carl shook his head. 'It wasn't like that. It was strange. My third night here and she came up to ask if I wanted anything to eat, and it just happened.' He sniffed. 'We just wanted to hold each other, I suppose, then . . .' He shrugged. 'It sounds stupid . . . but it didn't feel like sex – real sex, I mean. Not with a spraysuit – not remote, but connected.'

Terry grinned.

'Fuck off,' muttered Carl.

A plastic Coke bottle was produced. Even in the dim light of the oil lamp Carl could see that it did not contain Coke. Terry poured two mugs of Hendrik and Maganda's cloudy home-brew.

'Actually, it doesn't sound stupid,' he said. 'I swam out to the buoy at Heron Point the day after SCOPE happened, after I'd run into the redzone as far as I could. Nose was streaming blood, and I just ran down to the water, stripped off, and dived straight in off the rocks.'

He adjusted the flame of the oil lamp. 'So what are you going do about Simone?' He flashed an edgy grin. 'You could always run away.' He coughed and started laughing; took another draw of his spliff and passed it over. 'God knows when I'll get my next shag.' Before the evening progressed any further, Terry thought it a good idea to check what he had for breakfast the next day. If the cupboard was bare he could cadge an couple of eggs off Maganda, but he saw there was some mackerel left and the bag of peanuts he'd found earlier. That would be enough. He could at least satisfy that appetite.

19

'It's funny, but you still expect to offer someone a cup of tea when they call on you,' said Alec John sheepishly.

Carl shrugged. 'It would be nice, I suppose.'

'Yes,' said Alec John. 'I gave the last teabag to Maganda yesterday to put on her veg; I must have squeezed a dozen cups out of it.'

Of course: Alec John was one of the lucky few, an essential worker.

'How many teabags do the committee give you?'

'Three a week. I think they're getting pretty low on supplies now.' He smiled at Carl. 'I've always been fond of a brew.' He lifted his cap and smoothed his greying hair back. 'I have to admit that I do miss it when I don't have it.'

Carl stiffened. 'If that's all you miss then you're doing well.'

Alec John went through to the kitchen. He'd witnessed too many traumatic scenes over the last few months, and now he knew when to stay silent. He rummaged in a cupboard, searching for a distraction.

While Alec John was through in the kitchen, Carl looked around the small low-ceilinged living room. The place was dark, with only a small window facing the bay. On the deep windowsill there was an old ice-cream carton, half full of loose change. A tea towel depicting Morecambe Bay had been draped neatly across one end of a drop-leaf table. Carl guessed that Alec John sat there to eat, alone at the window, looking out over the bay. Framed photos, some of them black-and-white, hung on the wall, which looked as if it could use a lick of paint. Above the fireplace a wooden mantel clock sat, its hands frozen behind dirty glass at twenty past two. Carl leant closer, but heard no ticking within. More photos next to it. Among the clutter on the dark wooden sideboard there was a toy car, a metallic blue Mercedes, still in its box.

'You don't strike me as a fan of toy cars,' Carl called through to the kitchen.

'It's a bit of a relic, that,' Alec John said, abandoning his search for an early lunch. 'For my fiftieth birthday someone asked me what my favourite car was. It was Allan Robertson's son, he left Inverlair to . . .' Alec John paused. 'Anyway, he turned up at the door on my birthday and said come outside and see your new Merc.' He laughed. 'And there it was sitting on top of a fence post.'

Alec John turned a log over in the open fire. Warmth flooded into the room as the wood's red-hot underside was exposed.

'Terry said you might want me to help you with something.'

'Well,' said Alec John, 'you've been using his uncle's old air rifle, so I thought you might want to spend a day on the hill, see how you are with the real thing.'

'What – shooting? Shooting animals?'

There was a glint in the stalker's eye. 'No, clouds – for the sheer hell of it.'

'Oh,' said Carl, abashed. 'Right.'

Alec John grunted, left the room. 'Come or don't come. It's up to you.'

'But I've never fired a proper gun. Never even held one.'

The stalker came back with a few gutted mackerel in a plastic bag. He put a blackened frying pan on top of the stove. 'You can learn. There's more to being a keeper than just firing a gun – a lot more, especially now that every animal matters to us. But that's nothing you need worry about for now.'

'Listen,' said Carl. 'I don't suppose you know how to get a spring piston back into an air rifle. It came out yesterday.'

'Aye, there's a tool for it, but I don't have one. I can make something that does the job, though. Did you take the spring out?'

Carl nodded.

Alec John narrowed his eyes. 'What did you use?'

'A screwdriver.'

'You're lucky you never lost an eye.'

Carl nodded. 'Bloody thing tore a lump out of the wall.'

Alec John uncorked a wine bottle and poured oil into the frying pan. 'Where would we be without Adam Cutler?' he said as the oil spat. 'Our Lord and Protector. Do you want some mackerel?'

Carl laughed. 'You're not his biggest fan then.'

A grimace was the answer. 'Always been a bit full of himself,' said Alec John. 'Thinks he's lord of the manor. Tried to suck up to the Arabs, whenever they flew in.'

'Arabs?'

'The estate owners, from Kuwait.'

'Did they like to shoot?'

'Oh yes,' said Alec John, turning the sizzling fillets. 'But they didn't have the patience to stalk for long or do a spot of fishing. They got fed up quickly. So it was five minutes in the chopper up onto the hill, half an hour to kill the beast, then down to the big house. It's no big deal to shoot a red deer when you've shot elephants and tigers.'

From a cupboard, Alec John took out a small yellow block of waxy polycarb and cut it in two. 'The committee let me keep this.' One wedge he placed on Carl's plate, the other on his own, along with some cottage cheese from an old margarine tub and the fish from the frying pan. 'Wasn't that kind of them?'

Carl agreed. 'Generous to a fault.' He cut a slice of polycarb. It was bland and rubbery in his mouth. And there was something about it he didn't trust. It was the last of the old man's supply. But it was carbohydrate.

As he ate, Carl noticed a framed photo of a young woman,

long-haired and laughing. An obvious question occurred to him which, in his former universe, he would have come right out and asked. But this time his curiosity, the habitual probing, slipped out of gear and into neutral. There was no article here. No need to probe. There was very obviously no Mrs Stoddart around the house, and there could be any number of reasons for that. There was no need to find out the answer right now, so he left the question unasked. They spoke about Glasgow and white rust. And about Howard and SCOPE.

Finishing his food, Alec John wiped his mouth and laid knife and fork neatly together on the empty plate. It had been difficult for them not to gulp the food down.

'I've got to go to the boatyard for more biodiesel, and to see if they've fixed the argocat.'

Carl grunted, finished his own food, felt warmth spreading in his limbs. 'What time do you want me to turn up tomorrow?'

'If the weather's half decent, about nine. We're well into November now so it'll be getting dark mid-afternoon, though we can't go that far into the hills any more.' He took the dirty plates through to the kitchen and plopped them in the basin. 'Casper said he'd have the argocat fixed by today.'

They left the house and walked down the track together towards the main road. Carl squinted at the pitched corrugated roof of a stone shed, surrounded by nettles and bramble bushes, that stood at the bottom of the track.

'Have a guess how old the roof is.'

Carl shook his head. 'Dunno – thirty, forty years?'

'My grandfather put it on, not long after the First World War. He got the corrugated iron second-hand from Glasgow.'

Carl eyed Alec John. 'Is that what you used to tell the tourists?'

'If they asked me, yes.'

'And it's really that old?'

'It is.'

'It looks in a bad way.'

'Well,' said Alec John. 'Round the edges maybe, but it's dry enough inside.'

'You never thought of putting new iron on?'

'No. Why?'

Carl shrugged. 'I don't know. Some people might say it doesn't look good.'

'And who was going to see it?'

Carl raised his eyebrows. 'The tourists?'

They turned down into the gorse and alder-lined lane towards the main road. 'If it was a shiny, new roof,' said Alec John, 'do you think the tourists would have stopped to take a photo of it?'

They reached the bottom of the lane.

'I'm going to see Terry,' said Carl.

'No bother,' said Alec John. 'See you tomorrow. Nine o'clock, or thereabouts.'

•

It was warm inside the caravan: the tiny solid-fuel stove didn't have to work too hard to heat the space, despite the chill. Using a steel ruler, Terry ripped out another page of Leviticus, rolled some leaf and a sprinkle of bud, glue-sticked dabbed along the edge, and it was ready to spark. 'D'you fancy being a ghillie, then? The hours are long and, at six extra spuds a week, the pay leaves a lot to be desired.'

Carl was scrolling through the comedy section of Terry's film files, thousands of them on the palmpod. He accepted a puff from the joint. 'He invited me out tomorrow. Didn't say anything about being a ghillie, though.'

Terry frowned. 'No? That's strange. I thought he would've.'

'Why?'

'Well . . .' He looked at Carl. 'He didn't tell you?'

'Tell me what?'

147

Terry flexed the steel ruler he held in his hands. 'He's got emphysema. The nanomeds were keeping it in check, but Dr Morgan says there are none left.'

'Jesus,' said Carl. 'He didn't say a word.'

'Without treatment, he'll find it harder and harder to breathe,' said Terry. 'Eventually, he won't be able to walk twenty feet, never mind up in the hills. The old guy always sidles in at an angle to things. He'll want to see what you're like before asking you outright.'

'Fuck,' said Carl, stunned. 'I had no idea.'

They were silent for a while.

Carl considered what Alec John had said and, more importantly, why the guy had made his offer in the first place. What was going on here? What was in the stalker's mind? Maybe Terry was wrong, and there was no secret trial period that might lead to a permanent position. Maybe it was all a mistake.

Carl wasn't sure he even liked the idea; it sounded like another random event over which he had no influence. He'd endured enough of those to last a lifetime.

'I don't know the first thing about being a gamekeeper,' Carl said. He squinted at Terry. 'There must be other guys here. Better candidates for the job.'

Terry shrugged, relighting his joint with a taper from the stove. 'Maybe so. But you're the one he asked.'

What to feel? Confusion, anxiety? But there was pride too. It wasn't the easiest combination of emotions for Carl to deal with. He stood up. He sat down again.

There was a knock at the door, voices and laughter outside.

'Come in.'

The door opened and a teenage girl popped her head round. 'Hi,' she giggled. 'Sorry to disturb the mood.'

Terry sat up. 'I can't possibly imagine what you lot are after,' he said. 'You guys finished that half ounce already?'

'No way was that half an ounce,' protested the girl. 'Graham's got a set of scales.'

'Has he now?'

She nodded slyly. 'Uh-uh.'

Terry opened a drawer where some cannabis bud was drying. He took out a thumb-sized section of stalk and threw it to the girl. She was pretty, with short black hair and dark eyes, wearing a ragged denim jacket.

'I'm surprised you lot didn't float across the bay to get here.'

The girl smiled. 'Thanks.' She put her hands in her jacket pockets and took out an egg from each. 'Don't say we're not good to you.'

'I'd never say that,' said Terry, accepting the eggs. 'Cheers.'

The girl rejoined her mates, and the group shouted and goofed their way back up the track to the main road. Terry shut the door, held the handle for a second. If Carl hadn't been so focused on Alec John Stoddart, he might have picked up the electric shift in the air.

'You think you'll make a go of things with Simone?' Terry said, handling the eggs he had just been given.

Carl snorted. 'You're kidding, right?'

'You know,' said Terry, 'I tried it on with her, just after I moved up.'

'With Simone?'

Terry nodded. 'Yeah. Tried – and failed.'

'She blow you out?'

'Completely. Reckon she thought I was bit of a Jack the Lad. That's the thing with some places: you get labelled, and you soon run out of options because of it.' He sighed. 'Unless you're prepared to settle down with anybody who's just as needy and desperate as you are.'

Carl pursed his lips. Where was this going?

Terry considered the two eggs the girl had given him. He set them down gently in a bowl. 'You don't have many options, Carl. That's for sure. And Simone's a nice person, smart – usually. Maybe you don't see much of that, but it's there. She's a looker as well.'

Carl shook his head, incredulous. 'I'm sure she's all of that, but ...'

'People are clinging on to each other,' insisted Terry. He picked up one of the eggs again. 'Everything's changed.' He was speaking almost to himself now. 'You've got to take what you can – know what I mean?'

Unsure of what Terry meant, Carl agreed, though, unlike the first time, this time he felt the electric shift in the air, the misalignment of personal signals. If only he'd been aware enough to realise that the tension wasn't focused on him.

Terry put the cracked egg he was holding down on the worktop and, picking up a tea towel, discreetly wiped the slime from his fingers.

August

20

The meeting didn't so much end at an appointed time as dissolve, a crowd of a hundred or so evaporating over the course of an hour, dwindling to a dozen stifled souls. Onlookers, really. There was nothing to discuss. There was no gradual adaptation, no consultation. People could only absorb what they were being told. Then the last dregs wandered away, confused, into the summer haze that warmed the bay. Necessary business had been conducted in near silence, with Howard Brindley in the chair, the guise of formal proceedings ensuring a hushed acceptance. Six days had passed, and the delta field was still impenetrable.

After leaving the meeting, Carl made his way down to the pier. It was a beautiful still evening. In another time he would have watched, in awe, the bright horizon of shifting silver, and the sunset bloody on rags of high cloud. He might have relaxed, at another time. How long ago was that?

From the end of the pier he looked back down the length of the village towards the head of the bay, at the people drifting home in silence from the meeting. Nothing existed around him. Everything appeared to recede into the distance – even what was close at hand. It wasn't a dream after all. It was here and now, and he was in the middle of it. It was real, zooming in and out of focus, sharp and raw and then diffuse, dreamlike. Is that what shock does? Is that how it works?

He looked around, amazed at what he saw.

Ropes and prawn creels and piles of rain-bleached netting. They looked real. Apparently, that was the case. They seemed to retain an everyday purpose. That was how the world worked: it was composed of little details, like roads and cities and living people.

Carl stood with his mouth open, but no sound came out. Brindley's words from the meeting were buzzing in his head. One moment he was able to understand what had happened – he could grasp it. Then he found it so ridiculous he felt like laughing.

During the meeting, Howard had seemed in control, dispassionate. He'd organised it all, compartmentalised his numb flock to ensure their survival; had assumed the worst – that the masts would prove as durable as their manufacturer had claimed and the signal would last two to five years. Maybe this time the marketing hype would be accurate.

Two joiners, two bricklayers, four mechanics, an electrician, foresters, an architect, those with livestock, a doctor, gamekeeper, a retired district nurse, fishermen, gardeners. In all, thirty-eight names were read out during the meeting. Those with essential skills were identified, as were the very young and the very old and those too ill to be of much use. George Cutler's job, as emergency committee chairman, was to record all the names and their allocated tasks; a technician who could keep the water treatment works operating; guys who could hotwire the forestry machines. Now that the electricity was off, they'd need to use the solar freezers in the community centre.

The name Carl Shewan had not been read out.

He made his way back to the hotel from the pier, just the gulls wheeling in the air and a dog trotting along the shorefront. Standing in the silent lobby, he thought he heard a cry from the hotel annexe, a woman sobbing. Maybe the waitress, Simone.

Her body.

Her smell.

His semen on the floor, where she'd walked away. No underwear. A dream of oblivion within a real nightmare.

In Room 14, he counted back to the exact time when the delta field sprang into existence, and adjusted the timer on his palmpod accordingly. The on-screen seconds counted. Six days, eleven hours and seventeen minutes.

•

Look at her photo.

Don't look at her photo.

There was the committee to think about, George reminded himself through the tears. Planning and organising to attend to. He looked at his wife's photo, properly, for the first time in years. Depending on where she'd been when this SCOPE system was switched on, she could well be dead by now. If she'd been sitting on her sister's couch sipping tea, then she might still be alive. How could she be dead? How? She'd been forced to sleep by these delta waves. It caught him again, all thought of his official responsibilities rendered nonsensical. Worse: obscene. George cried again, sobbing quietly into his hand, a strangled high-pitched sound that he forced back down into his throat. Confronted with words like hypothalamus, sinusoidal and entrainment, he felt impotent.

Brindley and that journalist from Glasgow, they'd known about SCOPE for a long time, especially Brindley – he knew what the risks were; the thing about the crystal filters and magnetic resonance. He'd even worked on it, the bastard. George dried his eyes with a hankie, blew his nose, and washed his face.

Maybe Brindley had done all he could to stop it. Maybe the same went for Shewan. And maybe the pair of them should be strung up from the nearest lamppost.

Look at the photo. Listen to her advice, her instruction. Right, love, I'll get on it straight away.

Downstairs, Simone had also just dried her eyes, blown her nose, and was splashing her face in the kitchen sink. Isaac was playing outside, in the sandpit, with Pavel.

'You okay?' said George.

Simone's voice was thick and uncertain. 'Fine.' She grabbed two steaming cups of black coffee and headed outside. George watched Simone and Fiona, sitting side by side on the bench, their kids building their worlds in the sandpit. It was normal. Nothing out of the ordinary. Why pretend at being normal? Because if you believe it for long enough then that's how everything will turn out. That's how to defeat pain and grief – exorcise them with the spell of the ordinary.

George grabbed the folder containing the electoral roll, and set off for the community centre. There was nothing ordinary about this situation. But he was the chairman. That was his role. He had to concentrate on whatever it was he needed to do.

•

Howard Brindley studied the PowerPoint maps projected on to the wall. The emergency committee, he knew, were looking for answers; guidance. First, he outlined a computerised food rationing system, then he set out the geographical context – the main hubs of Berlin, Paris and London marked in blue; SCOPE's rural network of masts in red – down to the Scottish scale.

'This is not an exhaustive map of SCOPE transmitters,' he said. 'It was based mainly on our company's register, and we were only subcontractors for the northern region. I managed to get some info from the east, from a contact I had there. Even in Scotland we didn't have the whole sector. And there are thousands of smaller nodes in towns and cities, in lampposts, on street corners, made by other firms.' He turned back to the map. Nobody was really taking in anything he said. The copper was doing his best to pay attention, but George and Councillor Matheson and that retired architect, whatever his name was, were zombies. 'As I was saying,' said Howard, his voice dropping. 'There will be other notspots, but where exactly I can't say.'

He paused. 'I think mapping the extent of our own notspot would be useful. The delta waveform fluctuates, so to have an average of several sweeps would be needed.' He looked around. 'And . . . it's good that the community centre has photovoltaic panels on the roof. That's . . . good too.'

'You said sweeps?' said Gibbs.

Howard took a mobile out of his pocket. 'Yes, this will plot the field intensity, a reading every fifty metres or so will do it. Once I've done, say, four sweeps around the bay, I'll feed the readings into the palmpod to give us a map of our safe zone.'

George clenched, unclenched his fists. 'Safe,' he repeated, looking around as if he didn't know where he was. Who was safe?

'Yes,' answered Howard. 'Someone might get too close to the field. If there are fluctuations then it could be dangerous. It would also be useful to know exactly how big a notspot we're in, and what that means for our resources, living space, and so forth. We can't waste time waiting for the masts to fail. I imagine winters can be pretty harsh up here.'

This moment had occurred to Howard, again and again, over the last few months. Here he was, telling shell-shocked people about SCOPE and how to organise for survival. It wasn't a concept any more. He was here, and the thing he'd dreaded had happened. And now he found that he couldn't just get on with it. He'd thought about this so often that it had become polished, like a lecture he could just rattle through. But instead of attentive students, there were broken people in front of him. His cleverness hadn't taken that into account.

If he'd acted sooner, a lot sooner, then none of this would have been necessary.

He brought the meeting to end, saying that was enough for today, and trudged back to Room 22.

•

The tide was out, exposing mudflats at the head of the bay. Carl crunched along the shingle beach, past a line of small boats that had been dragged above the high-water mark. Paint peeled and flaked from two of them, exposing old rotting wood. The boats looked neglected, forgotten about. He stood, looking up at a big house, half hidden by trees, patio doors and a veranda facing the bay. He heard footsteps crunching on the shingle.

'Hi,' said Howard softly.

Carl barely acknowledged the greeting. He patted one of the boats on the gunwale. It felt solid enough, but blue paint flaked off in brittle shards as he touched the wood. He rubbed the paint to dust between his hands.

'Listen,' said Brindley. 'I've been speaking to the committee, but I don't know what information they've actually absorbed and what's going over their heads.'

Out on the mudflats Carl spotted what looked like an old bicycle, its rusted frame swathed in seaweed. The sea was burying it, making the bike part of itself. He watched wading birds, long-legged and slender-billed, probing the edge of the tide. He tried to focus on what Howard was saying.

'Anyway,' continued Howard, 'I told them it would be a good idea if we plotted the delta field. You can help me, if you want. First of all, though, I reckon we should take a boat and see how far we can get.'

Carl roused himself, responding to the idea behind the words. He stood straight, attentive now. 'Of course – a boat.' He smiled. 'A boat. Why didn't I think of that?'

Howard shook his head. 'There are coastal masts north and south of here, and masts on the islands you can see on the horizon. I wouldn't bet on a clear passage out of here.'

'But it's a possibility, right?'

'Yes, it's possible, though where we can go I don't know.'

'Somewhere. Anywhere.'

'We *are* somewhere.'

'Somewhere else,' insisted Carl, his voice rising. 'Taking a boat is a great idea.'

Brindley pursed his lips. 'OK, I've put the idea to the committee, and George Cutler said his son Adam would take me out in his fishing boat. It's a bit rough today, I was told. Maybe tomorrow, if the wind drops.'

'Can I come with you?'

'Well,' said Brindley, 'if there are fluctuations in the delta field – sizeable ones – then being in a boat might not be the safest place. There may be refraction effects because of the tide. We might not be able to turn the boat round in time.'

Carl shook his head.

'I'll take that chance.' He was staring at Brindley, face to face. 'Take me with you.'

Brindley nodded.

Carl pulled a single cigarette from his pocket. It was bent and crumpled. He looked at it for a second. 'Do you have a light?'

Howard shook his head grimly. Carl looked at the cigarette again and put it back in his jacket pocket.

'You know,' said Howard, 'maybe here is as good a place as any to pitch up. Inverlair is one of the biggest notspots, that's why I came here.'

'Yeah, well,' said Carl, picking at the flakes of paint. 'I came here because of you. And, if it's all the same to you, I'd like to get the fuck out of here as soon as possible.'

•

It was after 11 p.m. and still daylight, the southern headland of Inverlair black against the glowing west. Carl could still see his hand in front of his face, the path up from the shore and the forms of the houses. There were stars in the darker east, a gentle salty breeze and each seabird so clear in the calling as their cries pierced the quiet. The hours and days were mounting up, and the rest of the world was saying goodbye. For all Carl cared, Adam Cutler's fishing boat could drop him over the side where he belonged, down among the devouring shoals. Better the CivCon sharks than here, where there was no normal terror.

21

From an upstairs window Isaac watched his uncle's fishing boat come back into the bay. He ran down to the kitchen to pass on the news. 'Uncle Adam is back,' he said, pulling a disgusted face. 'With more fish.'

George was hunched over the sink, hands covering his face. He was shaking.

'Grandpa?'

Without turning round George straightened up, ran his hands under the tap. 'I dropped something.'

'What did you drop?'

George splashed his face with water. 'Never mind. It's fine.'

Isaac came over. 'Is it cut?'

'No.'

'Let me see?'

'It's fine,' he barked, quickly drying his hands and face. He threw the dish towel aside.

Before the boy's shock became tears, George whisked him out into the lobby, the mask of tolerance restored.

Down at the pier, a group of people had gathered. George gripped his grandson's hand, figured that if the boat was back so soon it must be bad news. The *Aurora* ploughed towards them, throttle easing back and into reverse as it neared the pier.

The expressions of those onboard told the story. Engines idling, the boat came to a stop, backwash lapping against the pier's barnacle-encrusted legs.

'Just over three miles,' shouted Howard. 'We went as far south as we dared and worked our way west and north.'

George sagged, letting go of his grandson's hand. His voice cracked. 'Could you see any other boats?'

Howard shook his head. 'Nothing.'

The sea looked inviting to George as the *Aurora* was tied up alongside. The urge to jump off the pier took hold.

He felt a little hand slip into his, squeezing. The pressure roused him.

'Well, we know what we have to do,' George found himself saying. He spoke loud enough for everyone to hear. 'We sink or swim. That's the choice. We were told it a few days ago, now we're hearing it again – that's all. We're going to get through this – all of us – together. We stick with the plan that Mr Brindley told us about at the meeting. Tomorrow we'll start organising jobs and work crews.'

Fair enough, that kind of pep talk. But what George really wanted to do was jump into the boat and race it out to sea as fast as he could, regardless of the consequences and blind to the reason for doing so. Despite that, his words had come out in a firm and clear voice. He wondered how that had happened.

George walked away, gripping his grandson's hand a little too tightly. As he climbed the rhododendron-lined path, he tried to remember when, exactly, the hotel stopped being a thriving business and became a huge empty building that ate his money. The process had been gradual. Like a heaving late-night party, people had slipped away, imperceptibly, until there were only a few stragglers left to face the dawn.

Inverlair Hotel had gone way beyond being a drain on his resources, he thought. It had become a mausoleum, and he was the caretaker.

•

Carl and Howard started their first sweep of the redzone at the roadblock, on the north road out of Inverlair.

'We'll head down towards the sea first of all,' said Howard. He nodded inland, to the brooding massif of Ben Bronach. 'Then we'll move up there.' He studied his deltameter-cum-phone. 'Look, the reading at the roadblock today is weaker than it was when Gibbs put the roadblock up. We'll need a few sweeps of the bay to get an average.'

On the grassy verge, a fat bee bounced from stem to stem. Howard's plan seemed like a good one.

'It's lovely here,' Carl murmured, looking out to sea. 'It was pissing down yesterday and now it's like the Bahamas.'

They left the single-track road and walked down the grass slope to the rocky shoreline, then came back up towards the roadblock, Carl entering co-ordinates on Howard's palmpod like he'd been shown. Sheep and sturdy black-faced lambs scattered as they retraced their steps.

'Don't take this the wrong way,' said Carl as they reached the road again, 'but why didn't you go to the media about SCOPE? Something this big is hard to ignore, even with the PLC on our case. Someone would have published, spun it as a managerial issue. There must've been some way of getting it out.'

Sweat glistened on Howard's hairless head. He took off his jacket. 'I was a partner in a firm, GeoByte Services,' he said. 'Three of us in a management buyout. The other two were more finance and deal-making, but I wanted to stay in product development. It was my job to iron out the signal noise from other telecomms on the site-share. Anyway, I went to Len, one of the partners, a guy I'd known for almost twenty years. I told him the modelling results confirmed the resonance in the diarite filters when the transmitters were networked. So he said he'd have a look at my results.'

Howard cleared his throat. 'A week later he still hadn't got back to me, fobbed me off when I asked him about the resonance results. Then, when I was about to go to him again, we got a visit from the main contractor, their head of procurement no less, who starts talking about a new contract, a bigger one, *if* we deliver on SCOPE. And that's when things got difficult for me. I went to Len again, but there was no budging him. I could see what they were trying to do, the contractors, so I went to the Security Ministry, and another sympathetic hearing took place.

'Two days later there was a break-in at the science park, my hard copies of the modelling report were stolen, and all my back-up data – three months of research – was wiped. Flash drives, cloud accounts, everything.'

Howard looked straight at Carl. 'I guessed then that CivCon would be monitoring me so I couldn't risk any kind of contact with you. And anyway, what would you have said if I'd phoned you up ranting about SCOPE and its two-hertz harmonic that might send people to sleep as they were walking in the street?'

'I would have thought you were nuts. If you were lucky I would have checked you out and asked for proof.'

'And I had none to show you.'

They pressed on in silence, Carl dropping back a little, lost in thought. What Brindley had said was plausible enough to dispel guilt, culpability. Could he have done anything different?

•

A few days later they were halfway through a second sweep of the bay. The first set of readings had given a maximum safe distance of 4.2 kilometres from Inverlair Hotel to the edge of what everyone now referred to as the redzone. They were about 400 metres above sea level.

'These are the exact co-ordinates, no doubt about it.' He handed the deltameter back to Carl. 'The field strength is much weaker than it was on the first sweep. Down to 120 microtesla again.' He frowned at the readings.

Here was something. Carl grabbed at the floating feather of hope with both hands. Twelve days and maybe SCOPE was conking out already. Never mind two to five years. Sitting on a moss-covered rock, Howard wiped the sweat from his eyes, frowning over his deltameter. Insects droned and hovered over the stewing bogs. He screwed the top back on his water bottle.

'Both the delta field's magnetic and microwave components are still present, which means the nearest transmitter is still working. I don't know why the signal strength has dropped off. There can be temporary attenuations in a signal for all sorts of reasons.'

Carl's head dropped. 'So, it's just a blip?'

Brindley pulled at blades of long grass. 'I don't know.'

'Why not? You built the fucking thing.'

'Incorrect,' said Brindley, glaring at Carl. 'But I think you know that . . . I think you also know that SCOPE was more than an emergency communications system. You *do* know that, don't you?'

Carl set off back down the grassy slope towards the village. He turned round, walking backwards. 'Well, if there's one man who can tell the rest of us what SCOPE really was, it sure as fuck isn't me.'

22

Grief belonged in the past. He had no use for it now. George kept telling himself that. It was too soon, that was the problem, and if he'd been given to platitudes, he would have said that time is the great healer, or something along those lines.

When he was alone he felt naked before grief. It had reduced him to the core of what he was. It was testing him, interrogating the workings of his soul, responses that he had barely given a second thought to before. It was testing his stitches. Was he held together properly? Would he come apart?

He would endure, withstand the punishment, or he would disintegrate. For the time being, he'd let grief take him, but he knew there had to be a way out of it, a way of confining it, mostly, as an experience that was based on memory, not raw actuality. George kept telling himself all that but, for now, it was no use. Maybe one day he would find himself entirely focused on what he was doing: the past's ability to hurt him reduced to an intermittent and fading signal.

The bench was warm. George sat with his face to the sun, an empty space beside him that he could picture being filled by Alison. So many times she had sat there and he'd hardly been aware of her; now that she was missing, he could hardly take his eyes off the space she used to occupy, when the weather had allowed.

Simone and Isaac were round at Fiona's, so he had cried on his own, a trickle this time, rather than a torrent.

He'd noticed that his daughter wasn't letting him look after

Isaac as often as she had; whenever she went out she took the boy with her. Did she think he was incapable of looking after his own grandson? Through his grief, George felt a surge of anger. It fired off in several different directions: at Brindley and the journalist, at the bastards who dreamed up the SCOPE system, at his own daughter. Himself. Alison had been pissed off with his moods, his sullen sarcasm. If it hadn't been for that, maybe she would never have felt the need to go to Edinburgh for a break in the first place.

He tried to focus. There were important things to do now. The situation is what it is, he told himself, and now we have to think of the future, like Brindley said. What was that stuff he'd been talking about the other day? Drawing up work crews. Rationing the food according to age and sex and usefulness. Okay. Lots to be done.

George cocked his head at the sound of his son's fishing boat returning, engine throbbing. It was too soon. The other day they'd reached four miles out. He stood up, blew his nose and wiped his eyes, and headed down to the pier to meet the *Aurora*.

Carl shouted something from the deck of the boat but George couldn't hear him above the engines. Adam eased back on the throttle, and guided the boat alongside, nudging the rubber casing. It was low tide and the *Aurora* was well below the top of the pier.

'There might be a gap, a way out,' Carl repeated. He scrambled up the metal ladder to join George on dry land.

Brindley doused some of their excitement. 'It can't be more than a few hundred metres wide,' he said. 'Hard to tell if it opens into the Atlantic. And if there is any kind of fluctuation in the field strength the gap could close in around you before you know it. There are refraction effects to consider as the tide rises and falls. You'd never turn around and get out in time.'

Carl stiffened. 'You said it was possible.'

'Possible, but extremely risky. A channel that narrow. In a boat.'

Howard shook his head. 'And there's no way of telling how far it extends.'

'There might be a way out,' urged Carl. 'That's what you said.'

'Sounds like a death sentence to me,' said George. 'And where would you go?'

Carl glared at him. 'Anywhere. West coast of Ireland – Howard's friends went there. Or Spain.'

George considered the horizon. 'I wouldn't like to sail to Spain in a tiny boat like that – especially if I have to head north to start with to get into the Atlantic. And don't they have that white rust fungus pretty bad down there?' He glanced at Howard. The guy was talking sense. 'In any case, there are over a hundred people in Inverlair and only three small boats.' George shrugged.

'So we just sit here for maybe five years, is that it?' said Carl, unable to believe what he'd heard. 'Shouldn't we, er, actually try to get out of here? There isn't much food, in case you hadn't noticed.'

Brindley guessed that George was thinking the same simple question. 'We can cope with the food we have, so I'm told. But why should we try to get out of here?'

Carl was flabbergasted. 'Why?' He shook his head. There were so many reasons to leave this place. Or at least Carl felt there must be. But when he needed just one of them, to slap down on the table as a trump card, he found himself unable to summon anything that sounded convincing. The places SCOPE hadn't blanked out weren't likely to be any better off than Inverlair. Further away, say north-west Africa, there might be a good life waiting – if a ten-metre fishing boat could make the 2,500-mile trip; if it could find a way out of the delta field and through the mountainous Atlantic.

'I don't know,' he said quietly. 'I just thought . . .' He looked at George. 'Don't you want to try and get to Edinburgh, to your wife?'

For a second, emotion charted a charmed route in George's heart, around Cape Wrath and the Pentland Firth.

'You won't be able to get anywhere near Edinburgh, or any other big town, for maybe ten years – I told you that,' Howard said to Carl. 'That much I can say with virtual certainty because of how SCOPE is configured in urban areas. I told you all this.'

Carl repeated the phrase, making the point. 'Virtual certainty. Virtual. But not absolute.'

His eyes wide, Howard waved him away. 'Oh don't be so bloody stupid.' He strode away. 'Go on then. Go. Take the boat and see how far you get.'

'Oh no, he fucking won't,' said Adam, climbing up onto the pier. 'No one's taking my boat anywhere.' He looped a thick rope from the *Aurora*'s bow around a metal cleat on the quayside. His father tied the stern line.

'There's a spot of lunch waiting,' George said to Carl. 'Not much, but it'll fill a hole. Brindley's right, you know. If it goes wrong, it's a death sentence.'

The boat nuzzled against the side of the pier, plastic squeaking on rubber, wet ropes taking the strain. A big seagull, snow-white chest, settled on a railing beside the men.

'It would be a quick death, at least,' said Carl. 'And that's better than the alternative.'

Saying nothing, George strode back to the hotel.

In the kitchen, they ate in silence. There was so much to say, and so many questions to ask. But instead of risking conversation, which might begin painlessly enough, saying nothing was obviously the safer option. Conversation could expose feelings, and feelings were hard to control, so the unresolved pressure of not talking swelled within the room. Isaac watched all the adults distill their private pain.

Eventually, Brindley spoke. 'It's still early,' he said to Carl. 'So I thought we could take some more signal readings in the hills, if you want to.'

It was unbelievable. Carl resisted the temptation to hurl his plate of food against the kitchen wall. Here they were, sitting nice and cosy around the table. Simone was being civil to him. But she was a door that had been closed and locked. He felt like saying: it was only a shag, and not a very good one at that. And that wee Isaac was giving him the evil eye as well. Little shite.

He nodded at Howard's suggestion. 'Shall we make a move then?'

Carl took his plate to the sink and rinsed it under the tap. The water was warm, the kitchen uncomfortably so because the fire was lit. From the window, Carl looked towards the summit of Ben Bronach. They would follow the line of the fence to the burn, then meet the forest track. From there it was up past the old stones and onto the shoulder of the hill, following the ridge, heading inland across the headwater streams that fed the river. He knew the way by now.

•

'I don't know if I'm imagining it, but is there something between you and Simone?'

It was another warm day, and plump lambs dozed by their chewing mothers. Carl figured there was no point in denying it. 'We had sex.'

Howard didn't know what to say. 'Oh.'

'She gave me a hug – that's how it started.' Carl's voice cracked. 'It was just comfort – closeness, y'know?' He felt tears in his eyes and his face reddening. 'But it doesn't matter.' He shook his head, annoyed with himself reacting this way. He was all over the place. 'Embarrassment is a pretty pointless emotion to feel, given what's happened, wouldn't you say?'

The slope was getting steeper now, grass giving way to heather. Howard stopped for a breather, taking out a hankie to wipe the sweat from his face and head. 'Your guess is as good as mine,' he said. 'I could never work women out.'

•

Five hours later Howard was flat out on the bed in Room 22, his legs and back aching, his neck sunburnt. Thank Christ he'd taken a baseball cap with him, otherwise his scalp would be toast. He felt good, though; physically tired, but relaxed with it. It was their longest stint yet, and they were well on with the second sweep of readings. He lay for a while, fully clothed, staring at the ceiling. Maybe he'd ask Adam Cutler if they could venture out in the fishing boat again, test the gap in the redzone to the north. Staying active made people forget – and that was good. If people did useful stuff, then so much the better. That was the only thing to do now: work. Survive.

There was a soft knock at the door.

'Come in.'

The door creaked open. 'Hello,' said George, peering into the room.

'Hello there.' Howard smiled. 'I can't seem to move.'

The smile was returned, weakly.

'I thought you might appreciate a dram,' said George, his voice low. 'If you feel up to it.'

Howard heaved himself up against the bedhead. 'Whisky doesn't really agree with me, but I'll make an exception, on the grounds that it may have some curative effect. I'll have a wash first. Freshen myself up.'

Ten minutes later Howard appeared in the residents' lounge, just as George cracked the seal on a bottle. An oil-lamp burned on the mahogany coffee table. George handed Howard his drink and gestured to an armchair. 'Carl said he would join us in a while. I prefer it in here to the annexe, although that didn't used to be the case.'

Gingerly, Howard lowered himself into the chair. He raised his glass of single malt. 'Cheers.'

Without any real enthusiasm, George returned the toast.

After a mouthful of whisky, Howard smacked his lips and held the glass up to the lamplight. 'Liquid gold,' he said.

George took another gulp of his drink. 'You guys must be nearly finished the second sweep of the . . .' He gestured towards vaguely towards the window.

'Redzone,' said Howard.

'Is that what you've called it?'

'We've marked it on the map in the community centre in red pen. I suppose we can't keep calling it "out there".'

'No,' said George. 'I suppose we can't.'

They fell silent. It was quiet enough to hear the wick burning in the oil-lamp. George swirled his whisky round the glass, felt the fire in his cheeks. 'Do you mind if I ask you a question?'

Howard stretched his tired legs in front of him. 'No,' he said, taking a sip of whisky. 'I don't mind.'

George let go a breath. His words, so carefully rehearsed, were jostling for position. 'People . . . some people . . . are wondering how you ended up in Inverlair. Why you didn't leave the country altogether if you knew this was coming – that kinda thing.' He waited for a reaction.

Howard smiled. 'People are suspicious of me,' he said. 'A stranger arrives and a terrible thing happens. The stranger was connected to the terrible thing. It makes sense.'

George poured another round of drinks and took a mouthful. 'You know how people are.'

'And what do *you* think?'

'Well, you worked on this system, you didn't like what you found out, and you tried to do something about it. But I do wonder why you didn't leave the country – go somewhere safe, I mean.'

Howard sat back in his chair, glass resting on his belly, stockinged feet on a footstool. 'We were working on SCOPE – this is about seven years ago – and my company was hired.'

'You owned a company?'

With a wave of his hand, Howard dismissed fifteen years of his life as 'nothing major'. He told George most of what he'd told Carl. The whisky worked its magic, and he kept talking.

'Some people, a few, were well connected enough to buy their way out of the country. People who knew what might happen. But I didn't have enough money for the traffickers. Even if I had, I was probably pretty high on CivCon's watchlist at that stage, so exit-point biometrics would have been primed with every move I'd ever made and an image of every pimple on my fucking face.'

He glared, briefly, at George, a gulp of whisky souring his expression, his voice rough. 'That's what gave them the initial idea for SCOPE. You can change the way you walk, your eyeballs, your whole face, even your fingerprints.' He tapped his temple. 'But you can't change this.'

George looked puzzled.

'Brainwaves. The active Beta range, to be exact.'

A bit clearer: but George was still missing the bigger picture.

Whisky storming round his head, Howard spoon-fed him the ABC.

'If you took an EEG of your brainwaves just now it would record a waveform which is unique to you. Between twelve and thirty-eight hertz is the beta phase of brain activity when the brain is alert.' Howard tilted his glass. 'Though we're getting less alert with every drop of this. Everyone has their own exact frequency.' He tapped his temple again. 'In here. Each emotion – fear, anger, even anxiety – has its own signature.'

Smiling was not something George felt like doing. He looked at his glass, a regular poisoned chalice; every mouthful of anaesthetic was bringing his pain into sharper focus. Only oblivion cancelled it out.

He became aware of another presence in the room.

'Hi,' said Carl. 'I feel more human after a shower.'

'The man himself,' called Howard, twisting round in his chair. 'The man who sniffed it all out.'

George poured another three-finger measure of whisky, handing it to Carl.

'Howard was telling me more about SCOPE.'

'So I gather,' said Carl. Something they had both agreed not to talk about was now being talked about. He accepted the whisky and sat down. Howard grinned as he finished his second generous measure.

'So SCOPE was designed to track people,' stated George, puffing at the reflux in his gut. 'Is that right?'

Howard helped himself to another drink. He was dog-tired and well on the road to being plastered. 'To begin with, that was the idea, but it became much more than that, Georgie boy.'

'We agreed, Howard,' said Carl firmly, staring grimly at his drink. 'We agreed. Certain things, yes?'

'Is that a fact?'

Before Carl could answer, Howard stood up, his index finger raised. He tottered, steadied himself. 'The questions we have to ask ourselves are: how do you control chaos? How do you manage the slow-motion train-wreck of civilisation? Fear and surveillance – that's how you do it. Fear makes people accept what you're doing, and surveillance keeps the money circulating – European research grants and Security Ministry contracts for everything from behaviour-prediction software to non-lethal weaponry for our militarised police forces. Not as much money as there was before, but enough to keep some important wheels going round.'

Tired now, and drunk, George sagged into his armchair.

She got on a bus. Got on a bus and didn't come back.

Howard lurched forward, waving an arm at Carl. 'There were no people anymore, no individuals, at the end of it – only data to be mined, targets on a screen. Our digital trails were actionable intelligence for certain interests. We weren't users of technology any more – we were its subjects. Finally, the right kit came along, advertising total control.' He wagged a bony finger at Carl, grinning.

'But they weren't as clever as they thought. Oh no. Hidden imperfection got the better of them. Carl there, he knew all about that. He knew what was going on with SCOPE – but he was too shit-scared to tell the rest of us.'

Carl drained his whisky. 'Fuck off. Don't give me the you-did-as-much-as-you-could crap. You worked on SCOPE for years. You were part of the whole fucking anti-terror show. SCOPE was originally a tracking system long before it was mood manipulation.' He stopped, glanced at Howard, went for a refill.

'The perils of dual-use technology,' declared Howard. 'Scientists could believe that everything military also had a civilian use – for the benefit of society. That's how we could do what we did with a clear conscience, more or less. But we couldn't see the bigger picture, not on this one.'

Howard was talking to George, but George wasn't really listening. He was too busy remembering.

'That's what we could tell ourselves.' Howard glared at Carl. He jabbed a finger towards Carl. 'You knew.'

Carl stood up. 'Look, you prick, what was I supposed to say to my editor? There's this new government communications system that's really an attempt at mass fucking mind control ...'

George looked up, aware of the fuss, but unsure of what he'd heard.

Howard was swaying with whisky and fatigue. 'I'll let our roving reporter tell you all about that little secret, George. It's time for my voluntary grave.' He aimed for the lounge door. 'A government contract is a substitute for intellectual curiosity,' he intoned as he tottered from the room.

Nonplussed, George looked to Carl. 'What was that?'

Whisky downed in two, Carl poured another. He started pacing the room, silently cursing Howard, slurping from his glass.

He could tell George the truth. He could tell him all about brainwave entrainment through pulsed magnetic induction. He could tell him about extremely low-frequency psychotronics, charting its history all the way back to the Russians in the 1960s and the CIA's MK-Ultra programme.

He stood at the bookcase, the shabby edition of *Highland Animals* at his fingertips. Where was *Vipera berus* now?

'Fear and money, George, just like old Ike said,' Carl said at last. 'And one hell of a ghost in the machine.'

23

It was 5.50 a.m. and a pale September morning was leaching into Inverlair Bay and into the hotel. Being awake at night was the worst; there was nothing but silence and uncontrollable thoughts darting in and out of existence. That was when sadness and terror stood tall by the bed and kept her awake. So there was nothing to do but get up. She could grab an hour's sleep in the afternoon. There was always something that needed doing, and doing something, anything, was better than lying awake in the dark.

Her mother. That journalist. The baby she was going to have.

Simone pulled her dressing gown tight around herself, more afraid than cold.

From the window of the residents' lounge, she watched dawn break over the village, heard the birds in full voice, light spilling into the bay, the tops of the far headland ablaze in the early beams. There was nothing unusual about any of it: day beginning and day ending, on a spool that replayed over and over and carried her along with it. She was now moving through days filled with other people and the things that always needed doing. People still had their needs, and their appetites. She tried to rationalise, to absolve, and she wondered if Carl was doing the same.

'Mum,' she whispered at the windowpane, cold glass under her fingertips.

She heard a noise behind her in the corridor and turned from the window.

Howard stood in the doorway wearing a grey tracksuit, a glass of water in his hand. 'Oh,' he said groggily. 'I'm sorry, I didn't realise there would be anyone else up.'

Simone caught sight of a coin-sized stain near Howard's crotch. For some reason, this put her at ease.

'It's beautiful – but very bright,' he said, gesturing to the window, squinting at the daylight.

'Yeah,' said Simone, turning back to the dawn. 'It used to attract a lot of artists. The quality of the light, and the colours.'

Groaning, Howard slumped into the chair he'd occupied the previous evening. Christ, what an arse he'd been.

'Too much of your dad's whisky last night. It's never agreed with me. Think I was a bit of an arse.'

'You're not the first person to turn into an idiot after a drink.'

'I suppose not,' said Howard. 'I'm stiff as a bloody board as well. All that walking in the hills.' He winced. 'Sunburnt too.'

They were silent for a spell, the only sounds the seagulls and the clock on the mantelpiece. Stirring from the window, Simone said, 'Where did you live, before you found out about SCOPE?'

Howard didn't really feel up to a conversation. He drank most of the water in three gulps. 'Near Reading. Private estate. Part of a science park.'

'Did you have anyone, a family, or . . .'

He groaned again. 'A father with Alzheimer's and a sister in New York.'

Simone nodded. 'Sorry.'

'Yeah.' Howard looked pained for a moment. He didn't really feel like elaborating. 'Haven't seen my sister for years. We lost touch.'

'Sorry, I don't mean to be nosey,' said Simone. 'It's just that you sit at our table every day, but I don't know the first thing about you, apart from your job . . .'

'You've got other things on your mind,' said Howard. 'I'm sorry about your mother.'

Simone chewed her lip.

'I've heard your father mention Hannah. Is that your sister?'

'Yeah,' she said. 'She's in Norway working as a translator. Maybe she still is.'

'Maybe,' said Howard. 'They didn't have SCOPE there. It was installed across Sweden though . . .'

Simone frowned, tightened her dressing gown around her. 'There's some tea. Would you like a cup?'

'Oh, yes please,' breathed Howard. 'That would be fantastic.'

When Simone went through to the kitchen, Howard picked up the empty whisky bottle and sniffed the smoky fumes. What an arse. What a loose-tongued vicious pain in the arse.

•

Carl waited on the pavement outside the hotel.

Okay, Brindley had said sorry and, yes, whisky brings out the demon in some guys, but he was a complete wanker for telling George about SCOPE, no two ways about that. With a bit of luck, George had been too pissed to realise what he was being told. Then again, maybe it was no bad thing if he did remember the previous evening, just so long as he didn't blame the obvious targets for not being heroic enough to stop it all. That's what they would've been if they'd blown the whistle on SCOPE: heroes. And not everyone can step out of the crowd like that, saying what no one else will say. Carl wondered if George would understand any of that. The risk and ridicule involved.

The hotel's front door squeaked open.

'You're keen to get started,' said Howard, without meeting Carl's eye.

Carl set off down the path towards the main road.

After a few moments, Howard caught up with him. 'I knew you knew what SCOPE was. I knew it. Listen, maybe it's no bad thing we told George.'

Carl snorted. 'No bad thing.' He shook his head. 'Do you realise that people are still wary of us? Do you actually get that? Some of them still think we had something to do with all this. And now George might be wondering why we waited three fucking weeks before telling him about the secret SCOPE upgrade. Do you want to get us lynched? These people are strangers.'

Howard shrugged. 'It won't come to that.'

A pick-up truck, piled high with logs, rumbled past them and turned into the boatyard. The driver was a heavy-set red-faced man in an orange boiler suit. He and his passenger jumped out, clattered open the truck's side-flap, and let sections of tree-trunk roll off, thudding onto the concrete forecourt. The driver eyed Carl and Howard with suspicion.

They passed the schoolhouse and skirted round the stalker's farm, leaving the bay behind.

Almost two hours later they reached the spot where the stream that fed the River Lair soaked away into the boggy uplands: fathoms of water-engorged peat that spilled and sprung their loads.

Howard consulted his deltameter. 'Twelve days ago, the delta signal dropped by 200 microtesla for a few hours. The signature was still there in the H-band, but a much weaker primary harmonic. Six days ago the same thing happened. And now again today. Some kind of pattern by the looks of it, every six days. I'll do a spectrum analysis later on my tablet, but I think we should wait here for a while, see what the main waveform does; there was marked attenuation for about four hours the last time it happened.'

Carl took out his palmpod and consulted the readings. As graphs, the signal behaviour was clear: there were dips in the primary signal every six days. But though each dip lasted four hours, their start times were unequal. First dip: 11.27 a.m. Second dip: 1.42 p.m. Third dip: 11.24 a.m.

'So the time now is eleven-thirty and the signal is going down. We could have almost four hours, or we could have two, or less or more.' Howard squinted at the sun. 'Not enough datasets to be sure.' There were clouds massing out at sea. Definitely a hint of autumn in the air. He looked across the bay to the fissured summit of Ben Bronach. 'We could perhaps try to get to that farmhouse today,' he said. 'It can't be more than four hundred metres into the redzone.'

Carl gestured across the bay. 'The farmhouse – behind Ben Bronach?'

'Yes.'

'It will take us well over an hour to get up there,' said Carl. 'If we wait another six days we'll know for sure.'

Howard shook his head. 'You said six days ago that some of the chickens at the farmhouse were dead. The automatic feeder must have broken or run out, and there isn't enough in the coop to feed them much longer. They might all be dead by next week.' He looked at Carl. 'Just think of it – we could probably carry half a dozen each, maybe more. Tie their legs together. More eggs. More flesh.'

'Yeah,' whispered Carl. He drank some water and stood up. Man brings food from hill. People would appreciate that.

'Okay,' he said. 'Let's do it.'

An hour and a half later, they were high on the ridge. Through binoculars, Howard studied the farmhouse in the glen. A few of the chickens looked very dead, and a few more looked close to it, scrawny and inert. He could see one, a hump of wind-ruffled feathers, pressed against the coop's wire fence, unmoving. The Land Rover had a flat tyre now and there was a ewe standing in the open doorway of the house, a former hunting lodge. The owner, or what was left of him or her, was probably lying in the house. Howard checked his deltameter, and they set off down the steep rocky slope.

As they descended into the glen the terrain gave way from rock to knee-high heather that made walking difficult. Hidden burns gurgled under hags of peat. It was hard going and they worked up a sweat. By the time they got to the farmhouse it was half past one.

'Jesus, Howard,' panted Carl. 'We're cutting it too fine, man.'

But Howard was already inside the hen-coop. 'Come on,' he shouted, chasing after a chicken that flapped clear of him. 'Give me a hand.'

After a few minutes they had grabbed and tied three birds each. And then the noise started, pricking in their skulls. They looked at each other, Howard with a panicky smile.

'Whoops.'

They bolted from the coop.

•

They were only 500 metres or so from the red marker stone that Carl had painted on their first sweep of the redzone. That was the distance to safety. But the ground was uneven, with hidden hollows and holes, sloping upwards to the mouth of the glen, and they had to hurdle through heather.

They ran with their feathery bundles of protein. After about 300 metres pain skewered Carl's temples, and his lungs were burning with the effort.

Fuck the hens.

He ran away from death, with every ounce of the strength he didn't know he had, and fell, semi-conscious, just metres from the marker stone, blood streaming from his nose.

•

Cold splashes on his face. Hard. Harder. Rain. Dark. Pain.

Carl sat up. It was pelting with rain and he couldn't see a solitary object or light, anywhere. Thrashing a hand blindly on the wet grass next to him he shouted for Howard, panic firing him awake.

He stood. His lungs ached from running. He was soaked to the skin, wearing nothing but a T-shirt and jeans. A gust of wind flung rain into his eyes as he began to run. He tripped and fell, braced himself for the impact, but there was only cold grass under his hands.

'Howard!' He tried to think. Howard had been behind him, running. They'd both been running.

Okay, okay, a bit of reasoning was required here. No need to lose the plot. Carl tried to visualise the glen in daylight: the red marker stone and the track that led from the farmhouse to the north road. If he walked and felt no pain in his head, he was safe, and if he hit the redzone he could about-turn and walk in the opposite direction. If only he could find the track, that would give him his bearings.

'Howard!'

There was no response.

'Jesus, man,' he wailed. 'Howard!'

He waited and shouted again.

After a few minutes, he knew he had to get under cover, out of the wind and rain. The nights were colder now, and longer. He knew he had to seek shelter. There was no question now of death being a viable alternative: he had to get back to the village. Wanting to stay alive, and the force of this impulse, took him a little by surprise. Dying out here, in the wet dark, was not an option.

Fuck that.

Edging forward in total blackness with his hands outstretched, it was slow going, and he was cold – dripping wet, blinking into the rain and wind, cursing, groping his way forward, afraid to take big steps.

He fell again. This time he wasn't so lucky, and smacked his forehead off a rock. He curled up on the sodden grass, nursing the point of impact and the percussive quiver inside his skull, tasting his own blood along with cold rain. After a few seconds, he lay back on the ground, the heavy drops cascading onto his face, into his open mouth.

Maybe he should wait until dawn. It couldn't be more than a few hours away. He could rest here.

Howard.

He shivered, teeth rattling. Was he going up the slope or down? Whimpering, he bit down on fear, head still ringing from the fall against the rock. He stood up again, edged forward into the black miles of steep hills and hidden streams, hands outstretched, feeling their blind way into the void.

Alec John found him seven hours later, barely conscious and huddled in a bank of heather, the groundwork for double pneumonia deep in his lungs.

December

24

At night he could hear the stags roaring out their challenges to other males. Procreation was everything, or at least insemination was, the urge that sprung open like a time lock every November. At this time of year, so Alec John had said, there was nothing but the urge. Stags were slaves to it. Everything, from fat deposits to the thickness of neck manes, was geared to besting their rivals and gathering as many females as they could.

Standing in the hotel garden, on a windless night, Carl could hear the snap of branches as they barged their way through the trees and bushes on the lower slopes of the hill. Brute power had the horn, and was looking for as many places to insert it as possible. But before that, there was the fear of violence to sow first. The urge to fuck was preceded by the urge to dominate. They were indivisible.

Out in the dark garden Carl shivered in the breeze. He zipped his fleece up and jammed his hands in the pockets. It had been a warm enough day, in the sun, but the breath of winter commanded the night air. His new room, number 7, was cold now, most of the time, as winter gales thundered in from the south-west, one charging storm front after another. Tonight there was a lull, and the few constellations that were now familiar to him stood out from the dense infinity of lesser stars.

Carl sat on the bench at the bottom of the garden, the smell of damp decay thickening the dark, until it got too cold to stay outside any longer. There was still a faint glow in the west, and it was amazing how people learned to cope in darkness that could no longer be banished with the flick of a switch.

He was getting used to moving around at night, sensing his way and what lay in the deepest shadows. Extra care was required on the stairs, however: that's where Isaac was in the habit of leaving bits of Lego, or worse, toy cars.

Carl stepped deftly up to the first-floor landing, where the moon waned behind the stained-glass window. In the room he set match to candle, took another swig of Hendrik's home-brew, and rolled himself up in the duvet. He lay, staring at the candle flame, in absolute silence, and thought about the day, and the days to come. Today, out on the hill, they'd crept up to this sleeping stag; its eyes were closed, jaws munching on cud and a thread of drool hung from its mouth.

'You can see how thin he is,' Alec John had whispered. 'He's run out – exhausted after all that shagging and squaring up to the others.'

They crawled through the heather for a while longer, elbows in the spongy moss, making sure to keep their arses down, until Alec John stopped. They were at the edge of a peat bank. Down below, and easily within reach, was their dozing target.

Alec John reached into his pocket, took out a coin and flicked it into the burn. The coin pinged off a rock before it hit the water, but the beast didn't move a muscle in response.

'Years ago,' said Alec John, raising his voice a little, 'in a different part of the estate, I saw one like that, fast asleep. He was a fourteen-pointer, and it turned out to be his last year as top dog.' He chuckled. 'I could've walked over to him and put the fucking barrel in his ear if I'd wanted to.'

He passed the rifle to Carl. 'Now's your chance. You won't get a better one. The rut's almost finished.'

Carl took the gun. He'd fired dozens of practice shots and now, maybe as close as he would ever get, here was the real thing.

'Remember,' whispered Alec John. 'Breathe easy, find the mark, and squeeze through it. Brace yourself, but stay relaxed.' He smiled. 'You know, I used to get a lot of Germans up on shooting trips. They're a hunting nation, the Germans, but there aren't enough animals in their own country to shoot. A lot of them were members of clubs and they all had medals, but they had never actually shot an animal. It was a big moment for them, to shoot a deer, and they were shaking.' Alec John chuckled. 'Half of them were so nervous they missed – more than once.' He considered the sleeping animal. 'So take your time, and relax. Regulate your breathing.'

Lifting his binoculars, Carl could see the saliva glistening on the stag's chin, long eyelashes glinting in the weak sun, closed eyelids, and the jaw muscles flexing, working, as the animal chewed. If Alec John was right, maybe he could walk down there, press the barrel of the .308 against the base of the stag's neck, and pull the trigger. Easy meat. His first kill. Protein for the committee to allocate, according to their affiliations. One squeeze of his finger would do it.

But it didn't seem right. The animal was asleep in the sun after getting its hole for the umpteenth time. If the beast had been active, alert, then he could do it easily, maybe, from this distance, though he wasn't entirely sure about that either.

He sighed. 'It doesn't seem fair,' Carl whispered. He squinted at Alec John. 'D'you know what I mean?' He shook his head, took in a breath of cool, clean air, his hands gripping the Ruger's walnut stock.

'That's just what I was thinking,' said Alec John, smiling. 'The time before, the one I just told you about, I didn't think it was right then, him just sitting there. He deserved a better death, I reckoned.'

'But we need the meat.'

'Well,' said Alec John, 'if we really needed the meat I'd say go for it. But the freezers are full enough and we'll need to save bullets.' He shrugged. 'Take him if you want. He's an easy target.'

Carl engaged the safety on the rifle. 'A fair fight, and all that.'

Alec John nodded. 'Come on then, let's go.'

Both men crept back the way they had come. The stag would sleep, recover his strength, and wake up none the wiser. There was still another season's peak performance ahead of him and enough strength to keep rivals at bay, this time. Then he'd be a target, sleeping or not, for a stronger power.

25

They had this game, the kids. Well, they weren't exactly kids. The guys were fifteen, sixteen, and one of them must have been six-two if he was an inch. The girls, one or two of them, looked like women. There was no beating about the bush where that was concerned; they looked older, though he could tell when speaking to them, the words they used, their awkwardness, and their concerns, that they were in transition. Gemma was fifteen. He knew that. He didn't know how old the other one was, but he guessed they were all about the same age. Terry could play the worldly-wise man and make them all laugh, and the boys, smart enough in their sullen way, were no real match for him in the one-liner department.

So, anyway, they had this game, the kids.

Terry had seen them come back down the road one evening. They'd pitched a tent down between the dunes, where they smoked his weed and messed about. He'd heard one of the guys snarking about not getting his blow job. It was their own private spot, their refuge, when they weren't required to work or account for themselves. Deprivation was making adults of them, drawing them into dutiful necessity and away from childhood. In their den, they could just chill out.

One evening they were coming back from their den and Terry was heading home on his bike, out of the saddle, desperate for the headland incline not to beat him in front of Gemma and her watching crew. They gave the old man a ribbing as he struggled up the road towards them. Thigh muscles burning, Terry stopped trying to turn the pedals, doing his best to act like he wasn't completely shagged out. As he got his breath back, he noticed one guy's white T-shirt had a splatter of red down the front.

'Is that your first shave, Hector?' he said, gesturing to the stain. 'You'll get the hang of it eventually, as long as you don't cut your throat first.'

'Hector got the flag record off Tony,' said Gemma brightly. At that, Hector started proclaiming his pre-eminence loudly. He'd clearly enjoyed a celebratory home-brew or two along with his smoke; his eyes were red and his voice hoarse. If he'd started to beat his chest and roar in triumph Terry wouldn't have been too surprised.

'Flag record?'

'In the redzone,' said Gemma, as Hector was thumped on the upper arm by one of his mates. 'He did a hundred and twelve metres before he had to turn back.'

Terry frowned, confused.

'He doesn't know,' said Gemma to her mates. 'Come and we'll show Terry the flag.'

At the roadblock on the south road they stopped, microwaves buzzing and clicking in their heads. Down the straight, level road – out in the redzone – fluttered a small yellow flag. 'Yellow's a positive colour,' said Gemma. 'Like in Buddhist countries they wear yellow. Red's so negative, you know?'

'So,' said Terry, mock-thoughtfully, 'the barrier isn't really a barrier, and by the power of positive thinking you'll make the redzone disappear?'

'No,' chirped the other girl, Annie. 'We're not fucking saying that.'

Terry looked down the road in disbelief. 'Let me get this straight: you run into the redzone, down the road, with the yellow flag. And how d'you get it back?'

Hector piped up. 'The challenger has to get it back.'

'You can have a rest though,' said one of the other guys. 'Before you try and beat the record. You need to have a rest cos of the nosebleeds.'

Some things that Terry had done in his life were inadvisable, to say the least. But running towards an excruciating head-bursting noise that would eventually kill you was not one of them.

Gemma brandished a wrist-phone. 'We get the distance from this. There's a pedometer on it. The flag's in a wee sack of sand so the wind doesn't blow it away.'

'Well, kids,' said Terry, trying to look impressed, 'that's certainly an inventive game you have there.'

'It's not a game,' spat Hector. The rest agreed.

'It's an ingenious challenge,' said Annie.

Terry smiled. 'With death the prize for the winner. If human ingenuity can get a man on the moon, then there's no telling what challenge we can meet, or where we can plant our poxy little flags of positivity.'

Gemma glared at him. 'Fuck you,' she said. She pointed down the road. 'You run out to that flag and tell us all about human ingenuity, with the blood pishing out of your nose because of SCOPE, or whatever it's called. What a brilliant invention.'

'Go, Gemma,' encouraged Hector.

At that, she quietened, uncomfortable with her power. There was a pause, as they all considered the little yellow flag, fluttering 112.56 metres down the single-track road.

There was an obvious question, so daft Hector asked it. 'Want a shot?'

For a second, the thought of taking off in pursuit of the course record actually crossed Terry's mind. It was soon put to bed. 'Nah,' he said. 'I've been known to try and swim across the bay when I'm fucking pished, but I don't fancy that, guys.'

'Pussy,' snapped Hector.

Terry glanced down the road again, unable to catch Gemma's

eye. He turned back to the boy. 'Maybe so, but you'll still be kissing my arse and saying sorry when you want a smoke.'

The group laughed, and Terry made his getaway while he could, his bravado intact. He found Carl in the caravan, stuffing a pipe with some dry leaf.

'You not out with Alec John?'

Carl lit the pipe with a taper, sucked in the smoke. 'He's not feeling too good, so we finished early.'

Terry poured some home-brew. Hendrik was confident, this time, that the demijohns had been cleaned properly, and that this batch would be less purgative than the last.

A couple of hours later it was dark, the wind on the move, surging and swishing around the caravan. The conversation turned to Howard, and the world before, and Carl's mood had soured. The same line kept running through his head: the machine gave us everything, then it took it all away. He wished he could stop thinking. Too much booze. Too much weed.

The wind-lamp brightened as the roof-mounted turbine whirled furiously in a gust, but the far end of the room, the tiny partitioned bedroom, a jumble of clothes and books, was in darkness. Carl felt tired, dead-beat, and talking about the past made him want to curl up, alone.

'I'm off,' he said.

Terry stayed sitting on a beanbag near the stove. 'Don't be daft, kip on the couch. What do you have to go back for?'

'I don't know.' He shrugged. 'Call it a homing instinct for somewhere that isn't home. Territorial urge.'

Carl shuddered at the thought of walking back to the hotel, groping along the road, afraid of where his next footstep was going to take him. The last time that had happened it had almost killed him, and his urge to leave the tiny caravan was stronger than the fear that it might. Carl stood, unsteady on his feet, and zipped up his jacket. It was black outside the window and he felt the wind give the caravan another shove. Maybe he should stay right where he was. He couldn't face feeling his way through total darkness, and if his wind-up torch packed in that's what he'd have to do.

'Right,' said Carl, his hand on the door. With light, he'd find his way. Opening the door, a fresh nor'westerly came diving in, fluttering curtains and paper, with the tide on its breath. The torch worked fine, its beam showing wind-tossed rhododendron and willow.

'Okay,' he said. 'See you tomorrow.'

On the road, Carl started to fret that the torch would stop working. A thick bank of gorse jerked in the wind and, for a second, Carl saw it as a crowd of onlookers jostling for a better view of this poor creature lurching past. He gave the charging handle a few more turns, but then worried that it might break because he had over-wound it. He was moderately pissed and fairly stoned – again. And the day ahead wouldn't be easier because of it.

The look on Howard's face, in the hen-coop, when he realised what was happening, what was about to engulf them. Call it a desperate smile. Whoops, I've just killed us. It all came back to Carl, no matter how hard he tried to keep it away.

Whoops. And then he was gone.

Carl kept the torch-beam focused on the road.

That's why people are afraid of the dark, he thought. They aren't in control, and they don't know what's in front of them or around them or where exactly they're going. An aversion to that level of uncertainty and powerlessness is hard-wired. Full illumination means freedom: people don't have to go to bed when it gets dark. Maybe Inverlair would reacquire that natural rhythm of responding to the night. It's dangerous to be in absolute darkness, with no possibility of light. Nothing bad can surprise you if the way ahead is clear, if you have a way of slicing through the unknown, making it visible and ordinary. Bad things hide from the light. He'd had light of his own to shine, once upon a time. Down the headland road he walked, curving round the loop to the other side of the bay, down past the shell of the old tourist information centre, blue-and-white signage bleached by years of rain. His torch-beam found the bus stop across the road from the copper's house: scorch marks from a vandal's gas lighter, graffiti on the few unbroken Perspex panels, Callum advertising buttfucking. Maybe Callum had no idea that his phone number and availability had been scrawled for all to see. Unless Inverlair was more relaxed that Carl gave it credit for. Offering sexual services in this way is common enough in Soho, so why not here?

Eyes. Silver-green. An animal, out in the darkness. In the woods near the bridge Carl caught the baleful eye-beams in the torchlight, then heard the hooves pounding and a quick thrash of leaves and branches as the animal bolted, making for higher ground through the gorse and bracken, out onto the open hill.

Carl burped, steadied himself, and lurched on towards the bridge at the head of the bay, through swirling scrap leaves, the river rushing underneath, its force dissipating in the salt softness of low tide.

In the south-east, as the wind surged through the branches, an electrical storm flashed, though it was too far away to hear.

Once he got closer to the houses, he could see a dim light from the PV batteries in a few of them. Electric lights were also on in the community centre. Probably the committee in there, cooking up more ways to expropriate some communal creature comforts. It's amazing how quickly dishonesty re-establishes itself, once officialdom takes hold and makes everything seem natural, rational and unavoidable. Food for the select few had been the norm, the last century and a bit notwithstanding. Normal dominion had been restored, after a reign of plenty.

Tomorrow there was the wedding. A dance in the community

centre to celebrate. Good for morale, he'd heard George say. Something to unite around.

Bollocks to that.

At first, Carl couldn't believe that there was going to be a wedding in two days' time. But now he figured that maybe George was right, and that it made more sense now, as a statement – call it a declaration of defiance – for two people to pledge lifelong fidelity to each other. The principle, he supposed, was admirable, even if, by all accounts, the bride-to-be had been having serious doubts before the redzone happened. The poor groom was clueless, apparently, and was telling everyone how love was eternal, and how lucky he was, even now. Especially now. Maybe the woman was right to play the percentages. Her options had narrowed, somewhat.

At the hotel's front door, Carl switched off the torch and stood there in the cold November black. The wind was really picking up now, and sleety rain started to spit on the windows and on his face. He felt a surge of remembered panic, fought to stay in control, feeling the hotel's rough exterior wall, the ordinary and safe under his fingers. In the pitch dark, he felt his stomach lurch, as terror gave him a squeeze to remind him of where he was and what had happened to his world, ninety-six days before. Maybe there was no redzone. Or maybe they were being imprisoned here, for some unfathomable reason. He turned on the torch again.

'They're not as clever as they think,' he muttered, climbing the stairs to forgetfulness, as quiet as any drunk can be.

26

There had been no-show from Carl today, so Alec John was out on the hill by himself. He'd seen the beam of a torch weave its way along the road last night, on the way down from Terry's. Maybe Carl wouldn't have been able to do much work today even if he'd wanted to come out: that home-brew was lethal.

From below the ridge, Alec John scanned Inverlair Bay with binoculars, out to the far islands and inland, across the moors to the jagged basalt teeth of the Needles, where the eagles nested. Further south and west was Glen Athar, where the nearest SCOPE transmitter stood. He knew it was there, had seen it on the map, though he couldn't see it. One day it would stop working, and they could see what was out there. It wouldn't be him though, not if the transmitter lasted the average of two years.

All was calm now, but the night before had been blustery. The bay was well sheltered, and Alec John knew that only a direct westerly gale could reach straight into it and do any real damage. Last night's wind had come from the north-west, brushing the last of the leaves from the alder trees near the road, pruning a few of the weaker branches. Doing its job.

He could see towards the south-east into the redzone, to the house of his former employer. Inverlair was sheltered from the north-west winds, but the sheikh's fourteen-bedroom holiday pile was not so lucky. It took a hammering in the winter. Maybe people would live in the house again, one day. It had stood for almost 200 years, after all.

Down at the community centre Alec John could see final preparations being made for the wedding reception. He shook his head at what he saw.

Bunting.

Can you fathom it? Probably the councillor's idea, or that stuffed shirt of an architect, Anderson. George would have gone along with it because he'd been so henpecked by his wife that he didn't have any thoughts of his own left. The good lady Alison said jump, and George didn't even have to ask how high. But he had loved her, and now she was no longer around to give him the orders he had come to depend on without even knowing it.

Alec John sighed, felt the tightness in his chest, his breath rasping, even when he stood doing nothing. George was doing his best, just like everyone else.

It was easy to forget that SCOPE had happened at all. Who, Alec John wondered, did he have to mourn? A few cousins in Glasgow and Canada; that was more or less it. He was sorry they were dead. Perhaps they weren't. But, in all honesty, he would have to say that he wouldn't be too upset if they were. To look at the world – the one he was used to – was to see nothing that different. It was just that he couldn't cross the estate like he'd been able to. Everything familiar to him was here, and everything from the first half of his life was strange and dead anyway, so there was no need to fret over it. It bothered him that he wasn't that bothered. He scanned along the village with his binoculars. There was activity at the boatyard. Washing on the line. Kids on their bikes.

'Bunting,' he said out loud. 'And where the fuck would you be going for a honeymoon?'

Looking at the hotel, Alec John could see George in the back garden. And there was someone else with a pair of binoculars, in a first-floor window. Carl was watching the hill.

•

There was a dusting of snow on Ben Bronach. Carl was at the window of Howard's old room, overlooking the back garden, with its clear view of the hills. This is the time of year when the deer come down to lower ground, Alec John had said. They'd even come as far as his back fence for food, not that there would be much of that this winter. What a racket the younger stags made at night now, crashing about in the trees, barging and bellowing. Showing off, like all young males.

There were wind-blown branches on the hotel's back lawn, and the leaves that had clung to the alder yesterday were now splattered all over the garden. Rain glistened on the grass.

George was out again with his rake and Carl watched him from an upstairs window. George would stop every now and again, stare into space and wipe his eyes, then carry on with the job. You had to feel sorry for folk like George. Married for years and then, all of a sudden, alone.

Nobody was really to blame for non-violent death, except maybe the person who died, but you could pin SCOPE down, attribute its malignancy to the nameless few. Blaming Howard was possible, though uncharitable: the guy had lost everything and the thing had killed him, far away from anyone that he might have called a loved one.

Was it unreasonable to blame himself? Could he have stopped SCOPE without any proof of what its real purpose had been? No. SCOPE's real purpose wasn't the sort of hypothesis to entertain for any length of time, not in a sane and rational mind that wanted to stay that way. In any event, minutes after the article had been printed, CivCon would have trashed the office and banged them all up for a Category 1 violation of the Emergency Order.

Carl lifted the binoculars to scan Bronach. He spotted Alec John looking at something with his own binoculars – the community centre, probably, judging from the direction he was pointing. Carl had heard they were even putting bunting up for the wedding.

He shook his head, wondering if that had been George's idea; the poor guy who was shuffling about in the back garden and who now looked every one of his sixty-four years.

Isaac ran out into the garden, followed by his pal from a few doors down. Simone and Fiona would be in the kitchen, talking about food, kids and the dickhead upstairs. It was a wonder his ears weren't ablaze.

He lifted the binoculars again to look at Alec John and saw that the stalker was looking straight at the hotel, and at him. Carl smiled and waved, before lowering the binoculars and heading downstairs.

Simone and Isaac were piecing a jigsaw together on the kitchen table when Carl came into the room. There was no sign of Fiona and her kid. Simone acknowledged Carl's presence by refusing to acknowledge him.

'I haven't seen one of those for a while,' he said. Simone clicked a jigsaw piece into place, picked up another.

'It's Grandpa's,' said Isaac, smoothing over the pieces that had been put in place, feeling the joins with his fingers.

'Does he like jigsaws?'

'He did,' said Simone, her eyes still fixed on the developing picture of a red racing car speeding round a racetrack. 'When he was a boy. This jigsaw is about fifty years old.'

Carl remembered jigsaws. He looked at Isaac and at the ragged outline of the racetrack, banners flying and crowds cheering. From out of nowhere, tightness took hold of his throat as he half remembered something from long ago.

'Oh,' was all he could say, a moist heat in his eyes. He turned his back and poured a glass of water at the sink.

'Let's go and see Grandpa,' said Simone. 'I think he wants to read you another story.'

Isaac shot out the door, delighted. Simone walked to the kitchen door, then stopped to make sure Isaac had run on ahead.

His back to the room, rinsing his mouth at the sink, Carl braced himself. Simone was watching him; he could feel her eyes on his back. She was gearing up for something big, and he could feel the weight in the air of what was coming.

The silence dragged on until it became obvious that he had no choice but to turn away from the sink and face her. Leaving the room would mean walking towards her, unless he went out the back door which, barefoot in a T-shirt and boxer shorts, would look pretty stupid.

He turned round, a glass of water to hide behind.

'I'm just waiting,' said Simone, 'to see how long it will take you to sit down and talk to me about what's happening.'

Downing the water, Carl wiped his mouth. 'You said you were keeping it,' he said. 'I don't know what more there is to talk about.'

'Yes,' said Simone quietly. 'I am. Wouldn't you like to know why?'

They stood there, the silence thickening again. There were no thoughts in his head and there were a million thoughts in his head.

He shrugged. 'What do you want from me? Shall we get married and settle down?'

'You're a funny guy – did anyone ever tell you that?'

Carl opened his mouth to reply.

'I want you to tell me how you feel about it,' said Simone, cutting him off.

'Delighted.'

Simone folded her arms. 'Probably as delighted as I am.' Her eyes widened. 'Do you feel happy, sad? Do you feel anything? Maybe you can't feel at all, and all you've got are crap jokes instead of real feelings.'

'Okay,' he raised his voice. 'I feel . . . sick. You happy now? I feel sick to think about being here and what happened and that there's a kid coming into this horrible fucking world because of me. There you go, now let's sign the register and jump in the limo. Let's call him or her something noble like, like, Gawain, or let's go all alternative and call it Sunflower or . . . I was thinking of mustard yellow for the nursery, with teddies . . . and rainbows splashed across the fucking walls.'

He stopped, aware that he was gripping the empty glass too hard and was brandishing it in Simone's direction.

'I hope being a total arsehole isn't inherited,' she said quietly. 'Isaac's a lovely boy, so I don't think it is. Because his dad was an arsehole as well.'

Her footsteps were quiet in the foyer, the fire door swinging open and squeaking to a soft close. Would she storm off to Fiona's? Unload on her? Would she throw him out?

Leaning over the half-completed jigsaw puzzle, Carl picked up a piece of red racing car. Something within him stirred, came to life. Shouting voices echoing from many years in the past, jigsaws fitting together under his concentration while his parents came apart. He gulped down another glass of water and went off to his room to wash. Face the day. All that shit.

In the reception area, a shaft of sunlight came through the frosted-glass window, lighting up the front desk. Carl went behind the desk, turned the guestbook to face him, its flat edge clearing the dust to reveal clean wood. He opened the book and signed in as 'Total Arsehole'. In the 'Number of Nights' column he wrote 'Indefinite Stay'. Three months ago he had signed 'Carl Shewan' for 'Three nights'. Now someone else had booked in, and there was only a passing resemblance to the other Carl Shewan.

On the shelf below the desk he spotted the ID scanner, an old model, like so many he had seen before in train stations and hotels and not paid much attention to. He took it out, the keypad and separate downlink processor, and laid them on the desk. After a bit of fiddling and forcing, he managed to prise apart the book-sized processor's plastic casing, exposing its circuitry. He squinted at the meaningless serial numbers and chip sets. Ingenuity, dexterity, made flesh, or at least memristors. Single-occupancy geeks or family men, who all had Government mortgages to pay off – they had made this, like they had made SCOPE and all the other kit that was needed to keep people safe from themselves. The people who had made the ID scanner were busy with their pieces of the puzzle. They only saw what was in front of them, the people who had been streamed into the only growth industry left, insecurity. They couldn't see the bigger picture.

Part of him wanted to crush the scanner under his heel, stamp on it, grind it into the dust. This gizmo should be obliterated, expunged from the cultural record: it was an aberration of nature. Instead of destroying it, he slotted both halves of the casing together again and put it back on the shelf. It didn't mean enough any more to bother with. The guys who'd invented it were just doing a job. It wasn't like they were guards at Auschwitz; they were just making little bits of rubbish, just as their training had shown them, and making precious money in the process. That was all. Maybe he should bury the fucking thing: HERE LIES FEAR – THE OLDEST TRICK IN THE BOOK.

He trudged up the stairs for a wash. The pressure in the tap was low again, and it took a good few minutes for four inches of water to dribble into the bath. He stripped off and climbed in, sat down in the cold puddle with his scrap of soap, removing the worst of the grime and stink of days. Cupping water over his head, the cold shock woke him up. His hair had grown to a soft crew-cut now and it needed cutting again. His beard was back. But what was the point in shaving? Why bother trying to look the way he used to look? Maybe he should start to sketch, like Terry, to forget who he was, to focus on something else that would eat up some time.

An hour later he was sitting up at the broch, watching, through binoculars, the crowd at the tiny church. He'd exhumed only two stones in the last week.

There was no minister or priest down at the church, so P.C. Gibbs, as the nearest thing, was joining together in matrimony the happy couple. There would be speeches. Looks like the local councillor is doing the honours: plastered in make-up, even now, hair solidly lacquered. It was scarcely believable.

Scanning along the bay, he saw Alec John was down at his house, spreading some scraps for the hens. Winter was coming and they weren't laying quite so often now. But Gibbs, and one of Cutler's mob, would still be round to collect; so said the Year 1 plan in Howard's survival strategy, and by Christ the committee were not going to deviate from it, in public at any rate. There was no chance of him pulling strings with George on anyone's behalf. Given Simone's condition, George was likely to use those strings to strangle him.

27

Carl had joined Alec John up on the hill; both men glad to avoid the wedding.

Within an hour, Alec John whispered, 'Down.' He pulled Carl by the sleeve and they lay still among the banks of heather.

'Over there,' Alec John said, pointing. Propped on his elbows, he raised a small pair of black binoculars.

Carl could see nothing.

'The wind's in our favour. Come on.'

Alec John crawled ahead and slid into a soft mossy gully. 'We'll have to wait, he's on the slope.'

'Can we not get any closer?'

'It's not that,' said Alec John, peering over the edge of the gully. 'The slope's rocky and it's too steep. If I take him there he'll roll all the way down and get smashed to bits. Bruised meat isn't very appetising, and he'll be harder to cut up. The slope's too steep for him if he goes further on ... He'll come back, if we wait.'

'For how long?'

'Until he comes back.'

Twenty minutes later there was sign of movement. The stag had been eating the juiciest patches of grass that were hard to reach. If he'd fallen, it would have been the end of him, but the reward was rich, undisturbed grazing. With autumn curdling the air, it was worth the risk.

Alec John inched backwards into the gully. 'He'll come on a bit and then hopefully stop once he's more exposed. He'll want to check around for a bit before heading down into the glen. We'll take him then, with a bit of luck.'

They watched the stag come closer, picking his way along the ridge, wary of every sound and smell. He stopped.

'Just a bit more,' said Alec John, his eye to the rifle's scope. 'Another few metres will do it.'

'Is he too far away?'

'Ten years ago I might have, but I'm not too good at that kind of range any more. I can hit him, but that's not good enough. He could be miles away by the time he dies.'

They waited.

After what seemed like an age, the stag finally walked on towards them. But he soon stopped again, his nose in the air. He turned to face the long curve of the glen, and stood, almost side-on to the gun.

Alec John jerked as he fired, and the crack nearly deafened Carl. The stag's legs buckled and he collapsed as if his feet had been swiped from under him.

Carl rubbed his ear. 'Jesus.'

'Ha,' said Alec John. 'Now that's not bad, not bad at all.' He clambered to his feet, pulled what looked like a stopwatch from his pocket, and strode away.

Something was dead, thought Carl as they rushed towards the animal. A huge living creature had been shot dead, right in front of him, and it all looked so ordinary, so workaday. Alec John was more interested in his pedometer.

'Will you look at that?' he said, stopping right next to the stag. 'A hundred and sixty-four metres. It's been a good few years since it was one shot from that range.'

There was no obvious hole in the deer, but then Carl figured that the exit wound would be on the other side. Still, there was nothing on the chest or head. He stooped to look at the beast, the mound of breeze-ruffled, brown-grey fur, and the staring eyes.

'Where did you get him?'

'Base of the neck. Severs the spinal chord and windpipe. I couldn't get a heart shot, and I knew he was turning for home. We were about to lose him.'

Alec John laid his rifle on the rough grass and took off his wax jacket. From the inside pocket he pulled a sheathed knife, a silver seven-inch blade with a plain black handle.

'We have to bleed him first,' said Alec John. He knelt by the animal's side. 'Find the breastbone, you're over the aorta, and then ... in you go.'

Alec John worked the knife a little and then pulled it out. Like a bottle of wine on its side, the blood poured out onto the grass. 'That'll take a few minutes.'

Carl felt his knees weaken. 'I didn't know ... Do you have to do it up here?'

'Of course.' Alec John squinted at him. 'I thought you said you weren't squeamish?'

'Not when it's ... meat, no. But this is different. A few minutes ago this was alive, eating and walking around. Now it's dead and we're sticking knives into it.'

At Alec John's insistence, Carl helped to manoeuvre the carcass onto its back. The stag was a good eighteen stones.

Finding his mark, Alec John set about the next part of the process. With a sound like tearing cloth, the knife was dragged along the deer's belly, opening the hide from dick to sternum. Taking great care, next he unzipped the fine membrane that encased the viscera.

'This is life,' said Alec John. He rolled the stag onto its side, and a coil of tubing slopped out onto the rough grass.

'All I can see is blood and death.'

'That's where you're wrong. This is life.' He pointed in the direction of the village. 'Our life. This is what's true now.' He continued to work the rest of the guts loose, switching knives to one with a curved blade.

'People have lived around the River Lair for thousands of years. It's only recently they started going to the supermarket. This is back to how it was. Help me or don't, but realise that.' He started to clean the knives with handfuls of grass. 'You might, in the middle of January, after a few months of fish and turnip. Now, you stay here, and I'll go and get the argocat.'

Alec John left Carl alone on the damp hillside with the dead deer and a pile of steaming organs.

•

Everyone was pumped up. There was a frenetic energy inside the community centre: the release of tension through vicious enjoyment. The bride and groom had long since departed, leaving a few revellers to warm themselves with dancing, home-brew and the few bottles of wine George had conjured from what he had previously said was an empty cellar.

Carl left the community centre, the sound of riotous fiddle, guitar and clapping following him into the fresh air. That kind of traditional dancing he'd never been able to master, and he certainly wasn't in the mood to try again. It was difficult for Carl not to view the whole event, both the ceremony and the dance, as some kind of hysterical, hallucinatory episode.

The night air was cold, and it sobered him up. The rain was on, just spattering, not the horizontal stuff of the week before. He'd had too much to drink. Should never have had that whisky either. Time to blow home.

'Home,' he said to himself. Pissed again, home to Room 7. Not to his flat with all his own stuff, with lenses and other distractions and fighting the good-but-pointless fight. In a way, he still yearned for CivCon, and food riots, and Eric arguing with the PLC. All that business had kept him alive and kept him thinking. Now he had nothing to think about except that past.

As he headed back to the hotel, he didn't see the couple skulking around the side of the community centre. A girl was giggling. Carl swung round, focusing on where the noise had come from, but there was no sign of anyone. A fading sign above the doorway read: AUXILIARY HIGHLAND RATIONING CENTRE 102. Maybe George and the committee would get round to a renaming ceremony to boost morale. That would be another item discussed, and another step towards the new normality.

He sucked in some cold, salty air to clear his head. Crossing the road, he leant on the seafront railing, nothing but the cold sea-night in front of him.

He didn't want to pick up a gun again. He didn't want to learn how to shoot deer, to have something die at his hands. Never mind sins of omission – he wouldn't go on with learning how to shoot and slicing animals open, and that was that. It was sickening.

Alec John would have to be told in the morning. Giving him a hand was one thing, but no way was he going to put a bullet in anything. Thanks for the offer, but no thanks.

Inside the community centre, the music started up again. Feet stamped and hands clapped, noises that indicated enjoyment. Not everyone, though. There were a few who wouldn't dance, who sat in corners, grimly sipping the rations the committee had released for the occasion. There were folk who hadn't turned up at all, not because they didn't like the bride and groom or hadn't been invited, but because they thought having fun wasn't right. Isn't that what some religious zealots thought, anyway?

Carl's dead editor had liked to dance.

What a colour piece I've got for you here, Eric, Carl thought. The resilience and resourcefulness of a community pulling together. Leadership in a time of hardship. It's all here. He spat into the sea. And just as much bullshit as you'll find anywhere else.

He stood on the pier for a while then went back along the shorefront, leaving the lights of the community centre behind. An owl hooted. Carl felt hungry.

There were footsteps behind him on the road. He turned.

Someone was there, coming closer in the darkness with the light behind.

'That you, Terry?'

The silent figure came closer without speaking.

Carl waited for a response. 'What're you creeping about for?' he said, relieved.

'Just heading home,' said Terry.

'Likewise. I've given up. Pretending to have fun is hard work.'

Terry walked away into the dark, switching on his torch. 'See you.'

'Yeah,' breathed Carl, watching the narrow beam of light move away along the shorefront. 'Yeah,' he said. 'Mañana.'

The ticking clock was the only sound in the dark hotel lobby. Carl stretched out his hand to feel the wall and the doorway to the residents' lounge, brushing his fingers over the framed photos. The place still smelled of fried fish from dinnertime. As he felt his way into the kitchen, he almost forgot to curse the darkness; he was getting used to moving about like this at night.

The wind was picking up now, pushing at the windows in gusts, getting stronger. Maybe it would clobber the hotel like it did the other night. Carl stood in the darkened kitchen. There was bound to be some fish, maybe some of that mayonnaise George had made, and a few bottles of lime-green fizz to wash it all down, if there were any left.

Standing in the lobby, Carl heard voices in the street, and footsteps running past the front door. A guy shouting, sounding none too pleased about something. Then silence. Some drunken rumpus. Ordinary aggression. He fumbled his way to steal more of George's booze.

•

Tongue: the wrong size and dust-dry. Throat: painful proof that he had, in fact, vomited until there was nothing else inside him to come out. Sitting up caused a bowling ball to shift position inside his head. At least there was no sign of puke anywhere near the bed, or on the bed, or on him.

Let's hear it for the committee, and their morale-boosting largesse. The wagon he'd been steering more or less on the straight and narrow was well and truly off the road now. Mixing different types of booze will do it every time, except there wouldn't be a next time, for a long time.

Alec John was expecting him today, though there was flexibility as far as clocking-in was concerned. Clouds were dark over the bay and it looked like it might rain. Maybe a hurricane would arrive and give him reason to lie, inert and suffering, for several more hours. He was going to call it a day with Alec John anyway. Enough with blood.

Tongue and throat demanded moisture. Carl sat up, groaning as the room spun and his head pulsed. Maybe he could ask at the community centre for some paracetamol. This time, the committee might take a kinder view of self-inflicted pain, given that its own generosity had been the cause. They might break out the painkillers. Maybe Terry would do him a fried egg. Eggs were good for hangovers – in the absence of any synthetic remedy.

With sledgehammer intensity, there was a sharp knocking at the room door.

He jerked himself upright, wished he hadn't, and quickly checked to see he was decently clothed, rubbing his face and smoothing his hair.

'Come in.'

It was Alec John.

'I didn't expect a personal wake-up call,' said Carl, swinging his feet onto the floor. He steeled himself for what he had to say.

Closing the door, Alec John stood, grim-faced. 'Something horrible happened last night,' he said. 'To Terry.'

Carl's hangover loosened its hooks. 'What do you mean – horrible? Is he okay?'

'Well, I heard different versions of what happened, but . . . it looks as if he's lost an eye.'

Carl mouth fell open. 'What?'

Alec John nodded. 'He's at Dr Morgan's now.'

'An eye?' Carl searched for his shoes. 'For fuck's sake. I saw him, I think, after the reception. What happened?'

'No one's sure. There was some kind of scuffle. It was pitch black and they ended up in the pine trees near the old bus stop. Casper says it was a branch.'

'Casper? You mean it wasn't an accident?'

Alec John shook his head, without any real conviction. 'I don't know the details.'

Carl pulled on his shoes, all trace of hangover purged by adrenaline. 'A fucking branch? Come on. Did Casper attack him?'

Alec John shrugged. He looked at Carl. 'Casper's cousin, this girl, Gemma, said that Terry raped her.'

Carl stopped tying his laces. He looked at his left shoe. The sole was starting to come loose near the ball of his foot. Maybe someone would have the right kind of glue to fix it, or any kind. Maybe there was some kind of plant resin . . .

'Who says it was rape?'

'The girl.'

'Any witnesses?'

Alec John squinted at him. 'Not as far as I know, no.'

'Right,' said Carl. 'So this girl says she was raped by Terry. There are no witnesses – but Casper attacks Terry anyway.'

'She's not known as a liar, Carl.'

'No one is. But everyone lies.'

Alec John got to his feet. 'I'm only going by what I hear. Terry's a nice guy but . . .' He shrugged. 'I don't know. These are . . . different times.'

Carl finished tying his shoes and grabbed his jacket. 'Yeah,' he muttered, opening the room door. 'But maybe not that different after all.'

•

Treating injured drunks wasn't that unusual for Dr Morgan, and she'd seen a lot worse than this during various stints in A&E. But it had been a long time since the last bad one in Inverlair, maybe three years or so. There was always booze involved and nearly always a fight between young men, though girls could be just as bad. And here it was again: the same ingredients in the same bloody mess, even after all that had happened. The disease had erupted again.

Dr Morgan gave Terry another shot of diamorphine. Not much left now. The orbital muscle in his right eye had been all but severed; sclera and cornea were in shreds. She pulled off her bloodied latex gloves and opened the pedal bin to drop them in.

She stopped. Maybe it wouldn't do to be so fussy about hygiene any more; there was probably no infection in Terry's eye, so the latex gloves could be saved, cleaned, for another time. She threw them in the sink instead.

The doorbell rang.

'What's happened to Terry?' asked Carl, as soon as Dr Morgan opened the door.

'He's resting,' she said. 'He's in shock, so it's for the best if he gets some sleep.'

'Is it true? Has he lost an eye?'

Dr Morgan hesitated. She considered inviting them inside, decided against it. Before she could answer, Carl said, 'Was it a knife?'

'I'm not sure,' said Dr Morgan, folding her thin arms. 'It could have been anything. Whatever it was, I had to take the eye out. I couldn't see any wood fibres, but that doesn't rule out . . .'

She smoothed her greying hair. 'It was something sharp, that's all I can say.'

Carl sighed. He glanced at Alec John. 'Can we see him?'

'You can,' said Dr Morgan. 'But please don't wake him up. He also cracked a couple of ribs, and dislocated his right shoulder.' She stiffened. 'I've also examined the girl, Gemma. P.C. Gibbs will interview her soon.'

'How is she?'

Everything was overlapping. Due process had no chance in this situation . . . Carl and Terry were friends, and Dr Morgan's examination would, ordinarily, have formed the case for the prosecution. Yet here was the prime suspect's associate asking how the victim was.

Dr Morgan shook her head and closed the door.

28

From within the broch's low walls, Carl watched the village. A roiling bank of cloud was swelling out over the Atlantic, threatening. It was bitterly cold, and he'd not put on a jumper under his Gore-Tex. Just his luck if he fell ill again. His lungs had been clear for weeks now. He wouldn't want to clog them up again with a cold, or worse.

With his binoculars, he saw Gibbs walk round to Gemma's parents', then to Dr Morgan's, and then round to Casper's house.

Different rules. That's what Gibbs had told him, making all the right noises about procedure and a thorough investigation. And then what?

Maybe the girl wasn't entirely blameless. He remembered the glint in her eye when she came round for Terry's dope . . . maybe it had just got out of hand. It felt plausible. But he felt uneasy with the thought. If Terry had raped her, he must be punished. That's what should happen.

Simone. How much interest would she expect him to take? What did she want? Carl couldn't conceive any answer that would make sense to him. There's nothing, physically, to be done about any of it, he figured. The other day she had asked him if he wondered if it would be born healthy or not, or if it would be a boy or a girl. He was finding it difficult to care about any of it.

She was having his kid, he wasn't about to run away anywhere, and there was zero chance of a relationship. All the salient facts covered, and there was no need to keep going over them.

'Different times, different rules,' Carl said out loud, blinking as the Atlantic air surged over him. No white boat was going to come. Howard's friends – what a fantasy that had been. No matter when SCOPE packed in, he would remain adrift and unrescued, and there was no point in believing anything else. He was a refugee.

Down in the village: a figure near the boatyard, just a glimpse of form. Carl lifted the binoculars again, but the person was now inside the boatyard. He cursed his wandering attention.

Maybe the figure had been a paunchy fifty-year-old copper on his way for a friendly chat. Maybe it was justice, hot-footing it to apprehend a lynch mob.

This is life, Carl thought. This is what's true now.

•

'Are you going to charge any of us, Mr Gibbs?'

Work came to a halt in the boatyard. Gibbs managed, just about, to project a gruff professionalism from inside his uniform. Cutler's greeting had made a civilian of him, but Gibbs ignored the provocation.

'Terry Noble lost an eye last night, Adam.'

'That's careless of him. We'll help him look for it.'

One of the work crew suppressed a snort.

'I would like to ask a few questions,' said Gibbs, who leant against a workbench with his arms and feet crossed. 'Just to clear up a few loose ends. Surely that can't do any harm.'

Adam nodded to himself, scuffed the ground with his work boots. Casper and the other guys exchanged glances, said nothing. Apparently deep in thought, Adam studied the concrete floor, considered the rafters and the tin roof.

Gibbs waited.

'Suppose,' began Adam at last, 'just suppose, that none of us want to answer any of your questions, then what?'

The men looked at Gibbs.

'That might mean you've got something to hide.'

Adam nodded. 'Would it now.' He fell silent again, then went over and continued to load ten-gallon biofuel drums onto a trailer. The first drum crashed down heavily on the trailer's metal floor.

'You sorted the chain on that saw yet, Gav?' said Adam.

Gav was in his mid-twenties, gold-stud earring; blond streaks in a mop of scruffy hair. He smirked at Gibbs. 'Fully operational, boss.'

Everyone except Casper went back to work. He didn't look too pleased with the situation.

'Come on, Brian,' said Gibbs quietly, dropping the nickname. 'Just a few questions.'

Casper pursed his lips. 'I didn't do it,' he said, frowning. 'I pushed him, I think. That's all . . . I was pissed.'

'Don't let him confuse you, Casper,' shouted Adam. 'That's how these bastards work. None of us want to answer any questions, Gibbs.' He stepped towards the door. 'If you want to pull us in, why don't you phone the nearest station for back-up?' He grinned, and went on with his work. 'Looks like it's all down to you, Cuntstable, and if you don't mind, given the circumstances, I don't think any of us are going to come quietly.'

Gibbs moved towards Adam. 'You're being very stupid, Adam.'

'Leave him,' growled Casper.

'There's fuck all you can do about it, Gibbs,' shouted Gav, tensing himself. He picked up a spanner.

Exasperated, Dennis groaned. 'Oh, for fuck's sake, behave yourselves.'

Everyone ignored him.

Adam smiled at Gibbs. 'Gav's right. We're busy here, so why don't you go and hassle the Dutchman for his eggs – impound his grass plants while you're at it. Now there's a real criminal for you, Constable, a real menace to the community. I assume you'll be arresting Terry Sullivan for rape, once the doc's finished patching him up?'

Outside, through the open end of the boatshed, only the birds and the sea made their noise. Gibbs would lose what was left of his authority if he backed off; yet there was no way he could handle the three of them. A dignified exit was the only option.

'This is not the end of the matter,' he said gravely. 'There will be consequences, guys. And I'll be having a word with your father, Adam.'

'I'm a bit too old to get my arse slapped, Mr Gibbs.' Cutler turned back to his work. 'Carry on.'

29

There had to be a chance. His son and the grandkids were in a village in Buckinghamshire. Maybe there, too, was a notspot. There was always a chance. They were in the countryside, maybe far enough away from a mast or a town. Maybe they were all okay and the boy just wasn't able to get in touch. Maybe they were alive. Gibbs tried to believe it.

On the computer screen, the slideshow of photos kept scrolling, though the accompanying soundtrack had been muted. Music could always push those buttons, switch the emotions off and on. Gibbs heard his wife come through the front door. He turned off the computer, picking up his needle and thread again as he wiped his eyes. Ellen appeared in the living-room doorway, watching her husband for a moment. Her hair was greyer, thinner now, and her face was lined; she looked years older in just three months.

'Have you told anyone yet, about the girl?'

Gibbs carried on sewing. 'No,' he said. 'I'm going to fix this first. I noticed the pocket had come loose earlier.'

He glanced up at his wife. 'Do you think I should still wear it? I mean, do you think there's any point?'

Ellen considered the uniform spread out on the table, knew that the confrontation with Cutler the other day had shaken him. 'If you feel you have a right to fill it.'

Gibbs put down the needle and thread. 'Does it make sense any more?'

Ellen touched the uniform. 'Maybe it makes more sense now than ever.'

'I've got a gun, of course.' He felt his wife hold a breath, then relax.

'A gun … what an excellent idea,' she said. 'Casper's got one too, and I'm sure Adam Cutler does as well. Why don't you go and shoot it out with them? I'll come along and cheer you on.'

'I don't know what to do, Ellen. There's no easy …'

There was a loud knocking at the front door.

'Now that doesn't sound very friendly,' Ellen muttered wearily. 'I think I know who that might be.'

•

Up at the edge of the redzone, Carl had felt his resolve waver. Could you still cling to the old idea of the law taking its course? But now he felt angry again, and Gibbs's frosted-glass front door took the brunt of it.

'I want to know if you intend to arrest Casper for what he did to Terry,' he said, as soon as the door opened. 'If you're not, I want to know why. No more excuses. I'm not leaving until you tell me what you're going to do.'

Gibbs took Carl into the living room. A glass of Amaretto was offered.

'It's been sitting in the cupboard for years. No one likes it.'

Carl refused.

'So,' said Gibbs, 'you'd like me to arrest Casper – all six feet four of him – by myself.'

'I'll come with you. Maybe we can get one or two other guys.'

'Maybe,' said Gibbs, inspecting his patched uniform by the light of the window. 'Casper's in his mum and dad's house. They might not take too kindly to seeing their son carted off – and to where? There are no cells in Inverlair.'

'We can lock him up somewhere. I don't know …'

Gibbs nodded. 'Maybe we can. Casper's dad's in his sixties but he's still a big fit man. Maybe his mum will weigh in as well. Do you think we can handle the three of them if Casper doesn't want to co-operate?'

'We can get others to help us.'

Carl wished he'd taken the offer of a drink, even if it was disgusting. He unzipped his jacket. The list of options all seemed to lead to painful, if not impossible, outcomes.

'Who should we ask?' continued Gibbs. 'Offhand, I don't know of anyone who would volunteer to tackle Casper and his old man, never mind Cutler and Gavin Marshall.'

Carl sat down in the soft armchair, staring straight ahead at the space in the corner where a TV had once stood.

'Now d'you see the problem?' said Gibbs. 'If they all stick together, we'll need at least five or six other guys to help us. Do you really want to start all that? A posse?'

'Do you have a gun? I've got one now.'

Gibbs stiffened. 'Don't be daft. Yes, I have a gun, but so does Casper, a shotgun, and I wouldn't be surprised if Adam Cutler had one too.' He looked around the room and sighed. 'They're just ordinary guys, Carl. There's nothing bad about them. Cutler's full of himself, but Casper ...'

'Has Catharine Morgan examined the girl yet?' said Carl.

'Yes.'

'And?'

'That's none of your business, Mr Shewan.' Gibbs put his hands on the windowsill, looking out.

There was a rain shower on its way into the bay, a fine haze drifting over Heron Point and the headland.

Clearing his throat, he studied his meaty fingers, splayed out on the sill.

'Seems it was consensual, to begin with, then Terry went a lot further than Gemma wanted. Casper is her cousin, and he found her crying, and not exactly sober. You can imagine how someone like Casper reacted. She told Dr Morgan all that earlier today. And Dr Morgan told me.'

Sleety rain slapped its first dabs onto the living-room window. In normal circumstances, Terry and Casper would be facing jail sentences. But the actual scenario, the chain of offence and revenge, was playing out in fast-forward. Carl could see it, understand it – accept it, even – until anger got the better of him. Terry had been disfigured for life, and there was nothing to show that he was guilty beyond reasonable doubt. He thought of Gemma, caught up in the moment then unable to stop it, and he felt revulsion at what Terry had done.

Carl zipped his jacket up, unsure of his next move. Gibbs told him about the confrontation with Adam at the boatyard, and Carl felt his anger and frustration rise again. Adam and the rest would make fucking mincemeat of him. He knew it. As he headed out into the squall, action and reaction formed a plausible truth, one he felt obliged to accept.

30

A few days later, a strong wind swung to the north-east, and it turned colder, drier. Clutching the deltameter, Carl trudged back over the northern ridge from the furthest edge of the redzone. One day, the signal would not register. One day, the horizon would recede, and he would be able to travel further than 2.26 miles. Right now, he would happily have left this hole of a place and never clapped eyes on it again.

He'd read somewhere about the fear of a north-easterly wind, back when the Vikings were doing their stuff as the latest incarnation of invincible power. A north-easterly pushed the Scandinavians where they wanted to go, across the North Sea, and they didn't need to waste so much muscle-power rowing the few hundred miles. Such a wind meant big trouble for the locals.

Folk would have seen the longships from up here, the first masts rounding the headland. Now there was terror for you, having that lot slide into view. What would he have done? Fight or flight? Where would he have run to? This would have been home, in the bay, with domesticated animals and shelter and family, so the men would stay and fight. And get slaughtered. Plenty of eyes gouged out in those days. Enough grief and death to go round. No scarcity as far as they were concerned.

He felt the nip of a wind that was pushing the clouds south-west, clearing the sky for night frosts. Three and a half months ago the land had looked like a green Mars. Now it was more like the real thing: barrens of brown, grey summits of scalped winter rock, ochreous mattresses of bog. The Vikings were welcome to Inverlair. They could have it.

In those houses without photovoltaics on the roof, or solid-fuel stoves, it would now be turning very cold. The community centre would be warm though, with bunks laid out for those who needed them. Maybe the winter wouldn't be that cold. Maybe everyone would survive; even the oldest ones who chose to stay in their unheated homes.

Dr Morgan said Terry was fit enough to go home today as the skinplast had taken. His cracked ribs were bandaged. Now all Gibbs had to do was let him. It wasn't as if he was going to run away, and Carl doubted he was a danger to anyone. All Terry had to do was walk home, along the shorefront, past the hotel and the community centre and the boatyard, a gauze plaster over his eye announcing to everyone that the rumours were true. They would assume he was a rapist. Maybe they'd lynch him from one of the ash trees at the graveyard. Then they could just drop him straight into a hole in the ground.

Gemma was full of herself; cocky and whip-smart. But when it came right down to it she was only a girl. The rules couldn't be that different; some of them had to be kept. They had to be. It couldn't just be the appetites that ruled. There had to be safeguards, a veneer of measured responses. There had to be control.

As he made his way down from the broch, picking up the forest track behind Alec John's, Carl remembered what Terry had said a couple of weeks ago, a conversation that had started off about sex, but which had strayed onto more emotional ground. To begin with it was sex and hunger – where people are most like animals. The worst was hunger, Carl had said, because you can go without sex for ages. Party World avatars more or less gave you the same thing anyway, if you had all the kit and the lenses and enough money for your own spraysuit. Hunger, on the other hand, was a different beast altogether. People could turn nasty if they were hungry. A day would do it: four missed meals, wasn't that what they said? Kill their own mothers for a slice of toast then, most folk would. He'd seen it happen. Well, maybe not mothers, but at Kelvingrove, before CivCon took over security at the rationing centres, he'd seen kids get elbowed out of the way for a few slices of bread by fully grown men.

So, there they were, talking about sex and death. Terry had been sitting stoned in the caravan in front of the tiny stove. He'd been talking about how people were clinging to each other and how that daft marriage was still going ahead, even though he'd heard the bride-to-be had been on the verge of calling it off before the redzone happened. Obviously, the groom was none the wiser about any of that. He was delighted, the sap, talking about how love and life have to go on. A nice speech, by all accounts. If only he knew how close he'd come to being an ex-fiancé.

'Maybe you can't blame the woman for reappraising her situation,' Terry had said. 'Her options are kind of limited now, unless she wants to shack up with a meathead like Casper or Gav. Instead of doing that, she's making the best of a bad situation.

'What's your least worst option, Carl? And what's mine? We both have to think about that – because we're men, not monks, you know what I mean? As long as we've got enough food to keep us alive, and a roof to keep the rain off, the other big appetite will need satisfied, sooner or later. That much never changes. Maybe you could be with Simone, I don't know. But what about me? What are my options in the female department?'

He should have taken the hint then, and at other times as well – those little silences and awkward moments between Terry and Gemma. Maybe the normal rules didn't apply any more. Maybe it was okay for a thirty-three-year-old man to have sex with a fifteen-year-old girl. Perhaps it was time to get back to a more basic version of human behaviour. Was nature that perverted? Did the Vikings worry about the age of consent?

There would be no legal ramifications, that much Carl was sure about, unless Gibbs decided to pick the easy target this time and arrest Terry for underage sex. Somehow, as Jess bounded across the field to meet him, Carl doubted that would happen. Gibbs, he figured, would probably prefer to forget all about the whole thing.

A coughing fit told Carl that Alec John was in his workshop. He didn't appear to be doing much, just moving things around. Carl watched him through the window, listlessly moving to and fro, picking up tools and opening drawers.

Without turning around, Alec John said, 'So ... you're back.'

'Well, only to say that maybe it's not working out. Maybe I'm not the right man for the job.'

'Is that so? Why d'you say that?'

'The gralloching, I don't know if I can do it. And ... the other day, this huge animal was alive, and then it was dead. I don't know if I can handle doing that.'

'So you'd rather not eat venison, or grouse?'

'I can live without them. Look, I've been thinking about what happened to Terry, and what he did. It's ... brutal. It sickened me.'

'It is brutal, yes. But the world can be brutal sometimes. You can hide from that or you can accept it.'

'I'm not hiding from it.'

'Of course you are. Your job was hiding in the shadows, and now you're out in the open and you don't like it. You need something to do, something to occupy your mind. If you can think of another job besides this one that's more useful, go right ahead – knock yourself out.'

Alec John wiped his hands on his padded checked shirt. 'How's Terry?'

Carl picked an adjustable spanner from its place on the wall, feeling its cool weight in his grip. Alec John had gone to the trouble of drawing a felt-tip outline around each tool. Every one had its allotted place from which to hang.

'Dr Morgan said he was well enough go home,' replied Carl. 'Gibbs said he could go home.'

'Has he spoken to Terry about what happened?'

Carl shook his head. 'He tried to, but Terry wouldn't say a word. I don't know what happens now. I don't think anyone does. I wonder if we should go and see him.'

Alec John stiffened. 'He might have raped that girl.'

'He might have, yes. But the only thing we know for sure is that he's been scarred for life.'

Alec John said nothing. The two men set off down the track to the main road.

'One day, maybe sooner rather than later, I won't be able to do this,' said Alec John. 'The doctor told me that herself.'

'I thought she couldn't say for sure?'

Alec John shook his head. 'The timing of it, no, no one can be sure of that. But without the medicine it'll come back. It already has.'

Carl glanced at him as they walked. 'Not bad enough to keep you indoors though.'

'No, not that bad. But I can feel it all the same, even on the lower slopes now, never mind the ridge. A shortness of breath that wasn't there a few months ago, before . . .'

They walked a little further along the main road, crossed the bridge at the head of the bay, the river in spate beneath it.

'There must be other people, better suited to it,' said Carl.

'There are. But it would benefit you the most.'

'I'm not ready for it.' But even as he uttered the words, Carl knew how weak they sounded. He wasn't ready for a lot of things. Stuff like tolerating the disfigurement of a friend, and the perpetrators getting clean away with it. He thought of young guys in Glasgow, getting killed in gang fights, and the coppers hardly bothering with a proper investigation, even if CivCon actually told them the murder had happened.

'Suit yourself,' said Alec John.

They walked past Cutler's boatyard and there was nothing doing, no sign of activity at all. Maybe folk knew that Terry could go home today and they didn't want to have to look at him. You'd think someone would come out, though, someone who cared to see how the man was feeling. Perhaps Terry had sacrificed the right to any such display. People could slake their curiosity from behind their fucking curtains.

Carl knocked on Dr Morgan's door. She answered, her face set hard, and told Carl and Alec John not to expect too much from Terry.

'He's still in shock,' she said. 'Post-traumatic stress, I'd say, though I can't be sure. He doesn't speak much.'

She led them through to the sitting room. Carl couldn't help but stare.

'All right, mate,' he said quietly to Terry, who was sitting, slouched, on a hard-backed chair, fingers splayed on his thighs.

After a second Terry looked up at the voice. 'Hi,' he said. There was something he wanted to say, but he wasn't sure what it was or why he should say it. He looked at the ceiling, down at his hands. No clues there. There was a pain in his eye. He was wearing a bandage. There was a reason for it all that he wanted to forget.

'Is there any more tea?' Terry asked Dr Morgan. 'Maybe they want a cup of tea.'

She nodded.

'They gave me half an ounce, so I should be able to squeeze another few cups out of it.'

Nice gesture from the committee, thought Carl: a few cups of tea for the inconvenience of losing an eye, the dependable fixer-upper that can soothe away all the bad things in life. He accepted the offer anyway, as did Alec John. Dr Morgan fetched the cups and teapot on a tray. Barely moving, Terry sat, head bowed.

After an awkward half-minute, Dr Morgan asked, 'Any luck with the deer today?'

Alec John took a quick breath. 'No,' he said, repositioning his baseball cap. 'Not today. They're mostly in the other end of the forest now, the part we can't get into. Maybe they're getting wise to where we can go and where we can't. Think I'll try out towards the Needles for a spell, give the forest a rest.' He glanced at Carl. 'One of us will, anyway.'

Carl tried to sound as upbeat as he could. 'So, will you be allowed to come home today?'

Again there was a wait while the question registered with Terry, winding its way towards an answer, which then worked its way mouthwards. Terry looked at Carl, and Carl wanted to look at Terry. But when you're looking into someone's face you generally scan across both eyes, the other person doing the same, and there shouldn't be just one eye, wide and wild, staring back, bandages over a raw hole where the other one should be.

Carl looked away.

'Yes,' said Terry. 'I, um, Catharine . . . Dr Morgan says that . . .' He nodded to himself, knotting his dirty-nailed fingers together. 'She says that. The copper says that. So that's what happening. I'm good to go.'

'Good,' said Carl, standing up.

Suddenly Terry sniggered, became alert. 'Fucking cyclops now, eh?'

The others exchanged glances.

'Bang goes my tennis game. You need binocular vision for that gig, eh? It's all about depth perception. Parallax. Still be good at pool though, because I always close my right eye when I take a shot. Save a fortune on lenses as well.' He sniggered again. 'Worse things have happened, eh? Worse things.'

No one knew how to react.

'Mine eye has seen the glory,' echoed Terry, snorting with laughter. He lapsed into silence while the others gulped their tea.

One their way out, Carl saw Simone and Gibbs walking towards the surgery. He waited for them, skipping the pleasantries when they reached the gate.

'Did you speak to your brother?'

'Yes,' said Simone, her voice flat. 'He had nothing to do with it.'

'Is that what he told you?'

Simone gave a slow deliberate nod. 'Yes. That's what he told me.'

Carl grunted. 'I'm only asking.'

'As I said the other day: if you grow a pair of balls – remember those? – you know where to find me if you want to talk about anything else that might concern you. Anything at all that might affect the way you live your life in any small way.'

'You don't even fucking know me, for fuck's sake,' hissed Carl.

Simone cocked her head. 'No, I don't – but I know your kind.'

Before Carl could answer, or ask what she was doing visiting the surgery, Simone went inside with Gibbs.

He refocused on what needed to be done. He could fetch Howard's car. If it would still start and its tyres weren't flat, he could get it out of Hendrik's lock-up and drive Terry home in it. That would mean no grand parade past all the houses. Better for Terry if they took the car home. But then Carl figured that those responsible should be forced to take a good fucking look at what they'd done. Did they think justice, whatever that meant, had been served?

31

Next day, Carl tried again with Gibbs. But the due process of law wasn't about to process anything.

'Gemma told Casper she'd been raped.'

'So that makes it okay? Taking someone's eye out and scarring them for life?'

Gibbs's eyes narrowed. 'I didn't say it was okay, Mr Shewan. It's very bloody far from okay. But there are different rules now, and I can't do anything about those. These are the hard-and-fast facts of life, I'm afraid. I thought you'd have grasped that by now. It is what it is, and there's nothing either of us can do about it. I'm sure as hell not going to start anything with Casper and Adam and Christ knows who else. We've been through enough. We've probably lost our son.' His jaw tightened, working on a pulse of angry grief. 'How do you think Liz would react if these bastards beat the shit out of me, or worse? Get a grip, man, and leave it alone. Perhaps you should spare a thought for a fifteen-year-old girl, rather than the man who might have raped her.'

Swallowing hard, Gibbs bit his lip and took a step back inside his porch. 'We've had enough pain to last a lifetime. You help yourself to more, if you feel up to it . . . And it sounds to me like Gemma was groomed – supplied with drugs – by your fucking *mate*.'

Gibbs slammed his front door. It had been over three months since the redzone had sprung up. Now Inverlair was right in his face again, as hostile as any microwave cannon.

•

'I can't believe there was no one else who'd do the job.'

'Well, there was maybe one or two. I was giving it some thought, before ...'

'Right.'

They walked on.

'So no one else will do it?'

Alec John screwed his face up. 'Well, I wouldn't exactly say that. I just thought that maybe you needed it more than most. Especially when you took the air rifle apart without a spring compressor.' He laughed.

'Very funny,' said Carl. 'But I was lucky the spring didn't take my eye out. And then Terry, you know? Whether it was deliberate or not I don't know, but it's odd, don't you think?'

'I'm not sure about that,' said Alec John. 'Maybe you're reading too much into it, over-thinking things, but maybe that's an occupational hazard with you. I think you're missing an opportunity up on the hill. I can feel my lungs getting worse and I need a decision. I need to take someone else on, if not you, then someone else.'

'No pressure, eh?'

'Yes, pressure. I'm not blowing my own trumpet, but this is an important job. You might not find it very pleasant, but you'll get used to it. It's also better than getting stoned all the time.'

Carl laughed. 'Hey, don't knock it until you've tried it.'

'Oh, I've tried it.'

'Eh? When?'

'A long time ago, before I came back here.'

'When was that? How d'you mean – came back?'

'You're a nosey bugger, aren't you?'

They passed through the forest-track gates and onto the road.

'Another of my old habits,' muttered Carl.

Alec John grunted, his heavy boots clumping on the tarmac as they rounded the bay. 'Well, since you're interested, I was twenty-seven at the time. My father took a heart attack, a bad one, so I came back, yes, almost forty years ago now.' He chuckled. 'I've tried a few things, for sure. Even after I came back, for a time.'

'What did you do before you came back?'

'I was a crane operator on a seismic survey ship.'

'Really?'

'Yes.'

'And your dad, he was the head gamekeeper here?'

'He was.'

Carl felt a tightening in the air. 'I thought . . .' He changed tack. 'Where were you a crane operator?'

'Where?'

'Aye.'

'All over. Oil companies, mainly. It was good in those days.'

'Good pay?'

'Yes, plenty of work in those days, before we drained the planet dry. We did some deep-water stuff off Angola, Spitsbergen. I spent a year in Baku, in the Caspian.'

'Really?'

'You sound surprised.'

They stopped at Terry's gate. What could Carl say – that he'd assumed Alec John had been born with heather sprouting from his ears? He fumbled for an explanation. But Alec John had moved on.

'How's Terry? I should come round more, but after being out with you on the hill, I'm tired.' He shook his head. 'It's a piss-poor excuse.'

'No, it's not.' Carl rubbed his face. 'He's okay, physically anyway. But it's affected him – there's no doubt about that. He doesn't say much and then he talks a lot of garbage, to be honest. Ideally, he'd get counselling . . . something.'

'Has he said anything about . . . that night?'

Carl sighed. 'It happened. They both had a bit to drink at the reception, went for a walk along the shore, started snogging and then ... it went too far. He said he felt horrible after doing it and he just wanted to get away from the girl as quickly as possible.'

'And so she went to tell Casper ...'

'No,' said Carl. 'Casper found her crying, by the side of the community centre. She told him what had happened.'

They were quiet for a spell at Terry's gate. Then Alec John brightened as he changed the subject. 'Do you see how important it is to stay low to the ground when you're crawling, especially your arse and your head?' He laughed. 'And will you try and remember: when you get the chance, go for a crow with the 10-bore, or a rabbit – that's why you've got it.'

Carl looked sheepish. 'Sorry. I forget.'

'You mean you don't want to,' said Alec John, a stern edge in his voice. 'You're going to have to make your mind up about that. Always take a crow if you can – that's the rule. You stick to them or you're no gamekeeper, it's as simple as that.'

'The poor old crow,' said Carl. 'Just trying to survive like everything else.'

Alec John shook his head firmly. 'They're vermin,' he said, shouldering the .308. 'I'll see you tomorrow, if you're still interested. I'll show you which areas to burn in the spring for the grouse. But you have to tell me one way or the other. Are you in or out?'

Carl said goodbye, watched the old man walk down the road towards the head of the bay. He was definitely slower now, less able, and more reliant on the argocat to get onto the hill. It was such a lurching uncomfortable ride that Carl would rather walk.

He went through Terry's gate and part way down the track. He stopped among the stand of alder where the earth and treacly leaf-mulch smelled of rain. This end of Terry's caravan had no windows. White smoke emerged from the tin chimney and vanished in the breeze. One-eyed Terry, who had stopped washing himself and was now mute – when he wasn't spouting gibberish – was in there.

Carl waited among the trees for a minute. Then he turned and walked back up the track. If he went quickly he would be at the head of the bay, beneath the big trees at the bridge, and Alec John wouldn't be able to see him walk back to the hotel.

•

From the window of Room 7 Carl watched Simone and Isaac set off on a visit. Down in the lobby he had been able to listen to her playing her flute through in the annexe, standing transfixed by the sound until it stopped. Then he'd hurried back upstairs to his room. It was the first time he'd heard her play, though he knew she did.

There was still no sign of a bump – when exactly did a woman start to show? But she'd put weight on, and there were hardly any in the village who'd managed to do that. As a pregnant woman she'd be getting extra food, according to Howard's system. Simone's right to calories was inviolable. Maybe they'd worship Howard as a god, as their saviour, in years to come. No. That was unkind.

Miscarriages happen in a high number of pregnancies. Carl had read that somewhere. But it was still there, no doubt about it, and pretty soon there would be no hiding it and then it would be a case of: here's this little baby and ooh and ahh and before you know it he's actually caring for it. That was the ever-changing world, making up new rules just as you're getting used to the old ones. He grabbed his jacket and rucksack, intent on heading out and up as far as he could, and he grabbed the 10-bore. Perhaps the time had indeed come to get rid of some predatory vermin.

Instead of heading straight onto the hill, Carl made his way along the edge of the northern headland, along the shoreline, past the roofless stone ruins of the old herring stations. There was nothing but time for him in Inverlair, an open-ended sentence stretching ahead. He might not even want to leave when the nearest base station failed. He shivered at the word: institutionalised.

What were the golden rules inside a prison? Watch your back. Keep out of trouble. Accept each day as it comes. Do your time. Keep active. Then what?

Howard had said that the masts would pack in within a few years. But approaching the cities and towns would take longer. SCOPE had numerous urban nodes, embedded in lampposts and on top of bus stops, so Howard had said, and they were all harvesting power from countless micro-renewable sources. SCOPE was a blanket of silence, with only a few small holes in the fabric. Years would pass before those holes got bigger, merged, then people would move back, recolonise; maybe they'd be non-Europeans. Carl smiled as he considered a racist's reaction on that prospect. Repatriation may no longer be an enforceable policy response.

Fissured cliffs of shale loomed ahead as the worn path beside the herring stations gave way to rocky shoreline. It took him over half an hour to travel along the base of the northern headland, over a jumble of rocks, and in that time the sky had darkened. A shower was on the way, but he had on his waterproofs, so he'd be dry. He sat down for a spell, an outcrop acting as a windshield, picked up a dark pebble and turned it over in his hand, staring up at the shale cliffs. The book in the residents' lounge had said this was the right kind of place for ammonites. Inverlair was littered with fossilised remains. He put the stone in his jacket pocket and sat there, staring at the waves.

The memory of a dream came to him. He was eight or nine and he dreamed he was standing at the living-room window looking out and up, terrified, at the bright sky, from which lasered a single, massive eye, watching him. He knew it was God's eye, up against the keyhole in the clouds, an unblinking all-knowing intelligence. And God, for whatever reason, wasn't pleased with what he saw. Carl remembered the dream because he'd had another one like it last night, only this time there had been no one eye in the sky, judging him, like when he was a kid.

But there was still something watching him, in the empty dream-streets of Glasgow, at Heron Point, or out on the hill, an invisible intelligence probing him, analysing him. Carl got the feeling that whatever it was hadn't quite made up its mind. A judgement would come, but there was still time for him to influence the outcome by adding to one side of the scales, or by taking away from the other.

In his new dream there was no god's-eye, only himself, and nothing obviously awry with the world apart from the fact that there was no one else in it. The streets were the streets and the sea was the sea. Yet his dream-self this time knew that something was present, undeniably so, something that was under the sea and in the wind-creaking trees at night and behind a thousand untenanted windows. It was in all those places, and in none of them. It might be God, or time, or death, or life. Something eternal, anyway.

He remembered a conversation with Howard, about SCOPE.

'There were people in the National Emergency Authority, officials who knew about black projects, who opposed SCOPE once they found out what it was designed to do.'

'So what did they do about it?'

Howard took a deep breath, resigned to the telling of it. 'They raised their concerns through the proper channels,' he had said.

'And then?'

'They were told that everything was in order, or that their concerns were being addressed.'

'And the opponents of SCOPE were happy with this?'

'Some of them were, yes. The ones with families to feed, mainly.'

'And those that weren't?'

There was a long pause as Howard looked out of the window, at the shifting light on the hills. He kept it simple. 'If they pressed too hard, they either died in accidents or killed themselves, or just disappeared.'

He looked directly at Carl, searching for the realisation that stopping SCOPE had been impossible. There was too much money and power behind it. And Carl had been made to understand the risks Howard had taken to warn people, to warn him.

Ammonite in hand, Carl shook himself at the thought of Howard, stood up and set off again for Heron Point, picking his way over the rocky shoreline, stooping every now and again to pick up an interesting stone or shell. He could see it now, see how it was going to be with the committee and Gibbs and Adam Cutler. It hadn't been designed to end up that way – he was sure it wasn't intentional. But the people who were running the operation, who were applying Howard's survival system, could enforce their will, if that's what they wanted. The law of unintended consequences had struck again. There was always a god's-eye, of some sort, trying to control how people behave.

The shoreline came to an end at the base of a spur that jutted from the headland, and he had to take an old sheep track that zigzagged up the rugged grassy slope and onto the headland's heathery peak. After climbing for a few minutes he stopped to look back. Through binoculars he could see a flotilla of ducks, close in against the shore. He'd seen geese head south the other day; maybe the ducks were doing the same and had just stopped for a rest.

He lifted the 10-bore. There was nothing pestilential about roast duck. If he crept back down the path he could fire down on them from a range of about thirty metres. With a bit of luck, he could chalk up another species on his hit list. They were just targets at the other end of a lens. Necessity dictated that he view them as nothing more. A man can behave like a machine, can act on what needs to be done, and there's no need to for conscience to come into it.

Isaac, cocooned in his hooded coat, looked up from his sandpit as the gunshot boomed around the bay. With three litres of home-brew inside him Terry slept on his couch, not hearing anything, except the dream-shouts of his pursuers, and the crying of a girl.

32

Christmas. He'd heard a kid, a girl of about five, say the word the other day to her dad, but the guy didn't know what to say in response. Others had mentioned the idea since then, mainly adults prompted by their kids whose kids had told other kids, and so on. What can you say when your son or your daughter asks about Christmas? Sorry, it's been cancelled. Maybe parents should say it's no longer appropriate to celebrate, or how there are no more toys because of what happened. Carl wondered how SCOPE and the redzone had been explained to curious young minds. Dad tells me X. A pal tells me Y. Put all the stories together, and the kids might end up concocting their own version of the truth. They might grow up believing any number of implausible reasons why the world became the way it is.

Christmas had once been toys – the bigger and noisier the better. Carl could remember a few of those must-have big-ticket items coming his way. Like a lot of parents back then, the amount of money his own had spent on presents was inversely proportional to the amount of time they spent with their kids. He remembered one girl in his student days, beautiful, brittle as sugar glass; her dad swam in Middle Eastern oil and he threw cash and presents at her, though he hardly ever saw her. He'd sent her a brand new top-line computer that had sat in the hallway of their shared student flat, boxed and unopened, for a week or more, until the Fairy Princess could be arsed to have a peek inside.

There had been money to spend and then, quite suddenly,

there was no money to spend. Cue stress and marital difficulties. How come it always seemed to be the guys that walked out?

The sharp, still world of frost and clear skies had given way to wind and rain, sluicing against the window of Room 7, but it was still very cold. On days like this there wasn't much he could do out of doors. He could see that now and he no longer had any real urge to go squelching around the hills repairing a Stone Age broch. Eventually, figured Carl, every animal, human or not, learns to accept captivity, though that doesn't mean to say there's no corner of hope. That nugget of hope can be kept and taken out every now and again and looked at, like a lover's photo in a locket. Then you close it up, put the nugget back in your pocket and get on with the grind.

He lay on the bed, fully clothed against the cold, a scarf around his neck. The other day Isaac had shown him some crayon drawings, and it made him half-remember his own offerings as a kid. What had his own dad said when faced with a page full of his son's scribbles? Maybe he said, 'Brilliant, son, well done.' Maybe he'd been genuinely enthusiastic about stick men with giant clubbed arms and tiny drainpipe legs, or big yellow suns and multi-coloured dogs with all their legs down one side. That response was possible, but Carl doubted that his own father – business going tits up, money worries mounting – would have been remotely interested in his son's early artistic endeavours. In any case, he couldn't remember any such encounter, traumatic or otherwise, with any degree of certainty. But he could remember snippets of arguments, sure enough, and to be honest, his dad did have a point. An ocean of liquid wealth had suddenly dried up, leaving a patchwork of puddles for little fish like him to gasp and flap in. It was almost funny. Servicing the insecurity industry could have given the man a good living, yet he'd turned his back on the Navy to buy a seafood restaurant in Leith. A little fish right enough, cursing his luck and the big ideas of his wife.

As Carl lay on the bed smoking a spliff, he got the feeling that Isaac had not been happy with his critique of his drawings: obviously a single cursory 'nice' just didn't cut it. But what can you say about stick men? You have a real eye for composition, young man. No. But the kid clearly thought his drawings were good enough to impress. Maybe Carl should have gone along with it by making generally encouraging noises, even though the felt-tip scribbles were just the basic elements of people and things. The kid was okay, once you got used to the fact that he was just a kid, and a confused one at that. They get hurt without understanding why.

Carl could relate to that. At least Isaac was past the shitting and crying stage. After a while, when Carl spent long enough in his company, he could see that there were thoughts in Isaac's head that were worth knowing. And they're honest, kids – they can't lie. Not when they're young.

Bugger it. Carl was stoned and cold, it was pissing down outside, and he was hungry. He checked the time. Pretty soon, Simone would be out around the village, helping to check on the older folk to see if they needed anything at the same time as George liked to read to Isaac sitting by the residents' lounge fire. Carl could creep into the kitchen and help himself to whatever food was available, just like old times. His habit was being fed: there was usually a bowl of something left out for him. It was better that way, better than sitting round the table, stewing in thick silence. George had said they'd write 'Carl' on a plastic bowl and leave it on the floor.

George, he'd noticed, had developed quite a skill for making him feel guilty for eating their food and for dirtying their sheets. Whenever someone in the village was ill, he would always refer to Carl's pneumonia, and slow recovery. Maybe the old prick reckoned on bully-boy tactics, just like his son: if you don't come to some kind of arrangement with my daughter, then we'll stop feeding you and we'll kick you out into the cold. Anyway, Carl had started to sneak down in the afternoons, about two o'clock, when no one was in the kitchen, as well as late at night. Looping his scarf around his neck, he padded downstairs, two pairs of Terry's socks on his feet.

The bowl of food was there, laid out for him in the still-warm kitchen. No name was on it, so far, and the bowl was on the worktop not the floor. Mutton and turnip stew. He grabbed the bowl and headed back upstairs to his room. When he'd finished, he sparked another joint, and lay back on his bed, the ache in his empty stomach drifting to the background again, though it was always there.

Rain on the window. Music from his palmpod. Tetrahydrocannabinol in his bloodstream.

The old is dead, and there isn't going to be any miraculous resurrection.

'It's nothing to do with me,' Carl had said to Isaac. 'Everyone crying and your granny leaving and not coming back – that wasn't my fault.'

But even as he'd said the words, part of him said yes, it was his fault, and yes, he could have made a better effort doing something to stop SCOPE. And there was Terry, sitting over in his caravan, not washing, smoking Hendrik's blow as soon as he woke up, if he slept at all. It was hard for Carl to watch that, even though he'd only known the guy for a while. Terry was lonely, and he needed a friendly face.

'Maybe they'll finish the job,' Terry had said, slumped in his chair, one day, wreathed in smoke. 'Adam and the rest will come for me one night and do me in.' He'd looked up at Carl. 'Now they don't have to worry about the consequences.' Terry laughed. 'Like CivCon, or the Gestapo. A knock on the door and the bastards'll black-bag me in a dawn raid and whisk me away. Shoot me in the quarry this time rather than slice my fucking ...'

'All right,' Carl had soothed. 'I don't think that's on the cards somehow.'

'Why not?'

Carl was silent for a moment, watching Terry flick his ash, tap-tap-tapping the joint on the rim of the ashtray, waiting for an answer. Tap-tap-tapping, even when there was no ash to flick. On edge.

'Why would they come for you?' he said at last.

Terry shrugged. 'Maybe they got a taste for it. Who could stop them if they came though the door, right now? You?'

Squaring up to Casper, let alone the rest of the boatyard crew, wasn't a prospect that Carl could imagine turning out in any way other than badly – for him. Maybe they did have a taste for it, and were enjoying flexing a bit of muscle, going round to polytunnels and greenhouses and hen-coops to see if people were hiding food. Enforcing Howard's system.

'You're just being paranoid,' said Carl. 'Besides, you said you couldn't remember what happened.'

Tap-tap went Terry's spliff on the ashtray. Tap-tap-tap . . .

'I can.'

They'd looked at each other.

'It's coming back to me, the more I try to remember, little snippets, in the dark, getting shoved around, and then the moonlight on something, flashing, a blade, you know, glinting in the moonlight . . .' Terry's voice broke, and the joint trembled in his hand. 'And, uh, then I was screaming and I, uh, could feel . . . I didn't meant to . . . I didn't . . .' His hand shook as he raised it to his eyepatch.

Carl felt the colour drain from his face. He pursed his lips. 'You sure?'

Terry sniffed. 'Yeah, I've been thinking about it, sitting here. I've remembered.' He gave a short laugh. 'Not much else to do but think.'

Now that he thought about that conversation, he wasn't sure if he trusted Terry's account of losing his eye. Can memories be recovered like that, after some blanked-out trauma? He sat up, went to the bathroom to splash cold water on his face. A knife glinting in the moonlight – how very cinematic.

There was a possibility, sure there was, but then he thought it might be a false memory because Terry wanted desperately for it to be the way he said it happened. To give matters their unvarnished truth, Terry might be lying. But he hadn't been lying about not using violence on Gemma. The rumours said Dr Morgan confirmed that the girl and Terry had sex, but there was no sign of force.

It was wrong. How wrong? Was the crime one of degree, of measuring initial intent, or was that just fudging the issue?

Carl tried to imagine someone being inside him when he did not desire it. When he wanted it to stop. What was he doing with Terry anyway? How could he associate with such a man?

He looked at his face in the bathroom mirror. The beard kept him warm, as did the hair on his head. There was no room for style or fashion any more. He'd forgotten why he'd shaved it off in the first place. There was only the simple truth of keeping warm in the winter. Maybe he'd shave it off for summer, like they did to sheep.

He set off for Alec John's. At least he'd spend today inside, learning how to saw a carcass, how to slice it into cuts and joints of meat.

It nagged at him, Terry and his flash of clarity. There was something about his way of telling it, something that wasn't obviously either a lie or the truth. Call it self-delusion. Was he supposed to spread the story around? Was he supposed to tell Simone?

He turned off the main road, just round the head of the bay, and walked up the gravel track to the stalker's farm.

He had to have the facts to stand up a hunch, and in this case his hunch was giving him trouble. There was no evidence to swing it either way; there had been no sign of broken glass or a knife in the trees in the clearing, just thin, sharp branches, sticking straight out from every conifer trunk. In daylight it was a pain to walk through; in the dark, and running, it would have been dangerous.

January–April

33

The sky cleared, and the temperature plunged. Two Celsius was the best the brief, crystal daylight could offer; by night it was sub-zero, down as low as minus eight. Clear skies meant crunching grass below and the full catalogue of constellations wheeling above, Orion rising in the east, where the ionosphere flashed and crackled every now and then to SCOPE's electric dance.

As dawn broke, a light wind rose. A mile above the stirring village a parachute opened, a silver cylinder suspended beneath it, glinting in the early sun. The canopy of white nylon drifted inland on the breeze, away from Inverlair, and sank silently out of sight.

Simone could hear Isaac humming to himself, as he thudded, one deliberate step at a time, down the stairs. Granddad would be down there, lighting the fire, wrapped in his dressing gown, with his balaclava on. He would probably tell Isaac off for coming downstairs without wearing any socks. Simone lay on her side, the duvet pulled up to her ears. At least she wasn't vomiting any more, that was something, and Dr Morgan had said everything was fine; everything, that is, except life in general. Simone tried not to think of her mum; tried not to picture what would be left of her after almost four months lying wherever SCOPE had sent her to sleep. There was her son to occupy her thoughts now, and the baby in her stomach, and her dad and her brother and other people to think about. They were here, and they were alive. Simone kept telling herself that she had to focus on the present, and that thinking about what had happened served no purpose. It would drive her mad if she let it.

What was she going to do?

She started to cry, her mother not present to make things right, to comfort and cuddle and nothing more, no, nothing more . . .

A crust had developed on her vulnerability, and no man would be allowed to penetrate it unless she, in full conscious realisation, wanted that to happen. She would keep her guard up, especially now, and her persona would bar the way to those who deserved exclusion. No outside force, no man, was going to make her feel bad again.

It was obvious to her that Carl was either incapable of opening up or unwilling to try. She lay there, wrapped in the duvet, staring into space. Fatherhood, to Carl, was just a frightening word with unpleasant connotations.

She hoped that her brother had told her the truth about Terry. It had been difficult enough to raise the baby subject before, to make it real for Carl, and now there was a reason for him to dislike her even more: Adam. She tried to see the justice in what had happened to Terry, but she found it impossible. He was a sad and lonely man.

She felt nauseous again, and her breasts were tender. Pregnancy was real enough for her.

At the same time that morning Carl lay in his own bed, fully clothed and hungry, trying to figure out how to start the day. He mustn't stop washing just because it was easier and warmer to get into bed at night with all his clothes on. An effort to keep clean should be made, bollock-freezing water or not. He wasn't going to stink like Terry. Days like this made him yearn for a coffee, a splash of Irish in it, just to keep out the chill. And carbs. Even the synthetic shit they used to hand out at the rationing centres. He would take a slab of polycarb right now, and a bucket of coffee, to kick-start his system. He was tired. Everyone was tired.

Something would happen, something that would make his spirit soar. There had to be that in life, an end to the staleness and sameness and discomfort.

This is how people used to live, he thought, his eyes fixed on the ceiling. They survived, cold and hungry, most of the time. Probably much worse back then, when there were no polytunnels or chest freezers or photovoltaics; no duvets or taps. And now an echo of the past had returned, making life what it had been for most of humankind's existence: a struggle. Nature used to dictate that there was less of everything in the winter, including warmth. And now the power of seasonal rationing was back, tightening its coils around Inverlair for the long cold squeeze, until spring.

He sighed. Why did she keep pushing him? She could be asking questions about SCOPE or Alec John or Terry one minute, then the next she'd ask about his own parents and the conversation, inevitably, would turn to children and the child that was on its way. He wasn't going to get pinned down like that. It was too much like losing control, and he'd had enough of that over the last thirty-eight years to last a lifetime.

In a minute he would fill a sink of water in the en suite, scrape together a film of soap from somewhere, and have a wash; then he would go and do something. In a minute he would do all that. Start the day. Perform an allotted task. He was starting to get the hang of things. Some of it disgusted him; the reek of steaming innards from a gralloched deer, or a snared rabbit, mouth full of its own blood. At least he was only answering to Alec John, not the committee – the self-appointed good shepherds. Maybe everyone needed that kind of authority, doing all the planning and organising.

The committee had stepped into the breach and were now enforcing Howard's survival plan, tweaked with their own sly modifications. Maybe that's just what happens: those who get to call the shots pretend that everything is okay and above board, while the folks at the sharp end just accept injustice as natural, so long as it isn't waved under their noses. Even gouging out eyes as punishment could be tolerated.

Maybe he should tell the rest of the village about Adam Cutler's food rationing stitch-up, and maybe enough of them would listen. But then what? Hold out the begging bowl and watch it get filled to the brim by a repentant committee? That sort of admission of culpability had never happened before the redzone, so why should it happen now? People look out for themselves; it only takes the right circumstances for the mask to drop, for people to regress to growling over a fresh kill.

•

Sunlight came streaming through the crystal-coated birch and into Alec John's living room. The sky was cloudless and the early afternoon had a piercing light to it. The day would darken in two hours, but for now it was blue around and above the frosting bay. Hungry birds – siskin, Carl thought – were squabbling in the leafless trees, oblivious to him walking past, crunching up the shell path.

Alec John was in his favourite spot, sitting at the window with a blanket round his shoulders and another over his knees, dozing, but not asleep. As Carl watched through the window, Alec John, his closed eyes dark and his skin stretched pale over the frame of his skull, grimaced and turned his head. But there was no respite from the discomfort, and the man's gaping mouth struggled to inhale what his lungs could barely use. This is how it would be, from now on: Alec John's breathing would get quicker and shallower and the lack of oxygen, once his emergency tank ran out, would mean even walking to the toilet would be a struggle. Without regular injections of nanomed to fight the good fight, his heart would soon no longer be able to pump oxygenated blood to his lungs. This disease had been exorcised by inexplicable magic – in Alec John's case administered five times a year by Dr

Morgan. But now it was creeping back, repossessing its human host. Undoubtedly, emphysema would bring a few friends along, and they'd all have a wild old time in their Highland retreat. They'd do their best to devour it.

Carl watched Alec John for a while. He couldn't help but think of Eric and Leslie. Did they die together? The question kept occurring. He shuddered at the image of a Glasgow filled with desiccated corpses, in beds, cars, offices and streets, lying where they'd collapsed, bones picked clean. There would be other notspots and, one day, he'd drive away and find them.

Carl went inside the house. 'Hello, it's me.'

Alec John stirred at the sound. 'Hello there,' he gasped. He coughed, spat into his hankie, a trace of blood and sputum clinging to his grey-stubbled chin. He lifted the face mask, took a few deep breaths, and sat up straight to focus on his visitor.

Carl noticed the bowl of soup, untouched, on the drop-leaf table. 'George will take that personally,' he said.

Alec John shook his head. 'I must have nodded off.' He straightened his back against the armchair, smoothed his thinning grey hair into place. 'I had some of the soup, and the bread – say thanks to George.'

He glanced at Carl. He was showing the evidence. Food? Keep my strength up? Look, Alec John was saying, I am nothing but skin and bone. I am already dead. One day soon, a shortage of oxygen will put me in a coma or give me a heart attack, and no amount of soup is going to stop that happening. He took a few sips of water. 'You have it.'

'Have what?'

'The soup.'

Carl hesitated. 'No, keep it for later.' He put another log in the stove. 'Heat it up whenever you're hungry.'

He stood at the fire for a moment, looking at the framed photos on Alec John's mantelpiece. Mother and father in black and white, wife and nephew in colour. The clock ticked and Jess panted in her basket.

'That thing the fishermen saw come down the other day, it's definitely a capsule – Russian, I think.'

Alec John brightened. 'Really? How do you know it's Russian?'

'I saw their flag painted on the side,' said Carl. 'It was too foggy yesterday to get a good look. There's a parachute attached, but it's too far into the redzone. Must have been dropped from very high up.'

'There could be all sorts inside, stuff we need.'

Carl nodded. 'They would've dropped important stuff – medical supplies, high-energy food maybe. But we'll have to wait a good while to reach it.'

Turning back to the window, Alec John said nothing more. Carl took the bowl through to the kitchen.

'Is Terry still the same?'

Carl pulled up a dining chair, turned it around, and sat with his elbows resting on the back. 'He's been okay for the last couple of weeks. He's started carving animals into logs, even into trees. They're amazing, really detailed.'

Alec John drank some more water, brighter now. 'Do you think he'll snap out of it completely?'

'I think he is. Part of him seems glad that he's been punished for something he's done wrong.' He looked at Alec John. 'He did have sex with that girl when she didn't want to. It was rape.' He paused. 'He's getting some odd ideas into his head though. Keeps going on about Celtic myths and old religion.'

Alec John sighed and shook his head. He kept his eyes fixed on the scrawny patch of hazel in the garden. 'Well, it was wrong, what he did, though not wrong enough for what happened to him.'

'Well, there are different rules now. That's what Gibbs said: different rules.'

'I suppose there are,' said Alec John, clasping his pale white hands together. Then he looked up at Carl, fixed his eye for second. 'Different rules.'

He took a breath of oxygen. 'Did you put the strychnine down for the stoats?'

'Yes.' Carl smiled. 'That American woman, the one who latched onto Adam, she was pretty horrified. Called it barbaric.'

There was a twinkle in Alec John's eye. 'Maybe she won't want any grouse then – if the stoats and crows leave us any. Did you check the Larsen traps up below the corries?'

'Yes.'

'And?'

'Two hoodies.'

'Good.' Alec John relaxed into the armchair again, licked his paper-dry lips, and collected his thoughts. 'In the corner,' he said gruffly, gesturing. 'You may as well have it.'

A gun in a leather case stood in the corner of the sitting room. Alec John had several guns, but Carl recognised the case. He picked it up, smelled the linseed oil on the cracked leather. He opened the straps and took out the Ruger.308. It was Alec John's own rifle. Not one of the .22s or a shotgun, but the man's weapon of choice. The magic meat stick, handed down from father to son.

'You may as well take it,' Alec John said.

Carl felt the gun, hard and cold, in his hands. 'This was your dad's.'

'Aye, and now it's yours.'

On the tip of Carl's tongue there hung a question, more a consideration, really: he wouldn't ask if Alec John was sure about giving the gun away, because that would mean raising the possibility of its rightful owner never firing it again. And that, they both knew, was probably the truth. He put the .308 back in the case and closed the silver buckles. Alec John said nothing, waved his hand to dismiss any protest.

'Thanks,' Carl said softly.

Pursing his lips, Alec John resumed his vigil with the crisp winter scene outside his window. What had to be done was done.

'You'd better make them count,' he said. 'There aren't too many left.'

'I'll pick my targets.'

Carl stoked the fire, turning the log so that some heat would flow into the room. Once the sun sank, the temperature would drop quickly.

'How's Simone?'

There were a variety of responses to this question, covering simple lies and complex truths. Carl opted for the simple truth. 'I don't know.' He cleared his throat. 'We don't really talk, or see each other that much.'

'Why not?'

'Well, because . . . because she always wants to talk about her condition, you know. I mean, what does she want? For us to settle down and pretend to be a happy family? That's not going to happen.'

'How do you know she wants that if you never talk to her?'

'What else is there to talk about?'

Alec John let out a short laugh. 'The fact that she's pregnant and you're the father?'

'But we know that, so what is there to talk about?'

'How the hell would I know? And you won't know either unless you talk to her. She might be terrified at the prospect of having another kid.' His face darkening, Alec John turned back to the window. 'You're going to be a father. That's something you should be thankful for.'

Carl snorted. 'Right. A kid is exactly what I need. And exactly what Inverlair needs.'

'Maybe it is.'

'No,' said Carl. 'It's not.'

Alec John reached for his oxygen mask and took a few puffs.

He was quieter when he spoke again. 'My wife died of a brain haemorrhage at the age of thirty-one. She was in the post office down the road when it happened, buying stamps. She had a bit of a sore head, I said goodbye to her that morning, went out as usual, and when I came back, the doctor at the time and the postmistress were waiting for me. Every day I think about her, even now.' He wiped his nose with the back of his hand. 'We couldn't have kids. It was my fault, and now here I am. You see, no matter where you go or what you do, you'll always be a father. There's no getting away from that.

'I never met anyone else after my wife died. I suppose that was my choice. But you don't have a choice now. It's all a question of what you do with the knowledge. I don't believe any man can just ignore his child and if he does, well, it'll have some effect on him, sooner or later.'

Sermon over, Alec John looked out the window, clutching the oxygen mask on his lap.

Carl got up and put his chair back under the table. He zipped up his waterproof jacket. 'I don't know,' he said, standing there. 'I don't know what to do.'

Staring up at him, Alec John settled the blanket round his knees. 'That's okay. It's fine not to know. But at least think about it.'

Carl shrugged. 'I shouldn't have upset you.' He turned to leave. 'I'll see you later.'

Alec John smiled. 'So I'm firing blanks as well as live ammunition, eh?' He turned back to the window. 'I'll be up and about tomorrow to joint that carcass, so you can watch how it's done again. You're still making a bloody mess of it.'

At the head of the bay, down on the main road, the shadows were already hardening as the icy night reasserted itself. With the sun up, there had been a hint of warmth in the air, an easing. But now, at just after 4 p.m., the cold was clenching again. At some point, perhaps in a day or two, the air stream would swing to the south and the clouds would come back and the temperature would rise. It would start raining again. This was the wisdom of those who had been here for far longer than he had. There were those who could see the bigger picture, who could see beyond the transient discomfort of a cold snap. They could read the secret signs that were invisible to everyone else, the subtle cues that suggested what was to come.

Carl had been good at that – the sense of what lay beneath the surface, finely attuned to the hidden language of true intentions. If he paid attention, maybe he could make it work – being here. He could get through this, whatever this actually was, by learning a skill. That's the way he had to look at it: learn what needs to be learned and then get on with it, keeping out of everyone's way in the process. It worked for Alec John, that kind of approach. Every man has dreams of power. It's how he reacts to powerlessness that defines the kind of person a man becomes.

Climbing the main road up the southern headland had warmed him up. Cold air clawed at his lungs, steaming hot billows into the cold. His stride slowed at Terry's gate, but quickened again, and he pressed on towards the roadblock. A little further and he stopped, just short of the painted boulders, feeling SCOPE in his right temple. Today might have been the six-day pulse, but it was too late in the afternoon to know for sure. Besides, he didn't really want to know about the six-day pulse any more. It was a deadly hope, and a false one.

Running. Running from the low-frequency wave that was breaking over him, and that was killing Howard. And then the darkness and the rain and the realisation. All of it came back to him if he let it, but there was no need to let it because he was moving forward into some kind of future. It was happening. He could see he had no choice. The alternatives were worse, on balance.

The deltameter showed the delta field was, if anything, a little stronger today.

The useless sun was slinking away back into its hole and there was fuck all for him to do but become proficient in something, the capacity to shoot and walk and watch that had fallen into his lap. He stamped on an ice-filled pothole, causing a crack, but not breaking through. His primary task was now maximising the supply of protein obtained through the flesh of dead animals. Those animals, in the main, had to be shot. The man who'd performed that task, dutifully, for almost forty years was more or less incapable of walking any distance, and he, Carl, had stepped into the role. He put the deltameter into his inside pocket and turned back towards the village. As the light dwindled behind the southern headland the shadow of night started creeping around the bay. Round and round the limits of its orbit, the world turned and the day went on into cold star-filled night. Carl lifted the binoculars, took a last look across the bay. There was that big fucking thug Casper, dumping more logs from the pick-up. The guy doesn't even bother to knock now, just marches straight into people's hen-coops or polytunnels, sees what there is, and loads up the trailer with plunder. There was no need for violence; he took the food because people believed the committee had a right to it. Yes, Carl could see the sense in Howard's system, in having a committee to ration everything – but fairly. This system wasn't fair. When is it ever?

George still enjoyed a whisky: the perks of the publican, perhaps, but surely conduct unbecoming for the chairman of the emergency committee.

Across the bay, Carl could see Casper talking with Adam and another guy. They could take over, he thought. Inverlair's own emergency authority could run the place in whichever way they chose. It was their choice. Gibbs couldn't do a thing about what had been done to Terry, and the committee wanted to smooth the whole thing over. Move along now, nothing to see here.

But there must be a consequence, a punishment. The evildoers must get what they deserve. Isn't that what happens?

Carl watched the men across the bay. Big dumb Casper and his little emperor. There would be a punishment. He would bide his time and then, when the right moment presented itself, enact his own version of justice.

Simone entered the binoculars' field of vision, dark orange scarf wound against the cold, a striped woollen hat down to her ears. He watched her say hello to her brother and the other two but not stop. She walked past the shorefront houses, past the boarded-up craft shop, Carl following her progress. She was pretty enough, and he liked her. There was nothing wrong with her, and maybe he'd accept the way things were, but then again maybe he wouldn't. There must be something left – some choice that he still had the power to make. Simone stopped at Dr Morgan's cottage.

Part of Carl hoped for the worst.

•

'This is a great little lamp,' said Dr Morgan. 'Remember that big power cut a few years ago, the first big one? My nephew gave me this for Christmas.' She switched on the lamp; it had a slender conical base topped with a wire-and-paper shade. 'Leave it on the windowsill to charge during the day and you get a good three hours of power at night ... Can I offer you a refill?'

Simone raised her dark eyebrows, an empty cup in her lap. 'Please, that tea was nice and fresh.'

Dr Morgan went over to the fire and lifted a pan of steaming water from the embers. 'Wringing out the last few drops,' she said brightly.

It occurred to Simone that tomorrow was the day for handing out tea and coffee rations. At this point in the week, a teabag would have been wrung out a few times to make a brew, by most people.

She watched the cups being refilled with hot water, steam rising as the cold ceramic was soused. She knew the food-rationing situation was wrong, but the fattening foetus inside her had its own needs, imperatives that she had to obey. And it was only a cup of tea, after all.

They sipped at their cups by the fire. Even though her face was warm, Simone could feel the chill at her back, where heat ended and a cold house began.

Delicately, Dr Morgan raised the subject of Carl, and Simone tried to make light of the situation. While talking, she became conscious of the fact that she was defending him, so she wound up the conversation with a shrug. 'There's not much I can do about the situation. We'll just have to see what happens.'

Barring any mishaps, one thing was certain to happen, and she was over halfway towards it, or towards *her*, as Dr Morgan's test had just confirmed.

34

On a bright spring day the lamb is born; and on the same bright spring day it dies.

Carl was too far away to help it. Through the binoculars he could see birds, bigger than crows – ravens, maybe – taking up position around the mother; one was even perched on her back. They were all waiting.

The sheep stood to give birth, its hindquarters thrusting towards the ground, mouth open, head tilted upwards, as a sausage of pliable waxy life unplugged itself from the birth canal and spilled onto the ground. Then the birds moved in.

Carl lowered the binoculars, his lips dry. The lamb was seconds in the world, and now it was out of it. Months to make, and all that energy, from sunlight to grass to foetus, was now being pecked back into death by the ravens. That, surely, was the point. The ravens had to live – they had as much right to life as the lamb, or as little claim on it. He could run over there now, take up a good position, and probably kill one of the birds, let it act as a warning to the others. The lamb would still have its eyes pecked out, but he could even the score. There would be no justice in it, because the birds weren't doing anything wrong, as such; it was simply that killing them helped keep death away.

Carl walked along the ridge, cutting down the track and into the boggy saddle between the peaks, inland from the head of the bay. There was warmth in the air, so he took off his baseball cap and unzipped his Gore-Tex to the navel. On a day like this it was good to be alive. He wasn't about to rush anywhere to waste a bullet.

The ewe had needed to give birth there and then, out in the open, just one dumb brute struggling by itself to produce another. The birds, too, had no choice – killing and eating a just-born lamb, fresh from the oven, was a simple risk-free way of eating. People talk about the facts of life, but it could just as easily be the facts of death. There was no escape from either, though there were rules of engagement.

Alec John had a choice: the moment of death was now in his own hands, thanks to Dr Morgan and 150mg of diamorphine. By controlling the 'how' he could control the 'when' and, thus, the 'where'. Death might be the strongest animal, but, if you're lucky, there will be time to tidy up before opening the front door to it.

At least Alec John could cut short the pain, any time he chose, though staying alive was becoming harder every day for him.

'Howard said between two and four years, but he also said the nearest mast might fail tomorrow,' Carl had argued. 'When it does, we can get the stuff you need, the nanomeds.'

Alec John had gone along with that, to begin with, but now pain and permanent immobility were proving too much. The fight to stay out of bed – which he saw as a step closer to the grave – was all but over. Most days Alec John couldn't make it into his clothes, or a chair. Even if the nearest mast failed tomorrow, it might not be enough to open the way to the next town, and the nearest doctor's surgery would not necessarily have the right kind of medicine. They both knew it was ridiculous to think otherwise.

Up on the ridge, Carl scanned along the shoreline with his binoculars, settled on Terry's caravan and then on Hendrik de Vries and his wife, who were fussing around in and out of their polytunnels. She paid regular visits to Terry, probably just to check on him.

On this side of the bay Simone and Isaac were in the back

garden, putting logs in a basket. She had her padded jacket on. It hid the bump but made her look twice as big.

There was no white boat on the horizon. And there never would be.

Just like Alec John, it could be any day now with Simone. One going out of the world and one coming into it. But at least the ravens wouldn't be waiting for either Alec John or the baby. Carl watched Isaac help his mum with the logs, watched how they acted together, the little actions that revealed their intimacy. Then he lowered the binoculars and began the long, hard climb up to the crown of Ben Bronach. After a spell, he veered left towards the gully and the river. Two days ago, when the weather broke, he'd taken an older hind here. He'd gralloched her with inexpert hands, still using the gut hook to detach the hot innards, blood-warm slime and intestinal tubing, scooping it all from the body cavity and onto the rough grass. For Alec John, such an activity provoked no reaction; pinched disgust was the best Carl was able to manage, even now. At least he no longer vomited.

Now, two days later, there was nothing of the hind's guts to be seen except a little dried blood and tufts of downy fur clinging to the heather. Who knows how many animals had fed off the remains? Maybe the guts had made the difference between life and death. A crow might emerge, alive, from the winter because it had eaten its fill here. That crow might kill a lamb. That lamb wouldn't grow up to produce more lambs. The struggle for flesh was open and constant.

•

Dr Morgan was relieved. This looked like a straightforward pregnancy. 'The head has engaged. BP's fine. Everything's normal.' She smiled at Simone.

Simone pulled up her jogging bottoms. Isaac was cackling out in the back garden with Pavel and Fiona.

Normal. That was a good one. She tried to smile at Dr Morgan, puffing and heaving off the bed. 'Thanks for coming round.'

'I was passing anyway. Just checking on Mrs Mackay.'

'Is she not well?'

'Oh, she's fine, a tough old bird that one. But her house is all electric, and it's been bloody freezing in there, though we're into spring now. She's in her eighties. It was minus two in Mr Cameron's bedroom when they found him. He was seventy-seven. And without treatment, the Armstrong boy's leukaemia will kill him in a month.' She rolled the latex gloves into a ball. 'Just another day at the office.'

Simone started to put her trainers on, but she was too big to reach down easily.

'Here, let me.' Dr Morgan crouched to finish the job and tie the laces. 'How does the father-to-be feel now?'

Simone considered her answer. 'I think ... I think he's resigned to hanging around.'

'What does that mean?'

'Well, he'll give it a go, I suppose.'

'There's a big difference between giving things a go and being resigned to hanging around, yeah?'

Pulling herself out of the chair, Simone pressed her fingers into the small of her back. She grimaced.

'He doesn't have kids, does he?'

'No,' said Simone.

'Did he have anyone special before, do you think?'

Simone watched Isaac out in the garden, climbing up the ash tree with Pavel. They were both laughing. 'No,' she said. 'Though I think there was someone a while back. She had an abortion and the baby wasn't his. He eventually found all that out.'

'He told you that?'

'Yes.'

Dr Morgan nodded, satisfied. 'He must have lost someone.'

'As far as I can make out, his boss was the most important person in his life,' said Simone. She waddled into the en suite bathroom and closed the door.

Claire Morgan wanted to say that Simone reminded her of her own daughter. There was a photo of Simone's mother on the bedside table. The natural links had been severed – for both of them – and she should say the thing she felt moved to say. Your mother and I are about the same age; I had a daughter too.

She should draw the comparison, build something, and Simone should do the same. Only good could come of it. Her Nancy was gone and so was Alison Cutler and . . .

The toilet flushed. Dr Morgan gathered herself.

'You know these spraysuits?' asked Simone.

'No,' said Dr Morgan. 'Are they for swimming?'

Simone smiled. 'No. It's mainly guys that use them. Stuff called neurogel. You bought a nebuliser and sprayed the gel on at home. There were also these contact lenses.'

'Porn, you mean?'

'Well,' said Simone, 'I suppose you could say that. But it's more than porn. It was like living with someone, if that's what the users wanted. It was for lonely people, I suppose.'

'Well, there are plenty of them still around. Did Carl have one, a spraysuit?'

'My dad seems to think he did. They were talking a while ago, before . . . before Terry.'

There was a sharp crack against the windowpane, as the first nugget of hail pinged off the glass; within seconds the shower swept in at full pelt. Simone watched as Isaac, Pavel and Fiona rushed giggling to the back door, holding their faces.

'Does Carl still blame Adam for what happened?'

Simone nodded, feeling exhausted all of a sudden. She sat down heavily in the bedroom's only comfortable chair, her breath condensing in the cold spring air. 'He thinks Dad could've done something about it, though I don't know what he had in mind. I mean, what could Gibbs have done anyway? Locked him in a cellar? I just get the feeling Carl wants Adam punished, somehow. He wants some kind of justice. But I say: what about justice for Gemma? If Adam or Casper get locked up why shouldn't the same thing happen to Terry?'

'And Carl can't get what he wants,' said Dr Morgan to herself, then louder, 'so things are complicated between you two.'

As quickly as it had started, the hail shower passed.

'I think they always will be,' said Simone, closing her eyes, her pale lips trembling. She tried to smile. 'We didn't have the ideal start, you know. I suppose I should be a little more . . . understanding.'

'Why?'

'He's used to the city. He doesn't belong here. The world for us maybe isn't so different; for him it's changed beyond all recognition, and everyone he knew in Glasgow is dead.'

'True,' said Dr Morgan. 'But it's been nine months, just about. Maybe it's time he started to accept the situation.'

'That'll happen, eventually,' said Simone, surprised by how confident she sounded. 'Even if he could leave here tomorrow, there isn't really anywhere for him to go any more.' She sat up. 'I'm not expecting anything to happen between us. I don't think I even want it to. I'd just like him to acknowledge this.' She patted her distended belly. 'And accept the possibility that being a father might actually mean something.'

Dr Morgan would have liked to talk more, but the sound of thumping feet and voices in the hallway helped decide the issue. She got smartly to her feet as Isaac and his pals burst into the room with a story about a dead bird they'd found in the garden.

'Sounds like a greenfinch,' said Dr Morgan. 'Birds get disorientated sometimes – no one knows why – and they fly into windows, into the glass, and break their necks.'

Ornithology by osmosis made her reasonably certain it was a greenfinch. If it hadn't been for divorce, she might have been an expert on birds by now. He'd always loved birds.

•

Terry's feet were on the windowsill, dust from sawn plasterboard on his boots and clothes, and in his tangled brown hair. There was old newspaper spread all over the floor of his uncle's house, not much furniture in the rooms, and everything smelled of new paint. The smell of past normality and the freshness of the future, each room a different colour, right down to the floorboards. A house of moods, and a room for each one, so said Terry.

'So, the trick is not to be afraid,' he said, taking another suck on his spliff. 'Open your mouth and your heart and your mind, and let the stuff just pour out of you. Say what you are moved to say. Take that first step towards not feeling stupid, by feeling stupid.'

Carl sat on the floor, against the wall. He grunted, too convinced by Terry for comfort. He didn't like the way everything was being smoothed over. The scars of knee-jerk justice were plain to see; the word rape conjured images of frenzied, feral violence. The truth of both was hard to fathom.

SCOPE was an invisible glacier, just another expression of force. But now he was in a place where forces had overpowered choice. Glaciers don't have the urge to dominate the rocks they grind to rubble. There's no other mode of being for half-mile-thick ice; grinding rock is what it does. It was the same with stags. They can't choose what they are; they can't resist the actions they are compelled to perform. They are their actions. That's what defines them.

People aren't just vectors of blind force. They can choose. It wasn't just a case of subjugate and inseminate.

Just for something to say, Carl told Terry about the crow in the Larsen trap, up on the moors. The bird had gone crazy when it saw

Carl approaching. He'd stood quietly, watching it from a distance. After a while the crow stopped flapping and clawing at the wire cage. It had been hard to tell if the thing was afraid; there was no trace of emotion in its gleaming black eyes, head cocking and bobbing, alert. To save shotgun shells, Carl was supposed to use the metal gripper to grab the bird by the neck, if he came across one still alive. Thus pinioned, the crow was then to have its brains stamped on.

'But I shot it instead,' said Carl. 'And I blew the bloody Larsen trap to bits as well. I felt sorry for it – even though they take grouse eggs and go for the lambs. It was just a young one. Alec John said the older ones know not to go near the traps. The death of a few crows teaches the rest not to go near them. It's like every so often they need a reminder of how to stay alive. A sacrifice. It was just trapped there, helpless, in the cage. I mean, I know it's a pest, but you're killing something that's just trying to stay alive, same as you are. Anyway, I made a choice, and it's been a while since that's happened.'

Terry passed Carl the joint. 'Everything is entitled to its share. Somewhere along the line I think we forgot that. We wanted it all for ourselves.'

Carl took a single draw from the spliff and passed it back. He shifted his weight on the hard floor, uneasy. 'Different rules now, in lots of ways, I suppose. But there are still some that carry moral force.' From this angle, and in profile, and with the light from the window hitting him straight on, Terry's eyepatch wasn't visible. But every so often, as people do when they're talking, he'd turn his head, and Carl would see the patch. Off had come the surgical gauze that Dr Morgan had supplied, and in its place Terry had drawn an oversized eye onto a triangle of pliable white plastic. He'd sewn a red glass bead onto the patch as an iris. The effect was disconcerting.

'I saw Gemma today,' said Terry.

'What do you mean – saw?'

'She looked terrified, then turned bright red, then looked as if she was about to burst into tears. She said sorry and ran away.'

Terry put the joint down in the ashtray and got up from the wicker chair, his red-bead eye matching the look on his face. He started measuring another sheet of plasterboard.

•

In the old quarry Carl watched sand martins swoop and frolic over the lagoon, shooting into their holes in the quarry wall, then bulleting out and up, dipping and circling. Spring is here, and this is how these birds behave. He watched them for a spell, at the centre of the sand martins' wild wheeling orbit, until he forgot what had been on his mind. As afternoon lengthened, he turned and walked back along the main road and up the northern slope of the bay. Near the red-boulder roadblock he stopped. The *Aurora* was close inshore, just sitting there in the calm sea. Through the binoculars he could see Casper fishing astern and Adam, shades on, dozing in a deckchair.

And then it took hold of Carl. The idea of what to do next got him like a heart shot.

He raised the binoculars again, his pulse quickening. The *Aurora* must be a good 200 metres offshore, apart from one spit of rock, where the distance was maybe half that. He could get down there in ten minutes if he moved quickly.

He ran down the uneven grassy meadow to the bottom edge. Crouching behind a fence, he cased the best route. What the fuck was he doing? Before he could find an answer, he set off again, running stooped to the gate that led down to the shingle and the rocks, slipping on the bank of high-tide seaweed as he rushed down to the foreshore. If he kept to the north side of the spit of rock the *Aurora* wouldn't see him, and when he got to the point he would be close enough to . . .

He splashed through rock pools, the .308 slung across his back, until he got to the cover of the spit. Maybe Adam and Casper had been fishing for hours and were set to go back to the pier. As he clambered over the dark rocks, the plan snowballed in his mind; each problem was met with a solution.

Afterwards, he could run back to the ruins of the herring station, grab the old dinghy and oars, row out to the *Aurora*, drop the anchor, and shove the bodies overboard. Then he'd head back to the boat, sink it, and tell everyone that he came across the *Aurora* aground on the rocks.

Afterwards. After what?

The further out the spit he went, the wetter the rocks became and the deeper the water. Once or twice he slipped and nearly fell in. Under his breath he started singing, softly, 'Set my people free, free, free, set them free' over and over again, barely aware that he was even doing it.

His heart was racing, lips dry, and he could feel his hands and legs starting to shake.

And here he was. And there they were, close enough for a shot. He caught his breath, peeping round the rocks every now and again.

Free, free, set them free . . .

It was a perfect spot: the rocks were arranged so that he could adopt an ideal firing position. Even the barrel of the rifle would have a shelf on which to rest. The earth and the tides had provided for him in his hour of need. It was preordained.

Free, free, set them free . . .

As he raised the rifle he found that his hands couldn't stop shaking. His heart was pounding in his throat and, even above the crashing surf he could hear it in his ears. Every time he tried to settle into position it would happen, his body shaking and his heart hammering against his ribs.

Adam dozing in the sun, shades on. Take Casper first in the

head, then down and to the left as Adam roused himself and – *bang*. He'd be doing everyone a favour.

Free, free, set them free.

Carl set the gun aside, and with a trembling hand wiped the sweat and snot from his face. He laughed to himself, unchambered the bullet, and turned away from his position.

He held the rifle in front of him to look at it, one hand gripping the rubberised stock and the other the barrel.

This gun was older than he was and it had never taken a human life. He'd had it all of five minutes and was already planning to do exactly that. Is that what he was going to do with the gun Alec John had bequeathed to him? Bloodlust wasn't part of the inheritance, surely. He could block that signal, if he put his mind to it. A man isn't a machine that can set conscience aside.

He put the rifle back into its case. It's easier, at the end of a telescopic sight, but not that easy. Adam was safe to throw his weight around until someone else threw it back at him. Let him sleep in the sun, saved for another day. Uncle Adam. The Big Boss.

Laughing softly to himself, Carl made his way back along the spit, through the foreshore rock pools, and back up to the roadblock. The *Aurora* was motoring back towards the bay now. He watched it approach the pier, throttling back.

Calmer now, his pulse back to normal, Carl made his way to Alec John's. Shooting animals was power enough.

Change had been thrown over him like a cloak of lead. The more he struggled under it, the heavier it got. Maybe if he stopped struggling, the future would lie lightly on him, and possibility would begin to flower once again. Lead would transmute, become lighter than air.

Jess came scrabbling down the shell path as soon as she heard Carl's footsteps. He stroked her, which set her tail to a joyful thrashing. Every time he saw Dr Morgan in Alec John's house he assumed the worst: that the old man had decided enough was enough and it was time to go.

'Well?'

Dr Morgan was in the sitting room, heating some milk on the range. She stirred the pan, ordered Jess into her blanket-lined basket. 'He's okay,' she said. 'He's got something to think about.'

'What d'you mean?'

'It's good news, maybe.' Dr Morgan brightened. 'I found a nanomed in the surgery. It's less than two years old. It wouldn't slot into the applicator as normal, so I just stuck it in a drawer ages ago.'

'Can you use it?'

Dr Morgan nodded. 'I think so. It's a fiddly job getting it into an ordinary hypodermic, that's why I didn't use it.'

Carl clapped his hands. Jess jumped out of her basket and gave a short bark.

'That's fantastic.' His enthusiasm waned when he saw Dr Morgan's expression. 'What's wrong?'

Warm milk was poured into a mug. 'Well,' she said, 'if he takes the nanomed in one go his lungs will be restored, almost, to the way they were. He'll have three good months.' Dr Morgan glanced at Carl. 'And then, unless the nearest mast fails – and assuming we can find more nanomed when it does – he'll have to go through all this pain and discomfort again.'

Carl sat at the table and stroked Jess at his knee. Death wasn't going to decide this one, not entirely.

'What does Alec John think?'

'He's not sure. I could give him it in two lots. He'd feel a lot better than he does now, but not well enough to go into the hills. He'll have a few months if I split it in two.'

Dr Morgan went through with the milk, Carl following her, to the end bedroom. 'He's asleep,' she whispered.

Propped on a bank of pillows, Alec John slept with his mouth open, thin hands splayed out on the duvet, ancient at sixty-six. His breathing was fast and shallow.

'I thought he'd be asleep,' said Carl softly. 'He can't sleep through the night so he dozes through the day.'

'Are you up with him at night?'

'Not often,' said Carl. 'He hates it when I come in. He was sitting in the chair the other night.'

'Really?'

Carl nodded. 'Yeah. He was just sitting there, both hands on his walking-stick, like he was just about to get up.'

'Did he?'

'No. He was back in bed half an hour later. Is there a drop of rum in that?'

'Yes,' said Dr Morgan with a smile. She walked back through to the stove with the cup of milk. 'You can warm it again when he wakes up.' She poured the milk back into the pan and put the lid on. 'You're very attentive.'

Carl shrugged. 'He's done a lot for me.'

Dr Morgan rinsed the cup under the tap, dried it, and hooked its handle on the stand. She picked up her jacket and put it on. They both stood there.

'In about two days' time, I would say, your daughter is going to come into the world.'

Carl pursed his lips. 'I'm staying. Whatever happens. Even if the masts failed tomorrow, where would I go?'

'Good,' said Dr Morgan. 'If you hang around for long enough, you might even try to make the best of it.' She buttoned her jacket, picked up her case, and patted Jess goodbye. Closing the front door, she was off, scrunching down the path.

Evening came down just as the low cloud lifted, fresher air sweeping in off the Atlantic, warmth in the spring air. Carl sat in Alec John's sitting room, by the warm stove, listening: to the old clock on the wall, logs settling in the grate, Jess breathing in her basket, the wind outside moving through the hazel.

He sat for a long time, drifting between regret and uncertainty, watching the wind at work as it roused the awakening earth.

New Life

Carl stopped the argocat and crept down into the open depths of the glen, keeping his eyes fixed on the middle distance. He had an idea what to look for now; the telltale signs and likely whereabouts of what he was driven to find.

After half an hour, he found it.

Crouching, Carl sank into a bank of heather. A single hind, quite young, was grazing down the slope close to a stream. As if sensing she was being watched, the hind lifted her head and scanned the higher ground. Carl dipped his head, waited then inched upwards until he could see again. She was thin, and clearly not pregnant. She'd come through the whole winter without being impregnated, which was rare, and was on her own, separate from the rest of the master's harem who were across the glen near the forest. He heard Alec John's voice telling him what a gift this was, winter-thin or not.

The lie of the land was such that Carl had to double back a little to the stream that rose on the sodden slopes. It was in spate, and the sound of rushing water would help mask any noise that he might make in his approach. The hind was a good 200 metres away, too far for a kill shot.

Following the stream down into the glen Carl crept along its hunched banks of rock and thin grass, stopping close to where the water slowed and opened out across beds of gravel.

There she was, down below, a fair distance away. There was a better way to come, he could see that now. But this was as close as he could get by following the water. Settling into a comfortable firing position, Carl sized up the target.

The hind was head-on so he would have to wait. It took another ten minutes for her to change her stance. Now they were ready.

Just above and to the left of the hip joint. That was the spot.

Now there was the slowing of breath, the emptying of mind; the universe packed into a square inch of grey-brown fur, the dead centre of extinction, where the energies of death and life were interchangeable.

'Thank you,' Carl whispered as he held his final breath, squeezing the trigger on the exhale. Twelve stone of deer dropped where it stood.

He clicked the distance function on the deltameter, and started off down the slope. Carl watched the figures mount. He touched the barrel of the .308 to the hind's staring eyeball. There was no response.

The reading said 137 metres. Alec John was right – Carl had a talent for this. In a different life, he could have made the Olympic team, but this was his truth now. He found the animal's carotid and plunged the knife home, indifferent to the blood that gushed out onto the grass. Carl had learned to live in this world. A truce had become uneasy peace. Back when it mattered, there had been different work that needed doing, and he'd done it until long after it became a pointless urge. After years of doing this other work, he'd realised there was a river of shit whose flow he was powerless to arrest. He'd take the odd bucketful, just to show people that what they were being told was pure water was, in fact, tainted. Septic with lies. But there was plenty more where the bucketful had come from. The river never stopped.

Wiping the lock-knife on his trousers he closed it and put it back in his jacket pocket. He watched, impassive, as the hind emptied her blood onto the new grass.

He had eighteen bullets left for the .308.

His work now was pure.

•

That evening he lay on the bed in Room 14 and looked at the ceiling. Paint was flaking from the cornices; and there was a dark stain from an oil-lamp that long ago burned by the bed while he burned and sweated in it. The room smelled of dampness now, or maybe it had always smelled like this and he had just never noticed before. On this bed and in this room. With sunlight in the window, shadow creeping along the wall, and that bloody painting. There had been no escape from any of it. But Boat At Rest hadn't run aground. And neither had he. Afloat, in one piece, but with no great voyage ahead.

Carl became aware of a presence in the doorway.

'Did you go somewhere?'

It was Isaac.

'Yes,' said Carl, lying on the sheetless mattress with his hands clasped behind his head.

'Did you go for a walk?'

Carl sat up. 'Yes,' he said. 'You remember Alec John?'

The boy said he did.

'Well,' continued Carl, 'he died, two years ago today, so I went to the graveyard to pay my respects.' He glanced at Isaac. 'Do you know what that means?'

Isaac said he did.

Sighing, Carl got off the bed.

'Are you going away?'

'It's not far,' said Carl, closing the window, securing the clasp. 'It's just a' – he searched for the right words, wondering how the boy might react – 'a little holiday. That's what people used to do. Take holidays from . . . themselves, sometimes.'

'Have you fallen out with Mum again?'

'You could say that.'

'So, you're going back to the other house.'

Carl nodded.

'Oh,' said Isaac.

'It's not far,' Carl repeated, and smiled. 'It's where Alec John used to stay. He gave me his house. Do you remember?'

For a split-second Isaac looked utterly dejected. 'All right,' he said, brightening in a flicker, fizzing from the doorway and down the stairs, whooping, 'I remember, I remembeeerrr ...'

Carl went down the hallway to room seven, and sat on the bed for a spell.

They'd been doomed, him and Simone, from the outset. Instead of all the preliminaries, like getting to know each other and living together, they had gone straight to pregnancy. Hardly an ideal beginning. They had never learned to be a couple, just the two of them, so being parents was just too difficult.

He picked up his bag, feeling the radiator for warmth, and went downstairs.

Oh well.

In the residents' lounge, George and Isaac had their game visors on and rifles at the ready. Sound effects – squawks and explosions and barked orders – boomed from the wall-speakers.

Carl left them to their mission and went on one of his own, to the kitchen.

'Is she asleep already?'

Simone was at the sink. 'She was tired today. Her last teeth are coming through and she didn't sleep well, not that you'd know anything about that.'

Carl shifted in the doorway, saying nothing.

Stains were scrubbed, angrily, from clothes, and the seconds ticked by.

'Where did you get the soap?'

There was no emotion in Simone's voice. 'A bottle of shampoo from the Mackays. A Christmas present they never used.'

In the sink, his daughter's clothes were taking a damn good

pounding. There were things that could be said, if he wasn't careful. He almost said them.

'Go on then – piss off.'

'I'll be round tomorrow,' said Carl. 'If that's okay.'

'Don't put yourself out on our account.'

Simone threw a rinsed-out sleepsuit down on the draining board. Who was this irritant taking up space in her kitchen?

'Oh, just go away, will you? Clear off to your pied-à-terre and do us all a favour, you self-centred arsehole. Off you go and enjoy your nice easy life.'

She stormed into the garden with an armful of wet washing.

'I'll see you tomorrow then?'

'Don't bother,' shouted Simone from the hall. 'We're emigrating, on the next luxury cruise-liner.'

Outside, the day was dry, though there was a haze of low cloud wisping over the headland and round Heron Point as Carl walked along the road. He said hello to the folk who were out. Some days he could pass the boatyard and not even think about the guys in there. Today wasn't one of those days. Part of him enjoyed glaring at Cutler or Casper whenever he encountered them, but the place was silent today. No swearing and shouting, no grinder shrieking against metal. The biofuel generator wasn't even running. He heard footsteps, light ones, hurrying behind him.

'Hey.'

'Hey,' replied Isaac.

Carl apologised for not saying goodbye, and they walked on.

'You were busy killing aliens with your granddad. Does your mum know you've gone out?'

Isaac nodded. 'It isn't aliens – it's World at War: Battle of the Bulge. I'm the Germans, and I'm winning.'

'Really?'

'Yeah. I'm in Ostend now.' He added casually, 'It's a town in Belgium.'

'Ostend, wow. That's bad news.'

'But I'm winning!'

'Well, in that case, Gruppenführer, go for it.'

'I am winning . . . but Granddad's visor is going fuzzy.'

'Oh. Can you not swap about to make it fairer?'

Isaac screwed his nose up. 'Nah. He gets the fuzzy one.'

They walked on, around the head of the bay, talking and laughing about nothing in particular. Climbing the track to the house, Carl stopped and picked something up off the ground.

'Here's your knife, you wally.' He handed the penknife keyring to Isaac.

'Brilliant,' said the boy, delighted. 'We couldn't see it the last time.'

'Sometimes you can't see things for looking. Then one day, when you aren't looking, you find stuff that was lost.'

Isaac opened the two-inch long blade and tested it. 'It's blunt. Will you sharpen it?'

Carl shook his head. 'It's sharp enough.'

'Will it cut into a deer, through the ribs, into the guts?'

'No,' said Carl, smiling. 'Not that you'd want to cut through ribs anyway, and not into the guts.'

They walked up towards the house.

'Will you show me?'

'Show you what?'

'How to cut through the ribs.'

'What is it with ribs? Leave the ribs alone.'

'You don't cut the ribs?'

'No.'

'Will you show me?'

'Show you what?'

'Where to cut into a deer and how to do all the cutting. You can still do all the shooting, if you like.'

'Gee, thanks. But you shall go to Oxford, young man, get

debagged, sent down, then take over at the old man's firm. No cutting ribs for you.'

'Oxford – is that a place?'

Carl stopped walking. A lump came to his throat as he looked down at the boy. Oxford may as well be on the moon; the outside world was just a concept, unknowable and unreachable. In all probability, Isaac would reach adulthood before having the chance to get within ten miles of Oxford, or any other town for that matter. The thought stuck in Carl's throat.

'Yes,' he said quietly, picking up the pace. 'It is a place.'

There were kids down at the shoreline, one of them carrying what looked like an oil drum.

'It's Pavel and Kieran,' said Isaac. 'We're building a raft.' He bolted back down the track, then turned and shouted, 'Bye.'

Carl raised his hand.

Sometimes he got the yearning for a cup of tea or coffee. People had become dependent on caffeine, of course, and some couldn't function until they'd had at least two strong hits in the morning; it would be nice, though, just to get a little lift every now and again. Thinking about good coffee, he looked up the slope to Ben Bronach, and along the dark line of the basalt ridge, and tried not to think about what he had to do today. Isaac was keen to learn, so that was good. Carl went inside. Maybe he should trim his beard.

Sometimes his heart felt so heavy, like it would sink down into his boots. Sometimes the old pain would take hold, and a black awareness would come over him. But he made it pass. It took effort, to shake off the mood, though these episodes were rare now. As memory pressed down on him, he would rise to meet it, strong enough to bear the weight. There was no reason why he couldn't exist like this way for years. It was possible. It could be done. For so long as he could imagine an end, when something better would arrive, he could go on without too much trouble now that he had acquired a way of living.

But that kind of thinking only took him to one place.

Clearly, it wasn't going to work out with Simone; it was Alec John's anniversary; the Oxford thing with Isaac; and earlier on he had thought about Howard and Eric; it was a witch's brew of all the negative stuff. But then there was his daughter's smile of recognition, her soft, pink feet in the cot as she slept; that was like mainlining an antidote to misery.

That kind of thinking took him to a better place. If she were lucky, she would grow up with all the good stuff that a parent can give to a child. Everything grows from inheritance.

There was also a carcass in the cold store, waiting to be butchered, some weed in the house, and a 1,000-film cine-viewer that someone had lent him. The accessible half of Inverlair estate could do without him for one afternoon.

In the upstairs bedroom he'd already prepared the essentials: fresh white sheet pinned flat to the wall; heavy dark blankets pinned and taped to the window, a big comfy chair, and speakers in the corner. Now all he needed was the stepladder from the shed.

A problem presented itself.

The best position for the ladder and cine-viewer was behind the comfy chair and against the bedroom door. The door would have to be closed to keep out the light from the landing, and that meant that if anyone came into the house they'd come upstairs, maybe without him hearing, and barge into the room. In all likelihood, the bedroom door would push the ladder over, and that was not good news for the cine-viewer sitting on top of it.

Simple: he'd lock the front and back doors so that no one could come in.

He fetched the metal folding ladder from the shed. As he turned the key in the front door of the house, he stopped. Locking a door. Turning a key. Keeping something out.

'What the hell,' he muttered, turning the key. He needed some time to himself, some harmless escapism.

He bounded upstairs for three hours and eight minutes of *The Fall of the Roman Empire*, Alec Guinness giving good stony Stoic Emperor. Marcus Aurelius wasn't afraid, if you believed his *Meditations*. Maybe the fear simply hadn't made it into print, and all that the emperor left to posterity was a carefully polished image of himself, redacted in all the right places and purged of all weakness.

About two hours into the film, Carl heard a banging from downstairs, at the front door. He groaned.

'Pause,' he said. A two-metre wide, impossibly beautiful Sophia Loren froze.

'Coming,' he shouted. 'No need to break the bloody door down.'

He should remain stoic, accept with equanimity the fact that his film, his time off, impulsively taken, had been interrupted.

It was Old Bead-patch himself at the door, and Carl felt his anxiety return.

'Didn't see you head up to the ridge today,' said Terry. 'Thought you might be ill or something.'

'No,' said Carl, leaning on the door jamb. 'Christopher Plummer is up to no good.'

Terry looked blank.

'Watching an old swords-and-sandals classic. *The Fall of the Roman Empire*. Alec Guinness plays ...'

'. . . Marcus Aurelius,' said Terry. 'The passing of an empire. It happens. Now we can start again.'

Carl nodded, one hand on the door handle, closer to closing it than to throwing it wide in welcome. That much he made obvious.

Today, Terry's eye patch was orange with green beads. Earlier in the week it was white beads on black. Maybe the guy really had made one for every day of the year, like Carl had heard. He'd have come from the village hall, where his young flock gathered to hear their shaman's drug-fuelled gibberish.

'Will I leave you in peace, brother?'

'No offence – but yes,' said Carl, keeping his voice level, his

287

eyes scanning the horizon. 'It's been ages since I've had a bit of downtime. Absolutely ages.'

'That's not a problem,' said Terry. 'Are you staying here now?'

Carl ignored Terry's sudden grin. 'For a while, at least.' He bristled, feeling he should downplay the significance of his living arrangements. 'We'll see what happens.'

Jess waddled up to the door, nudging Carl's legs.

'Right,' said Terry, his wry amusement fading. He nodded. He understood how things were, finally, after weeks of trying to inveigle his way back into Carl's company. Or recruit him to the cause, as Carl suspected. 'I'll catch you later then.'

'Sure. I'll be along at some point.'

As Terry walked back down the track, Carl felt relief, and a surge of guilt. A line had been drawn, and it was obvious now on which side each belonged. Unless he apologised for not inviting Terry in, and quickly, the insult would harden into a barrier, a permanent separation. Perhaps that's as it should be. Best leave Terry to his sordid little arrangement with Hendrik and Maganda, and his new religion that involved Gemma and a few other kids, and peyote, although Carl didn't know for sure what was going on. He didn't want to. Bizarre what some people would believe when there was nothing left to believe in. Carl ruffled Jess's ear, then closed the door. He turned the key in the lock.

'Do I hear a sigh of relief?'

Jess padded through to the kitchen and flopped into her basket.

'Not impressed with my hospitality, huh?'

The dog gave a deep, shuddering sigh, and curled up, cosy by the warm stove. Carl poured a glass of water and took it upstairs to his private Odeon. Sophia was still looking worried, eyes and mouth wide. Marrying Omar Sharif's wily provincial potentate, rather than Stephen Boyd's dashing but irrelevant Roman noble, was clearly giving her trouble. Film might be a world of illusion, but good ones had a grain of truth, emotional or otherwise. It was great to lose yourself in films. To forget. That's what good ones did: they flowed over you like flashing water and made you forget who you were and the fact you were watching a film. Is there anything wrong with that? Is there any harm in forgetting, for a while, your space and place in time, even now?

Carl stuffed a few more leaves into his pipe and lit up. There was only a splash of fuel in the lighter he'd found in the shed. Chuckling, he thought of the folk in the village who were trying to invent matches by taking the phosphorus out of old lifeboat flares. If they couldn't perfect their technique soon, maybe they'd all have to wait for lightning to strike a tree. Thank you, great Sky God, for sending us the power to cook and stay warm. Prometheus, or whoever, could then set off with a flaming torch, running from house to house.

'Play,' said Carl.

Sophia Loren took up where she left off. King Omar Sharif was given the girl. No contest, when there's an empire at stake. After a while he shouted, 'Pause.' He sat there, listening to the sound of the house, another man's house, settling around him. He chose some Led Zep from Alec John's old CD collection and thrashed about on the drumkit for a spell.

With the thick end of the drumstick, he crashed down, hard, on the cymbal. It bucked and gonged and quivered into silence. He sat there, the drumsticks in his hands, another man's house around him and around that, another world that wasn't his world. No matter how long he stayed here he would always feel that he belonged somewhere else, that he was an outsider. He had tried hard, and had learned a new set of rules; he had focused on his daughter, on Isaac. Kids are so impressionable, they absorb habits and opinion, distill it all into their own poison, their own love. It was all transmitted, from one mind to another. It was all in the implanting.

Carl got up and went downstairs to the living room. In a black bin bag, taken from Terry's uncle's house, he found what he was looking for. He smoothed the old newspaper – yellow and brittle round the edges – flat on the drop-leaf table. His first big story. His first front-pager. Just short of nineteen years ago.

'And over the top he went, fighting the good fight,' he muttered to himself. Jess came shuffling through from the kitchen; he reached down and scratched behind her ear, the way she liked. From the drawer of the dark sideboard he took a pair of scissors.

'Just in case you take me for granted,' he said to the dog, cutting round the article. 'At any point I could resume my flourishing career – so watch out.'

The dog breathed heavily at his feet, unconcerned.

Out in the shed, he found a box of Alec John's stuff and, in it, an empty frame. Two years ago the photo of the long-dead Mrs Stoddart had been placed tenderly between her husband's folded hands. They were together, not far from Howard. In place of the photo he positioned the newspaper article, clicked the glass back into the frame, and hung it on the same hook in the porch. Through the window he saw two kids, a boy and a girl, running up the track from the main road. Carl went outside to wait for them and noticed Isaac ambling some way behind his friends, whacking bramble bushes with a stick, trying to look cool.

'If there's a party at mine,' said Carl, 'then nobody invited me.'

'It's Gary,' said the girl, out of breath. 'He's run into the redzone and hasn't come back.'

'What?' Carl started off down the path then stopped, turned and ran back into the house. 'What did he do that for?'

Isaac ran after him. 'Is it Pulse Day today?'

'Um, no, I don't know,' said Carl, rummaging through the side pockets of his rucksack. 'What was that stupid fu—' He shook his head. In truth, he had no idea when the next pulse in the delta signal was due. He used to know, used to have it marked out months ahead on the calendar. He found what he was looking for.

Car key. Deltameter.

Bolting from the house, he ran down the track to the stone byre. Both doors were flung apart and he whipped the dustsheet from Howard's car. Every so often he turned the engine over, checked the tyres. If the thing started now, when he actually needed it, he could be at the roadblock in seconds.

'Get in.'

Isaac and the other two got in. As she climbed into the back seat, Carl saw a fresh scar on the girl's pale upper arm.

'You kids still playing your stupid games, cutting yourselves open?'

The girl, Katy, pulled down her sleeve and glared at him. Carl jumped in. The car started first time.

'We don't need the safety chips any more. Gary said adults had put them in to keep us prisoners,' she said. 'Gary said we should cut them out.' Then she shouted, 'You made the world the way it is, fucking adults, so don't start giving me advice and telling me what to do.'

Carl said nothing. The car swung out of the old byre and bounced down the rough stony track. They sped off up the main road the mile or so to the roadblock.

'Maybe Gary won't be giving any more orders,' he muttered, eyeing the sullen girl in the rear-view mirror. He wondered if Isaac had asked for his own chip to be cut out. The idea made him queasy.

At the line of red boulders Carl stopped the car and they all got out. There was no sign of Gary, or the rest of the kids. Carl took out the deltameter.

Nothing.

He searched through the log, worked out when the last pulse should have been. Two days from now. Not today.

Not today.

'There they are,' shouted Katy, pointing down towards the sand dunes. 'Gary's with the rest.'

With the older boy in tow, she climbed the roadside fence and ran off down the field of thistles and reeds to join their friends, past the quarry. Oblivious to Gary and his pals, Carl looked along the stretch of road to where it curved round a long sloping outcrop of rock and grass, before vanishing inland among the hills. Gary and the other kids, jumping and running in the sand dunes, were at least 500 metres inside the redzone.

Carl stood, motionless and quiet, and looked down the road.

'What's wrong?'

It took him a few moments to register that Isaac was still beside him. 'In you get,' he said quietly.

There was not a flicker on the deltameter, right through the sinusoidal spectrum. If it had been Pulse Day, the signal would be back to full strength by now. But there was no sign of it. He licked his trembling lips.

'What's wrong?'

Carl put the car in gear and drove, taking it slow, doing 20mph, checking the deltameter as he went. At 30mph he reached the curve in the road; he checked the mileometer. A mile. Around the curve and on and down through a long dip and across a short bridge by more pine trees and then uphill again.

He stopped the car.

Two miles. Nothing. They were a lot closer to the Russian capsule now. The thick silver torpedo had not moved from its spot on the hillside for over two years, though the parachute had long been shredded by the wind. But that was a good half-mile away from the road. The capsule would keep. There was another village, he remembered, a few miles away.

Carl smiled, though tears were welling in his eyes. He coughed, blinked, his voice hoarse and uncertain. Solid plates were shifting again, as they always must, grinding towards a new alignment. Change was here. The wall of silence had opened, by how much it was hard to say.

With his left hand he reached over and grabbed the passenger seat belt, swept it around Isaac, and clicked it into place.

'What's that for?'

'So you don't get hurt.'

'Where are we going?'

'I don't know,' whispered Carl. He put the car into gear again and drove on, his hands shaking. 'We'll find something useful, and bring it back.'

Acknowledgements

I would like to thank Joan Michael, David Robinson, Jan Rutherford, Alison Rae and Neville Moir. You all played your part in making this possible. I am grateful.

M.F.R.

Also by Lucy Powrie

The Paper & Hearts Society
The Paper & Hearts Society: Read with Pride

the PAPER & Hearts SOCIETY

BOOKISHLY ever AFTER

BOOK THREE

LUCY POWRIE

Hodder

HODDER CHILDREN'S BOOKS

First published in Great Britain in 2021
by Hodder and Stoughton

1 3 5 7 9 10 8 6 4 2

A CIP catalogue record for this book is available from the British Library.

ISBN 978 1 44494 927 8

Typeset in Wilke LT by Hewer Text UK Ltd, Edinburgh
Printed and bound in Great Britain by Clays Ltd, Elcograf S.p.A.

The paper and board used in this book are made
from wood from responsible sources.

Hodder Children's Books
An imprint of
Hachette Children's Group
Part of Hodder and Stoughton
Carmelite House
50 Victoria Embankment
London EC4Y 0DZ

An Hachette UK Company

www.hachette.co.uk
www.hachettechildrens.co.uk

For Tabby, Olivia, Cassie, Henry and Ed
– thank you for changing my life.

And for Polly Lyall Grant – the best editor I could
have wished for. Your kindness, friendship and
belief in me has meant the world. I will always
be grateful to you for showing me the way.

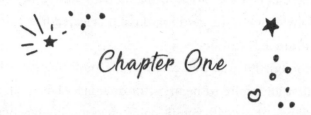

Chapter One

'Dearly beloved, we are gathered here today to celebrate the life of our treasured friend, Edward Eastfield,' Olivia Santos said, reading from the piece of paper in her hand. She wiped a solitary tear from her eye. 'Ed tragically passed away in a horrific murder incident not long ago, the circumstances of which remain a mystery to this very day. He will be sadly missed.'

The aforementioned Edward Eastfield had to stifle the giggle bubbling up in his chest. From his position in the makeshift cardboard coffin, placed on two dining room chairs, he couldn't see the others' reactions, but he had no trouble imagining them: each of their faces would be a picture of intense mourning. He kept as still as possible, so as not to dispel the illusion of his death, biting the inside of his cheek to force the laugh away.

Olivia went on. 'In life, Ed was a good friend, who cared deeply about animals, Shakespeare and doughnuts. He was kind, compassionate—'

'And handsome,' Ed murmured with barely moving lips. Olivia kicked the cardboard coffin, cleared her throat and continued with her eulogy.

Although Ed was dedicated to his performance – he did, after all, aspire to be an actor one day – lying still in a cardboard box with white paint covering his face was getting boring now. Turns out, being a fake murder victim wasn't fun when your only scene direction was playing dead.

Ed was beginning to regret allowing Olivia to host the latest meeting of their book club, The Paper & Hearts Society, at his house. He'd agreed on one condition: that she let him be the victim in her Agatha-Christie-inspired murder mystery party. How long was he going to have to lie like this? Olivia had already taken over the whole house, planting clues for their friends to investigate, and now she was taking an age!

He opened one eye and moved his head a millimetre, so he could get a better view of the proceedings. Olivia was standing in front of the coffin, and Ed's other friends were facing her, lined up on the opposite side of the living room, all dressed in black. Henry looked even taller than usual in his smart, dapper suit, his hair falling into his eyes. Tabby, Henry's girlfriend, and Ed's best friend in the entire world, stood with her arm in Henry's, her dress floating down to her knees. Finally, there was Cassie,

Olivia's girlfriend, who had gone to town on her outfit – a luscious velvet suit and her signature Dr Martens floral boots.

Oh, Cassie, how nice of you to use my death as a fashion statement! Ed thought, because he couldn't say it out loud without ruining the effect.

Olivia had drawn the curtains to create a sombre mood but had vetoed his idea of lighting Gothic candles. Apparently she didn't trust him around flames. *Probably wise, to be fair.*

'I'm sure you'll all agree with me that such a tragic loss deserves to be avenged – and that the murderer *must* be discovered,' Olivia was saying, leading up to her dramatic murder-mystery declaration. 'We cannot let our friend die in vain.'

Fair play, Ed thought. *Olivia doesn't have terrible acting skills after all. Maybe she should join me when I rise to acting stardom. We could play Romeo and Juliet at the Globe!!*

'OWWWWW!' Suddenly, Ed was seized by a cramp in his leg so painful that it felt as if his calf muscle was going to explode. He sat up so quickly that the dining room chairs gave way, and he fell out of the cardboard box, landing on the floor. Everything went dark as the box followed him to the ground, covering Ed from head to toe.

'Ohmigod!' he heard Tabby shout, and footsteps approaching, but he was focused on getting out from underneath the box, while clutching his leg, which throbbed unlike anything else he'd ever felt before.

Maybe I'm actually dying. Maybe my fake funeral will become my real funeral! This is SO PAINFUL. Owwwwwwwwwwwww!

Olivia, always on theme, cried out, 'He's alive! Ed's alive! It's a miracle!'

Ed was far from impressed to hear Cassie's wheezing laugh, as if she was trying to hold it in but couldn't.

'Are you all right?' Henry called over the commotion. He sprang forward and knelt down to Ed's level, but Ed was writhing around too much to help, ignoring Henry's question.

'Oh.' Just as quickly as it had arrived, the cramp had disappeared. 'Cramp,' he explained weakly. Now he felt deflated – there was only a shadow of pain to prove it had ever been there, as well as a small ache where he'd landed on his side. 'Don't worry about me. I'll live.'

His friends said nothing as Ed scratched his head and gazed at their sceptical faces.

Olivia looked put out. 'On that note . . . Well, you've kind of ruined the dead part, Ed, but there is still a mystery to solve.'

'I can pretend to be dead again?' he said, and put his hand up to his forehead, faking a backwards swoon to the floor.

Tabby poked him with her foot and this time he didn't hide his grin. Suddenly, he had an amazing idea. An idea so good that he had to act on it *immediately*.

'Be right back,' Ed said, and raced out of the living room.

Olivia called after him, 'No snooping in any of the rooms!'

He went into the hallway and then up the stairs to the airing cupboard at the end of the landing. He rummaged around, coming up trumps when he found an old, slightly yellowed bed sheet screwed up into a ball at the back. *Mum won't need it, will she?* Ed dashed across the landing to the bathroom, where he cut two circles out of the fabric. And then . . . the finishing touch! In the cabinet was a fake moustache he'd bought for a practical joke a few months ago. It was *perfect*.

He tossed the bed sheet over his head, adjusting it so he could see through the two holes he'd made, and then peeled off the sticky backing of the moustache, attaching it underneath the eyeholes.

'OoOoOoooO!' he said to the mirror over the sink, waving his arms about. It was brilliant – ghostlike but not terrifying! The Paper & Hearts Society were going to love it.

Not wanting to keep his friends waiting any longer, he rushed down the stairs, picking the bed sheet up so he didn't trip over it. But the eyeholes kept slipping down past his nose, so it was quite hard to see. He jumped down the last step and turned towards the living room.

'OW!' Ed said, not for the first time today, rubbing his side where he'd bumped into someone. 'Mind my precious being!' He tugged the back of the sheet so that the eyeholes migrated upwards and he could see.

'Mind where *you're* going!' Cassie sounded very disgruntled.

'It's me,' he hissed. 'It's Ed. I'm a ghost.'

'Who else would it be, Ed? Don't be ridiculous. Only you would do something this weird.'

Ed smoothed his moustache. 'Just because you're jealous, there's no need to be mean.'

'Yes, I'm very jealous of your costume.' Cassie crossed her velveted-sleeved arms over her chest. 'Because I too would like to wander around underneath an old sheet.' She laughed. 'Come on, we're waiting for you.'

As Cassie turned away to go back into the living room, Ed saw his opportunity.

'GHOST HUG!' he cried, throwing his arms around her neck and enveloping her tightly in the sheet. 'You can't see me, but I'm right here!'

'Get off!' Cassie cried, but she was laughing and spun him around. To get her own back, she started tickling him, which she knew he couldn't stand.

Ed let go instantly, howling in a mixture of delight and pain ... *Was it pain?* He couldn't quite tell as he tried to dart out of the way.

'Are you two coming back anytime soon?' Olivia arrived in the doorway, her hands on her hips. She stopped as she took in the sight of Ed. 'Um ... Ed? Why do you have a moustache stuck on a sheet over your head?'

'GHOST ATTACK!' he shouted and chased her back into the living room. He was enjoying himself. *When I get cast in* Hamlet *one day at the Globe Theatre, I can say that my future was decided in this very moment, with my best friends.*

'What are you wearing?' Tabby laughed.

'OoOoOoO!' he replied.

They all cracked up.

'Wow,' Henry said, 'for a moment there, I thought I saw a ghost!'

'You did,' Ed replied. 'And a *very* realistic one at that. I think this is a trend that could catch on.'

Olivia clapped her hands for attention, as if she were their school teacher and they were her pupils. Ed couldn't help noticing she was in her element. The ultimate organised Olivia was coming out today.

'Okay, Paper & Hearts Society! We had a break, but now listen up! We are here to solve a murder, and we only have limited time to crack the case. You'll have to go through room after room as a group looking for clues, but be warned: red herrings may throw you off the scent. It's up to you to figure out the murder weapon, the conditions in which the murder took place and who did it. And just remember' – Olivia lowered her voice, and looked at each of them in turn – 'that the murderer could be walking among us even now.'

'OoOoO.' Ed couldn't resist.

While the others laughed, Cassie rolled her eyes, although Ed was sure she too was laughing deep down. Olivia handed each of them their own magnifying glass and a 'clues sheet' to write down their theories and make a note of anything important.

'Just so you know, I'm going to cheat by looking at yours,' Ed said to Tabby, leaning his head on her shoulder.

She patted the top of his head through the bed sheet. 'Ghosts are allowed to cheat now and again. Nobody can see them anyway, right?'

'Result!'

They made their way through to the kitchen. It was usually fairly tidy, but Olivia had worked her magic and turned it into a room fit for any budding detective. The stone work surfaces were covered in flour, there was jam

– or blood? – in splodges on the centre island, and yellow crime-scene tape was covering the back door and stuck to the kitchen cupboards.

'How should we do this, then?' Cassie asked, surveying the room. 'Split up and cover the room individually, or move as a group?'

'You know I love working with you, Cassie,' Ed teased. 'We're such an excellent team – how could you even think of tearing up our bond? No, let's work together – remember, one of you murdered me. I want to keep a close eye on all of you.' He made his eyes wide through the holes in the sheet and pointed at each of his friends in turn.

Ed picked up a pen from a little pot on the side so he could keep track of everything. He studied his clues sheet while Cassie, Henry and Tabby looked around, trying to discern where to start.

'Why don't we begin with working out what these letters mean?' Ed said, nodding over to the work surface, where he'd noticed individual letters written in the flour. 'It might be some kind of word puzzle that we need to solve – what do you think?'

Cassie and Tabby moved over to get a closer look, while Olivia and Henry stood off to the side, giving the others room to work.

'Good plan, Ghost Man,' Cassie said. 'Livs, couldn't you have made things a bit . . . tidier?'

'It wasn't me! It was the murderer!' Olivia protested.

'Well, the murderer can clean up afterwards or my mum will go mad,' Ed said.

'Z,' Tabby read, then, 'X, W, F, D, C, A . . . Cassie, is that a B or an E?'

Ed was jotting everything down, making sure he heard correctly; he didn't want to be the one who messed up.

Cassie bent her head down to inspect the letter and then nodded. 'It's a B. And that's the final one, too. We've got all the others.'

'Great,' Tabby said.

'So what does it mean?' Henry said, looking over Ed's shoulder – which he could easily do, being the tallest. 'Is it an anagram?'

'Sorry to break it to you, but I don't know any words with both "Z" and "X" in them,' Ed said with a shrug. 'And I don't think we have time to look through the entire dictionary.'

'Maybe we'll find more letters as we go on,' Tabby suggested, as she looked around the rest of the kitchen, pulling drawers out and removing things from the fridge.

Ed really was hoping the murderer – and the investigators – would help to tidy up afterwards.

'Can't you give us a clue?' Ed asked.

Olivia looked very pleased with herself. 'A clue? Why would I be able to give you a clue? It's a murder investigation – I haven't had anything to do with it!'

'Paw prints!' Tabby exclaimed. 'Look, leading out to the garden. Do you see?'

There was a trail from the fridge to the back door, which looked like a sort of powdery brown texture, like mud.

'Well, Ed does have a cat,' Henry said with a shrug. 'Mrs Simpkins might have left those – it's not necessarily a clue. I think we need to take a look at the jam – sorry, *blood* – over here.'

'If you're sure that's a better bet . . .' Tabby conceded.

Ed pushed Henry and Tabby out of the way and made for the jam blood himself. But he was disappointed to find that there were no more letters – only punctuation symbols like exclamation points and squiggly question marks.

'A red herring,' he suggested, with one more stroke of his moustache.

'Damn it, I really thought we'd get more letters,' Tabby said.

Meanwhile, Cassie had pulled away the tape covering the back door and tugged it open, brushing down her suit afterwards. 'After you, sleuths,' she said, waving a hand through the door. 'We'll have to check everywhere, just in case we miss something.'

Tabby went first, then Henry, then Cassie and Olivia, and finally Ed.

11

The cool January air hit them keenly, and Ed was suddenly glad of his ghost sheet, wrapping it around himself tightly. His garden had a small patio area at the front, which neither he nor his mum bothered with. There was a neglected, peeling set of wooden garden chairs, and weeds poked through the cracks of the paving. Down two concrete steps was the overgrown lawn, edged by flower borders that had seen better days, but in the middle of the lawn was Ed's pride and joy: the hammock where he would curl up with Mrs Simpkins and a good book in the summer.

Today, though, they didn't make it down to the lawn because on the patio was a drawn outline of a body, arms and legs sprawled out at strange angles.

Ed clutched hold of Tabby's shoulder. 'It's just too much for me, seeing the place I took my last, shaky breath. Please, Tabby, hold on to me – I think I might faint.'

He added a wobble to his voice for extra measure, and she grinned at him. 'Don't worry, you can faint against me and I'll catch you. We wouldn't want Ghost Ed injuring himself – or messing up his very fine moustache.'

Ed stroked the fake moustache, exaggerating the movement. 'I knew you were taking a shine to it! Maybe I should grow one. What do you think, Tabitha?'

'Good luck with that,' Cassie interrupted, putting her arm around Ed's sheeted shoulder. 'Don't you remember when you tried before? It was an epic fail.'

Olivia clapped her hands together again. 'No distractions now! You have to focus! The murderer is among us! They could strike again! We have to keep searching!'

'I thought the afterlife was supposed to be relaxing,' Ed said. 'So far, it's just like real life. Where are the cats? Where is my own personal library? Why is Shakespeare not here?! I thought he would at least turn up for me.'

'Aha!' Tabby said, reaching down into a stone flowerpot. She pulled out a cat collar and held it between her fingers in the air. There was a tuft of cat fur clinging to it, and a brown-paper label that definitely wasn't usually hanging on Mrs Simpkins's collar. But Mrs Simpkins's glow-in-the-dark collar it definitely was . . .

'Did you rip my cat's fur?' Ed hissed to Olivia. 'If you've harmed Mrs Simpkins, I swear—'

'Of course not!' she objected. 'What do you take me for?'

'A murderer, perhaps?' he suggested.

'Trust *no one*,' Olivia hissed back, sounding as menacing and ominous as possible.

Tabby passed around the collar so they could all get a look at it. Ed had seen the collar many times before, but he tried to scrutinise it for clues, anything that might be out of place.

He turned over the brown-paper label. 'More letters!' He transferred them on to the clues sheet, just underneath the original set they'd found.

GUKVUTSQ

'Is it just a super weird anagram, or did we decide against that?' Cassie asked.

'It must mean something,' Tabby said, taking the sheet from Ed. 'Have you tried writing them out differently?'

'Like mixing and matching them?' Ed said.

'Maybe it's all just one big red herring,' Henry said. 'Maybe the letters are trying to throw us off the scent – they look like a load of nonsense to me. Let's search somewhere else.'

Cassie bent down to get a closer look at the body outline on the ground. 'Don't you think it's weird how its left hand is touching its neck?'

'It?!' Ed protested. 'That's me you're talking about! I'm not an "it"!'

'You're ruining my train of thought,' Cassie said with a roll of her eyes. 'Tabby, you found the cat collar discarded in a bush, as if whoever put it there didn't want it to be found.'

'Well, I definitely didn't put it there.' Ed shrugged. 'So what – it's the murder weapon? The cat collar?'

A hush descended as Cassie said in an ominous tone,

'The evidence suggests that Ed was strangled with that very cat collar. Think about it! If this is where the body was found, it seems too much of a coincidence. We can't ignore a clue or think anything is too inconsequential. Isn't that right, Livs?'

Olivia was keeping tight-lipped but a proud little smile formed on her face. Cassie must be on the right track.

'Strangled with a cat collar,' Tabby said with a shudder. 'What a way to go.'

'Although I have no memory of it, it was extremely traumatic for me,' Ed said. 'But what about this bunch of letters?' The clues sheet was really beginning to bug him – he just couldn't work out what any of it meant!

'Let's continue our tour and see if you can piece this all together. We haven't looked upstairs yet,' Olivia said.

Ed took double the time to get up there because he was determined to scrutinise all the furniture on the way with his magnifying glass. In the end, Cassie had to drag him along to hurry him up, which only made him stare at *her* through the glass.

Once upstairs, they found more crime-scene tape covering Ed's bedroom door. There was something hanging from the lampshade on the high ceiling of the landing, too. How Olivia had managed to get it up there, Ed had no idea, but now their problem was how to get it down. It *must* be a clue.

'Go on!' he said to Tabby, kneeling down. 'Climb on to my shoulders and you'll be able to reach!'

Tabby clambered on and Ed grabbed hold of her legs to keep her steady.

'To the left! No, to the right a bit! No, go forward – I can't get there!'

He resisted the temptation to burst into laughter. He was sure they looked like a slapstick comedy duo, not serious crime detectives.

'How the hell did you get this up here, Livs?' Tabby moaned, trying to reach for it but not helped by Ed, who couldn't easily keep his balance.

'No, Ed! Just forward a little bit more! There! No, not quite like that!'

'Don't look at me,' Olivia said, 'I had nothing to do with it. It was the murderer, obviously.'

Ed could feel Tabby slipping from his back. Quickly, he bent down so she wouldn't have as far to fall, and she landed on her bottom, sighing loudly as she came away empty-handed.

Henry eventually reached up, pushed his weight into his feet, and jumped, grabbing hold of the paper. It revealed yet more letters.

POLM

Ed helped Tabby up before looking at the piece of paper. 'Molp?' he said. 'Lopm? Olmp? It can't be an anagram! This makes no sense whatsoever!'

'Try writing them out alphabetically,' Cassie suggested. 'That's an awful lot of letters now, and none of them are repeated. Maybe we should be looking at which letters are missing, not the ones we have!' He did as he was told – he usually did when it was Cassie asking. She was bossy, but he loved her nonetheless.

'E,' he said aloud, running his finger along the line. 'H, N . . .'

'We need to see if there's more clues that will make it clearer,' Cassie said, and they all moved into Ed's bedroom.

Tabby was rifling through the room, looking high and low for further clues. Ed watched out of the corner of his eye as she bent down and pulled something out from under his bed.

'Ed, you don't keep a diary, do you?' Tabby asked, holding a ring-bound notebook in her hand.

'Not one like that,' he said. 'Mine is fluffy and pink with a heart-shaped padlock on it, obviously.'

Seemingly satisfied that she wasn't going to uncover his deepest, darkest secrets, Tabby flicked the pages open and skimmed through.

'Ohmigod,' she said, her mouth hanging open. 'I can't

read it out loud – you'll have to read it yourselves for the full effect.'

I didn't mean to do it - it just kind of happened. I had seen Ed with Mrs Simpkins, how much he loved her - and this wave of jealousy overtook me. The next minute, he was dead. I panicked and tried to think about how I could make myself seem innocent. I had to frame the cat.

Ed burst out laughing. 'Olivia, this is amazing!' he hooted. 'Mrs Simpkins, the cat murderer!'

'Don't ruin the fun, Ed!' she giggled. 'This is the murder confession! I didn't have anything to do with it.'

'But you did,' Cassie said, scratching her head. 'Is this why you asked us for a sample of our handwriting last week? It's not mine.'

'And it's not Livs because hers is much neater,' Ed said.

He continued tracing the letters on the clue sheet, finding a missing 'R' and then finally a missing 'Y'. It all clicked into place.

Tabby raised her eyebrows. 'And it's not my handwriting.'

Ed, Tabby and Cassie – as well as Olivia, even though she had orchestrated it – turned in one synchronised line to stare at Henry.

Who let out a long, evil laugh, throwing his head back and grinning wildly.

'You?!' Ed said. 'You murdered me?! That is so, so, so wicked! You're my *friend*. How could you?!'

Henry shrugged. 'What can I say, Ed? I was just jealous of your relationship with Mrs Simpkins. I wanted her all to myself. The easiest way to sever your bond was to . . .'

'To sever my life! Right! You're asking for this!' And with that, Ed took off his ghost sheet, reattached the moustache to his face and charged towards Henry, tackling him to the ground.

Henry tried to push him off, but he was laughing too hard, and then Olivia decided to join in too. Before long there was a Paper-&-Hearts-Society-shaped giggling pyramid of bodies on Ed's bedroom floor. 'Your toe is in my ear, Ed!' Cassie protested, and Olivia took the opportunity to steal his beloved moustache.

Once Henry managed to push them off, they all retired to the living room, where Ed passed the biscuit tin around and they drank tea, spread out on the sofas. Ed took the prime spot in his armchair.

'Are you nervous to start work tomorrow, Ed?' Tabby asked, brushing biscuit crumbs from her dress. She took a sip of the extremely milky tea Ed always poked fun at her for and put her head on Henry's shoulder. 'I still can't believe you get to work in Woolf and Wilde. An *actual* bookshop! You're so lucky.'

Ed had been so caught up in the Paper & Hearts Society meeting that he'd hardly thought about it, but now it was at the forefront of his mind. He couldn't believe that tomorrow would be his first day working at Woolf and Wilde, their favourite bookshop in town.

His interview had been before Christmas, and he'd been *so* nervous. He'd searched for part-time jobs for months and hadn't been successful – not at two of the local supermarkets, at the pet shop down the road and in the clothes shops he would have been terrible working at anyway. Then he'd seen the advert for a new Woolf and Wilde bookseller while he'd been browsing for books one day, and he knew he wanted the job more than anything else in the world. And he had been determined to do anything to get it. Maybe that was what they'd seen in him when he'd interviewed – despite the nerves, despite the fact that every single book title had slipped his mind, he'd let his passion for books shine through, and they'd rung him up the next week to welcome him to the team.

Ed shrugged. 'Nervous? What have I got to be nervous about? I'm going to be the best bookseller the world has ever seen! Trust me, by this time next year, I'll be so successful they'll have to rename the shop Woolf, Wilde and *Ed*.'

'It does have a certain ring to it.' Olivia laughed, sipping her tea, the other hand resting on Cassie's knee next to her.

'Don't get ahead of yourself,' Cassie said sarcastically. 'You're not exactly in the same league as Virginia Woolf or Oscar Wilde, are you?'

Ed scoffed. 'Maybe they're not in *my* league. Ever thought of that? They'd have begged me to be their friends.'

Olivia, giggling, said, 'Too bad they're both dead. But then again, you were dead an hour ago and look at you now!'

Ed put his tea on the coffee table and threw his arms in the air. 'A fine figure of health!' he declared. 'It is indeed a miracle! I am immortal!'

'Not for long if you carry on being irritating,' Cassie said.

Ed dunked a chocolate biscuit in his tea. 'Maybe I am a little nervous for tomorrow,' he admitted.

'You?' Olivia said, clapping him on the back. 'Nervous?! Never!'

Henry laughed. 'Good joke, Ed.'

He smiled weakly. 'Ha ha, yep, you're right. Just joking. I had you fooled there, didn't I?'

He wasn't fooling himself, though. He had definite butterflies in his stomach. But if The Paper & Hearts

Society didn't think he should be nervous, he'd have to just not be nervous, or at least not show it.

If Ed could pretend to be a ghost, he could act his way into being a bookseller. How hard could it be?

Olivia: Good luck Ed!!!! You are going to rock it today!

Henry: You've got this, pal. You're going to be amazing.

Cassie: you'll be alright i guess 😌

Cassie: (good luck!)

Tabby: We believe in you!!! :D :D

Chapter Two

It was way too early to be awake on a Saturday morning, but Ed was excited. Today was THE DAY.

I'm going to be a bookseller, baby!

'Oh, my little boy, off into the scary world of work! Let me take your photo – go on, please,' Mum fussed, jumping up from the sofa as Ed walked into the living room. In the doorway, she licked her thumb and attempted to smooth down his eyebrows, but he was having none of it. He sidestepped out of her way, leaving her pouting.

Ed and his mum shared the same thick blonde hair with a slight wave to it and the same smattering of freckles covered their pale white skin, but Mum was shorter than Ed, only just reaching his shoulders, and he'd inherited his dad's murky green eyes, instead of her bright blue ones.

'Don't be nervous now, don't be nervous at all, you have nothing to be worried about,' Mum chattered away, running a hand through her short hair. 'It's okay if you're nervous, you just have to remember to breathe and make sure any nerves don't cloud your judgement. They are completely natural! And it's fine if you make mistakes – it's also completely normal and to be expected – just don't panic, you'll be great. This isn't at all like the time you took that group on a tour of the school during the open evening and locked those poor people in the store cupboard. You've matured a lot since then.'

'Mum!' Ed said.

'What?'

'If I wasn't nervous before, I am now!'

'It will all be fine. What's the worst that could happen?'

Not helping!! Ed had visions of accidentally burning the bookshop down, or pulling down an entire heavy bookcase on top of an unsuspecting customer, leaving just their arms and legs poking out from the corners, like the patio crime scene yesterday.

But that will not happen because I have NO REASON TO BE NERVOUS. Ed Eastfield, nervous? IMPOSSIBLE. He blocked from his mind the fact that he'd chewed all his fingernails, and had slathered on what felt like an entire roll of deodorant to disguise the fact that he was sweating profusely.

He reversed back out into the hallway to put his coat on and found Mrs Simpkins sitting at the bottom of the staircase, her tail flicking back and forth. He leant down, picked her up in his arms as if she were a baby and cooed,

'Now, don't miss your father too much while I'm gone! I'm going out to earn a living so you can keep eating your premium cat food!'

She meowed, and he gave her an extra-squeezy hug before putting her back on the ground, where she trotted off down the hall towards her food bowl.

He picked up his car keys from their place: a gold dish in the shape of a pineapple, on the sideboard.

'Be good! Sell lots of books!' Mum said.

'See you later,' Ed said, putting his coat on. He wrapped one arm loosely around his mum and kissed the crown of her head. And with that, it was time to head off to his new life.

BOOKSELLING, HERE I COME!

See, absolutely no nerves. I am cool, composed and ready to face all the challenges of selling books. Nerves?! What even are they? They have no place here! I'm absolutely fine! Everything's great!

Ed had been told to wait in the staffroom of Woolf and Wilde until Dinah, the owner, came back. It was a small room on the second level of the bookshop, with just enough space for a battered purple leather sofa, an armchair, a sink and a fridge. He couldn't face sitting down, so he paced the floor until he thought he might end up wearing a thin patch in the old grey carpet. Earlier, when he'd followed Dinah up the winding flight of stairs and noticed the STAFF ONLY sign on the door, he couldn't help but grin, thinking, *This is actually happening. To me.*

At half-eight in the morning he had stood opposite Dinah, with her dangly earrings, curly dyed reddish hair and long flowy skirt, nodding along as she'd mentioned the fire exits and who was on shift, when he'd get his breaks and what they had on that day.

Please don't let there be any actual fires where I have to use the fire exits because this is a lot of information to take in. He'd tried to remain composed as he'd said, 'All sounds cool to me!'

And then Dinah had left Ed to put his stuff away. He'd breathed a sigh of relief and thought, *Ohmigod, can I really do this? Am I really here?*

Ed noted the view from the aged windows: an alley at the back of the shop, where no customer could see, and he saw why – a dustbin from the restaurant next door overflowed with rubbish. It was in stark contrast to the view from the cafe downstairs, looking out on the pretty old cobbled streets of the Dorset town, giving customers the warm fuzzy feeling of being in a period drama.

There's something about this view that lessens the magic of Woolf and Wilde slightly, he thought. *I feel as if I've lifted the curtain back and can see the puppet master pulling the strings.* It was like the time his mum had informed Ed the Easter Bunny wasn't real; it was just too much to take in.

The sun shifted and Ed caught his reflection in the window, hoping to see his appearance smart and ready . . . and that was when he noticed the cat hairs over his new black shirt, the one he'd spent half an hour trying to iron the creases out of the night before.

He rushed over to the mirror hanging above the fireplace, furiously rubbing at the shirt as he went, but it was no use. He'd have to pick every hair off individually, and that would take ages! Time he most definitely didn't have.

Mrs Simpkins, I love you, but why did you have to do this to me? And THIS MORNING, of all mornings!

The door swung open and Dinah came back in, flashing her kind, broad smile. She walked over to the kettle and flicked the switch. 'Everything okay, Ed?'

Don't look at the cat hair. Do NOT look at the cat hair. Nothing to see here. Ed spun around slowly and leant against the fireplace. If he were a hero in a movie, he would look suave. But Ed was no movie hero, and Dinah would surely see through him.

'Everything's hunky-dory,' Ed said, as he surreptitiously picked off another cat hair. 'Absolutely fine. Fantastic.'

Dinah poured the water into a mug that read: 'World's Best Bookseller'. 'Now, don't forget, if you need something or are unsure of anything, all you have to do is ask; there's always someone around to help.' She let out a small chuckle and raised the mug to her mouth, before changing her mind and putting it down on the side. 'I remember my first day as a bookseller. I misheard a customer and found them a book about *sex and relationships* instead of the *history of saxophones* that they were looking for. You should have seen this man's face. He went all tight-lipped and as red as my hair is now. Funnily enough, I never saw him in the shop after that.'

Ed's feeble laugh led to an awkward silence.

'Right then. No need to worry – you'll do great,' Dinah said, 'and as it's Saturday, we'll give you someone to shadow. Hannah's the same age as you, so hopefully you'll get along. She'll be here in a minute. Just let her know when she comes in.'

Dinah picked her mug back up. 'Good luck, Ed, and welcome to the team!' The door shut behind her and, once again, Ed was left on his own to wonder who Hannah was and whether he'd survive the day.

Pep talk time. *You have got this, Edward. If Shakespeare can write at least forty plays and some of the best sonnets in the English language, as well as being an all-round awesome human being, then you can spend a day working in a bookshop. Sell those books! Organise those shelves! You have got this!*

He was giving the air a fist punch just once for good measure when the door burst open and a girl with long chestnut-coloured hair appeared. Her cheeks were rosy red from the winter cold, and she wore a fluffy grey coat and a black backpack.

Make a good impression. Turn that charm on! Think about what Shakespeare would do.

'Hey!' he said. 'The name's Ed.' *Why did I say it like that?! I'm not James bleeding Bond.* 'I mean, I'm Ed. It's Hannah, right?'

She nodded and inched forward a step, before turning towards the lockers. Hesitantly, she said, 'Who are you?'

'I'm the new bookseller – I think I'm supposed to be shadowing you today? Like I said, I'm Ed. Or Edward. Eddie. But probably just Ed.'

ED. PLEASE. He had to stop this habit of just blurting out whatever came to mind. Most people found it funny, but she ... Well, she wasn't laughing.

There was a moment of silence, which she filled by blinking.

Oh, great. Look what I've done. 'Just Ed is fine. Ignore everything else I said.' He'd probably been really confusing. What if she now decided to call him Eddie? He wasn't exactly keen on that as a nickname.

He followed her gaze to the window but couldn't see what she was looking at. 'Dinah said . . .' Had he got the wrong end of the stick? But Dinah *had* said it, he was sure. 'You are Hannah, aren't you?'

'Yeah, I'm Hannah.' She took another step forward, removing her backpack and unbuttoning her coat, and pushing her stuff inside one of the lockers. Hannah turned back to face him, and he noticed she was moving her fingers frantically, thumb to index finger, then middle finger, then the next, then her little finger, and back to the index again. Over and over.

'Um. Are you okay with me shadowing you? I'm sure if we spoke to Dinah . . . I mean, I don't want to put you to any trouble!' Ed gave a small laugh. 'Not that I'm any trouble, not really, although my friends would probably disagree with me on that one.'

He expected her to laugh in return. Nothing. If Cassie were here right now, she'd tell him to shut up and he'd deserve it. His mouth had clearly disengaged from his brain. 'Are you okay?'

Hannah frowned. 'I just *really* hate change and this is . . . Well, this is very unexpected. Dinah didn't warn me. But it's *fine.*'

It didn't look fine, but Ed wasn't sure what to say.

'Come on. We need to get started. We haven't got all day.' She turned and headed to leave the staffroom, opening the door and swinging it back so he had time to follow. 'There are only ten minutes until the shop opens and I've . . . we've . . . got a lot to do.'

Ed followed Hannah down the stairs. 'It's nice to meet you,' he said, close at her heels. 'I'm really excited to start work because I'm always here as a customer anyway – I couldn't believe it when I was told I got the job. How long have you worked here?'

'Just under a year,' Hannah replied, and ushered Ed to go through to the shop floor first.

'That's cool. So what do you like reading? I remember during the interview I completely blanked when I was asked that question.' He laughed. 'Every single book slipped my mind.'

Hannah didn't reply – hopefully not because she didn't want to chat, but because Dinah had spotted them and was waving them over to the counter. 'Ah, I see you two have met! It's nice to have some young faces around here.'

Ed winked. 'I have been told that I have a baby face. It must be my smooth skin and cute looks.'

Dinah laughed. 'Ha, I like it!' Ed loved making people laugh; being liked gave him instant gratification. He waited for Hannah to join in the joke, but she didn't.

After a silence, Dinah spoke. 'All set then, Hannah?'

'All set,' she replied, gathering some books and heading off in the direction of the History section.

Ed followed, thinking he would have his work cut out if he was going to bring Hannah on side.

First job of the day: sorting out the morning's orders and shelving the new books in the right place.

'So you do it like this,' Hannah said, taking a piece of paper from the first box. Ed looked at it, over her shoulder, but moved back a couple of steps when he felt her bristle. He hadn't realised he was that close. 'We get a new order in almost every morning – some are to restock the shelves, others are books that customers have requested – so we first need to separate the customer orders from the list. See, this little mark here.'

Hannah ran a finger down the list of book titles, ISBN numbers and figures, and stopped on an asterisk. She continued, 'This means a customer has requested it, so if you put those books to one side, you can contact them after we've gone through the list to let them know their order has arrived.' She took out a highlighter from a pot on the desk. 'Highlight those on the page, so they stand out clearly.'

'Right, I think I can manage that,' Ed said. He grinned. *How difficult could it be?* Maybe this really would be the relaxing bookshop job he'd always dreamt of.

'Once you know a book on the list is included in the delivery, mark it with a tick. We've had some missing before, so it's important to check everything.'

I am a cool, capable bookseller. Shakespeare would be able to do it. 'Righty-o! It's easy, really, isn't it? Just a few books and a bit of highlighting.'

Hannah raised her eyebrows. 'In that case, can I leave you to it . . . Ben?'

Ben?!?! 'It's Ed,' he said. It was only two letters! Was this some kind of psychological tactic to test him?

There was an awkward silence. 'Oh, right. Well, will you be okay?'

'Uh, yeah, I'll be fine.' He laughed breezily after her as she walked away. 'I'll be done in no time!'

But as soon as she walked away, Ed's mind went blank. Dinah was busy behind the till, so he couldn't ask her for help. He started taking the books out of the boxes, stacking them to look at the titles on the spines. There were thickly bound history books, bright and beautiful children's picture books, and titles that suggested swoony romances and epic adventures, fictional detectives and walks through nature. Books Ed had heard of and ones he hadn't, covers that shined with foil and others that felt waxy to the touch. He was having great fun.

Once the box was empty, he looked at the two heaving piles he'd made that took over a large section of the desk, leaving barely enough room for highlighting the order invoice.

Right then ... First book. And then the next, and then the next, and the next ... *Wait. I swear I haven't checked this one off, so why have I highlighted it? Does that mean I've missed one out? Argh! Oh great, Hannah's coming over.*

'How are you getting on?' she said.

'Super-duper! All fabulous over here!'

Hannah looked at the page, and as she did, Ed realised it looked as if the pink highlighter had thrown up on it. 'There surely can't be that many customer orders,' Hannah said. 'There are never that many.'

'Uh ... orders?' Ed said. *I knew I was going overboard on the highlighting!*

'You're supposed to tick off the books that are present, and only highlight the customer orders.' Her face looked pinched. 'Tick, and then highlight. Not scribble over the entire thing. This is ... this is a mess!'

'So I guess it's not all fabulous after all?'

'It's fine, it's fine,' Hannah said, but it clearly wasn't. She picked up the pen and hastily scribbled asterisks next to the customer orders. 'Just ... just ... I'll put the books away, and you can start calling the customers using the order list.'

Ed didn't mind phone calls but he knew that, without any instruction, he'd make another mistake. Or waffle on and on at the poor customer at the other end of the line. 'What should I say?'

'Oh, good point.' Hannah reached for a Post-it Note pad tucked under the counter. Grabbing a pen, she scribbled away, and then ripped it off, handing it to him.

Hello, this is Ed from Woolf and Wilde. I'm calling to inform you that the book you ordered is ready to collect ... Have a good day!

After Hannah left to go back to her task, Ed realised he had forgotten to ask where the phone was. Dinah headed past him to the door, turned over the sign to read 'OPEN' and then positioned herself back behind the counter. 'Everything okay, Ed?'

'Yep,' he said. 'Um, could I possibly have the phone? I don't know where it is.'

'Ah, Hannah got you on the phone, did she?' Dinah chuckled, and reached behind her to remove the shop phone from its cradle. Before handing it over, she teased, 'Now, Ed, do you know how to use one of these? It's very simple: all you do is press the numbers you want and wait for it to ring. Then you speak into the little microphone bit here. Got it?'

Ed grinned, moving behind the counter. 'Could you explain that to me again?'

Dinah laughed, handing him the phone. 'Just teasing,' she said. 'You've got this, I can tell.'

He braced himself, reading over Hannah's script. Short but precise, that was what he had to be. Not too charming, just professional. With maybe a fabulous Ed flourish thrown in for good measure.

He dialled the first number on the order list and listened to the call tone. Then it clicked and there was a scrambling noise on the other end. Ed paused, waiting for the right time to speak.

'HELLO?'

'Hello?' Ed's brain froze and he had to get it back on track. He looked down at the script on the Post-It Note. 'Um, this is Ed from Woolf and Wilde here. I just wanted to inform you that your book has arrived and is ready to collect.'

'Who?' the voice squawked down the speaker. 'Who's there? What do you want? I'm not accepting nobody selling me stuff over the phone!'

'No, no, Mrs Lomax, I said, it's *Woolf and Wilde here* to tell you that your book order has arrived!'

'What? What was that? Who did you say you were? I'm telling you now . . . I've already got everything you're selling! I'm not interested!'

'It's *Woolf and Wilde. WOOLF AND WILDE!*'

Next to him, behind the counter, Dinah was holding her stomach, doubled over from laughing so hard.

There was no response for a second. And then, 'Woolf and Wilde? Well, why didn't you just say so? There's no need to shout now.'

I did say so!!!!!! And I was only shouting because you were shouting!

Ed raised his voice to land somewhere between his original tone and the shouting. 'I'm sorry to bother you, Mrs Lomax, but the book you ordered has arrived and it's ready to pick up.'

'Book? What book? I haven't ordered any book.'

He took a glance at the title and lowered his voice again. 'It's ... it's a book on, well, on incontinence in the elderly.'

'What? What? Speak up, boy!'

'It's a book on INCONTINENCE IN THE ELDERLY!'

Tears streamed down Dinah's face as she gave Ed two thumbs up. A customer had just walked in and he could see the horror on the woman's face – the first thing that she'd heard was Ed screaming about incontinence. He put his hand up as if to say sorry while he continued the phone call.

'I haven't ordered no book on incontinence – don't be so impertinent, boy!'

Oh great. From somewhere, he remembered the phrase *the customer is always right*, even though all he wanted to do was protest.

'Oh, well, okay then, Mrs Lomax,' he said, clawing back control. 'I must have got the wrong number. I'm sorry to have bothered you. Have a good day!'

'GOODBYE.'

The line went dead. Slowly, Ed lowered the phone from his ear.

'Wow,' he said to Dinah, feeling as if he'd worked up a serious sweat, though he tried to style it out with a shrug and a giggle. 'That was . . .'

'Oh, Ed, you've made my day. No need to explain,' Dinah laughed, patting him on the back. 'Count it as your initiation. We've all been there with Mrs Lomax. And not to worry – her son will be in to collect the book for her by the end of the day, you mark my words. It happens every time.'

But Hannah saw the order list. If she knew Mrs Lomax was an awkward customer, why didn't she warn me? Has she got it in for me?

Ed was snapped out of the thought by Dinah's voice. 'Don't worry. Finish the other calls – I promise they won't be half so awful – and then go on upstairs. Not long until the readalong. You'll love it! The kids get so excited.'

Ed took a deep breath and dialled the second number. Dinah was right – the others weren't so bad – some customers were even so nice that Ed had to ease himself out of the conversation because they wanted to chat for longer. It restored his faith in the Woolf and Wilde customer base.

*

39

The readalong was held in the children's book nook on the first floor, a circular room with rabbit-warren-like corridors lined with books leading to the main hub. At the front, Hannah was sitting on a small stool wearing rabbit ears to match the picture book in her hand: *Guess How Much I Love You*.

'Did you finish the calls?' she asked, looking up.

Ed took a deep breath as he approached her. 'Why didn't you tell me how awkward Mrs Lomax was to speak to on the phone?'

She shrugged. 'She can be grumpy. It wasn't a problem, was it?'

Through gritted teeth, he responded, 'No. Not a problem at all.'

The children and their guardians started filing in. The adults ushered their kids to sit on the beanbags or rocket-shaped carpet, while they took seats on the benches at the side. Ed squeezed on the end of one of the rows.

He watched in amazement as Hannah transformed from aloof teenager into animated bookseller. She knew most of the kids by name, asking if they were comfortable and smiling at their guardians, before starting to read in an enthusiastic voice.

It was as if she were a completely different person. Then it hit him. *Oh god, it's me. I'm the problem.*

For the rest of his shift, Ed tried to put it to the back of his mind. But he was rattled. *Why doesn't Hannah like me? Oh god. Does Dinah secretly feel the same? It's only my first shift and already I'm more fail than fantastic. OH GREAT.*

Tabby: How was your first day, Ed?

Ed: It was marvellous! You know, I really think I've got the hang of this bookselling stuff. It's like I've worked there all my life!

Tabby: <3

Cassie: did you ask about the friends and family discount? you can fix us up. i have an expensive graphic novel habit that needs supporting

Ed: Not yet. I can't have them thinking that's the only reason I'm working there!! I'm a PROFESSIONAL don't you know

Olivia: When's your next shift?!

Ed: Wednesday! I only have college in the afternoon so I can work the morning, CAN'T WAIT!

Olivia sent a photo.

Olivia: Here's a picture of my very long wish list so if you'd like to get me a bookish present, Ed, you can!!

Tabby: . . . Does that list take up the entire length of your desk, Livs?!

Olivia: Quite possibly!

Ed: I'm going out to EARN MONEY not SPEND IT on all of you, WOW

Chapter Three

'GO, MRS SIMPKINS, GO! I BELIEVE IN YOU!'

The living room door swung open and Mum stared at Ed, rubbing at her face as if she had a headache. 'Is there a reason you're shouting so loudly? I can hear you upstairs through my headphones.'

'Yes, there is a very good reason, actually,' he replied, holding up the cat treats and catnip in his hands. 'I'm teaching Mrs Simpkins to fetch her mouse toy and bring it back to me. It's taken all morning, and I've had to rearrange the living room so she has more space, but look, she's finally getting it.'

To demonstrate, he threw the toy and Mrs Simpkins ran after it. 'You can do it! You can do it! That's it! You've got the hang of it now!'

'Great, but can you . . . not shout?'

Ed thought Mum was being a little unfair. It wasn't shouting; it was extreme enthusiasm! When it came to Mrs Simpkins, he couldn't dampen his enthusiasm. She was his baby! How could he not be like a proud parent on sports day?

'You won't be saying that when I'm a world-class cat trainer,' he said. 'You'll be more encouraging then.'

Although, now he thought about it, maybe he was being slightly loud in his excitement.

'Did you ring your dad like you said you would?'

Ah. Way to put a dampener on my good mood, Mum. He was reminded of the fact that his dad had hardly ever cheered him on at any of *his* sports days.

Ed huffed. 'Yeah, I did it last night,' he said, 'but he didn't answer.' The agreement between him and Mum was that Ed would visit his dad every three weeks for the weekend, so long as Ed could keep living with Mum the rest of the time. It had been that way since he'd started college, and before that it had been every fortnight. Ed also had to call Dad once a week, which was proving difficult when there was no reply. At least he'd see Dad this Saturday.

'Oh, I'm sure he was just busy.' Mum didn't sound convinced, though. She never spoke a bad word against Ed's dad because she said he was no longer any of her business. After all, they had been divorced for five years. Still, she always sounded weary when they talked about him.

Yeah, right. He's just conveniently busy and not picking up the phone on the one night we agreed to speak to each other.

44

Mum perched on the sofa arm. 'You can always try again later. You might just have picked a bad time yesterday.'

No, because the football will be on and it is always more important.

Mum sighed and made to move away. 'Do you want me to make you a cup of tea?'

'No, thanks.'

Ed suddenly felt very grumpy. He didn't feel much like continuing with Mrs Simpkins's training now. She stared up at him from across the room with her large, beady eyes, her tail flicking from side to side as she waited impatiently for her next treat. It was all right for her – she had an excellent cat father who never ignored her or pretended she didn't exist. In fact, if anything, she had the opposite problem – Ed never left her alone! It wasn't as if Ed's dad ignored all his children. Whenever his older brother Daniel wasn't at university, he stayed at their dad's. Just thinking about it made Ed's throat tighten up and his eyes start to sting. He headed for Mrs Simpkins to give her a gigantic squeezy hug.

His phone started buzzing from the sofa. An incoming FaceTime call. 'Tabby' read the caller ID, showing a picture of her Ed had taken seconds after he'd jumped out on her in a bookshop. He laughed every time he saw her scared, surprised face.

'Hey!' Tabby said, smiling enthusiastically and waving from her gran's living room, in front of the window that looked over the front garden. Her hair was pushed up in a messy bun. 'I thought it would be easier to call than message. How are you?'

'Hi!' Ed replied, alongside a meow from Mrs Simpkins. He chucked her a treat from the little bag. 'Oh, you know me. I'm all right.' He mustered a smile, which wasn't so tricky now he was talking to Tabby. He always found something to smile about when she was around. 'Just keeping on keeping on!'

'Sure?'

'Absolutely! Hey, is that a new pair of curtains behind you?' Not the best deflection, but maybe Tabby wouldn't realise.

'Ummm . . .' She craned her neck to get a better look. 'Nope? Maybe it's just this light?'

'Ah, that's what it must be! Maybe I need to turn the brightness up on my phone.' He pretended to fiddle about with the screen, but Tabby probably wouldn't be able to see anyway.

'So, how does it really feel to be working at Woolf and Wilde?' Tabby asked. 'And don't give me nonsense about how you're the best bookseller in the world and it's *your* dream come true, plus *their* dream come true to be working with you. Honest answers, please!'

Ed grinned, fighting the urge to ask Tabby if he was really that predictable. He knew he was. 'It's obviously their dream to work with me; that is an honest answer! But yes,' he said, 'it *is* a dream come true, but there's also so much to *learn*. Bookselling isn't just about selling a few books to customers. Take Dinah, the owner, for example. She has the most extensive knowledge of books! She rivals Olivia, and I didn't think that was possible. I feel as if I've got a *lot* of catching up to do if I'm ever going to be good at it.'

'You've only had one shift,' Tabby consoled him. 'You can't be expected to know everything.'

'Pfft, I do know everything!' he joked. 'I am the world's cleverest person! There is not a piece of knowledge I don't know.'

Tabby laughed. 'You already knew that I knew that about you. If you know everything, that is.'

'But . . . I felt a bit of a nuisance,' he admitted. 'There's this other girl that works there. Hannah. I don't think she likes me.'

'Everyone likes you,' Tabby replied unhelpfully. 'What's not to like?'

A LOT, he thought but didn't voice. He bet Hannah had gone home and told all her friends about how annoying and incompetent he was. They'd have a right laugh, especially about how after the readalong he'd led a customer to the history of war section instead of the gardening section, and made up for it by trying to convince them that a book on the Crimean War would be suitable for their aunt's birthday, until Hannah had intervened.

'I don't know,' Ed said. 'Maybe I'm just making it seem bigger in my mind than it really is.'

'Probably,' she said, moving to the sofa where she blew him a kiss through the screen. 'You've just got to have more faith in yourself.' Tabby gazed at something off-camera. 'Here she is!'

Another voice came over the phone. 'Who is it? Is that my Ed? Ed, is that you?' Tabby budged up on the sofa and Gran sat down next to her, snatching the phone from her granddaughter.

Ed wasn't close to his grandparents, and he loved Tabby's grandmother so much that she was 'Gran' to him too. Anyway, Tabby was like a sister to him, so it definitely counted. Seeing them together on the screen made his heart feel full; he was so lucky to have them in his life.

'Hi, Gran!' Ed said, catching the huge grin appearing on his face in the tiny box in the corner of the screen. 'You're looking exceedingly beautiful today.'

He watched as she blushed. 'Oh, stop it, you charmer. How are you doing, my love? Tabby says you started your new job! We'll have to pop in and see you when you're working, won't we, Tabby dear?'

'You can visit whenever you like and I'll give you a personal tour,' Ed said, switching on the charm even more than usual. Gran brought out the best in him. 'It's tiring, but I think I'll do just fine. Wait. No, no, Mrs Simpkins! Stop!'

The phone fell out of his hands as Mrs Simpkins jumped on the sofa and began to attack the bag of cat treats he still had in his hand. 'Stop!' he cried out. 'Tabby, Gran, I'm going to have to go! Mrs Simpkins, no! You can't have any more!'

But Mrs Simpkins wouldn't stop, even when Ed stood up. She scampered around his feet, rubbing up against his legs, always one step ahead of Ed's movements. 'No! Don't do that!' he kept saying, as Tabby's and Gran's laughter sputtered out of the phone speaker. 'It's not funny! She's trying to attack me!'

But it worked. He chucked the bag of treats to the floor, just to get Mrs Simpkins away from him. He was out of breath, in slight shock and feeling much distressed. Meanwhile, Mrs Simpkins looked as if she was having the time of her life. She hoovered up the treats as quickly as she could possibly manage, meowing in gratitude.

'That cat is the boss of you,' Gran said, just as Ed collapsed back on to the sofa.

'Oh, I know,' Ed said. 'Trust me, I know.'

Mrs Simpkins knew it, too.

Ed: Hi Dad, I've tried to ring you but you don't seem to be
answering? Hope everything's okay? See you Saturday?

Read 13:34

Chapter Four

Ed was prepared to be the best bookseller the world had ever seen as he entered Woolf and Wilde for shift number two. He was dressed in a newly washed and ironed shirt that wasn't covered in cat hairs, and armed with the lunch his mum had made him – because she still insisted on treating him as if he was at primary school. He was taking his duties very seriously and was determined not to show himself up. Or to irritate Hannah any more than he had done during his first day.

He really couldn't bear it if he didn't make some progress with her today. *I just want to be friends!! Or not even friends – just friendly acquaintances would do me fine!* He was like one of those annoying dogs who kept batting you with their paw if you ignored them.

Dinah instructed Ed and Hannah to man the till together. Ed noticed Hannah had rolled up the sleeves of her polka dot dress, even though it was cold inside the bookshop today. She explained what each button on the till did, as well as the ones he definitely shouldn't press. Hannah's hair was tied back in a way that faintly resembled a pineapple, but it really suited her, Ed thought – not that he'd risk telling her.

After she'd finished instructing him on the till, they waited for a customer so he could practise. But every customer that came in only browsed and then left. And every time they did, a blast of cold air would shoot through the door and Ed and Hannah were left in icy silence.

Ed couldn't stand it any longer. 'What's your favourite book?' he asked as Hannah clicked around on the computer.

'What?' She looked up quickly, surprised he'd spoken.

'What's your favourite book?' he repeated.

'Oh,' she said, 'I like Eva Ibbotson's books.'

He expected her to say something more about Eva Ibbotson, but instead she started showing him the database page, moving the cursor over one of the fields. 'So you type the book title in here,' she said, 'but you don't need to use words like "the" and "and". So if you were searching for *Charlie and the Chocolate Factory*, for example, you could just put "Charlie Chocolate". It will come up whatever.'

'Okay, got it,' he said. 'So what do you like about this Eva Ibbotson's books?'

Hannah didn't reply.

Ah, so it's going to be like that. He ventured another comment. 'You've made me hungry by mentioning chocolate now.'

'It's not long until lunch.'

They lapsed into silence again, listening to the tinkling of coffee cups and the murmur of voices in the Woolf and Wilde cafe on the other side of the wall.

Not easily defeated, Ed tried again. 'So, how old are you?'

'Seventeen,' Hannah said. 'You ask a lot of questions, do you know that?'

That was more promising. 'And you don't ask many questions. Did you know that? I'll ask them for the both of us. Tell me five things about yourself. They can be super boring, but it's got to be five things.'

Hannah shook her head. 'I don't think so,' she said, readjusting the display on the counter. 'We have work to do.'

'Three things, then. If you haven't noticed, there aren't any customers in here.'

She raised an eyebrow as she stacked the books into neater piles. 'Will you leave me alone if I do it?'

'Yes, I promise.'

'Fine, then.' She seemed to think for a few seconds, then she held up her index finger. 'One: my name is Hannah.'

'That doesn't count!' Ed spluttered, and it was the first time he heard her laugh – light and airy, carefree – which in turn made him laugh too. Ed noticed that when she laughed, it was with her whole face: her eyes lit up, wisps of hair fell over her features and slight dimples appeared in her cheeks.

'It counts, okay?' She shook her head, as if she felt betrayed by her own laughter. 'Two: I have sixty guinea pigs. And one dog called Indiana Bones.'

'Sixty?! Sixty?!'

'Yes!'

Ed's mind was well and truly blown. That wasn't just a few pets ... she had an entire herd! 'Wooooowwww! What are they like? Do they all have names? How do you know which is which?'

Hannah scoffed. She didn't meet his eye as she answered, and instead looked around the bookshop floor, then down at her hands resting on the counter. 'It's like, well, do you know all the people you're friends with? Can you tell them apart?'

'Yes, obviously I can. We have a book club called The Paper & Hearts Society. All members have really obvious characteristics. Take Olivia, for example: she's really enthusiastic about li–'

'Cool. Well, it's the same with guinea pigs: they all look different, they have different personalities and you grow to know them as individuals. And yes, they all have names.' Her voice was kind of flat, with only a little rise and fall, but Ed liked it.

'And what about your dog, Indiana Bones? That is such a cool name!'

Hannah pinched the bridge of her nose. 'Indiana Bones is a German shepherd who wreaks havoc wherever she goes and doesn't know her own size – but I would protect her with my life.' She held her hand up. 'Right, that's enough questions now. You need to learn how to use the card reader – I swear I am not rescuing you if you charge someone one thousand pounds for a single book.'

Ed shrugged. 'At least it would mean more profits for Woolf and Wilde?'

Hannah raised an eyebrow. 'And at least you'd be off my back when you were arrested for defrauding customers.'

He hoped she didn't mean that.

As the day went on, Ed realised that Wednesday mornings in the shop were ... well, quiet, so there wasn't much opportunity to practise his newfound bookseller skills. One woman had deliberated between two books for half an hour and in the end left empty-handed, and there was an elderly man who bought an Ordnance Survey map for a hike he was about to embark on, but that was it. Ed was disappointed; it was very unlike the hustle and bustle of

Saturdays in Woolf and Wilde, and vastly different from his dreams of the exciting life of a bookseller.

Ed was hit by another blast of freezing air as the shop door flung wide open. *A customer!* A middle-aged woman wearing a thick red scarf entered, giving them a quick smile as she removed her gloves and headed upstairs.

Ed sighed and leant over to rest on the counter. 'Maybe we should guess what each customer is going to buy,' he suggested. 'And whoever gets the closest is awarded a point.'

Hannah sighed. 'Are you ever serious?'

'Now who's the one asking questions?' Ed grinned. He stood up straight and stretched out, his shoulders aching from being cooped over the counter all morning. 'I can be serious, but why would I want to be? I'd rather be funny and make people happy!'

Hannah shook her head. 'I do . . . not understand you. Like, at all. Just saying. I don't hate it, but I don't get it whatsoever and right now I feel just a little confused.'

'Because I've dazzled you with my charm?'

Hannah snorted. 'In your dreams, *Ben*.'

'I do not look like a Ben and I will die on this hill,' Ed muttered. 'This is an absolute injustice. The name is Ed!'

Hannah gave a small laugh. 'And here's an extra fact, just so you'll leave me alone: I have a blog all about bookselling.'

The woman in the scarf came back down the stairs and, just like that, their conversation was cut off. 'Excuse me, but is this the cheapest price?' She spoke as she walked towards them at the till point, holding out a huge gift edition of *A Game of Thrones* that she could barely hold in one hand.

Hannah smiled, stood up tall and took the book from the woman. She turned it over. 'The price on the back is the recommended retail price.'

Underneath the counter, Ed noticed Hannah's fingers flicking back and forth, but the customer couldn't see this.

'This price?' The woman tapped the back of the book.

'Yep, that's the one. Shall I ring it through for you?'

The woman pulled out her phone. She held it out on the buying screen of a well-known shopping website and waved it at their faces. 'I don't think I should have to pay full price when I can get the content somewhere else for far cheaper. Don't you want to keep your customers?'

Ed felt Hannah tense beside him and noticed her hand flicking movements speed up.

'I'm sorry,' he jumped in, 'but the recommended retail price is what you pay in a good independent bookshop. We'd love to be able to offer the same discounts as big online retailers, but it's just not possible.'

He wanted to add, 'Why wouldn't you want to support your local independent bookshop?!' But he didn't.

'Oh,' the woman said. 'Well, never mind then, I'll just order it online.' She left the book on the counter and with that, she flounced out.

'Wow,' Ed said. 'Was she for real?!' He deeply resented the chill she'd let in – both by opening the door and with her unbelievable behaviour.

'Oh, she was for real, all right,' Hannah said. 'She isn't the first and she certainly won't be the last customer to complain like that. I hope her book gets lost in the post.'

Ed was getting used to the unglamorous side of bookshop life – the staffroom, especially – and it wasn't so much of a surprise to learn that the job wasn't about reading books all day. He was growing quite fond of his little locker, from where he retrieved his lunchbox. He made his way over to the old sofa, which sank down so much he could have almost been sitting on the floor, and opened his lunch.

Oh great, tuna – thanks, Mum. What an attack. Why would you send me off with the stinkiest sandwiches around?

He opened the window a crack, but that didn't seem to do much except let in the cold, so he closed it again. In between taking bites, Ed checked his phone for messages.

Cassie: alright pals, i've got a good idea for a paper & hearts meeting this week. are you all free tomorrow

afternoon? i know it's short notice, but you'll just have to
deal with it.

Olivia: Ooh, a Cassie Paper & Hearts Society meeting!! I
am here for it!!!

Tabby: I was only planning on hanging out with Henry. So
we're both free!

Henry: Only! What a cheek!

Ed: LET'S DO IT!!! Let me know details Cassie and I'll pick
you up after college?

Cassie: great! well, that was easy. it's a deal, ed.

He'd devoured half the sandwich by the time Hannah
came in. He put his phone away so as not to seem
rude.

'The . . . smell . . .!' Hannah said, and backtracked into
the hallway. He could hear her steps as she went back
downstairs. *Great, Ed. You've messed up again, just when
you were getting somewhere.*

'How did you find today?' Dinah asked, as Ed was
clocking off his shift. 'Hannah said you had an awkward
customer.'

'That customer was . . . well, I haven't got the words.'

Dinah patted him on the shoulder. 'You're doing a
great job, Ed. It will feel more natural soon, I promise.'

Is it really obvious that I'm not finding it natural?

'Thanks, Dinah – see you at the weekend. Is Hannah around? I should say bye.'

'She's already gone, love,' Dinah replied, prising a book into a too-small slot on the YA shelves.

And just like that Ed was wrapping his arms around himself, preparing to be hit by the freezing cold air of the winter evening.

Ed: CASSIE WHERE ARE YOU

Tabby: We're just on our way now!

Tabby sent a photo.

Tabby: Henry and Olivia are being slow though as they're too busy arguing over who is the cutest in a picture of them in the year 6 Christmas play?? Don't ask!

Ed: We haven't left yet, don't worry! CASSIE HURRY UP. I can feel the cold in my bones standing here! (Henry was the cutest)

Henry: Thanks Ed!

Cassie: i'm waiting outside the cafeteria ed. where are you??? are you ready to take me to my paper & hearts meeting. i've been organising it for weeks, the least you can do is pick me up

Ed: I'm waiting by my car! Come and FIND ME I am NOT walking back all that way

Cassie: fine, be there in a minute

Chapter Five

'So this is where you're hiding,' Cassie said, smirking at Ed as he leant against the bonnet of his car. She was wearing a fluffy grey coat open over a pair of black corduroy dungarees, with a tote bag slung over her shoulder that displayed one of her art designs. Her bobbed black hair tickled the top of her coat collar and the look was completed with fierce red lipstick and a black flat cap.

'It's my car, Cassie. Where else would I be?'

Cassie shrugged. 'We need to go. The others will be there way before us at this rate.'

'It's far too cold to be standing around outside for ages,' Ed grumbled as he got into the driver's seat, and Cassie climbed in on the other side. He turned on the engine to switch on the heater.

'Well, some of us can't organise meetings at our house. You should have worn an extra layer for the park!' Cassie snapped, raising her feet up so that her shoes made dusty feet marks on the panelling. She rubbed the side of her face, avoiding her eye make-up. 'Sorry, that was uncalled for. It's been a busy week and I'm tired.'

'Want to talk about it?' Ed asked. They teased each other rotten, but Ed hoped that Cassie knew how much he cared, deep down. He'd realised by now that if he invited Cassie to share with him, then it was best for her to feel as if he wasn't staring or pushing her to answer. All in her own time. Over a year ago, Cassie's dad had passed away suddenly, and ever since, Cassie had been looking after her mum, who had been diagnosed with depression. Ed knew it wasn't easy on Cassie, but that she wouldn't have it any other way – she loved her mum and wouldn't hear a bad word spoken against her.

'I've got a doctor's appointment with Mum in the morning and she's getting a bit worked up. It sounds hopeful, though – last time, they said they'd try out some new medication, and she's slowly coming around to the idea of bereavement counselling. I promised I'd go with her for the first session, and it seemed to do the trick.'

Ed changed gear, and they made their way across town. 'That all sounds positive,' he said. 'How do *you* feel about it?'

With Ed's focus on the road, he felt Cassie shrug. 'I don't know. I don't want to get my hopes up, but it feels as if we're turning a corner. And she's been letting more people in the house, which is nice. There are so many aunties who want to fuss around us, and I'm enjoying all the food they bring with them.'

'Well, if you've ever got any going spare . . .'

The further into town they drove, the busier the roads were. Ed and Cassie were both silent, looking out of the window at children in school uniforms running around, people carrying shopping bags and beaming babies in buggies.

'Anyway, this is going to be the best meeting, just you wait and see,' Cassie said with a smirk.

'Oh, yeah?' was Ed's response. 'That sounds like a challenge to me.'

'Watch and learn, Ed. Watch and learn!'

Ed put his arm around the back of Cassie's seat and reverse parked in the same spot he used when he was going to work. Ed locked up, and they walked the short way down the high street, past Woolf and Wilde and the library, before crossing over to reach a paved path that led to the park's entrance.

He'd always loved the park, begging his parents to take him there after school and at the weekends as a kid. There were benches dotted around, as well as a playground with climbing frames and swings at the other end. He remembered wanting to be pushed higher and higher on the swings, so high he'd have to grip extra hard on to the metal chains, excited and scared in equal measure about flying into the sky. *Dad was pushing me . . .*

But no, Ed got choked up when he thought about that. He never, ever allowed himself to go there. Ever.

'Over here!' It was Henry, waving his long arms about wildly in their direction, standing next to their fellow members of The Paper & Hearts Society. It made Ed feel all nostalgic to see them gathered by the large oak tree, where they'd had their first ever meeting. It was good to replace difficult memories with new, happier ones.

'Hey!' Olivia walked in their direction and wrapped her arms around Cassie. Ed turned away from the PDA, as if he were a kid watching a romantic movie with his parents, embarrassed that such things happened. He often did the same when he was around Tabby and Henry. He was happy for his friends, but they were his *friends*. It grossed him out if he thought too hard about what they got up to in their spare time.

'I'm looking forward to what you've got planned,' said Tabby to Cassie, once she'd extricated herself from Olivia.

'Today we are going to be doing a cover recreation competition,' Cassie replied, addressing the whole group, chucking her tote bag on to the ground. 'I've come with lots of props, and your job is to work in pairs and think of a book cover. Then you either recreate it, or make one that's even better. Finally, you take a photo of the finished cover on your phone. Got it? Good. Because I can't be bothered to explain it again.'

Cassie picked up her tote and removed the items inside one by one, chucking them on the grass. Ed saw the glint in everyone's eyes as they each realised that they were going to have to grab things speedily, in case someone else took the prop they wanted.

'And it's first come, first served with the props, so no fighting,' Cassie said. 'You can choose whatever book jacket you want to recreate, and you'll be judged on your final photos. I want to join in too, so we'll all judge each other's.'

Ed looked around at the others, wondering who'd be best to pair with. They'd all take it seriously – but who would go the extra mile? Olivia, most likely.

But she was already sticking her tongue out at Cassie to suggest they partner with each other. And when he looked towards Tabby, she was linking arms with Henry, clearly already whispering ideas to each other.

Great. I'm not even the third wheel. I'm the useless fifth wheel that gets forgotten in the boot of a car and gathers dust and cobwebs! He dismissed the thought. His friends loved him and he had no reason to feel inadequate. It was just a fact that there were five of them and that meant splitting into pairs became basically impossible.

'Ah, Ed, you're on your own,' Henry pointed out. 'Do you want to—'

'Nope, I am perfectly fine on my own, thank you,' he said. 'I'll just have to win and then I'll be able to say I'm the single-handed champion, putting in even more work than everyone else. An excellent strategy!'

'If you're sure . . .' said Tabby.

'We haven't got that long until it starts getting dark, so I'm going to set the timer for half an hour, including time for taking the pictures,' Cassie said.

They moved to stand in their pairings – or singles, in Ed's case – each at a fair distance from Cassie's stash of props.

'Is it going to be a fight to the death? Because if so, I need you to know that I'm extremely fierce,' Ed said.

'No,' Cassie said witheringly. 'There will be no fighting to the death today.'

'*Three . . . two . . . one . . . go!*'

'Yes, Cassie!' Ed shouted, punching the air with enthusiasm.

They had enough room to spread out in the park, and Ed kept darting looks around to see what Olivia and Cassie, and Tabby and Henry were doing. Both the pairs were riffling through items – he wouldn't admit it, but Ed did feel like Cassie had a clear advantage, having known from the start exactly what she'd brought with her.

He looked down at his own selection, which didn't look up to much: a black, velvet-like material, enough that he could possibly fashion it into some kind of cloak, a stuffed cat toy, a beaded necklace and one of Cassie's small jumpers that he wouldn't be able to get on. It was starting to get really chilly in the park, and Ed considered wrapping himself in the cloak and sitting down, defeated.

'What are we going to do with this?!' Tabby said. Out of the corner of his eye, Ed saw her lift a Viking-style hat to her head, and then heard her laugh.

'Suits you, though,' Henry replied.

No distractions, Ed. Think! The task is to put our own spin on something. So which book covers do I like the most?

'No!' Olivia was attempting to shove Cassie's arms through a waistcoat. 'Livs, you agreed you were the one posing!'

'No, I didn't! Just do as I say – do you want to lose?!'

Ed knew that Olivia's desire to win was just as great, maybe even greater, than his own. Their competitive nature saw them clash in a way that nothing else ever did. *That's why we should have been paired together! Eyes on the prize, Ed. Think harder!*

Maybe he was on to something with turning the black fabric into a cloak. It would be the perfect dramatic costume and he could couple it with the stuffed cat to . . .

Yes! That's it!!! YOU GENIUS, EDWARD.

He'd had the most marvellous idea, an idea he was sure would see him crowned the champion.

He took his college exercise book from out of his rucksack and ripped a page from the back, then tore two tinier pieces of paper from this sheet, shaping them into white paper fangs. He hoped these would stick over his actual teeth without getting soggy and disintegrating.

Please stick, PLEASE stick, he silently pleaded.

Now, he just needed one more thing to complete the look.

'You don't have your red lipstick in your bag, do you, Cassie?' Ed asked.

Cassie was looking less than impressed after being forced into the waistcoat by Olivia. 'Um, yeah, why?'

'Can I borrow it?' Ed could see her reluctance and pressed his hands together in a praying motion. 'Please, please, please,' he begged. 'I'll look after it! I only need it for a few seconds, maximum.'

'Fine,' she said and, after rummaging around in her bag, threw it to him.

Ed caught it first time, and used his phone's selfie camera to look at his reflection as he drew extra thick lines of red down the sides of his mouth to his chin.

There was a half-scream, half-battle-cry from Cassie as she noticed what he was doing. 'What the hell, Ed! I am going to kill you! You're running my lipstick down. I'll never be able to use it now! Do you know how expensive it is?!'

Ed threw the lipstick back to Cassie. 'Do you have any make-up wipes?' he asked. 'Or I might be stuck like this for ever!'

'I'm not going to dignify that question with an answer,' Cassie replied. 'Right – you've got fifteen minutes left, people! Let's get a move on! And don't forget to add your name and title of the book on your pictures, please!'

As long as Ed's soggy fangs stayed on, he'd be fine. The final things to do were throw the fake cape over his shoulders, grab the cat and take the picture. He played around with draping the cloak in different ways so it would look more effective, using selfie mode to get the best angle. Then, with the hand that wasn't holding his phone up, he lifted the cat toy to his face, positioning his mouth so it looked as if Ed the vampire was trying to suck its blood.

Sorry, fake cat! I feel very bad! At least you're not Mrs Simpkins!

'No, Tabby, move back a little!' Henry said.

Ed tried not to get distracted by the others, but they weren't making it easy for him. Henry kept calling out instructions and, on his other side, Olivia was bent over laughing as she took photos of a very grumpy Cassie, then kissed her cheek to cheer her up.

After snapping a few pictures, Ed sat on the grass and looked at his camera roll. While they did look cool, he wasn't sure they were exactly right. It looked as if he was in the middle of a park dressed as a haphazard Dracula, and the cat wasn't helping matters. There was a limit to how menacing you could make sucking the blood of a fluffy toy look.

He messed about with the filters, trying to find the darkest, gloomiest and most Gothic one, then started snapping away all over again, aiming for the right look and feel. *Aha! Perfect! I really do look like Count Dracula*, he thought.

Now to add the title and author's name to the image. Ed wasn't amazing at design things. He'd never paid attention in art, nor IT, but right now he was wishing he'd done both. He downloaded a free photo-editing app and opted for basic fonts: a dripping, horror-style for '*DRACULA*' and a formal handwriting font for 'BRAM STOKER', placing the former at the top and the latter at the bottom.

'Not bad!' he said, aloud on purpose, rising to his feet. 'Be worried, foes, for I have created a masterpiece!'

'Well, at least someone has!' Tabby replied, giving a pointed look to Henry.

'Hey, ours isn't that bad!' he said, ruffling Tabby's hair.

'Yeah, okay. I believe you,' said Tabby, but she didn't sound convinced.

'Okay, time's up, folks! Gather in! Stop fiddling with your phones. Henry, I saw that! Time is *up*! Do you want to get disqualified for cheating?'

'Absolutely not, Cassie.'

'Good!' she said. 'Now, who wants to share theirs first?'

'Me, me!' Ed said, getting the picture up on his phone. 'Now, are you ready to behold my masterpiece, the greatest creation of my life?'

Not waiting for his friends to reply, he handed the phone over to Cassie, who looked at the photo and said, 'Not a poor effort!' then passed it on.

Tabby, standing next to Ed, gazed at him, then back at the phone. 'I love the look,' she said, patting his makeshift cape. 'Very Gothic. And the cover is very convincing too!'

'If you threw some sparkles over yourself, you'd look as if you'd stepped out of the pages of *Twilight*,' Olivia teased. 'Edward Cullen eat your heart out!'

'I am a very serious vampire,' Ed said, picking up the cat toy from the ground and baring his soggy fangs, 'and if you're not careful, you'll be my next victim.' He hissed for added effect.

Olivia laughed and linked her arm in Cassie's. 'Right! Why don't we share ours?' she said, grinning.

I love my weird bunch of friends. Who else would do this?

'Do we have to?' Cassie said through gritted teeth, but even Ed knew it was all part of her act. A glimmer of a smile was blowing her cover.

'Do not judge us,' Olivia prefaced, loading the photo and passing it to Ed next to her. 'We got the *worst* props possible and had to come up with something at the last minute!'

'Yeah, it was a nightmare!' Cassie agreed.

Ed wasn't entirely sure what he was meant to be looking at. On screen Cassie leant against the oak tree and one of them had drawn a speech bubble coming out of her mouth, which read, 'Can I have some more?'

'It's supposed to be *Oliver Twist*,' Olivia said, 'but really it just looks like Cassie posing for a cover shoot wearing a waistcoat, flat cap and rolled up trousers – doing a very bad job at pretending to be Oliver Twist.'

Tabby turned her head to the side to see it from a different angle, which Ed didn't think was a bad strategy. He tried the same, but it still didn't look wholly convincing.

'Well, I like it,' Henry said. 'Although ours is, of course, marginally better. Tabby, do you want to do the honours?'

'Sure, partner! Here we are, everyone.' Tabby held out her phone. 'Don't get jealous now, Ed! And thank goodness for photo timer!'

Tabby wore a plastic crown and was stood back from the lens. In front of her, Henry held up a playing card that showed the Queen of Hearts, so that it looked as if Tabby was wearing it.

'That's a brilliant optical illusion!' Olivia said. 'I would never have thought of that!'

Tabby took a little bow. 'It was all Henry's idea. Sorry for annoying you, Henry. I know it took me ages to actually stand in the right place.'

He put his arm around her. 'A bit annoying, but I'll forgive you.'

She laughed. 'Good, because I really didn't want to have to tell everyone that it was the Queen of Hearts who ruined our relationship in the end.'

Everyone laughed but Ed couldn't wait any longer. 'So who's the winner?' he asked, trying to sound casual.

'Well ...' Cassie said, 'I may have lied.' She reached down to her bag, where she pulled out five bars of chocolate. 'The winner is all of us!'

'What a cop-out!' Ed protested, dropping to the grass. 'I won that hands down!'

Cassie raised an eyebrow. 'So you don't want the chocolate?'

'I should get *all* the chocolate! I would have won if we'd voted on it! You know I would have done!'

He got to his feet and stomped his foot to prove his point, but Cassie raised her eyebrow further.

'I didn't think I'd ever see Dracula throwing a hissy fit,' Olivia said, 'but stranger things have happened!'

'It is not a hissy fit – it's an artistic dispute!'

'Well, artistic disputes don't get you chocolate,' Cassie

pointed out, 'so you'd better think carefully about stamping your foot again anytime soon.'

'Fine,' he said, 'I'll accept your decision, but I know, deep down in my heart, that I was the true winner.'

Tabby took the crown off her head and placed it, lopsided, on to Ed's. 'There you go,' she said, laughing, 'my true champion. I would have voted for you, Dracula.'

'See! Thank you, Tabby. That's why we're friends.'

The afternoon was drawing in and the temperature seemed to have plummeted further. They huddled together and ate their chocolate bars, looking back over their photos and pointing out tiny details that they were extremely proud of; in Ed's case, the accidental feature of a creepy looking crow that had flown past just as he was taking his picture.

'Thanks for a lovely meeting, Cassie,' Tabby said. 'I value these even more now we're all so busy with school and college – and work, in Ed's case.'

Cassie gave Ed a pointed look. 'All Ed values is winning.'

'I must say, all I value is chocolate right about now,' Henry said, popping another square into his mouth. 'There's nothing better.'

Ed suddenly had a brainwave. 'We need a shelfie for The Paper & Hearts Society scrapbook!' he cried, jumping up and down. He wished he had the selfie stick with him that he'd bought on their literary road trip last summer. It was likely gathering dust under his bed but would have been perfect for this moment. Instead he turned his phone on to selfie mode, and ushered everyone even closer than they already were. 'Gather in!'

He grinned, still with the lipstick blood marks on his cheeks and Tabby's crown atop his head, while the others pulled funny faces.

'Take the photo then!' Cassie moaned. 'We haven't got all day!'

Ed knew when to do what he was told; he clicked in quick succession until he got the shot he wanted. He hadn't expected today's meeting to involve so much photography, but he'd enjoyed it; it had been a great and funny creative task. Hats off to Cassie, she'd excelled herself, while staying true to her artistic talents.

Ed added a filter, so there were hearts falling over their faces. 'I'll put it on my Instagram and send it to the group chat too,' he said, and pressed 'Post'. 'Done!'

While The Paper & Hearts Society chatted away, Ed found himself looking at the recent Stories tab. His brother, Daniel, was in various photos taken last night, clubbing at university. Ed rolled his eyes, but felt his stomach drop when the last picture in the story appeared – it was of two lattes, tagged at a cafe shop in his university town centre with the caption: Cheers Dad! 👍

What the?! Ed zoomed into the picture, moving it closer to his eyes to get an even better view. Sure enough, that was Dad's tanned arm coming into shot, his chunky silver watch visible. *HAS DAD FORGOTTEN HE HAS TWO SONS? Why is he hanging out with Daniel, and not even answering my calls? Have I done something wrong?* There were those memories again, trying to force their way into his brain.

'All right?' Henry asked, clapping Ed on the back. 'You look as if you've seen a ghost.' He chuckled. 'Or a vampire!'

'Yeah,' Ed said. 'Fine.' And when it seemed Henry was going to ask again, Ed put on his best Ed smile, thinking, *How would I even put this into words?*

It suddenly got dark and the street lights by the side of the park lit up. The Paper & Hearts Society headed back through the park. Tabby asked if Ed wanted her to get him something from the ice cream parlour, Brain Freeze. For the first time possibly ever, his answer was no.

'Are you sure you're all right?' Henry asked.

'Yeah! Promise! I'd say if there was something up, wouldn't I?'

@cassie.artx: amazing time with the paper & hearts society, even if @TheIncredibleEd is trying to bite my neck here. congratulations to @WhatTabbyDid and henry for winning!

@WhatTabbyDid: CHAMPIONS!

@bookswithlivs: I love this so much!!

Mum: While you're out, can you stop by the supermarket for
me?

Mum sent a photo.

Mum: Here's the list xx

Chapter Six

I am not in the mood for this, Ed thought as he dodged around screaming, demanding kids in the supermarket. He was ready to snap.

I should be at home practising my dramatic monologue for drama tomorrow, not rushing around here. Although, come to think of it, he wasn't sure he'd be able to put his all into his performance. All Ed could think about was the fact that his dad and Daniel were together, acting as if they weren't just father and son but best friends, and Ed couldn't even get a message back from his dad.

He was barely looking where he was going as he rounded the corner down the health and beauty aisle to look for the very specific brand of shampoo Mum had asked for. But then he happened to lift his gaze and his eyes met a sight he was far from expecting to see.

Hannah.

Oh no. Ed panicked. God knew he'd manage to mess up again this time and say something stupid and it would make things even more awkward during their next shift.

He didn't know what came over him, but Ed suddenly felt sick at the thought of bumping into Hannah with his trolley full of cat food and toilet rolls. It just didn't seem right, seeing her outside the bookshop, as if they were somehow crossing a boundary or acknowledging the other's existence out of their usual environment.

He held on to the trolley and was about to do a dramatic U-turn, in the direction of the opposite aisle, when Hannah looked up. She blinked, as if she was questioning whether he was real or an apparition, and then grinned. 'Ben,' she said, with a smile that told him she definitely knew his real name by now. 'Hi. What are you doing here?'

Ed grabbed the nearest item on the shelf.

'Oh hey, Hannah!' he said, feigning nonchalance. 'I'm . . . well, I'm shopping. What are you doing here?' To demonstrate his point, he waved his hand about and gestured to the box he was holding.

Jeez, Ed. What is wrong with you?

'Are you . . . okay?' Hannah asked. She nodded towards his hand. 'Umm . . .'

Ed's gaze dropped to the box in his hands. A box of laxatives. A box of laxatives that he was gripping on to, which he had been waving around.

'They're for my . . . cat,' he said. *Why didn't I say my mum?!*

'Your cat?'

WHAT IS WRONG WITH ME? 'Yep, she has terrible constipation, so . . .' The phrase 'digging a hole' sprang to mind. 'Yeah. She's normally got excellent bowels, but, well, this morning she was meowing in agony what with all the . . . waste product in her . . . bowels. It was dreadful. She must have tummy trouble. Does your dog ever have bowel problems? Oh wait, you probably didn't come to the supermarket to chat about that, sorry.' *How many times can one person say 'bowel' in a conversation? I think I must be going for the world record.*

'Oh.'

Shut up, shut up, shut UP, Ed! She looks scared – oh my god, she looks SCARED. Because of me and my total inability to stop talking when I really do need to stop talking!

'I'm sorry about the other day,' Ed said, 'with the sandwiches. I didn't realise just how smelly they were.'

'It's fine,' Hannah said. 'It really is, but it was pretty disgusting.'

He grinned sheepishly. 'You're not wrong; imagine eating them.'

Hannah began to look as if she might be sick. First he was talking about constipation, and now he was going to make her ill with his tuna sandwich chat.

Ed threw the laxatives into his trolley. *Think of something else to say. Change the subject, Edward!*

'So, what are you doing here?'

She's shopping, Ed. What do you think *she's doing here?!*

'Buying groceries,' she said, tilting her head to the side to look at him funnily. 'Look, I'm really bad at small talk, so can you just ignore me if I say something weird?'

That worked for him. Hopefully she'd do the same and completely block the laxative chat from her mind. 'Of course,' he said. 'Are you okay?'

'I just feel bombarded in here. My brain really hates bright lights, strong smells, changes in temperature and lots of people jostling about. The supermarket is like all of those times a million.'

'*There* you are, Hannah.' An older man with white hair and a friendly face – who looked around the same age as Tabby's gran – walked towards them, shopping basket in hand. 'I was wondering where you'd got to.' He looked from Hannah to Ed. 'Is this a friend, love?'

'No, we work together,' Hannah said.

At the same time, Ed reached out a hand and said, 'Hi, I'm Ed.'

Ouch. That stung. She'd dismissed any idea of friendship between them just like that. Well, he had been waffling on about cat constipation for the last five minutes, so he couldn't fully blame her.

'This is my grandad,' Hannah explained, gesturing briefly to him and then looking at her boots, tapping one of them on the linoleum floor.

'Nice to meet you, son. So you're Hannah's colleague, eh? Bet that's a lot of fun, working together in the bookshop over in town.'

'Oh yes!' Ed said, leaning on his trolley. 'I love working at Woolf and Wilde; it's a cool job. We're very lucky.'

'Well, then . . .' Hannah said. 'We'd better get—'

Her grandad turned to her. 'Has she told you about all her guinea pigs, Ed? Hannah, have you told him? She must have told you, son – oh, it's so nice to meet one of your friends, Han.'

'I told you, Grandad,' she said quietly, rolling her eyes, 'we just work together.'

Ed tried not to flinch. 'Yeah, Hannah mentioned them. I think it's awesome! I love animals, too.'

'You'll have to come over and meet them one day,' her grandad went on. 'Oh, and, Ed, if you work in the bookshop, you must have read Hannah's wonderful bee-log? She shows me her posts sometimes; it's very good.'

Hannah's eyes were wide, but her grandad didn't seem to pick up on the fact Hannah wanted to stop the conversation. 'Blog, Grandad. It's called a blog,' she mumbled. 'And I'm sure Ed doesn't want to read it. He's got better things to do.'

'No, I'd love to!' Ed said. 'I think you started mentioning it the other day, but we were cut off.'

'See, I keep telling you, Han. People *are* interested!' Her grandad looked very pleased with himself. 'Here, son, I always keep the details with me so I can tell anyone I meet.' He reached inside his coat pocket and handed Ed a small piece of paper with a website address scribbled in biro on it.

'You can read it – it doesn't bother me,' Hannah said, meeting Ed's gaze.

Ed grinned. 'I can't wait!' He meant it sincerely too – he wanted to find out more about Hannah, get to know her better.

Ed noticed how Hannah's discomfort wasn't easing and, remembering how she'd confided in him about hating the supermarket, gestured in the opposite direction. 'It's been lovely meeting you, and so great to see you, Hannah. Do you mind if I head off? My mum's expecting me back and she'll get anxious if she doesn't hear from me. I should pay and load the boot.'

'Not at all, son,' her grandad said. 'It's always nice to meet a friend of Hannah's. It doesn't happen very often. I guess she thinks I'll embarrass her.' He chuckled to himself.

Ed smiled and lifted his hand. 'See you on Saturday, Hannah.' Ed waved, and she waved back, looking somehow totally embarrassed yet happier than when he'd originally bumped into her.

As he walked away, Ed tried not to panic as he heard her hiss, 'Grandad, you didn't need to invite him round or tell him about my blog!'

'I'm *hooommeeeee*!' Ed called as he put the shopping bags down in the hallway and shut the front door behind him. He unlaced his trainers and chucked them on to the rack, putting his car keys on the side before entering the living room.

'Where are you?!' Ed found Mum lying on the sofa, scrolling her phone in the near-dark. He flicked on another lamp. 'All right? Earth to Mum?' he said.

'Oh, sorry. Hi, Ed. Yes. Fine,' she said, running a hand through her short hair. 'Did you get everything on the list?'

'Almost – they were out of fish cakes so I got fish fingers instead,' he said. He was still processing seeing Hannah, so decided not to mention it. It wasn't relevant, was it? Of course not – they were just colleagues.

'Thanks, Ed, I appreciate it. Was the supermarket busy?'

He sat down on the opposite sofa and watched as she tried not to look at her phone lighting up every three seconds from the arm of the sofa. 'Yeah, a little, but I didn't mind. Look,' he said, 'I'll put the shopping away and then I think I'm going to find Mrs Simpkins and have an early night. Do you mind?'

'That's fine,' she said, 'you've had a busy day! I'm going out tomorrow night, by the way. I forgot to mention it to you earlier. Are you okay with that?'

'Sure,' he said. 'Why wouldn't I be? Going anywhere nice?'

'Oh, just out with some friends. We thought we'd go for a meal! At the new Italian place in town. I've heard they do really good spaghetti – but then again, I might have the lasagne. Or try the pizza!'

Okaaayyy ... I really do not need a breakdown of the menu. Why are you rambling so much?

He shook his head. 'Mum?' There was one last thing he had to ask.

'Yeah?'

But how could he possibly ask her about Daniel and Dad? Mum might think it was nothing and that would just make him feel worse. No, he'd push it down and forget about it. It was the best way.

'No, don't worry about it. I've forgotten – ha!'

As Ed walked across the living room, Mum picked up her phone again. He walked past her and she was typing away, adding to a long stream of messages.

Weird. Mum hates messaging – she's always telling me to call my friends, or meet up face to face instead. Ed picked the shopping bags up, and took them to the kitchen. *Why isn't she helping? Maybe she finally trusts me to do it for once*, he thought as he put the peanut butter away. *Yes, that's it. I'm old enough to do this responsibly and not mess it up. It's good that I'm considered reliable.*

Mrs Simpkins pushed her way through the cat flap at the perfect moment, just as Ed had put the last of the items away in the freezer. He picked her up and carried her upstairs, where he collapsed on his bed. Mrs Simpkins stretched out on top of his duvet, licking her paw and rolling on to her back. Ed gave her a quick tummy tickle, and then reached for his laptop, retrieving it from the desk next to his bed. He took the piece of paper out of his pocket and typed in the website address. His monologue drama revision would have to wait.

Come on, internet! The browser seemed confused; it was stuck on the loading page for what felt like five hours – but in reality was thirty seconds max.

Finally, the website burst to life. 'Wow,' he said under his breath. It was an extremely professional-looking page, with a large header, multiple tabs for different sections and bright photos. He scrolled right down, until he came to the very first post, and began to read.

Hello! My name is Han, also known as the Autistic Bookseller. Welcome to my blog, where I hope to share what it's like to work in a bookshop. For my first post, I thought I'd share a little bit of my backstory so you can get to know me. Who am I? What do I like reading? Why have I decided to start this blog?

Like I said, my name is Han, and I'm a teenager from the south-west of England. I live with my parents, my grandad, my dog and lots of guinea pigs. I'm seventeen now, but when I was fourteen I was diagnosed with autism spectrum disorder (which is sometimes abbreviated to ASD). I like to say that I am autistic, rather than that I have autism, because it's not something that I can change; it's as much a part of me as the colour of my eyes or my age. It means that I see and experience the world a bit differently from people who aren't autistic, but that's not necessarily bad – while things can sometimes feel difficult, I wouldn't change who I am for the world. It's made me who I am!

I began working in my local bookshop a few months ago and I love it. I love reading books with lots of animals (because I am a HUGE animal lover!), as well as historical fiction. It's also great to read books with neurodiverse protagonists because there's nothing like reading a book with a character like you.

It's a very common misconception that autistic people don't experience empathy, but if anything, I have too much of it – I get so engrossed in stories that it feels as if I'm living in the book myself. I can spend hours and hours reading, and when I turn the last page, I look up and suddenly remember where I am and all the things I've forgotten to do. And please, if you know me in real life, do not interrupt me when I'm reading – because it makes me extremely grumpy!

I've started this blog to document my experiences not just as a bookseller, but as an autistic one, too. I'd love to encourage other autistic young people to follow their dreams – and dream big! I'm following mine and it feels amazing.

I hope you'll enjoy my bookselling journey!

Your autistic bookseller, Han x

I didn't know Hannah was autistic. But Ed was glad that he knew now. She had such a natural writing voice that it almost felt as if she was in the room, talking directly to him. It was incredibly comforting.

He stroked Mrs Simpkins, who was steadily purring, and scrolled to the post below, the second she'd written.

Hello!

First of all, thank you for the supportive and kind comments you left on my first post – I didn't expect that people would be reading my blog already, but I really appreciate it!

I don't want every post on my blog to be specifically about being autistic, because it's tiring delving into the deep crevices of your personality and identity constantly, but I did want to talk a bit more today about my experiences so far – because maybe there are some of you who are autistic and want to become booksellers, too. And then next week, who knows?! Maybe I'll just share a long, long post full of pictures of my guinea pigs!

So there are two main ways that my autism affects my bookselling:
1) I can sometimes find social interaction pretty difficult
2) I have MEGA-SUPER-sensory skills, so I have a very strong sense of smell, sound and touch (and taste – but I don't exactly go around tasting the books!!).

Something I've found that helps with the first thing is that I've got lots of little scripts in my head. So when a customer comes in, I'll say, 'Good morning!/Good afternoon! Please let us know if you need any help.' And when customers come up to the till, I ask, 'Did you find everything you were looking for?' Relying on a script can be frustrating and even funny sometimes, though – because the customer doesn't know the other half of the script, so they often say unexpected things that completely throw me off!

The second thing can be a pain because my life is basically one big bombardment of my senses. When I first started work, the shop would play classical music by the counter, which ran on a loop all day, every day. It was nice for the customers, but by the end of my shift, I felt like crying because there had been absolutely no respite from it. It got to the point where I'd dread having to look after the till because it felt as if I couldn't breathe. Too much noise, or certain smells, or anything that feels scratchy or itchy causes me to feel actual pain; it's not me just being a bit particular or fussy. Luckily the bookshop owner was super understanding when I finally told her, and so now the only place that plays music is the cafe at the side of the shop.

Even though some things are pretty annoying, being autistic has also made me a far better bookseller. For example, lots of autistic people have what are called 'special interests' – things we are really passionate about. This makes it really convenient when recommending books because I can draw on all the weird, interesting facts that I know, and my brain remembers tiny details very easily. Some of the kids who come in for story time each week love me because they think I've got magical powers as I always find them books they love. (I just hope they don't get disappointed when I eventually recommend them something they don't like!)

When I set my mind to something, I'm pretty good at following through with it, no matter what. When I'm given a task, I can focus really well on just that one thing – which is why I'm really good at stock-taking and shelving. I love how repetitive shelving is; you just work through the pile until you get to the last book and, unless you get distracted by a customer (the worst!), you can zone in on the task, and drown out everything else – you can just get on with it.

Thanks for reading!
Han x

As Ed closed his eyes, he felt grateful that he'd bumped into Hannah at the supermarket. And relieved that he might have been misreading the situation at work. He bookmarked her blog to return to later, excited to read more before his next shift. There were so many more posts, about everything from tips on how to create the perfect window display to how to deal with annoying customers.

Instead of going to sleep thinking about Dad that night, Ed fell asleep thinking about Woolf and Wilde.

Ed: Tabby what should I do if I've made a fool of myself in
    front of someone

Tabby: . . . What have you done this time?

Ed: Brandished around a box of laxatives in front of
    Hannah, the girl from work and told her they were for my
    cat

Tabby: Is Mrs Simpkins constipated?

Ed: NO, THAT'S THE POINT

Ed: I PANICKED

Tabby: Ohmigod Ed

Tabby: This is AMAZING

Ed: It's not! I'm going to have to quit my job!

Tabby: Question: were you seen as a professional before?
    Be very honest with me now

Ed: Okay probably not but STILL

Ed: How did your appointment go with your mum? Hope it
   went WELL!

Cassie: it did actually, thanks! she got given some new
   medication so hopefully if it works, things should be a
   little better for her. here's hoping!

Ed: That's great news!

Ed sent a photo.

Ed: Mrs Simpkins is happy for you too, here she is

Cassie: . . . she looks constipated, not happy

Ed: HAHAHAHAHHAA you do NOT know how funny that
   really is HAHAHAHAHAH

Cassie: okay that's not weird at all

Ed: Don't worry I'll explain some other time but right now I'm
   too busy LAUGHING HAHAHAHAHAHAHAHA

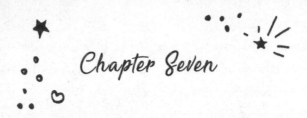

Chapter Seven

Nearly . . . done . . . There we go. Completing the finishing touches to the sociology essay due tomorrow, Ed put his pen down and stretched out his neck and shoulders. It was getting dark outside, the winter afternoon giving way to winter evening, and he was glad to be done with all his college work. After he'd delivered his drama monologue today, his brain wanted to get everything else done – so at least then he'd have less to think about. Between work and The Paper & Hearts Society meetings, he barely had enough time as it was.

The monologue had gone well – it was nice to be another character, step into someone else's shoes and lose yourself in the moment. Ed rarely got nervous performing because it was what he loved most in the world. And it had given him perspective, too: why was he so worried about Dad not getting back to him, when he'd see him soon anyway? Maybe his phone was broken. That would be it. He was overthinking it.

There was a knock at his bedroom door; Mum didn't wait for him to call her in, instead parading into the room with her arms wide.

'What do you think?' she said, pointing at her outfit. Ed blinked – she really was made up quite fancy, in her smartest dress and even a chunky beaded necklace and earrings.

'Bit dressed up for pizza, aren't you?' he said, but regretted it as soon as her face dropped.

'What do you mean?'

'Well . . .' How to say this tactfully? 'Your friends aren't all going to be lipsticked up, are they, or wearing their nicest clothes? I just . . . Why don't you put on some jeans, relax a little? It's not like you need to impress them!'

Mum bristled. 'Thanks a lot! So I can't look nice now? I should have asked Mrs Simpkins – she'd have been a bit fairer.'

Ed shrugged. What did he know about fashion? 'Have a nice time, anyway. Don't be back too late or you'll be grounded!'

'Ha ha. See you later. There's a vegetable lasagne in the fridge for you. Be good!'

'I always am! You have nothing to worry about, Mum.'

He was relieved when she left, and he could do one last read through of his essay, just to check for spelling mistakes. He always rushed these things and paid the price for silly errors, eager to move on to the next thing.

Finally finished, Ed's stomach growled as he stood up.

Pizza would be so good right now. Can't Mum bring some back for me? But the vegetable lasagne would have to do; Ed was never one to turn down a meal, anyway. All food was good food as long as it ended up in his tummy.

He switched off his desk lamp and shuffled the papers into a pile, then padded out of his bedroom in his warm, fluffy socks. With a yawn, and ruffling his hair, he made his way downstairs at a leisurely pace, although he picked it up when he felt – and most definitely heard – his stomach growl for a second time, like a hibernating bear that had just woken up and was very aware it needed food.

Mrs Simpkins was waiting for him by her food bowl in the hallway.

'Hey, you,' he said, scratching her behind the ears. She meowed up at him and brushed closer to his touch. 'Do you want your dinner now?'

She followed him into the kitchen, where he took out her cat biscuits from the dedicated Mrs Simpkins cupboard, filled with her food and treats. She flicked her tail back and forth as she watched him go back and fill up the bowl.

'Aren't you hungry?' Ed cooed, looming over her with his hands on his hips. Sometimes he almost expected her to answer him and was kind of disappointed when she never did.

Oh, well. If she didn't want to eat it, he couldn't force her. He had his own stomach to answer to. From the tall fridge, he carefully carried out the vegetable lasagne Mum had left wrapped up in tinfoil in a glass container, and shut the fridge behind him, very aware that the last thing he wanted to do was drop it on the floor.

A third stomach growl echoed around the empty kitchen. He lifted the foil and practically salivated as he gazed down at the culinary delight.

Riiiiinngggg, riiinggggggg! Riiiiinnnggggg! His phone was upstairs and it was going mad.

'Who's that now?' Ed said to Mrs Simpkins, who was gazing up at him from the kitchen floor. He put the lasagne down on the side, quickly chucking the foil back over it, and rushed up the stairs to grab his phone before it stopped ringing.

Luckily, it was still going by the time he swung open his bedroom door and dived for the phone on his bed.

He answered it before the ringing ceased.

'Son.' His dad's voice was gruff and harsh on the other end. 'You took your time.'

'Yeah, sorry. Hi, Dad.' Ed really was not in the mood to speak to him. He was drooling at the idea of the lasagne downstairs and his day had been long enough without an awkward conversation on top. Plus, it was the first time they'd spoken in weeks.

'Look, you can't come here on Friday. Change of plans. Sorry about that.' But Dad didn't sound sorry in the least.

'What do you mean? Do you want me to come another time? I can come on Saturday instead – it won't be a problem. I hadn't heard from you for ages, so I just . . .'

There was a pause on the other end, a pause that Ed wasn't unfamiliar with, as if they were both using the time to work out how polite they needed to be to each other.

He'll never understand me, Ed thought, but he stopped it in its tracks. Otherwise his eyes would begin to sting and his voice would crack. He didn't want another wobble. Not now.

'No, I'm busy this weekend.'

'Oh, right. What about next weekend?'

But by this point Ed knew what the answer was going to be. 'No, I'm busy.' Short but most certainly not sweet.

Ed couldn't help himself; his reply just came out. 'You had the time for Daniel, though. When you visited him at uni. I bet you didn't cancel on him.'

'I can't help it if I'm busy this weekend, can I? It's nothing personal. Your brother wouldn't make a fuss.'

'Oh, right. Nothing personal. Sure,' he responded sarcastically.

'You know your problem, Ed? You've got to stop being so needy and be more of a man. You're not a little kid any more, son.'

Ed pulled the phone away from his ear, as if it had burned him. Dad – and his brother, Daniel – were always making hints and suggestions that he should 'man up' more, but this was the first time Dad had come out and said it directly. And 'stop being so needy'?!

Ed went to hang up but found that his dad already had. He fell back on the bed, his whole body tense. How did Dad do that: convey so much meaning in so few words? Ed didn't even want to consider why his dad felt the need to favour his brother over him. *But I'm obviously far less important than anything they've got going on. I know how wanted I am.*

Frustrated, he scrubbed at his eyes with his hand, letting out another big sigh, before getting up and heading back downstairs. He'd almost forgotten his hunger. Almost, but not quite.

Mrs Simpkins's food bowl was still full up; that wasn't like her. 'You haven't eaten your dinner yet!' he called, but the only answer was a scraping sound that wasn't dissimilar to the rattling of china. He froze. Had someone broken in? Was there somebody else here?

Ed took a reluctant step forward towards the kitchen, his socks slipping against the wooden floor. Closer and closer he edged, until his back was pushed up against the kitchen door. He took a deep breath in, gearing himself up for attacking the potential intruder. Could he do that?

He peered around the door frame.

'OH. MY. GOD.'

What was going on?! He couldn't *believe* this! It was ... impossible! There was no intruder. There was only ...

'No, no, no, no, no!' he screamed, coming face to face with the sight of the empty lasagne dish. And Mrs Simpkins leaning over it, licking her lips. As she turned to gaze up at him, she grimaced and then let out a little burp.

Ed thought he might cry. One: there was no more lasagne. Two: was it even safe for Mrs Simpkins to eat all of that?!

'What have you done?!' he cried.

He rushed over and picked up the dish, which had been licked clean. There was barely any evidence that there had even been a lasagne in there; Mrs Simpkins had clearly got very carried away.

Ed was exasperated. 'Why would you do this?' he said. But Mrs Simpkins, obviously, didn't answer him. He coaxed her off the top of the counter, where she wasn't allowed, and chucked the empty dish into the dishwasher, so he no longer had to feel sick at the sight of it.

I feel so betrayed! And so annoyed and frustrated and millions of other adjectives to describe irritation. WHY?! WHY WOULD THIS HAPPEN?!

His unrelenting stomach growled with hunger once more.

'Don't you dare even think about eating any more of my food,' he scolded Mrs Simpkins, who was sitting on the floor looking as if butter wouldn't melt. Or maybe the phrase should be changed to 'looking as if the lasagne hadn't been eaten'. That was far more accurate.

He'd have to find something else to eat, but the last thing he wanted to do right now was cook an elaborate meal. What he needed was comfort food of the highest order.

He practically sprinted over to the bread bin to pull out the loaf of bread he knew was sitting inside. He hugged it to his arms and would have showered it in kisses if Mrs Simpkins hadn't been watching, and judging, him.

He found nestled in the corner of the tin cupboard the holy grail of food: a can of baked beans. Glorious, glorious baked beans. He snatched it out and was overcome by his imagination picturing the scene: baked beans on toast, warm in his empty stomach, eating quickly at first but slowing down later to savour the taste.

Perfection.

Thinking only of his hungry, grumbling stomach, he popped the can in the microwave and set the timer. He would wait to prepare the toast, lest Mrs Simpkins decided to jump on the counter and help herself to seconds. He wouldn't put it past her, and there was no way he was taking the risk.

Ed went to the living room and turned on the TV, deciding to watch a Shakespeare documentary he'd recorded last week while he waited for dinner. He loved Shakespeare more than anything else – his plays, his intriguing and often secret life, the way his writing still seemed relevant today even though he had created his plays hundreds and hundreds of years ago.

When he'd visited Stratford-upon-Avon last summer with The Paper & Hearts Society, it had only made him love Shakespeare more. Visiting the place of his birth, seeing where he'd grown up and lived, had been magical. Ed didn't think he'd ever feel quite that sense of wonder again.

He pressed play and settled back, letting himself relax for the first time that day. When he was watching anything to do with Shakespeare, he was able to forget all about homework and essays, all about his dad and why he was never that bothered about seeing his youngest son. He felt as if he was able to just exist, without any of the pressures. It was amazing.

On screen, the presenter wandered about the streets of Stratford-upon-Avon, and if Ed blurred his focus just enough and focused his brain, he could imagine that he was back there, too. Maybe, if he closed his eyes and leant back, he could even imagine that he was Shakespeare himself, traversing the Elizabethan streets, dodging around rotten waste, escaping the hooves of horses, and . . .

BANG!

What *was* that?!

The next second, Ed was plunged into total darkness. The lights all went off and the TV went dead. He couldn't see a thing. He scrambled around on the sofa next to him for his phone, and fumbled to switch the torch on. His heart was jumping out of his chest. He was sure he'd forgotten how to breathe, as if his breath had been stolen from him. In shock, he was unable to move for what felt like hours, but in reality was only a minute. Then he rushed up and out of the living room, heading down the hallway in the direction of the explosion.

He wasn't ready for the sight that met him as the torch illuminated the room – the microwave door had been thrown open, the tin was lying near to it, mangled and distorted, and there were small tendrils of smoke rising from the appliance. He picked his feet up and grimaced as he realised he'd stepped through escaped baked beans, which littered the floor.

'What the hell do I do now?' He fought against the choking sensation in his throat. *What the hell is wrong with you, Ed? You can't even cook beans on toast properly! What is Mum going to say when she comes back?! You've really done it this time!*

Think, think. What can you do?

Ed: Um asking for a friend of course but what would
      someone do if they technically had blown up their
      microwave and made all of the electricity in the house
      stop working ASKING FOR A FRIEND REMEMBER

Henry: . . . Ed. Seriously?

Ed: SERIOUSLY. It's for a friend

Cassie: a friend called ed?

Ed: THERE'S NO TIME FOR THAT HELP
      MEEEEEEEEEEEEEEE!!!!!

Olivia: I cannot believe you!!!!

Henry: How badly has the microwave blown up?

Ed: Let's just say there are baked beans EVERYWHERE

Olivia: Did you

Ed: Was I not supposed to do that?!

Henry: NO

Olivia: NOOOOOOO!!!

Tabby: No, Ed!!!

Cassie: most definitely not

Ed: It would be nice if you were all agreed on something for
      once.

Well, they were no use. It was no good chastising him for
what he'd done – he couldn't change anything or go back
in time.

He positioned the torch on his phone so that he could
illuminate the mess, and carefully worked his way over to

the door leading outside, which he swung open; the last thing he needed was for the smoke alarm to go off. His feet, covered in gloop, felt disgusting, but he couldn't afford to think about that. Tentatively, he went back to the microwave and slowly, so slowly, pulled the plug from the socket. Should he move it?

He was scared to touch it, so settled on cleaning instead. He grabbed the mop from the cupboard under the stairs and began to scrub at the kitchen tiles, but it wasn't really effective; it just pooled all the gloop together.

I have really, really, really, super messed up. My god, Mum will never leave me alone again! How am I nearly an adult? How will I ever be a responsible citizen? I'm a danger to myself and other people!

It seemed to take hours to get even the floor free of baked beans and he found more and more as he went along. Even once the mopping up was done with, he had to wipe down the kitchen surfaces and the walls and then go back over the floor. It wasn't an easy job in the dark; Ed was aching by the time he'd finished from all the skidding over the tiles he'd done.

Afterwards, he sat in the dark living room, chewing on a slice of bread to appease his still empty stomach. His heart hadn't stopped racing, but it was also accompanied by a headache of epic proportions, the kind that was only ever brought about by stress. He was certain his face was covered in bean juice, and Mrs Simpkins had decided that she would climb all over him, despite the angry vibes he was giving her.

This is all your fault, you silly cat!

Ed heard a key scraping in the front door and, not for the first or even second time that day, he jumped. Mrs Simpkins flew off his lap and ran out to the hall, and Ed slowly got up and stood in the doorway.

Mum closed the door behind her and eased off her heels, not looking up. It was strange watching someone when they didn't know they were being watched – you noticed all sorts of things about them that you would never usually see. Like the little smile that lit up Mum's face and the glow in her cheeks that he could make out even in the darkness. Now, he'd have to ruin that for her.

'Hi,' Ed said. His voice cracked.

'Ohmigod! Ed! You terrified me! What are you doing in the dark?!' Mum clutched her chest in fright.

'Mum,' Ed said with a gulp. He had to come clean. 'I'm really sorry but I've blown up the microwave.'

He did not like the weary look his mum gave him. As if she wasn't at all surprised. 'Right then,' she said, raising her eyebrow. 'We better have a look at that, hadn't we?'

Ed nodded. Maybe he'd hold back from telling her about Mrs Simpkins and the lasagne too.

Olivia: How are you now, Ed?! Did you get it sorted?!

Ed: I knew there was a reason I had to get a job. I've got to pay for a new microwave

Henry: Try not to blow up the new one?

Ed: To top it all off, THE POWER CUT MEANT THE RECORDING OF MY SHAKESPEARE TV PROGRAMME DISAPPEARED!!

Tabby: Wow, it really is not your day today!

Ed: Not my day? It's not my LIFE Tabby! IT'S A DISASTER

Cassie: too bad

Ed: DISASTER

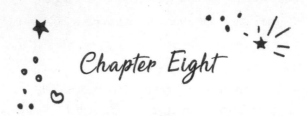

Chapter Eight

'Please do not use the microwave at work today,' Mum said, holding the front door open to let Ed out. 'I do not want to turn on the news and find out you've blown up an entire bookshop.'

Sheepishly, Ed promised not to. 'That seems a bit extreme, even to me. I'm not *that* incompetent . . . Am I?'

Mum quirked an eyebrow. 'Better not to put it to the test.'

To be fair, she'd been pretty good about it, once everything had been cleared up and the microwave had been dumped. Ed had had to buy a new one out of his savings – which basically meant that now all his earnings from Woolf and Wilde were gone – and then he'd had to endure a tutorial on how to use it *properly* without any explosions, but she hadn't got super angry with him. Well, not until Mrs Simpkins vomited lasagne all over Mum's clean bedding. That hadn't been a pretty sight to behold.

'Thanks, Mum,' he said now, feeling a little like a balloon inside him had deflated. He felt a kind of quiet sadness that could only be solved by the person who knew him best – his mum. Even though he was taller than her, even though he wasn't a child any more, she recognised whatever was going on in his head, and wrapped her arms around his middle; she couldn't reach his shoulders easily these days.

'I'd better leave or I'll be late,' he said, but didn't make any move to go.

'What is it?' Mum asked, reaching up and smoothing his hair back with a mother's affection. 'You look as if there's a black cloud raining down over you.'

He shook his head and grimaced. *Just come out with it, Ed.* 'Mum, do you think I need to man up?' he said. 'Not be so sensitive?'

Mum looked confused. 'What? Has someone told you that? Of course you don't! Why would you need to "man up"? Nobody ever tells anyone to "woman up"!'

'Oh well, I just, it's nothing . . .'

'You spoke to your dad, then?'

Did she have magical powers? Mum could read every expression on his face, analyse every little moment and hear every change in his voice to know what was up without Ed saying a word.

'Yeah.'

'Well, that's a load of nonsense, Ed. Just ignore it. I'm sure he didn't mean it. He loves you – he's your dad.'

Yeah, so he has to. Doesn't mean he likes me.

Ed shrugged it all off. There was no point crying over it because that would just make him feel as if his dad was right; and he'd be late to work and that would just make everyone grumpy. He couldn't fail Dinah like that.

'I'm so glad I can trust you, at least,' he said. 'I know you'll never let me down.'

'Go on, go off to work and have a good day. Then why don't we have a movie night tonight? I'll even let you choose. It'll be just the two of us – and Mrs Simpkins, of course.'

'Thanks, Mum,' he said, kissing the top of her head. 'See you later.'

The question was still going around his head, though, as he drove into work: was he really just a big, sensitive baby who needed to turn into a proper adult? He turned off the radio and let his thoughts take over until, by the time he pulled into the car park, he was ready to scream at himself to shut up.

He slammed the car door shut, not realising how loud it was, and startled a woman and her child walking past. He locked the car and walked down the alley, to the back entrance of Woolf and Wilde.

'Morning, Ed!' Dinah was piling a big colourful stack of books on the counter. 'You don't want any of these, do you? They're proof copies that publishers send us to see if we want to stock their books. I'm afraid Hannah's already had a riffle through, but you're very welcome to anything else that takes your fancy.' She took one more out of a jiffy bag and added it to the pile. 'Can you do me a favour and take them up to the staffroom with you on your way up?'

'Will do. Thanks!' Ed said, gathering the towering stack in his arms. 'Could you ... possibly open the door for me?'

'Oh, of course!' Dinah laughed at the sight of him with the books tucked under his chin for balance. 'Ah, the picture of a bookseller. You're doing just fine, Ed.'

'Thanks,' he said. He appreciated Dinah's support more than anything. 'I'll just take these up and then I'll be back down.'

He headed up the winding stairs to the staffroom and pushed the door open with his elbow. Hannah was perched on the edge of the old sofa, eating the last mouthful of her cereal bar.

'Hey,' he said, slightly out of breath from the stairs. 'Where do you think I should put these?'

She put the wrapper in her bag before pointing to an empty box in the corner. 'In there's good, just make sure the spines are facing up so people can see the titles.'

He bent down and put the pile of books he was carrying on the ground, so he could get a better look at what was there. Adult fiction, books for kids, non-fiction and a few with plainer covers that he couldn't categorise. He picked out two YA proofs that he liked the look of and put the rest spine out in the box. It felt like a real honour that Dinah had allowed him to take some; he was starting to feel truly part of the bookshop.

'So, I read your blog . . .' Ed left it at that, waiting for Hannah to pick up the conversation if she wanted to. He didn't want it to seem as if he was intruding. *Reading blogs isn't very manly, is it?* Ed could imagine his dad saying. But he pushed that thought well away.

'Oh.' Quiet. And then, in a hushed tone, she said, 'So what did you think?'

'I *loved* it. It's so professional! And you're such a natural writer that it felt as if you were in the room reading it out to me, rather than me reading it myself. You'll have to tell your grandad thanks from me for sharing the link to your bee-log.'

She laughed. 'I keep telling him it's called a blog, but he never listens! I think he knows secretly but enjoys me whining at him to get it right.'

'Seriously, it's amazing. Everybody should read it. I didn't know you were autistic, but if I had, I definitely would have been more careful with my stinky tuna sandwiches and incessant, overwhelming questions.'

'Thank you,' Hannah said sincerely.

'What for?'

'Well, most people say things like, "But you don't look autistic!" as if it's something I can get rid of at the drop of a hat – or even, once, "I like you in spite of your autism." They thought that would be a comfort to me. But you haven't said that.'

Ed shrugged. 'Why would I be dismissive of you? I enjoyed reading your posts. God knows I need some help on the bookseller front; there's still so much I feel like I don't know.'

Hannah smiled, so warmly that it made Ed instantly smile back, as if they were sharing in something.

'I'm glad it's made you see sense with the tuna sandwiches. But, for the record, I'm getting used to the constant questions. I don't really mind.'

He didn't have time to reply because she got up and headed for the door, turning back as she pushed the handle. 'I'm happy to do the orders this morning! Dinah said she'd like one of us to do a once over of the children's section – apparently there were some untidy kids wandering around yesterday. Do you want to head up there?'

'Sure, I'll do that now.' Hannah had already gone, the door closing quietly behind her. He put his bag away in his locker, banging it shut.

By the time the shop had opened, Ed had managed to tidy the children's area and the entirety of the top floor, and now he was back downstairs to find out his next task. A bulk order of Woolf and Wilde bookmarks had just arrived, so Dinah asked Ed to sort them into a pot on top of the counter, and to place the remainder into a box underneath it.

He'd not noticed before now that there was no music playing, despite always noticing it being on when he'd visited as a customer, often humming as he browsed. He thought back to Hannah's blog post. They were lucky to have such a supportive boss.

'I've got so many of these at home; I find them everywhere,' he told Dinah as he fanned the bookmarks out in the pot.

'So that's where they've all got to! I was beginning to wonder!'

The bell tinkled over the front door. A dad walked in, his little boy in tow, animatedly chatting away, holding each other's hands. Ed froze, as if he'd been plunged into a freezer and was now an ice cube. The world was still moving around him, but it felt as though he was no longer a part of it.

'Good morning!' Dinah trilled. And then, just like that, it was over, and he had arranged his face into a tight, customer-facing smile. The only feeling left was a tightening in his heart, prickly and painful.

'That's a lovely job,' Dinah said, turning back to him. 'Do you think you can run up to the top floor and put some of these bookshop event leaflets out? I probably shouldn't admit to this, but I always forget! Then, after Hannah's done with the readalong this morning, I'll get you both on the till while I sort out some problems in the cafe. Sound okay?'

'Yeah, sounds good,' he said, but he wasn't entirely sure what he was agreeing to. Dinah could have said anything, and he would have nodded.

The thought kept going around his head when Ed was upstairs: *I wish I was that little boy with his dad, going into the bookshop to spend a Saturday morning together. We never had that kind of relationship. He thought books were too girly.*

Dad had always forced him to watch sport or fix something, things that he had absolutely no interest in. When Ed had ever mentioned anything, even as a child, he'd dismiss or ignore him.

When he looked down, he found that he'd crushed one of the leaflets in the palm of his hand. He crumpled it up into the pocket of his trousers, like the crumpled hope of his dad ever listening to what he had to say.

The truth was that his dad's recent dismissal of Ed had brought back memories of the divorce. And while he tried to focus on the fact that he still had his mum, that didn't make it hurt any less. And now he had a stinging paper cut as a reminder.

Tears pricked at his eyes. But he focused on dotting the leaflets around the top floor and then made his way back down the stairs. Well, he was trying, but he was caught up in a dawdling stream of kids heading in the same direction after Hannah's readalong. It took twice as long as it usually would, and each added second gave him even more time stuck in his swirling, spiralling mind. *I don't want it to get me down like this; I don't want it to ruin my day at work.*

Finally, he thought, jumping down from the last step, relieved to find Dinah waiting for him.

'Do you mind looking after the till?' she said. 'Hannah will be back in a bit, but I know you'll manage just fine on your own.' She was already looking towards the cafe entrance. Ed knew he should feel proud of himself that she trusted him, but he didn't think he would ever feel proud of himself again.

The first customer was fine – he made polite conversation about the pile of books she'd selected for her book club, rung the books through correctly and printed out the receipt for the customer, putting the second printout in the till. He even remembered to put one of the new bookmarks inside the first book and packed them neatly inside a paper bag so the books wouldn't get ruined. A job well done.

But all good things eventually had to come to an end. And, unfortunately for Ed, the end was in the shape of a kid. He was asking for the same book over and over again, through tears, while his mum said she wouldn't buy it for him because he'd chosen three others already. She came over to the till carrying a small stack of books, her son whinging on her hip.

'I'd tell him to shut up if that was my child,' Ed said, and his mouth fell open. *Oh my GOD, I did not just say that out loud.*

The mother glared. 'Excuse me? What did you just say about my child?'

Ed felt nauseous. 'Uh . . .' *How do I sort this one out?!?! ED. WHY?!*

Luckily, Hannah appeared at that moment, and must have overheard. 'Hello, little Tommy!' she called. 'Did you enjoy the readalong this morning? Why don't I ring those through the till for you?'

The glare of his mother softened as she turned to Hannah and handed the books over.

'Ed, could you put this back for me over there?' Hannah said, shoving a book into his hands and pointing to the furthest end of the room.

'I'm so sorry about that,' he heard Hannah say, 'he's new, that's all.' Ed felt terrible that she was having to pick up the pieces after him, just as things had been beginning to work out as a bookseller. Had he not learnt anything after all? *I'm going to have to quit . . . that's if I don't get fired first.*

Dinah came back then from the cafe. *What if Hannah comes clean about what happened? I suppose all I need to do is grab my bag from the locker. How will I explain this to Mum?* Ed fiddled with his staff badge, about to remove it.

'Can we take our break a little early this morning, Dinah? Do you mind?' Hannah said quickly. 'We won't be long, but the readalong was busy this morning. I'm never going to be able to give customer recommendations effectively if I can hear Ed's stomach rumbling.'

Ed joined in. 'Yeah, the cake in the cafe does smell very good today.'

Dinah checked her watch. 'Oh, I suppose it is that time! Ten minutes early won't do any harm – there'll be a little lull now anyway, before we get going again at lunch. Go on, why not?'

Hannah twitched her head in the direction of the staff-only door. *Let's go*, her eyes said, and Ed felt, rather than prompted, his body follow hers.

They didn't say a word to each other until they'd entered the staffroom, Hannah closing the door behind them and leaning against it. Ed threw himself on to the sofa and groaned. He wasn't so much panicking as feeling an enormous sense of dread taking over his entire being. 'Oh god, what if Dinah had heard me? I would be sacked!'

'Dinah wouldn't sack you,' Hannah said, matter of fact, 'but I don't think she'd be impressed. But it's fine – Dinah didn't hear, and I just saved you.'

'You're my knight in shining armour,' Ed tried to joke, but his heart wasn't in it. Subdued, he said, 'I really messed up, didn't I?'

'Yeah, it wasn't exactly your best moment.'

She sat down on the other side of the sofa while he buried his head in his hands, enjoying the darkness behind his closed eyelids. They weren't touching, but he felt that Hannah was close, and that was enough. Her presence was putting a stop to the total mopefest he would otherwise have descended into.

'So what's up?' she asked.

'Nothing.'

'Am I really supposed to believe that? You're the most enthusiastic person I've ever met, but right now, you look terrible. Look, we all have bad days in the shop. It's perfectly normal. It's how you move on from it that matters most. Now, tell me what's going on, and we can sort it out.'

'Just a few bits at home,' he said. 'But it really is nothing; you don't want to hear me moaning on.'

'You can talk to me, you know. If you need to. I'm sure you've got loads of friends to talk to, but I'm here, too.'
Yes, but my friends have their own problems; I don't want to overburden Olivia after the trouble she had at school last year, and I don't want to risk Tabby getting anxious, or add to Cassie's own home issues.

How could he possibly explain to Hannah that he cared about his friends so much that he was scared they'd leave him one day too, just like he cared about his dad and he had walked out of the door?

He settled on, 'Thanks, you don't know how much I appreciate it.'

He heard Hannah get up and open her locker, then felt her plonk back down next to him. 'Do you have Instagram? I'll follow you, then you can see lots of cute animal pictures if you follow me back.'

The thought did cheer him up a little bit. 'It's @TheIncredibleEd. Just don't scroll back too far!'

'Tempting!'

Slowly, he lifted his head from his hands, sitting up to full height and looking across at her as she found his profile. 'Does this mean we're friends now?'

'Don't get too carried away,' she said with a lopsided grin, but he detected the humour in her voice, and it brought a smile to his face too.

Maybe we all need to take a backwards step sometimes

to realise how much we want to keep moving forward. Maybe this is just a little blip and Hannah's right: it's how I move on from it that matters.

He was encouraged by her smile. 'You know, I thought you hated me when I first started.'

Hannah broke into a full-on grin now. 'Not going to lie, I kind of did! You were a very big change to my quiet shifts. But I guess I'm learning to adjust to this new, Ed-shaped normal. Now enough of the sincerity or my brain might explode. Let's go and get back on with it. You can't hide up here all day.'

'Yes, boss!'

And with that, Ed dusted himself off and made a mental note to himself that it would never happen again.

Mum: I'm going out for the evening but I need to speak to
    you about something. Are you home from college late
    tomorrow?

Ed: Nope, it'll be normal time! Where are you off to tonight?
    I thought we were doing movie night! You're never home
    at the moment! You're not going out for pizza again, are
    you?

Mum: Oh, I'm sorry! I completely forgot! It's a networking
    thing for work that I can't miss. I might be back a little
    late but I'll be home tomorrow, ready and waiting. We
    can have our movie night then.

Ed: Sounds good! Have a nice time, Mum!

Ed: I'm sat in the car park waiting to leave work but I made a bit of an idiot of myself today and I just wanted a virtual hug

Tabby sent a gif.

Tabby: Better – a GHOST HUG just for you!

Ed: Awwwwww thanks Tabby <3

Olivia: What's up Edward?! What happened?

Ed: My dad's just been a bit weird with me and I was upset and kind of took it out on a customer. It's nothing I guess but I shouldn't have let it get to me. Hannah at work helped so it was fine in the end

Henry: Your dad? What happened?

Olivia: Ooh Hannah! Is she nice?

Ed: It's really nothing. He just won't see me, that's all, Henry

Tabby: That doesn't sound good. Did he say why?

Ed: Got to go or I'll be late home! Thanks for the virtual hugs!

Chapter Nine

Ed crashed on his bed when he got home, logging into Netflix on his laptop and selecting a cheesy Christmas movie, despite the fact that Christmas had already been and gone. There was just something about Christmas films that made his brain switch off. He was working his way through a packet of cookies; Mrs Simpkins brushed against his hand every time he got another one out.

'No, you silly cat,' he told her. 'They're all for me! You've got your biscuits downstairs.'

With the tinkling Christmas soundtrack as background noise, he picked up his phone and opened up Instagram, immediately seeing the follow from Hannah, waiting.

He clicked on her profile and followed her back. Hannah's Instagram was packed to the brim with pictures of her guinea pigs, possibly the cutest things Ed had ever seen in his life – apart from when he looked in the mirror, of course. And obviously Mrs Simpkins, who was the cutest of all. There were baby guinea pigs, fully grown guinea pigs, ones with short hair, ones with sticky-up hair and others with long, flowing locks. There were group shots of guinea pigs together as well as individual photos which looked as though the guinea pigs were posing.

Ed LOVED it. He thought it was the best thing he'd ever seen – all this cuteness in one place, all their squee-worthy faces gazing up at the lens with bright, button eyes. He clicked 'like' on a few of them.

He scrolled down, trying not to audibly gasp from adorability overload. Interspersing the guinea pig pictures were photographs of her dog. Indiana Bones, wasn't it? A large, very loveable-looking German shepherd, who in one photo was even grinning at the camera.

Love of my life ♡, it was captioned. The way Hannah talked about her animals was the same way Ed talked about Mrs Simpkins, and there was nothing that made him happier than people who loved their animals.

He smiled as he saw the notifications pop up in his Instagram message inbox.

Hannah: So you couldn't resist guinea pig pictures?
Ed: They're SO CUTE, I LOVE THEM. I WANT THEM ALL
Hannah: Sorry, they're all mine!
Ed sent a photo.

Ed: This is my cat, Mrs Simpkins. I don't think she'd be very
happy if I brought a guinea pig home with me. She likes
all my attention to herself

Hannah: That is a ridiculously fluffy cat, look at her little
face. She doesn't look at all constipated in this picture

Ed: I'm never going to live that one down, am I?

Hannah: Haha I don't think so, no. It was pretty weird and
usually I think I'm the weird one

Ed: I'm always the weird one in most situations but I promise
I don't usually go around buying laxatives for my cat

Hannah: Okay I believe you . . .

Hannah: Are you all right after work today?

Ed: Cookies have considerably helped, not gonna lie.
There's nothing a good cookie can't solve

Ed liked Hannah over message. She was funny and quick in response, and there was no risk of being interrupted by a customer disturbing their conversation. He waited for her to reply but it looked as if she wouldn't, seeing as she'd read it but gone quiet. It wasn't a question, thought Ed, so it made sense she wouldn't reply.

The film was drawing to a close too, so he kicked back the duvet, got inside and just lay there, staring up at the ceiling, Mrs Simpkins keeping his feet warm at the end of the bed. 'Well, that's that then, Mrs Simpkins,' he said, feeling his eyes close.

What a bittersweet day. Out of all this rubbish, at least I've got closer to Hannah. Things will be fine from here, right? They've got to be. I won't let Dad get to me any more.

He had to just keep pushing the feelings down, until they didn't upset him. That was the way to do it.

Mum: I got back later than planned last night and you were
asleep and then I overslept this morning! Sorry! I want to
talk to you when you get home later though.
Ed: Cool! I'm just heading into drama so can't text but I'll
speak later

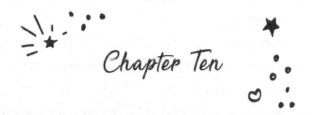

Chapter Ten

Do. Not. Spill. Do. Not. Spill. The mantra played itself over and over again in Ed's head as he carried the two mugs of tea out to the living room. One for him with two sugars, one with just milk for Mum. He carefully kicked the living room door open with his foot, and put both mugs on the coffee table without a single spillage.

'Thanks, love. Come and sit down,' Mum said, patting the sofa cushion next to her. She looked kind of expectant, kind of . . . happy. *What was this all about?*

'I've got something to tell you.' *Are we getting another cat?! Have we won the lottery?!*

Ed moved one of the scatter cushions to one side, and sat down. 'I'd really like a ragdoll breed next. Have you seen how cute they are?' he burst out, feeling suddenly nervous.

'What?' Mum said.

'I thought we were getting another cat . . .'

'No, no, Ed, listen . . .'

'Oh.' So no new cat, and he was guessing they *hadn't* won the lottery . . .

'Ed,' she began, and he stared back at her as she spoke, as if he was challenging her: *Go on, tell me. I dare you, Mum. I dare you. What is it?*

'Ed, I've got some news that I'd like to share with you. I've thought over the best way to say this, and I've decided I will just come out with it. Then if you have any questions, you can ask me. Okay?'

He didn't nod.

'Right,' she said to his non-response, picking up her tea and taking a sip. 'You see, Ed, I've met someone. Someone I like.'

'What, like someone in the supermarket? Someone in the street?'

She smiled softly. 'N-no,' she said. 'Someone *romantically*. We met online actually, and now we've met up in person a number of times. We get on well. Really, really well.'

Ed clenched his fists in his lap.

'He's lovely, Ed. I think you'll like him – Phil, his name is. He's got a child, a little girl, so he knows what it's like to be a parent. I hope you'll be supportive of us.'

'What the *hell*!' Ed shot up off the sofa.

Mum is in a relationship?! This man has a small child?! What, does he expect Mum to parent her too?

'I'm really happy, Ed,' Mum said. 'I wouldn't tell you if I wasn't sure it was serious, but I am. I don't know if I've been this happy for a long time.' A pause. 'And I'd really like you to meet him.'

I have a family! A father and a sibling – I really do not need another of both. I won't be told I'll like this . . . this usurper!

'I need to . . . I need to . . . go.' Ed lurched out of the room as quickly as he could, grabbing his phone from the sofa arm as he went.

'Go?' Mum shouted to him. 'Go where? Ed, it's getting dark!'

'I've . . . got to . . . I can't be here,' he said, more to himself than her, his heart thumping in his ears. He grabbed his house keys, pushed a random pair of shoes on his feet and staggered out into the night.

He ignored everything around him as he nearly tripped over the threshold of the front gate. Ed looked down and realised too late he was wearing his house slippers. He continued up the pavement, putting as much distance between himself and home as possible. He had to get away.

'Ed! Ed, come back!' His mum's voice echoed behind him, but even though he registered it, he chose not to hear it.

She can't do this, he kept thinking as he walked up the street. *She can't tear our little family apart – Mum and me.*

I thought we were happy as we were. I thought everything was okay. She can't do this to us. To me.

The fresh, cool air, away from the stuffy, claustrophobic house, helped to bring Ed to his senses slightly. When he'd walked far enough to catch his breath, he found himself outside the children's play park where Mum had brought him a lot when he was little. It wasn't as good as the big park in town, but it still felt nostalgic. He had always been allowed to ask Olivia to come out to play, and they would spin around together on the merry-go-round, or Ed would guard the climbing frame as if it were a castle and Olivia were the queen.

He pushed the squeaky gate and entered the play area, feeling the familiar squishy texture of the ground beneath his slippered feet.

He sat down at the bottom of the slide, remembering hurtling down as a kid, thinking it was the most exciting thing in the world. He sighed; possibly the longest sigh that had ever existed on Earth. He pushed all his anger and grievances out through it, but it didn't work. He felt just as distraught.

His thoughts started spiralling – flashbacks to his mum and dad's divorce, memories of all their fights and how he'd tried to stop them; when he'd told them that he loved them both, so they couldn't fall out – surely if they loved him back, they wouldn't do this to him, they would stay together. Daniel had never seemed to get upset; as he'd been older, he'd understood more that it was best for both of them if they weren't together. Yet, he'd never tried to stop Ed from getting so upset.

'*Please,*' he remembered begging, tears streaming down his face just like they were beginning to now. '*Please stop!*'

His parents' arguments had scared him – he was sure the neighbours had heard every single word through the walls. It had only ever been voices – never physical – but Ed had never known when it would stop, never known what he could do to stop it. He'd known if he'd turned his back, went upstairs to hide under his duvet, then maybe things would have got even worse and he'd never have been able to live with himself.

He felt the same kind of frantic now. *What if Phil hurts Mum? What if he tears apart our little family? What if Mum asks him to move in and then the house seems too small for all of us? What if Mum doesn't want me, just like Dad? It will just be me and Mrs Simpkins. I don't want to leave home – everything's been fine up until now. Why does it all have to change?*

Maybe Phil would be like his own father was. He'd tell him he was weird for liking drama and Shakespeare and try to get him to watch the football with him, then attempt to humiliate him when Ed didn't know what the offside rule was. Yes. That was how it would go. And Mum would watch and let it happen. Because she loved this man out of choice.

Ed shakily took his phone out of his jeans pocket, and brought up his contacts list, hovering over the only person he could face speaking to. There was the steady sound of the call tone, and then a crackling static as the call started.

'Hello? Ed? What are you doing calling so late – has Mrs Simpkins finally mastered her new trick?'

'Tabby,' Ed said, suppressing a sob.

'Ed, are you okay? Where are you? It sounds as if you're outside.'

'Tabby, I don't know what to do. I feel so lost . . . I don't know what to do . . . I just can't do this . . . I can't do this any more . . . I can't, Tabby. I can't.' His voice was breathy, his words joining together into one messy line.

He heard rustling. 'Ed, where are you? I'm putting my coat on now – I'll come and find you.'

'No, no,' he said, 'don't. I want to be left alone. I'm fine. I just wanted to talk. It's nothing, honestly. I'm just being silly.'

'It doesn't sound as if you're being silly; it sounds as if you're upset and I don't like the idea of you being all alone when you feel like this. You'd do the same thing for me.'

'Maybe,' he said, and then, 'Tabby, am I a good friend?'

'Ed,' she said immediately, 'are you serious right now? You're my best friend in the whole world and I love you more than anything. Of course you're a good friend! You are the kindest, most generous, loveable and caring person in my entire life. What's this about, Ed? Just tell me where you are.'

'I'm okay,' he said. 'I promise I am. It's just that everything's gone wrong, absolutely everything, and I don't know what to do – I don't know what I can do. I feel as if everything's falling apart and I can't stop it.'

He didn't know what came over him, but he began to laugh as he continued. 'I'm sitting on a slide,' he said, and suddenly it really was the funniest thing he'd ever heard. Here he was, sitting at the bottom of a children's play slide, in the cold on a winter's night, and now he was laughing so hard that an explosion of tears ran down his cheeks.

He stood up and walked around the base of the slide, taking a deep breath. 'And my mum has got a bloody boyfriend who has a small child and I'm sure she thinks that I'm getting older and I'll be gone soon, and so she may as well replace me while she's got the chance, because who cares about Ed and his feelings – who cares that Ed only feels comfortable at Mum's house not Dad's and that now he'll be pushed away from the only place he truly feels at home, and ...' He gasped, sitting down on the slide again, and unhappy tears fell unbidden. 'Oh god, Tabby. I don't know what to do. There's nothing I can do. Everything's gone wrong. Mum's done this and Dad doesn't want to see me, and most of the time acts as if I don't exist. I've got nobody!'

'Oh, Ed,' Tabby said. 'Ed, my lovely, I wish I could hug you. I wish I were with you right now. I wish I could take away some of your pain. I know it's not easy, but it will get better, I promise. In this moment, it feels as if your heart is being ripped out of your chest, but it won't always feel like that. Why don't you go home and get into bed and try to sleep some of this pain off?"

'I can't go home right now. All I keep thinking is that I should have been better,' Ed choked out. 'I shouldn't do silly stuff all the time without thinking about what I'm doing. Then maybe none of this would be happening right now.'

'That is one hundred per cent not true. We love you for your silliness – never let anyone tell you otherwise. Do you want to stay here? We can make the sofa bed up for you.'

Ed didn't know what to say.

'Just take the first step,' Tabby said. 'And then the second step is to get in your car, and then the third is to drive here. One step at a time, Ed. You can do this. Go on.

I'll stay on the line until you get there. I'm not going anywhere.'

First step. Then the second, then the third, just as Tabby said. He was chilled to the bone, but it helped, in a way. It mirrored the numb feeling that had set in.

Tabby talked to Ed the whole way back; even when he stopped as his house came into sight, she coaxed him on with her warm words. 'I'm here,' Tabby whispered down the phone as he stood facing his house from the bottom of the path. 'I'm here, Ed.'

He made it to his car and started the engine, quickly reversing out of his parking spot before his mum heard him. He knew he'd soon feel safe with Tabby, and it would all be okay.

'I'll see you soon. I'm going to hang up now, okay?' Tabby's voice came through the car speakers. 'And then we'll speak properly when you get here.'

What would he do without his best friend? He couldn't imagine a world where they hadn't met.

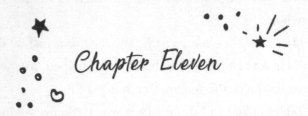

Chapter Eleven

Tabby was outside the door and ready to greet Ed as soon as he pulled up. He was here. Finally. He walked up the path of Tabby's gran's house, lined with cheerful white snowdrops that almost glowed in the dark. They were the exact opposite metaphor for his current mood, but they made him smile nonetheless.

'Oh, Ed,' Tabby said, pulling him into a tight hug. He surrendered to her love and felt all the composure he had left dissolve. 'Are you okay? You're here now, Ed; it will be okay. Come on, come inside.'

She led him indoors, where Ed took off his slippers, now caked in a thin layer of mud. He knew full well the consequences if he got Gran's cream carpets dirty. The TV, blaring out sound, quietened as they walked into the living room. Ed took in the sight – the fake fireplace with its tall flame, giving off a warm heat through its vents, and Gran sitting in her armchair with her feet up on a green velvet footstool.

'Ed, my darling, how are you?' Gran said. She looked as if she was about to get up, so Ed quickly went to her and gave her a kiss on the cheek.

'Sit down and get yourself comfy,' Gran said. 'You're in the right place; we'll look after you.'

'Do you need anything?' Tabby asked him, feeling his forehead to check if he had a temperature; she seemed satisfied. 'Biscuits?'

'Do you have any paracetamol?' Ed said, sinking into the huge leather sofa. 'I don't have any in my bag and I can feel a headache coming on.'

'I'm on so many tablets,' Gran said with a laugh, 'that I rattle whenever I get out of this chair. Go and get him some from the cupboard, Tabby dear. You'll have to play nurse to this poor patient, won't she, Ed?'

'I don't mind,' Tabby said. 'He's worth it most of the time. And I know he must be feeling awful because he just ignored the offer of biscuits. It must be serious. Shall I make you a cup of tea?' Tabby offered.

He nodded. *Yes, please.* But he didn't have any words left.

He never could have imagined feeling as if his whole world had been tipped upside down and he was holding on for dear life, as though if he let go he'd fly through the atmosphere and into space. Maybe space was preferable. Could he get a little astronaut costume for Mrs Simpkins? That would be cute!

'You should let your mum know you're here,' Gran said, and her words were so soft and caring that they were almost as if she was giving him a hug, despite the fact she was still in her armchair. 'She'll be worried about you, even if you don't think she will be ... Send her a little message if you can't face talking to her over the phone,' Gran suggested, obviously noticing Ed's look of defiance. 'It will do more harm than good if you don't; she'll think you've run away and she'll worry herself sick. I know what that's like as a mother and grandmother.'

'Okay,' he said, and prepared himself. He took his phone out of his pocket.

Mum: Ed, where are you? Please just let me know you're okay.

Ed: I'm safe and I'm spending the night at Tabby's but I don't feel like I can speak to you right now.

Her response was immediate.

Mum: I hope you're okay. I'm sorry if you're upset. Mrs Simpkins is missing you. xxxx
Mum sent a photo.

Oh no, no, no, Mum, why did you have to do that? I don't want to cry AGAIN! But seeing Mrs Simpkins lying on his bed looking forlorn, waiting for him to get home, made Ed's heart crack. He quickly wiped his eyes with the back of his hand before Gran or Tabby could notice the moisture in them.

'Here you go,' Tabby said, 'strong with two sugars, just how you like it!' She padded across the room in her slippers and presented him with a steaming mug.

Ed felt his face wobble and a lump appear in his throat. The next minute he was full-on crying and there was no way he could stop.

'Give the boy a hug, Tabby,' Gran said. 'I can't get out of the chair quick enough these days or I would do it myself.'

Tabby did as she was told, and he let himself be comforted, while trying not to wipe his nose on her sleeve. There was a pain in his chest over his heart; he was worried that he might never stop crying and would just end up as a puddle of salty tears on the floor.

'There,' Tabby said, patting his back, 'let it out, Ed. Let it all out.'

Now he was safe, here with Tabby and Gran, he let the memories flow unchecked, the ones he'd hidden away in the deep and dark cellars of his brain:

His dad, during a fight with his mum when they had all been living at home, spitting his acerbic words. 'Nobody will ever love you if this is how you act.'

And afterwards, as she'd silently sobbed on the sofa, Ed had sat next to Mum and whispered into her hair, 'I'll always love you, Mum. I'll never leave you. I'll always love you. It will just be me and you, and that will be okay, won't it?'

And she'd replied, 'Just us, Ed. Of course that will be okay. In fact, that's perfect.'

He'd tried to protect her when Dad had shouted, when Dad had threatened to take Ed and Daniel to live with him, leaving Mum alone. Until the day Dad had moved out. Daniel had said he'd split his time equally between the two, but Ed hadn't wanted to do that. He'd kept his promise to Mum: he'd never left her on her own, apart from the weekends when he'd had to go to Dad's, which were now even less frequent. It had always been Mum, Ed and Mrs Simpkins: their own separate, untouchable family.

'Come on,' Tabby said, pressing a tissue and the paracetamol into his hands. 'Try to have something to drink; it's okay to cry, but you've got to keep hydrated, too.'

'Yes, nurse,' he replied with watery eyes. 'Why does it hurt so much, Tabby?'

Ed knew from her look that she could tell exactly how he was feeling. 'Because you care, Ed, and that's never a bad thing. It hurts because you have so much love inside you, and because your mum is important to you. But don't ever apologise for that.'

'We all have to go through change,' Gran added, 'but that doesn't make it any easier. You just have to ride the storm, young man, and make it out the other side. It will get easier eventually.'

That made him think of Hannah; she hated change just like he did. He knew exactly why: change led to the unknown, and the unknown was scarier than anything.

As the evening went on, Tabby wrapped a blanket around him and he snuggled down on the sofa. Later, when Gran went to bed, Tabby got under the blanket and cuddled into him as they watched some light-hearted TV. He was grateful for her presence, even if they said very little.

'Thank you, Tabby,' he said. 'I don't know what I'd do without you.'

'It's a good job you'll never find out, then,' she said. 'I'll always be here for you, Ed. Just as I know you'll always be there for me.'

'Even when we're all old and wrinkly?'

'Especially when we're all old and wrinkly. They'll have to put us in a care home together because we'll never be separated, and we can have adjacent rooms and never leave each other's sides.'

Ed laughed. 'As long as you're there and there are cats, I don't mind,' Ed said.

'Lots and lots of cats. *All* of the cats. And we can have a little door that goes between our rooms that we keep open.'

This was why Tabby was his best friend: because she knew that sometimes he just wanted to chat about absolute rubbish to take his mind off the things that were bothering him. He also knew that if he wanted to change the subject, steer it back into serious territory, she'd be fine with that too.

His phone flashed with a message and he leant forward to get it from the coffee table, dislodging Tabby from his side.

A flicker of a smile appeared at the corners of Ed's lips.

Hannah: How are you today? Hope things are feeling a little
    better!

'Who's that?' Tabby asked; he could tell she was trying not to sneak a peek.

'Hannah from work,' he said, clearing his throat. 'She wanted to see if I was feeling any better.'

Tabby nodded against his shoulder. 'It's nice of her to be worried about you.'

'Yeah, she's decent.'

Ed: Thanks for checking in, you didn't have to! I'd feel better
    for a picture of a cute guinea pig, I'll be honest
    Hannah sent a photo.

'She must care about you, to see how you're doing.'

Ed shrugged against Tabby. 'She's a good colleague, just checking up on a fellow colleague. That's it.'

Tabby burst out laughing. 'A *good colleague*?! Oh, Ed ... Wow. I can't believe you just referred to her as a *good colleague.*'

'Because she is!' Ed threw Tabby a moody pout. 'I take my job seriously, Tabby, and that means getting along well with everyone.'

Tabby rolled her eyes.

'Get some sleep, pal,' she said, pulling the blanket off and getting up from the sofa. She blew him a kiss, and he pretended to try catching it but miss.

'Things will be better in the morning.'

'I hope you're right. Night!' Ed called after Tabby. 'Sweet dreams!'

After she'd retreated down the hall to her bedroom, he settled back on the sofa and waited for sleep to reach him.

His phone didn't flash again; he waited for it to, but it never did.

Instead, he turned to another of Hannah's blog posts.

Seeing as I am a bookseller, I thought today I'd offer you some book recommendations. There's no feeling like seeing yourself represented in a book, and I've taken great comfort from reading books with autistic characters – characters just like me, who understand that touch can be painful if it's not done in the right way, that the world can be overwhelming, and that there's nothing better than having a special interest in which you can lose yourself.

#1 – *The State of Grace* by Rachael Lucas

This is one of my favourite YA books and when I first read it, I thought the author must have looked into my brain and decided to write about me. I loved the main character, Grace, and, as an animal lover, I loved reading about Grace's love for horses. This is a must-read!

#2 – *A Kind of Spark* by Elle McNicoll

Addie, the main character in A Kind of Spark, is such an amazing protagonist. In the book, she's fighting to have a memorial set up to remember the women who were burned in the Scottish witch trials. Her passion and belief are inspiring! We all need to be more like Addie. I was rooting for her all the way.

#3 – *Can You See Me?* by Libby Scott and Rebecca Westcott

My favourite thing about this book was the diary entries of the main character, Tally. They have a truly authentic voice – and even made me feel as if I wanted to keep a diary (although I guess this blog kind of counts as one?!). I think it's very important that when you read books with autistic characters, you also support authors who are autistic – and all the authors in this post are.

#4 – *Diary of a Young Naturalist* by Dara McAnulty

This is a beautiful book all about nature and the environment, written by an autistic teenager. Being outside, surrounded by nature, is such a relaxing activity and whenever I'm out (and not bookselling!) I find so much peace – I never find nature overwhelming, instead I forget all my troubles. In this book, the author's passion for the natural world shines through.

Let me know in the comments if you've read any of these and, if so, what you thought!

Han x

Ed slept well after that, with Hannah's voice floating through his mind, comforting and familiar.

'Wakey-wakey, Sleeping Beauty.'

What's that noise?

'Rise and shine!'

There's definitely a noise coming from somewhere. And maybe a poke. I hope Mrs Simpkins is okay.

'Ed,' a voice said softly. 'Wake up.'

Ed blinked awake; Tabby loomed over him, but she was smiling, which made him smile back.

'Hi,' he said, rubbing his eyes. He attempted to stretch out, but his feet hit the end of the sofa. 'What time is it?'

'Eight in the morning,' Tabby said. 'I didn't want to wake you, you looked so peaceful, but Gran will be up in a minute and I didn't want her to poke you awake.'

'Like you just did?'

She grinned down at him. 'It doesn't count when it's your best friend.'

Tabby was wearing Lycra leggings and a warm hoodie, as well as a winter hat. He spotted her trainers by the door.

'I'm going out for a run,' Tabby said. 'Do you want to come? I'll go slowly, just for you.'

It wasn't that Ed didn't like exercise, he just really didn't want to be doing it first thing in the morning. And this morning of all mornings. He shook his head. 'No, thanks, if you don't mind. I'll stay here and get myself sorted.'

'Okay,' she said, and prepared her phone so she could listen to music. 'I won't be long; I'll just go around the block. Gran'll be up in a minute, and there's bread in the bread bin out in the kitchen. Make yourself some toast if you want. I think we've got strawberry jam in the cupboard.'

'Are you trusting me with the toaster?' he said in disbelief. 'You know what happened to the microwave.'

'Ohmigod. Was that a joke?' Tabby teased. 'Somebody's feeling a little brighter this morning.'

Now Ed thought about it, maybe he was feeling a bit better.

'Don't touch the oven, though!' she called from the hallway, laughing as she shut the door behind her. Ed watched as she stretched outside the window, and then jogged out of the front garden.

I'd better get some breakfast, then. His stomach did feel as if it needed filling up, so he made his way off the sofa and into the kitchen. *Hopefully I can make toast without setting the fire alarm off.*

Halfway through waiting for his toast to pop up, Gran came in wearing pyjamas that, if Ed didn't know better, looked like fitness gear.

'How is that head of yours this morning?' Gran asked, and without waiting for a response added, 'Can you pop two more slices in and boil the kettle, love?' And with that she made her way to the living room.

He was happy to oblige – him being here would let Tabby have some time to herself without feeling guilty for leaving Gran, and he felt useful.

Ed took their tea and toast into the living room, passing Gran's to her before taking a seat on the sofa.

'It must have done you some use to let all that emotion out,' Gran said, taking a sip of tea. 'It's not good to bottle it up, as I always tell Tabby. If it's in there, it's going to come out one way or another.'

'I'm not very good at that kind of thing usually,' Ed admitted.

'That's okay – it comes with age. It will get easier.' Gran finished her last mouthful of toast. 'Right, young Edward.' She reached forward and took an iPad out from its charging point. 'Tabby's out, so you can help me work this technology. I'm not terrible, but I can never find the right buttons on the YouTubes.'

'Of course,' Ed said, and Gran handed the iPad to him. She told him the passcode, which he typed in, and then directed him to YouTube.

'Tabby has set up a playlist for me,' she said, 'called "OAP Zumba". Find that please. And then stand up and prepare yourself. Oh, and can you pull the coffee table to one side to give us some more room? Thank you, Ed!'

He found the playlist that Tabby had set up and clicked on the first video, where a woman in a hot-pink Lycra all-in-one suit played up to the camera. She swished her ponytail around as she chirpily explained the basics.

Gran started squatting, circling her arms in time to the music.

'Time to Zumba!' Ed said, pretending to be more enthusiastic than he really was.

This was maybe the weirdest thing he'd ever done – and would ever do – in his life: Zumba with his best friend's grandmother. As the video went on and on, the level of exercise required grew increasingly more intense, until he could feel sweat prickling down his neck.

'That's it!' Gran said. 'You've got it, Ed!'

He really did not feel as if he'd got it; if anyone had it, it was Gran! She was outdoing him at every step.

Ed was relieved when there was a tap at the window and Gran paused the video, going to the front door so she could investigate.

'Come in,' he heard her say, and the next second an elderly man was standing in the living room.

'Ed, this is my neighbour Mr Helstone from across the road,' Gran said, a redness rising to her cheeks that couldn't only be explained by all the Zumba. To Mr Helstone, Gran shouted, 'This is my Tabby's friend, Ed.

We were just doing a little bit of Zumba to start our morning, weren't we, dear?'

'We certainly were,' Ed said, trying to catch his breath. 'Gotta love a bit of Zumba.'

'Is this Tabby's young man?' Mr Helstone had a gruff way of speaking that made everything he said sound as if it had just a hint of aggression behind it, but Gran didn't seem to notice or care.

'Oh no,' Ed said. 'We're best friends – it is *not* like that.'

'Don't you have a young lass?' Mr Helstone asked Ed, eyeing him up from head to toe.

An image flashed in his head, a face that was becoming more and more familiar to him, but he very swiftly dismissed it and wouldn't give it another thought. Ed shook his head. 'N-no, I don't. I, uh, I'm not really interested . . . I mean, I haven't met anyone that I . . . feel that way about . . . sir.'

'It weren't like that in my day,' Mr Helstone said. 'If you saw a nice young lady, that was it, you'd be married within weeks. And happily married I was until my Mavis left me five years ago for another man. A dancer, he was. Ballroom, not Latin. Well, she did me a favour, in a way; it's given me more time to spend on my garden, and I'm hoping for some good runner beans this year.'

'Absolutely dreadful,' Gran said, tutting. 'But yes, your runner beans should be *spectacular* this year. Not that they weren't last year!'

Ed didn't know what to say.

He didn't care how sweaty Tabby was when she stepped through the door – he was so relieved to see her he could have given her a hug, although he realised he must have been pretty sweaty from the Zumba too. He wasn't sure how much more OAP Zumba or OAP questions about his love life he could take.

Gran and Mr Helstone went to the kitchen, leaving Ed and Tabby to it. 'I bumped into Olivia and Cassie on my run! They were taking pictures for Cassie's latest art project and Olivia mentioned they were going to go for a walk with Lizzie the dog later – do you want to go along? We can let Henry know, too. It might do you some good to get some fresh air.'

Ed hung his head. 'That sounds nice. But I'll need to go home and get changed first.'

'It'll be fine,' she said, reaching out and squeezing his hand. 'If your mum is there, just be civil and try not to get worked up. I need to shower and get changed too, so that'll work well – do you want to meet at your house in an hour-ish?'

Ed said his goodbyes to Gran and Mr Helstone, who seemed to still be talking about runner beans, and headed off with the promise of seeing Tabby and The Paper & Hearts Society later. *I'm so lucky to have such good friends.*

Chapter Twelve

The Paper & Hearts Society were wrapped up warm and waiting outside Ed's house to head out for their walk. His mum hadn't been in – she'd left a note for him 'just in case you come back', and he'd breathed the biggest sigh of relief. He wasn't ready to face her yet.

'Wow, I am so embarrassed to be seen with you,' Cassie said, standing at the bottom of Ed's path and gazing up at the sight of him on the front doorstep. 'Please walk ten steps behind me at all times. I have a reputation to uphold.'

'I think it's cool!' Tabby said. 'It's . . . different, certainly, but there's nothing wrong with that. If Ed is happy, then that's all that matters.'

Lizzie, the little Jack Russell Terrier, began to strain at the lead, and her low growl turned into a sequence of yappy barks.

'Lizzie,' Olivia hissed, 'you'll scare Mrs Simpkins!'

'Actually,' Henry pointed out, 'Mrs Simpkins is the one giving Lizzie the evils.'

Giving Lizzie the evils?! Ed thought. *How could Henry say such a thing?!* 'She is *not* giving anyone the evils! She's an angel; she wouldn't do that!' Ed was fiddling with Mrs Simpkins's collar, tightening it to fit properly so she wouldn't run off. He'd never forgive himself if she got lost. He eventually got the collar at just the right tightness and clipped on the lead. Mrs Simpkins let out a grumpy meow and flicked her tail at him.

'She looks so cute,' Tabby cooed and bent down to scratch her behind the ears.

'You never say that about me,' Ed joked.

'You always look cute; there's no point saying it because it's just assumed,' Tabby said, pretending to scratch him behind the ears, and making Ed laugh.

'Let's do this, Team Paper & Hearts Society!' Olivia called. 'A stroll with friends and pets! What could be better?'

Henry and Tabby walked along arm in arm while Olivia and Cassie chatted away. Olivia passed Lizzie's lead to Cassie, and Cassie passed it straight back to Olivia.

Ed walked behind with Mrs Simpkins, who looked far from impressed.

'Where are we actually going?' Henry asked.

'I thought we could head over to the fields at the end of the cycle track,' Olivia said. 'There's a good path that goes that way, and a picnic site where we can sit down when we get there. Sound okay?'

'Sounds good to me!' Tabby said. 'I'm still trying to explore more of these places you guys just seem to know about.'

Wow, that's further than I thought. Ed looked down at Mrs Simpkins and wondered when her resolve to walk would run out. Surely she wouldn't make it all the way to the picnic site? But it was better than the alternative: Ed moping around at home, hiding away in his bedroom.

'Mrs Simpkins looks as if she's having a great time,' Tabby said to him, unlinking arms with Henry and walking back to keep Ed company. Mrs Simpkins looked as if she was getting the hang of it. She trotted along at his side, while he encouraged her by jingling the lead about so that she'd know he was there.

The group slowed their pace. 'I got an actual decent mark on my physics test this week!' Olivia threw her hands in the air and whooped. 'Can you believe it?!'

'That's amazing!' Ed said as Mrs Simpkins stopped to rub up against a lamp post. 'Wow, Livs, you must be so pleased.'

'I am! I had to do a double take when I saw the result! I nearly fell off my stool.'

'That wouldn't have been good,' Cassie said. 'You'd have knocked all of the science facts out of your brain. My god, I feel so pleased I don't have to remember that stuff any more.'

'Do you want to take Lizzie?' Olivia asked Henry, and he took over. He wasn't as natural as Olivia was, but still didn't do a bad job. 'We can take it in turns; I'll make sure everyone gets a go, don't worry.'

'Sorry to hear about your mum,' Henry said to Ed. Tabby must have filled them all in – which was nice of her as he didn't really want to have to explain everything – because they all looked as if they were paying extra attention to how Ed would answer. 'Well, not sorry for her . . . but sorry for you. That can't be easy.'

Ed shrugged. 'Well, she doesn't care how I feel or she wouldn't be doing this to me – so I don't see why you should care.'

'Of course we care!' Olivia said. 'Your problems are our problems – you should know that by now.'

But Ed didn't want to talk about it. He was supposed to be having a good time with Mrs Simpkins and The Paper & Hearts Society. He wouldn't let the thought of Mum ruin that.

As they made their way past the entrance of the park, Ed heard one little girl shout, 'Is that a cat on a lead?! Cool!' to her mothers, who were swinging her by the arms, just as his parents had done for him when he was younger. The two women gave Ed a very odd look.

It was almost as if Mrs Simpkins had noticed the attention too, as she had fixed her paws to the spot, refusing to go any further.

'I don't think she wants to move, Ed,' Henry pointed out. It wasn't helping that Lizzie was being the perfect pet, eagerly walking through the entrance, and wagging her tail at everyone that passed.

'You need a little backpack for her,' Olivia giggled. 'You know, one of those bags that looks like a spaceship, so the cat can look out of the window!'

'Come on, Mrs Simpkins! You can do it! Just one more step!' Ed tugged at the lead, but Mrs Simpkins had decided that she wasn't going to budge. She was light enough that when he pulled, she slid along the floor, but he was worried he would hurt her if he dragged her too much.

'This isn't going to work,' Ed said. 'I'm going to have to take her back. We'll never get anywhere at this rate. Just go on ahead of me, and I'll come and find you once she's at home again.'

'Can't you just pick her up?' Cassie suggested.

But Ed looked at the miserable expression on Mrs Simpkins's face and knew that carrying her wouldn't be a good decision either.

'No, I really will take her back.'

'Are you sure you want us to go ahead?' Tabby asked.

'Yeah!' He nodded. 'It'll be fine; I'll be able to catch up and, if not, don't worry. We can do this another time.'

With unsure glances, the other members of The Paper & Hearts Society headed off towards the picnic site, wandering into the open countryside.

Mrs Simpkins seemed perfectly fine with walking if it meant going in the direction of home. What must he look like, Ed wondered, wandering the streets talking to a cat on a lead?

'Thanks a lot, you silly cat,' he rebuked her. 'I would be on a walk with my friends right now if it wasn't for you playing up like this. Why would you embarrass me like that? Don't you care about my feelings?'

Mrs Simpkins practically ran all the way home, which made him even madder. 'Oh, so you want to move your legs now? You don't want to lie on the floor like you were doing ten minutes ago? I thought I was a good cat father to you! I thought you'd at least try! I feel so let down, Mrs Simpkins. You aren't the cat I thought you were.'

Ed deposited Mrs Simpkins back home, the cat running down the hallway to be reunited with her biscuit bowl, then he started off again at a quick walk. But by the time he'd got to beyond the park, The Paper & Hearts Society were still nowhere to be found. He was in a terrible mood, wandering around in an unfamiliar part of town, convinced he had the start of a blister on the back of his foot. On one side of the field was a housing estate, and a large playing field was on the other. Ed was sure that if he took the path leading through the middle, eventually he would reach the picnic site.

As he was busy gazing into the distance, a great big black and tan-coloured dog that looked like a German shepherd came bounding up to him. It circled round his body, sniffing at his coat pocket.

'Hey, you,' he said, not sure whether to stroke it or not – some owners were funny with things like that. But the dog wouldn't go away, looking up at him as if it wanted something. He still had a cat treat in his pocket – maybe that was it?

'Ed?'

He looked up, straight into the eyes of . . .

'*Hannah?*' *What were the chances?*

'Looks as if Indiana found you!'

'This is Indiana Bones? Oh wow, she's even more awesome in person!'

Ed might have been a cat person at heart, but he could still appreciate a cute dog when he saw one. He crouched down so his face was level with Indiana Bones.

'Nice to meet you, Indiana Bones,' he said. The dog sat down and, much to Ed's delight, held out a paw, which he proudly shook. 'I'm Ed and I am honoured to finally be in your presence.'

Hannah laughed. 'Seems as if she likes you. What are

you doing here? I haven't seen you around this part of town before.'

He nodded in the direction of the path. 'My friends have gone for a walk and I was supposed to be with them, but I had Mrs Simpkins on a lead, and she really hated it, so I had to take her home. I was going to catch them up, but I have a blister, and I really just can't be bothered today.'

Indiana Bones was now eagerly jumping up at Ed.

'Indiana, down, that's it. Please can you stop annoying Ed?'

'Like dog, like owner,' Ed teased, getting down to Indiana's level again and stroking her. Hannah rolled her eyes at him, but she seemed genuinely pleased that he was there. At least, he hoped she was.

'We've got to stop this habit of bumping into each other,' Ed said, thinking back to the supermarket. 'People will start talking.'

Oh dear. That sounded a lot more . . . well, romantic . . . than I wanted it to be.

'It's okay, I know you're obsessed with me – I get it,' Hannah said.

Ed loved this new banter between them; it felt different when they were away from the bookshop and didn't have to think about customers, or shelving books incorrectly, or Dinah getting them to do the next job, and the next job, and the one after that.

Ed felt himself blush. 'Obsessed with you? More like obsessed with your dog.'

'I don't blame you really; I'm obsessed with her too. Would you like to meet the guinea pigs? I only live around the corner.'

OHMIGOD, SHE'S GOING TO SHOW ME THE GUINEA PIGS!? 'Are you sure?' Ed asked, trying to play it cool.

'Come on,' she beckoned, leading Indiana Bones back in the direction they came. 'Follow me.'

While they made their way through the estate, and Hannah stopped to deal with Indiana Bones needing the toilet, Ed had just enough time to message The Paper & Hearts Society.

Ed: Not to abandon you because YOU KNOW I LOVE YOU
     but I don't think I'm going to be able to catch you up now.
     I am completely fine with this though so please don't feel
     like you can't have fun without me
Ed: (although I hope you all start crying because my
     absence is too painful)
Tabby: Are you OK?
Ed: ABSOLUTELY!
Olivia: Noooooooooo! We're crying already!!
Cassie: speak for yourself

Ed caught up with Hannah, who was now slightly ahead. They formed a little line; Indiana, the leader, certainly knew the direction home.

'Here we are,' Hannah said, as they turned into a cul-de-sac, past a house on the left and towards a tall wooden gate right at the end of a creosoted fence. She twisted the metal handle open, unclipped Indiana's lead and ushered Ed in after her.

The gate led into the back garden, where there was a lawn strewn with wood and mesh hutches and a shed that stretched over half the garden.

'Ready to see the guinea pig palace?' Hannah said. She was grinning wider than he'd ever seen her before, and it made him grin too.

'So ready!'

She led the way down the middle of the lawn, over the stepping stones packed into the grass.

Hannah and Ed stepped inside the shed, greeted by the smell of fresh hay and vegetables.

Surrounding them were long hutches on both sides, divided up into segments depending on how many guinea pigs were in each. The central walkway led up to a window at the end, and halfway down was a store box with a bale of hay and lots of leafy green vegetables. Ed was completely blown away at how amazing this was; it was a dream as an animal lover! He loved how they had that in common.

'This is guinea pig *heaven*,' Ed exclaimed. 'Hannah, I think I might faint right about now because this is *so insanely cool*! How do you ever do anything else other than be in here all day?'

'Trust me,' she said, 'it's a wrench. I'd spend all day in here if I could. So, the tour . . .' Hannah started by taking one of the hutch doors down, and a smooth cream and white guinea pig with flecks of silver immediately stuck its head out. He sniffed the air and looked very content as Hannah tickled him under the chin before popping his head back inside. Hannah reached out and held him to her chest.

'This is Bertie and he's very cheeky. If you can believe it, he's being a little shy because he knows you're somebody different. But he plays up to the attention if it's someone he knows well.'

'Hello, Bertie,' Ed said, but resisted the urge to shake his tiny little paw as he'd done with Indiana Bones. The German shepherd had followed them into the shed and was rolling around on the floor, hay collecting in her fur.

Hannah popped Bertie back inside, lifting the door back on to the hutch, and moved to the next. 'And this is a family group: here we have Hazel, her granddaughter Saba, and Saba's daughter Betsy. You shouldn't have favourites, but . . .'

She pointed to each in turn so that Ed could get to know them properly. He'd already seen a picture of Hazel, with her orange and white fur. Saba had a long, flowing mane the colour of chocolate grizzled with grey, and her daughter Betsy was white with stripes of black and a patch of orange over her eye.

Hannah was beaming now, so much so that Ed thought her face must ache, and she was a lot chattier too. And open to his questions.

'Can I – can I *hold* one?' Ed asked, his eyes wide with excitement and confidence building. 'I promise I'll try not to drop them. I swear I'll be really good!'

'Oh, I know who you can hold! You'll love her.' Hannah moved on down the shed, to the hutch at the end, and lifted a smooth-haired tricolour guinea pig out. She was black, white and a golden brown, with bright, beady eyes. 'This is Hermione and while you'll be fine to hold her, be warned, she's a known escape artist. When she was little, we had two hutches side by side and she managed to squeeze out to steal food from the other, and hop back in when we weren't looking. When she's out on the lawn, she's always trying to escape, too.'

'She sounds like a girl after my own heart! They've all got so much character,' Ed said. 'How do I . . . how do I hold her?'

'Like this,' Hannah demonstrated, holding the guinea pig in her arms, Hermione's little paws digging slightly into her skin. Ed hoped her claws weren't as sharp as Mrs Simpkins's. 'Make sure to support her properly, and hold her close to your chest. Keep a firm hand over her body, but don't be too rigid or she'll know you're scared. Got it?'

'Got it.' He took a deep breath in, and then Hannah lifted the guinea pig into his arms. At first, he panicked and wasn't sure if he was doing it right, but then he relaxed and loved the feeling of Hermione's soft fur.

'Take a picture, take a picture!' Ed was excitable, but he didn't want to be *too* enthusiastic – what if he forgot he was holding Hermione and threw his arms out wide in all his elation, and she went flying? He wouldn't put it past himself to do something stupid like that.

Hannah held her phone up and snapped some photos.

Here, in her own environment, Ed noticed she was more relaxed, more . . . *at home* – but then she *was* at her home, so it was no wonder really.

Ed inspected the creature in his palm. 'I always thought guinea pigs had tails,' Ed said, and Hannah gasped in response.

'Tails?! Guinea pigs don't have tails! Cover your tiny ears, Hermione!'

Ed laughed. 'And they're awake in the day. I thought guinea pigs were only awake at night, going round and round on little wheels.'

'Please give my guinea pig back and get out,' she said, shaking her head. 'Please get out now because I cannot believe you just confused guinea pigs with hamsters.'

Ed bent his head and whispered an apology to Hermione.

'But they are quite similar, you have to admit.'

'They are worlds apart. Ed, this is unbelievable!' Hannah said, crossing her arms, an eyebrow raised. 'Hamsters are not the same as guinea pigs. Cover your ears, all of you piggies. Don't listen to a word he says. This is such a disgrace.'

He chuckled and carefully handed Hermione back to Hannah. 'Do I get to hold another one now? I want to share my love between them all!'

Ed was given Elsa to hold next. She was actually very heavy for such a small creature, and Ed was glad that she was happy to sit in his arms while Hannah finished the tour.

Other guinea pigs included satin-coated Englebert, whose coat shined the brightest of all, who had his own hammock hanging from the hutch he shared with his brother. There was Emily, Anne and Charlotte, named after the Brontë sisters. And Leveret, who yawned like a lion when they passed her cage, which she shared with Raven and Beatrix.

There was a punnet of strawberries resting on one of the hutches and Hannah took one, holding it out to Ed. 'Elsa will eat it out of your hand if you hold it still,' she said. He was aware of being careful not to touch her hand, only the strawberry, as he took it from Hannah, so that he wouldn't surprise her with his light touch. Ed was delighted when the pig started to sink her teeth into the juicy flesh of the fruit.

'This is the best day of my life,' Ed said. 'Honestly, I mean that. This is incredible. Can I move into this shed?' *I'd prefer it to having to confront Mum when I get home.*

'If I open the door in the morning and you're hiding in here, I'm going to kick you out,' Hannah kidded. 'Shall we put Elsa back now?'

Feeling braver and surer of himself with the guinea pig in his arms, he turned away. 'No!' he cried. 'I love her too much! You can't take Elsa away from me!'

'I can! I will!' Hannah was laughing, and dived for Elsa. She could only grab her by putting her arms around Ed and effectively hugging him until he conceded the guinea pig.

'Oh,' she said and jumped back, but not before Ed had turned bright red and surrendered the guinea pig awkwardly.

She took Elsa from him and put her back in her rightful place. Neither of them said anything.

'Do you want some cake?' Hannah asked as she turned back around. 'I made a Victoria sponge last night.'

'Jeez, this really *is* the best day of my life! Guinea pigs and cake?!'

Yes! A joke! The awkward atmosphere between them disappeared. Ed tried not to think about why he was so embarrassed, why he was wishing for . . . *No, Ed. That's a weird thought to have about someone you work with.*

They put the shed awkwardness behind them and Hannah told him to take a seat at the table outside, while she went inside to cut the cake. She came out a few moments later carrying two plates, with two blankets strewn over her shoulders, and handed Ed his cake and a blanket, sitting down opposite him.

'It's easier to talk outside,' she said. 'I hope you don't mind: Indiana Bones starts barking for attention if a guest comes in.'

'I don't mind. You are spoiling me with cake, after all,' Ed said through a mouthful of gooey cream icing. 'Did you *really* make this?'

Hannah smiled. 'Do I not look as if I could be a *Bake Off* contestant?'

'I don't know, but I couldn't be,' he said, 'seeing as nobody trusts me to step inside the kitchen these days. I'd never pass the risk assessment.'

'Stick to bookselling,' she said with a smile. 'You can't burn books in the oven.'

I wouldn't put it past myself!

'I love how passionate you are about your guinea pigs,' Ed said, taking another bite. 'It shines through. Like, I can tell you love bookselling, but when you speak about your animals, you come alive in a completely different way.'

She laughed, putting her plate on the table. 'Sometimes I forget that other people are around me when I'm thinking about or discussing my special interests.'

'Special interests?'

'It's what some people call the obsessions – or passions, I prefer that – of autistic people. We get very fixated on certain subjects such as, in my case, guinea pigs. It's why I know so many random facts; it's why I care so much. When I'm around them, when I'm thinking about them, nothing else exists apart from this ball of energy, and it makes me want to keep talking and just living and breathing my special interests. It's pretty cool, to be honest. I wouldn't ever want to change it.'

'Good!' Ed said. 'I wish more people were like that – so passionate about something. It makes conversation easier, for one.'

'Right?' Hannah smiled and tucked a loose strand of hair behind her ear, and Ed could see her fully again. 'You know how much I hate small talk – it makes me want to scream or cry – but I could talk all day, every day about animals or guinea pigs or certain books that I really love.'

Ed held a hand over his heart. 'Like me and the love of my life, William Shakespeare,' he said.

'How are things at home now?' Hannah asked, the one question Ed dreaded.

But he had to answer; he couldn't exactly refuse. 'Complicated,' he said. '*Way* more complicated than I had anticipated. Everything's the same with my dad, but as it turns out, my mum has a boyfriend. I did . . . not see that one coming.'

He took another bite of cake for something to do as she replied, 'Wow, that's rough. Sorry.'

He shrugged. 'What can I do? Please tell me you have a less complicated family situation. I envy you if you do.'

'I guess,' she said. 'My grandad lives with us now after my grandma died, but otherwise things are pretty uneventful. He really liked you, by the way – he'll be so pleased to know you've seen the guinea pigs now.' *Uneventful. Wow, I'd love that.*

Long after the cake had been eaten, and when the afternoon was beginning to draw to a close, Ed checked the time on his phone and audibly gasped. *Is that really the time?!* He hadn't thought about how long they'd been sat outside, chatting in the cold, because he'd been cosy under his blanket, and completely swept away in the moment. He gulped.

Should he feel guilty about ditching his friends? He would have had fun with The Paper & Hearts Society today, but this was a different kind of fun. Cuddling guinea pigs, eating cake, spending time with Hannah ... He couldn't remember the last time he'd had such a good time.

'Sorry! It's been ages since I got here. I think I love your guinea pigs more than anything else in the world,' Ed said, pushing his chair back and getting up. 'I really enjoyed this; thank you. You didn't need to bring me here, but it was cool.'

Hannah led Ed back through the gate. 'It was fun,' she said, standing at the end of her drive. 'I enjoyed myself. A lot. I don't have loads of friends because wow, that's a lot of effort – and none of them have ever even attempted to memorise the names of all my guinea pigs. But this was fun. I had a good time – and Indiana Bones here likes you, too.' She held on to Indiana's collar to stop her running off. 'And I trust her judgement.'

'She clearly has good taste,' he said with a laugh, and shook Indiana's paw as a goodbye.

'See you!' Hannah called, and Ed turned towards home. He walked down the street with a skip in his step, not even noticing the blister that had developed. Ed thought it must be the excitement of meeting so many guinea pigs at once . . . But it wasn't only the guinea pigs he thought about when he got home. Hannah floated in his mind – the way she cared so much for her beloved animals, how she brought their personalities to life by her very being, and how happy she'd made him; how at peace he felt in her presence.

How does that happen? I was feeling miserable and now suddenly I don't feel half as bad.

Hannah sent a photo.

Hannah sent a photo.

Hannah sent a photo.

Hannah: I have never seen anyone so excited to hold a
guinea pig in my life

Ed: Ahh I LOVE these pictures I'm going to frame them and
hang them all over the house

Hannah: Your mum will be ecstatic, I'm sure!

Tabby: Hey! Thought I'd check in with you to see if you're
okay? We really did miss you, I promise! Are you sure
you weren't upset that you didn't catch up with us? I
don't want to have made your day worse!

Ed sent a photo.

Ed: Trust me, I love you guys but I was not upset

Tabby: Is that a GUINEA PIG?

Ed: YES IT IS

Ed sent a photo.

Tabby: Where did you see all of these guinea pigs? Omg
how many are there

Ed: A LOT

Tabby: Did you break into a pet shop or something?!

Ed: I bumped into Hannah when I was on my way to catch
you up and she let me go to her house

Tabby: 'Bumped into' SURE

Ed: I SWEAR it was entirely innocent. We're colleagues! Of
course I like her – she's cool, we work together, we have
similar interests. What's not to like?

Tabby: Fine, I'll drop the subject. For now! But I am telling
the others about this

Ed: TABBY!

Ed: I know I said it before I left but thank you so much for having me earlier. If I didn't have Mrs Simpkins, I would be begging you for guinea pigs right now

Hannah: Don't worry, there was nothing else I would have preferred doing. It was good. And I'll keep you on the guinea pig waiting list!

Chapter Thirteen

Ed spent most of the following week at work and college, eking out every second and putting in extra time so he wouldn't have to go home to the Arctic conditions that Mum had created. *She only has herself to blame.* When Ed had finally got in on Sunday evening, he and Mum had eaten their meals together in complete silence, only commenting on what was happening on TV. Whenever he was home, Ed spent as much time in his room as he could, using revision and homework as an excuse. And now, Mum was acting sheepish and he couldn't be bothered with it.

Today's Woolf and Wilde shift had been extra exciting. Dinah had shown Ed how to select which books to order and allowed him to curate his own section on the 'Staff Picks' shelf, but all good things had to come to an end.

'Hello, you,' he said to Mrs Simpkins when he got in. She was lapping up water from her extra water bowl by the front door. 'Have you had a good day?'

Ed stopped. On the other side of the wall, he could hear his mum on the phone in the living room, a call that she was hastily trying to end. 'Look, Phil, I've got to go. I'll ring you later, if that's okay? Yes, he's back. Yes, speak soon, bye now, bye, bye.'

Remember to breathe. Act as if you haven't heard anything. It would be better to pretend as if nothing had changed, as if he'd never been told about *that man*. Easier said than done.

'Is that you, Ed?'

Who else would it be? I can't exactly ignore her. Can I?

'Yeah.'

'I thought you were back. Was work okay today?' she called.

Ed shrugged off his coat and hung it over the bannister. 'Yeah.'

He bent down to scratch Mrs Simpkins under the ears and ran his hand across her back and up her upright tail. She turned around and stared at him with her loving beady eyes.

'Are you coming in?' Mum asked.

Ed took a deep breath and went into the living room, where Mum had muted the sound on the TV quiz she was watching. Ed could see her sitting on the armchair out of the corner of his eye, but he didn't look at her, instead going to draw the curtains against the dark and turning on a few extra lamps.

'Did you sell lots of books today?'

'Uh-huh,' he said, shaking things up from his usual 'yeah' as he repositioned the vase on the coffee table.

'Do you want to sit down?'

'Not really.' But he perched on the sofa.

'Ed, please let me talk,' Mum said. 'I don't want things to be awkward between us.'

'I'm not ready.' He got up, and made to leave. 'I need some more time and space. Come on, Mrs Simpkins, it's homework time.'

'Okay, I can give you time,' Mum said, 'but not indefinite time, Ed. That's not fair on me.'

'If you need me, I'll be in my room.'

'Ed . . .'

Ed made his way upstairs, Mrs Simpkins following obediently behind him. He made sure to shut the door behind them, then closed his blinds and crawled on top of his duvet.

He *could* do homework tonight, but maybe he'd try to do some reading for pleasure instead. He had that stash of proofs from the bookshop to go through. He reached over to his desk and piled them on his bed. *I could look at the first chapter of each and decide which one to read in its entirety first!*

His phone flashed.

Hannah: I saw this cat video and thought of you! It reminded
me of that meme of the cat with its head in a slice of
bread

Ed: Hahahaha I LOVE it! Is it stuck in that cardboard box?!

Hannah: I think so! I think these videos should come with a
'NO ANIMALS WERE HARMED IN THE MAKING OF
THIS' warning though. Poor thing!

Ed sent a photo.

Ed: Mrs Simpkins did something similar once and my mum
took this photo as I was rescuing her. I panicked so
badly! I can't imagine not having an animal in my life.
She means everything to me

Hannah: I'm the same. Even when people are confusing
and I'm having a bad day, I know my animals will be
there to comfort me at the end of it. They've helped me
more than they will ever know.

Ed: I love that. Animals are amazing, aren't they?

Hannah: A customer came in asking for a book about
guinea pigs when you were on your break earlier and
I had to stop myself from screaming lots of very
random guinea pig facts at them! Did you know that
all guinea pigs have a little bald patch behind their
ears?

Ed: Really?!

Hannah: Yes! And, just like humans, guinea pigs can't store
vitamin C so they need a constant supply of veg to keep

them healthy. They eat better than I do – I'm a super
fussy eater

Ed: Are you just a walking library of guinea pig information?
It's very cool! I wish I had a memory like that

Hannah: Something like that!

Ed suddenly realised that when he was messaging Hannah, he didn't feel as if he needed to tell lots of jokes, and his style was different. He wasn't writing in caps. It all just flowed, as if the phone wasn't really there at all. He loved chatting to her, especially sharing cat and animal videos. Apart from Olivia with Lizzie, none of his friends were super into animals like he was. He remembered the looks on their faces when he brought Mrs Simpkins out on the lead the other day. *I can tell that deep down they think I'm silly for loving Mrs Simpkins as much as I do.*

Ed: Do you want to do work with animals? I know you have
the job at Woolf and Wilde (haha, obviously!) but is that
what you'd like to do? You'd be very good at it!

Hannah: I'm not sure! Maybe! I'm just trying to get through
college first. I hate it. The end of next year can't come
soon enough

Ed: Really? I don't actually mind college – yes it can be
annoying sometimes, but on the whole I don't mind it

Hannah: I'm okay if I'm straight in to my lessons and out
    again but I don't like to hang around for too long because
    there's always too many people in the corridors and the
    LIGHTS
Ed: The lights?!
Hannah: They're like super strength bulbs or something and
    they give me a headache
Ed: So no 'light bulb moments' for you?!

While he was waiting for Hannah's reply, Ed crept downstairs, behind the wall of the living room, where luckily Mum was watching her quiz show at full volume again. He grabbed a big bowl of cereal to take back to his room . . . and then sat back on his bed, moving the pile of proofs on to the floor – they had been long abandoned in favour of his fellow bookseller.

Hannah: Hahaha certainly not!
Hannah: I've got to warn you, I am liable to sometimes
    forget to reply to your messages, sometimes I write a
    reply in my head and don't realise that I've not actually
    typed it out and hit send. It's a PROBLEM
Ed: So it's not because you really hate talking to me and are
    going to ghost me for ever more?
Hannah: No I don't actually mind talking to you

Oh. He hadn't expected her to say that. It made him feel ... Well ... Happy? No, it was more than that. Ed hadn't even realised he was smiling down at his phone until his face muscles began to ache.

'Night, Ed,' Mum called through his bedroom door, but he pretended to already be asleep. When he heard her footsteps retreat across the landing, he picked up his phone again.

Ed: A compliment! A compliment! It's a miracle!

Hannah: Oh shush! I'm nice to you!

Hannah: look I better go to bed or I'll never get up in time to feed the guinea pigs or walk Indiana Bones in the morning

Hannah sent a photo.

Hannah: she's sleeping at the bottom of my bed

Ed sent a photo.

Ed: Mrs Simpkins is doing exactly the same!

Hannah: They look as if they'd be the best of friends but in reality I think Indiana Bones would try to eat Mrs Simpkins

Ed: ...

Hannah: hahaha! Now I really do need to sleep!! Night Ed!

Ed: Night Hannah!

He put his phone down on the bedside table and lay back on the bed, staring up at the whorls on the ceiling.

*All is not so bad in the world after all. I like Hannah?
It's just weird that I keep getting this strange butterflies-in-
tummy feeling whenever she's around, and talking to her is
by far the brightest part of my day. IS THIS WHAT IT FEELS
LIKE TO HAVE A CRUSH? Do I have a crush?*

Oh god, I do.

Mrs Simpkins, what the hell am I supposed to do now?

1) *It's not all about books – it's mostly about learning how to cope with aching feet.*

Whenever I tell people I'm a bookseller, they usually think it's glamorous, as if I lounge about in the bookshop all day, reading in a comfy armchair. In reality, it's a bit like a workout: the weights are the piles of books you have to carry; the cardio is running up and down the stairs to go between customers who demand your attention; and at the end of the day, your feet feel as if they're going to drop off because you can't remember the last time you sat down. (But I wouldn't exactly change it.)

2) *The customer is always right . . . almost never.*

I'd love a pound for every time a customer has tried to convince me of a book's title or the author and I know they're wrong but I have to act as if they're correct. Then I'll lead them to the right section and find the right author, and by this point, I've perfected a brilliant eyebrow raise, just enough to convey my satisfaction. They always look a little sheepish. The customer isn't always right; you're the one who has been hired for your passion for books.

3) *Listen to the kids; most of the time, they know their own minds.*

My absolute pet hate is when parents bring their kids

into the bookshop and tell them to choose a book, but don't actually let them have any of their choices. They'll say things like, 'But you're too old for that book – it's for babies!' or, 'No, that book is meant for girls and you're a boy. Find something else.' It really winds me up! I hate the disappointed looks on the children's faces. Sometimes, I've had to diffuse the situation with another book recommendation.

4) *It's the best job in the world!*
Despite my grumbles, I can't imagine wanting to do anything else. I'm so glad I decided to apply for the job at my local bookshop because it's changed my life. There are good days and definitely bad days, but I wouldn't swap it for the world. It's made me more confident – I meet lots of new people, and I've also discovered so many more books.

Han x

Chapter Fourteen

On any other dark and rainy day, Ed might have felt miserable, but there was something extra magical about a dark and rainy day spent in Woolf and Wilde. Amongst the books, with the soft lights illuminating the shelves, the tinkle of coffee cups from the cafe and the occasional jingling of the bell as a soggy customer came in, there was a cosiness that felt as if it could only exist in this moment.

'These are great!' a boy of about nine said. He was beaming up at Ed, showing off the gaps in his mouth where teeth should have been. He clutched the *How to Train Your Dragon* series in his arms, and his mother next to him looked grateful. 'I'm going to love these so much!'

'I really hope you do enjoy them,' Ed said. 'I loved them when I was your age. You'll have to come back in when you've finished them and let me know what you think.'

'I will! I will, won't I, Mum?'

'Yes, darling. Say thank you to the nice man, won't you?' Ed didn't really feel as if he was old enough to be called a 'nice man', but he accepted their gratitude.

As they took their books downstairs to pay, Ed was left in the children's section. He'd originally come here to tidy up and gather his thoughts, but had been sidetracked by the mother and son. Now they were gone, he had time to himself.

Hannah looked . . . lovely this morning, in a flower-print dress with slightly puffy sleeves. He almost couldn't bear to look at her, she was so pretty. As soon as she'd walked into the staffroom to put her stuff away, he'd had to stop himself from screaming some rambling rubbish in her face, had to tamper down this new feeling of joy and excitement whenever she was around. He didn't want to scare her, and he was scaring himself. He felt very flustered all of a sudden.

He cringed now as he thought back to what he'd said: *'Hey! It's the guinea pig girl!' Why can't you just be a normal human being who doesn't make a fool of themselves at every turn?* he'd cursed. *Why am I LIKE THIS?*

Hannah had screwed her face up, in definite cringe-mode. He'd turned away, quickly busying himself, straightening out the pile of books on the table next to him so she wouldn't see how red his face had turned.

Ever since, he'd tried to keep himself out of the way: offering to take leaflets for the Woolf and Wilde spring

190

literary festival into the cafe and arrange them nicely; running up and down the stairs with this morning's new stock. Anything that would mean it got his brain concentrating on something other than Hannah.

But now he was done with all his tasks and had to head back downstairs, where he noticed Dinah behind the till. Hannah was also down there, tidying one of the shelves. *Just be cool and normal, Ed. Okay, maybe not cool because that might come across as creepy. ACT NORMAL AND CASUAL. Do not, I repeat, DO NOT, embarrass yourself! You do not want to mess this up!*

'Greetings, fellow booksellers!'

Okay, that was definitely not casual. He had to stop speaking before he'd actually engaged his brain.

But instead of cringing as he thought she would, Hannah waved and replied with her own, 'Greetings! Why are you looking so cheerful?'

'It's just a joyous day to be surrounded by books, that's all!'

Ed couldn't help but grin; in fact, his face hurt from all the grinning it was doing today. Things might have been terrible at home, but this, right here, was magic.

'Hannah,' Dinah said, ushering them both over. 'You couldn't sort out the window display for the Books of the Month, could you? Ed'll help you, won't you?'

Ed nodded. 'Yeah, I'd love that!'

'Okay, cool,' Hannah said. 'Ed, why don't we go upstairs and raid the props cupboard? You can be the muscles of the operation; I'm not carrying everything down the stairs if I can help it.'

'Let's do it!'

It felt like an honour to be asked to help with the window display – it was what the customers saw as soon as they turned the corner into the street, their first impression of the shop. He remembered a display in the window when he was little: a library-themed doll's house, all lit up with the doors propped open by books, so you could see inside. He'd dragged his mum to see it every time they were in town, and Daniel had laughed at Ed, saying, *'Why are we here again, looking at this stupid house with the tiny books and tiny bookshelves? We get it, it's tiny!'* Ed had wanted to shrink down and step inside the doll's house, become the tiny librarian, looking after all the tiny books, to be on the inside looking out.

Now *he* was going to get a say in making a window display up. He just hoped he could focus on the task at hand and not all the weird, confusing thoughts that were going around in his head.

Ed didn't mind climbing the stairs again, even though he would usually complain about it. He took them two at a time, even trying to outdo himself with a huge three step. Hannah laughed at him and shook her head in disbelief.

'You'll do yourself a mischief,' she said, but even she jumped up two steps to the top, with a giggle of her own.

'See! It's fun!'

'Not when you break your neck because you're too busy showing off to think about your safety.'

Ed clutched a hand to his heart. 'Hannah, I didn't know you cared!'

'I don't!' she joked, pushing past him to reach the props cupboard first, which she unlocked with a key from her pocket, before walking in. It wasn't exactly roomy, but it was big enough for them both to stand up in side by side.

The cupboard was stuffed with the most random items: feather boas, stuffed animals, tiny doll's house furniture and what looked like a mini fridge. Whatever you could think of, it was probably sitting in the props cupboard.

'Our Books of the Month have quite a natural theme to them this time – they're about the environment, mostly, or are set in the great outdoors. So the plan is to invoke that in the window display – we'll bring the outdoors indoors!'

'Love it,' Ed said. 'Do we, like, keep the top windows open and bring the rain and wind in too? Or maybe we could put so many huge plants around the shop that people feel as if they're in a forest, not a bookshop.'

'*Sensible* suggestions are welcome, of course,' Hannah said, scanning the built-in shelves for what she needed. She picked a few items from the top and asked him to hold them, to which he obliged. 'Although maybe instead of opening the top windows we could just take the glass out altogether, really leave things open to the elements. I'll ask Dinah and see what she thinks.'

That took Ed by surprise. 'Ha! I knew you'd come round to my idea.'

'See what you're doing to me – you're making me think all these silly things! I can't believe I actually just said that.'

'You love it really,' he teased.

For the second time that day, she surprised him with her answer. 'Yes,' she said, 'I must admit, I do.'

He felt himself blush, self-conscious over the sudden turn the conversation had taken. Suddenly, this tiny cupboard felt way too small for the two of them. Hannah seemed to feel it too because the next moment she was loading a huge papier-mâché tree into Ed's arms and getting the final props she needed – what looked like a bag full of fake leaves and felt mushrooms.

'Right, let's go,' she said. 'That's about all we need for now.'

Ed's arms were laden as Hannah directed him down each step. *No showing off now!* He really might break his neck – and the shop had filled up with customers. Not that Ed could see many of them from behind the tree; it obscured most of his view.

'Ed! We didn't know you worked here!'

'Uh, hi! Hi! Who is that?' he said, fumbling around with the cumbersome tree before Hannah said, 'I'll take that from you now.'

Ed grinned as he saw the two people standing in front of him, although he hadn't failed to notice Hannah's swift departure, over to the window.

'Rocky! Nell! Hi!' He was pleased to see the two members of Olivia's Read with Pride group, the one she'd formed to take on her school library's discriminating system. 'Are you book shopping? Can I help you with anything?'

'We're just browsing,' Nell insisted.

But at the same time, Rocky, looking more than guilty, said, 'Well, actually . . .'

Nell shot them a dirty look, but in the end gave up with a roll of her eyes. 'Oh, just tell him.'

Rocky leant their body closer to Ed, darting a look to check nobody else was listening in. 'We're on a secret mission – Oscar and Alf are in the cafe and we think they're on a date! They were being very secretive about it but we wanted to check everything was okay. So we thought we'd *casually* pop by Woolf and Wilde.'

'A total coincidence,' said Nell.

Ed had got to know Rocky and Nell, as well as the other members of the Read with Pride group, through helping Olivia out with her mission to make her school more LGBTQ+ friendly – and he'd grown rather fond of them. Even though he was still concerned after Olivia had burned out with stress, he loved how passionate Read with Pride were – and so he couldn't be more pleased to see two of the members in the shop.

'Wow!' Ed said. 'That's certainly exciting for them! Do you want me to hand over the CCTV footage or . . .?'

'Could you do that?' Rocky said, so hopeful until they saw Ed's face and figured he was joking.

'Sadly not,' he said, 'but I wish you luck in your quest. And also wish you luck if they find out you're spying – I can't imagine either Oscar or Alf would be too happy about that.'

'It'll be fine,' Nell said, linking her arm through Rocky's. 'Come on, Rockstar. Let's see if we can spot them.'

'Nice to see you!' Ed called with a wave, and Nell and Rocky went off to peer around the cafe entrance.

He practically skipped back to Hannah at the window, so excited to get started.

'Friends?' Hannah asked. She had taken the old display out while he'd been talking, so they were left with a blank canvas to begin working on.

'Sort of,' he said. 'My friend's friends, but they're cool.'

'I thought maybe they were part of your book club. Which I've been meaning to ask you more about, as it goes.'

'Trust me,' he said, 'you'd know if it was The Paper & Hearts Society in here. There would be no books left on the shelves, for one thing; we can never resist a good book shopping expedition. You must have seen us in here before!'

'Probably,' she said, 'but I'm not the best with faces. They're all blurry in my brain if I try to remember them. Can you help me string up this bunting? I think it was used for a harvest festival thing one year, but it fits our theme so we may as well reuse it.'

As Hannah handed it to him, their hands brushed; Ed shot his back.

'Sorry!' he said quickly.

'No, it's fine,' she said with a smile that melted his heart. 'Thanks for remembering.'

I need to pull myself together!

Being taller than Hannah, he reached up high to pin the bunting in place, while she made sure it didn't get tangled in the process. Then they moved on to setting up the papier-mâché tree, right in the centre of the display.

'I saw some of your Society meetings on Instagram,' Hannah said. 'They do seem very cool – did you really go on a literary road trip?'

'So you've been stalking me! Can't get enough of me? Is that it?'

Hannah laughed. Was it wishful thinking that the fact she didn't instantly disagree meant it was true? No, he was reading into it too much.

Once Ed had started chatting about The Paper & Hearts Society, he couldn't stop. He told her about their road trip, Olivia's Read with Pride campaign, and their latest murder-mystery and book-cover-recreation meetings.

'We always try to live our best bookish lives,' Ed said, wrestling with a toy squirrel, pretending it was a real animal while Hannah held back a giggle.

'Will you leave Squirrel Nutkin alone?' she scolded. 'It certainly sounds as if you're all living your best bookish lives. I'm exhausted just hearing about it.'

He wondered if he'd ever get to invite Hannah to a Paper & Hearts Society meeting. *Would she want to come? Would they let her?* But the two happy parts of his life joining up would make his world complete.

One of the books going in the window display was a children's non-fiction title about volcanos, with a red-hot lava-spewing volcano big and bold on the front cover.

'Bet this is an *explosive* read,' Ed said, wiggling his eyebrows.

Hannah groaned. 'That is the worst pun I have ever heard.'

'What do you call a cute volcano?'

'Don't know – what *do*—'

'*Lava*ble. Get it? Like loveable! But lava!'

'I can't take any more!' she said, laughing. 'They're too awful! Save me!'

After they had finished and Ed went back to serving behind the till, he was buzzing. He'd just helped with a Woolf and Wilde window display! What a dream come true! Afterwards they'd both – along with Dinah – gone out to look at it from the other side and, other than a few tweaks, mainly due to Ed forgetting the attention to detail, it was perfect. A bright, natural display that would hopefully draw potential customers right in.

'Good work today,' Hannah said, leaning past him to put the scissors away in their pot. They were so close, Ed could feel her body heat next to his, which was getting warmer by the second. Had someone turned the central heating up in here?

'Wow, praise?' he said, hoping and praying he wasn't blushing. 'Can you just repeat that so I can record it and remember it for posterity?'

'Ha, ha,' she said with a sarcastic shake of her head. 'I thought you'd have figured out that I don't hate you by now. In fact, I rather like you, Ed. Maybe I got lucky when you were hired. Woolf and Wilde wouldn't be the same without you.'

Ed thought he might faint. What had she said? Now he really did want her to repeat it. But she'd turned away to neaten up the counter and the opportunity was gone, not that he had really been considering it.

Oh wow, I think I'm in trouble! I've never felt this way about anyone before. WHAT AM I GOING TO DO?

Ed: Henry are you at home?

Henry: Yes, why? I'll be here all afternoon and evening.
  Everything okay?

Ed: Is Tabby with you?

Henry: No, she's coming over for dinner, but not for a
  couple of hours

Ed: I'M COMING ROUND RIGHT NOW

Chapter Fifteen

'To what do I owe this pleasure?' Henry asked, letting Ed in. The lenses of his glasses were dirty with fingerprints, highlighted by the glare of the setting sun.

'Oh, I just want to hang out with my best buddy,' Ed said, putting his hand forward for a fist bump. Henry shot him an odd look.

'Ed . . .'

'Honestly, I just wanted to hang out, the two of us, on our own! Do I need an ulterior motive?'

'I suppose not, no.' Henry thought about it, and then bumped his fist against Ed's. The two of them headed to the conservatory at the back of Henry's house.

'You can relax, you know,' Henry said, when Ed sat down on the small sofa in the conservatory. Ed hadn't realised how tense he was, so he let himself sink in, and tipped his head back. He didn't have a headache exactly, but it did feel as though his brain was spinning around up there, or maybe doing a merry little dance.

Ed cleared his throat. 'Um, Henry, how did you, uh, know that you liked Tabby?'

'We all liked Tabby,' Henry said. 'Didn't we? You liked Tabby when you met her. I think it was impossible to dislike her.'

This was true: Ed had instantly liked Tabby, and had never once questioned whether they could be friends or not. She'd fitted right in, as if she was always meant to be there.

But that wasn't what Ed meant. 'No,' he clarified, 'I mean "like" as in ... feelings that ... aren't friendly.' *No, that's not what I mean, it sounds as if I don't like Tabby!* 'I mean, how did you know you, um, felt a spark between you?'

Henry stared at Ed from the armchair opposite him, before picking up his glass of water from the coffee table and drinking it down in one. 'If you're trying to tell me you've got a crush on Tabby, Ed, then this is going to be strange. I don't really want a weird love-triangle situation going on.'

'No, no!' Ed waved his hands around in panic. 'I love Tabby! God, I love her, but I'm not *in* love with her, Henry! Although, just saying, I think I could beat you in an arm wrestle.'

Henry's shoulders relaxed, and he burst out laughing. 'In your dreams.'

'In your nightmares! Anyway, that's beside the point. What I'm trying to ask is how did you know that you were, ahem, romantically attracted to Tabby and wanted to pursue her hand?'

Henry once again burst out laughing. 'Ed, why are you speaking like a Victorian?'

Ed lowered his voice. 'I'm trying to speak to you! I'm trying to have a man-to-man chat!'

Henry coughed. 'Ed, I wouldn't exactly call either of us pictures of masculinity, would you? You don't need to put on that gruff voice. I've known you long enough to work out when you're putting it on.'

'Okay, okay.' Ed waved his hand. 'I'm just trying to be serious! Was there a moment when you, like, realised that you fancied Tabby?'

'Uh, yeah, I guess there was,' Henry said. 'It wasn't love at first sight; we became good friends first, as you know, got to know each other slowly, and then I suppose . . . Actually, no, there wasn't one moment; it was a collection of moments that fitted together and made me realise that when I was with her, I was at my happiest.'

Ed nodded. 'And how did you know that she'd feel the same? Were you worried she'd reject you?'

Henry's expression changed. 'Ed, what's this about?' He looked concerned, and Ed didn't want him to be concerned. Ed wanted him to keep talking.

Ed sighed. 'Well . . . uh . . . See, the thing is, I've decided to write a book and it's a very big deal. I want to get the storyline accurate, so I thought I'd ask you some questions.'

Henry looked far from convinced. 'You're writing a book? *That's* really what this is about?'

'Yes, so for research purposes, were you worried that Tabby wouldn't feel the same?' Ed prompted.

Henry leant back in his chair. 'Of course I was worried,' he answered. 'But I respected Tabby enough to know that if she didn't feel the same, then I wouldn't let it ruin our friendship, or our friendship group. To be honest, I thought there was no way she'd be interested in me because I was boring and she was too good for me.'

'You're not boring!'

Henry shrugged. 'Some people would say I am. I'm not outgoing like you or Livs, am I? I haven't got a lot going for me.'

Ed was outraged. 'Don't be ridiculous! Henry, just because you're quiet doesn't mean you're any less than those of us who are probably too loud for our own good. It takes all sorts to make the world; we need people like you or there would be too much noise pollution from the rest of us non-stop talking.'

Henry chuckled. 'Maybe you're right. But what I'm saying is that yes, I did doubt myself, and sometimes I still do, but I love Tabby and I hope she feels the same. It's good to have that doubt though. It makes you think about what's important to you in a relationship; it should feel a little scary because it means you care.'

'What is important to you in a relationship?' Ed got out his phone, and made it look as though he was typing out notes while Henry was talking.

Henry thought about it and then said, 'Honesty. Trust. Feeling comfortable enough in the other person's presence that you feel you could tell them anything. Knowing that when you need them, they'll be there; and knowing for sure that when they need you, you'll drop everything and go to them.'

Oh, right. That wasn't really the question he was asking. He rephrased it. 'I guess it comes down to what I originally wanted to know: how *did* you know that you and Tabby were compatible? How did you stop making an absolute fool of yourself every time you were around her, once you'd realised that you liked her, and not do things like topple over an entire display of books, and speak a load of nonsense that not even the world's cleverest person could discern?'

'Ed . . .'

'That was, of course, just a made-up scenario. FOR MY BOOK. I am not talking from personal experience, obviously.'

'Ed, listen to me now, and answer me truthfully. Is that the real reason you're asking me all of this? Because I can help you if you tell me, but my superpower is not mind-reading, so if you don't tell me, I can't.'

'Yep!' And with that, Ed stood up from the sofa, clapping his hands against his thighs. 'And, you know what? I really should be getting home to write my next chapter. This conversation has really got my mind working; thanks, Henry! Very useful. I'll put you in the acknowledgements. Thanks again! I'd better get home!'

Ed affectionately tapped Henry on the shoulder, then walked quickly through the front door and out on to the street. *Well, that wasn't as helpful as I thought it would be. Oh god, what if Henry saw through my white lie? Looks as if it's just down to me and my lack of common sense to work out what to do! Please, Edward, from one man to another, do not mess this up!*

Cassie: ed why are you acting so weird

Ed: What do you mean?!

Cassie: henry just told me you turned up at his house and asked him loads of weird questions and said you're writing a book???

Ed: That TRAITOR! I thought we were having a confidential conversation!

Cassie: ed what's going on

Ed: I'M WRITING A BOOK. YOU ARE MY MUSE, CASSIE

Cassie: i am giving you so much side eye right now. well, i'm here if you want to talk SENSIBLY. and none of this book nonsense. you couldn't sit still long enough to write a book

Ed: My book is NOT nonsense! It will be a bestseller! Mark my words!!

Ed sent a photo.

Ed: This is Mrs Simpkins after she brought in a mouse this morning which was ALIVE and started running around the kitchen and I had to trap it and catch it and let it outside. She was sulking because I took it away from her

Hannah: Oh my god how did you manage to catch it?

Ed: Hahahaha WELL that is a good question but you did ask . . .

Ed: There was lots of screaming involved (yes, my screaming), but once I had it under the washing basket I managed to slide the basket along the floor towards the back door but the first time I attempted that IT ESCAPED AGAIN so I had to trap it a second time. And then when I finally got it to the back door, it ran back in!!! After the fifth attempt, I was finally successful

Hannah: How do you end up getting yourself in these situations?

Ed: I think I just attract chaos? I don't know!! It's always been the same!

Hannah: I'll leave the chaos to you. I'd rather have everything go to plan! But then I guess you can't plan a mouse visitor? Anyway, your chaos is pretty funny, I must admit

Ed: FUNNY?! Are you laughing at me Hannah?!

Hannah: Oh I totally am and you know it! 😂

Chapter Sixteen

'Oh, history!' Ed cried, throwing his arms out dramatically and only just missing Cassie. 'You are such a mystery! I can't remember dates; you make me want to . . . escapes!'

Cassie was drawing next to him in her sketchbook, while Tabby and Olivia sat opposite, going over a French conjugation table together. The table between them at Olivia's house was covered in paper and Post-it Notes, pens and revision cards. There were only a few months to go until exams began, and if they were going to spend time revising, they may as well spend it together. It was good to keep an eye on Olivia, too, and make sure that she didn't become too burned out like last year.

'Thanks, Ed, I'll use that one,' Henry said wryly, before screwing up his face in frustration. 'None of these dates are going in!'

'I think Ed's on to something with his rhyme,' Olivia said. 'You're good at poetry, Henry, so pop the important dates into a poem and then memorise it.'

'Yeah, Henry, I'm proud of my rhyme!' Ed puffed out his chest, but Henry just went back to glaring at his timeline. Hmmm, maybe he should get back to his own revision, Ed thought. Or, more likely, his own procrastination.

Cassie put her pencil down. 'So Yaz from my art class is having a party at the weekend,' she said. 'It's at her massive house with loads of rooms. She always has amazing parties. What do you think? Are we going?'

Olivia pulled a face. 'You know I don't ... *love* that lot.'

'I know, but it's not as if we have to hang out with them. We can do our own thing. And if we all go, it will be even better.'

Ed looked around at each of them in turn, but nobody looked super keen. Parties weren't exactly Ed's favourite thing in the world; he always ended up stressed before, during and after. But if nobody wanted to go with Cassie, maybe he should ...

It would be easier for him, anyway, because it would mostly be people from college there. 'I might be interested,' Ed said.

'I guess I could tag along too,' Olivia said.

'Well, if you're both going ...' Tabby said, but she didn't seem sure. She looked to Henry. 'We could ...?'

Henry shrugged. 'Yeah, I don't mind. And it will be cool if we all go.'

'That's decided then!' Cassie grinned. 'You'll all be fine once you're there. You don't have to sound so begrudging. It will be fun!'

Cassie resumed her sketchbook work. The others went back to their revision. Ed's heart was not in his English language test paper. That was most definitely – most *definitely* – the only reason he was so happy when his phone, facing him on the table, lit up. He grabbed it so quickly that the rapid movement dislodged a stack of sketchbook paper on to the floor and he had to scramble to pick it up quickly before Cassie had a go at him.

Hannah: I think I'm going to suggest to Dinah to start an
employee of the month board in the staffroom
Ed: Even though you know it would be me every month?
Hannah: Can you stop typing so quickly so I can finish?
Now you've stolen my joke! It would be me every month
of course and you'd have to stare at a huge picture of my
face and admit that I am the ultimate bookseller
Ed: That won't be a problem because it will be me crowned
the ultimate bookseller and you'll be staring at my drop
dead gorgeous face

They were talking to each other a lot outside work now. Like, a lot. Ed hoped that Hannah liked what she found out about him as much as he liked what he found out about her. Or maybe she was sick of seeing pictures of Mrs Simpkins. WHO KNEW? Wow, this was all so stressful.

He tried to tamper down the grin he was sure was on his face so The Paper & Hearts Society wouldn't ask him why he was smiling so much.

> Hannah: I taught you everything you know about
>   bookselling!!
> Ed: Pfftt, really? I was a NATURAL, admit it
> Hannah: Hahahaha now I know you're really joking! You so
>   were NOT and you know it!

'You'll never get all your revision finished if you pick up your phone every five seconds,' Tabby pointed out. 'Come on, Ed. Stop your procrastination!'

He stuck his tongue out and ignored her, and peace descended on the table for another few minutes while Olivia, Tabby, Henry and Cassie went back to their work.

They're so serious about it. But they won't be when I tell them that my drama revision is performing a one-man play in the middle of the kitchen.

> Ed: What are you up to this afternoon? Other than cuddling
>   many, many guinea pigs as I assume you already have
>   done?

Hannah: . . . Am I really that predictable?

Ed: Yes!

Hannah: Haha I know it! Well I've got some proofs that
Dinah asked me to read to see if they're worth ordering
in for the children's section, and then Indiana Bones will
need walking. How about you?

Ed sent a photo.

Ed: This is the revision table I'm currently sitting around,
failing to do any revision while my friends give me dirty
looks because I'm putting their productivity to shame

'Ed,' Tabby said with a nudge.

'Yes?' He looked up from his phone.

'Come on, then. Tell us who you're talking to. We're
due a revision break – spill.'

Olivia put her elbows on the table and her head in her
hands, leaning forward eagerly. 'Yes, who's the mystery
person that's got you all dreamy-eyed and asking weird
questions, Ed?'

Ed threw his hands up in the air. 'Thanks a lot, Henry!
Did you tell *everyone*? I thought you were supposed to be
trustworthy!'

'I am,' Henry said, surrendering. 'But, you have to
admit, you were acting pretty weird. I was concerned. You
kept asking how I "pursued Tabby's hand" and then ran off
in a hurry.'

'You guys are the worst,' Ed grumped. 'Can you not let me just live happily in peace without interfering?'

'We're your friends,' Tabby said. 'Interfering is what we do best.'

'Well, there's no need to.' Ed – who thought highly of his acting skills – tried but failed to act blasé. 'I'm just talking to a phone I have connected to Mrs Simpkins and when I send a text, it reads them out for her. It's a very complex technological system, with the hope of one day discovering that cats are able to communicate with us.'

'Ed.' Tabby didn't look impressed. 'Honesty. You owe us honesty.'

Urgh, I really do not want to do this, but they aren't going to shut up until I tell them, are they?

'Well . . .' He had no clue where to start. 'Um. Right. Yes, well, I am messaging somebody from work. That's all you need to know.'

Hannah: Revision? I don't envy you! I hope you've at least
    got some good revision snacks?

'Is that them?!' Olivia squealed.

Can't they just butt out?

Cassie glanced over Ed's shoulder. 'Hannah. And she just mentioned snacks. Ed must be smitten.'

'You know, I'm starting to think this is very mean,' Ed said, 'all of you being nosy with my private business.'

'Okay, we're sorry,' Tabby conceded. 'We won't say any more about it.'

They all went back to their revision in silence, apart from the scratching of Cassie's charcoal against her sketchbook and Olivia slurping from her mug of tea.

Ed was aware that they were darting looks to each other out of the corners of their eyes. It made him want to reveal everything, and at least then he wouldn't have to go through all of these new feelings by himself.

Just tell them. They're your friends; you know they'll support you. 'Fine! Fine!' Ed said. 'I'll tell you.'

The Paper & Hearts Society sat up straighter in their seats and focused their gazes on him. It was worse than being stuck under the hot spotlight on the drama department stage with nowhere to hide.

'I met this girl at work,' he said.

'Hannah, the one you were telling me about?' Tabby asked.

Ed nodded. 'Some of you might have seen her in Woolf and Wilde. Yes, her name is Hannah and she's a fellow bookseller. She showed me the ropes when I started. I think I got on her nerves at first, especially when I assaulted her sense of smell with some very stinky tuna sandwiches, but then, I don't know, we've been getting on well. Like, really well. But I don't know if she likes me, or we're just friends because we work together. It's hard to tell.'

'And you like her?' Tabby asked. 'You know I've had my suspicions.'

Ed nodded again.

'Ed!' Olivia squealed. 'Why didn't you say anything to us?!'

Ed smiled and then put his head in his hands. 'I don't know. I don't what to do!' he cried. 'I'm so hopeless! I just make a fool of myself and I'm worried I'm going to scare her off by accidentally blowing up the bookshop or hugging one of her guinea pigs and strangling it by mistake!'

'Yeah, that probably would put her off,' Cassie said. Olivia shot her a look that said, *Unhelpful, Cassie*, which echoed Ed's sentiments exactly.

'Don't be so hard on yourself,' Olivia said. 'You're very loveable! Yes, you might *occasionally* cause minor explosions, but that makes you even better in my eyes. A bookshop romance! It's like a modern-day Jane Austen novel!'

'You've just got to be yourself,' Henry added. 'If she doesn't like that, then she's not worth it.'

Ed thought back to the awkward moment between them in the guinea pig shed, when Hannah had tried to lure the guinea pig away from him, and that half-hug-not-hug. He felt his cheeks rise to a blush. *What if it was like that all the time?*

'It's simple,' Cassie said. 'All you've got to do is invite her to the party. Then, while you're there, explain how you feel.'

'But Hannah's autistic. She doesn't like the kind of parties you go to, Cassie – they're always packed with people and noisy. She doesn't even like it when the bookshop is busy. It's not as easy as that.'

'Maybe not, but you can still ask,' she replied. With a swish of her hair she added, 'Trust me, I'm an expert at these things.'

Olivia laughed. 'Who knew you were a dating expert?!'

'Oi!' But Cassie was laughing too. 'We're going out, aren't we? Look, Ed, I'll show you how it's done.'

Ed didn't realise what she was doing until it was too late, Cassie's hand snaking past him towards his phone. He made a grab for it, his heart thumping in his ears.

'No, no! Don't!' But Cassie was too quick for him. She turned around and held the phone tight to her body.

'Cassie, stop it!! Give me my phone back! Give it back!' Ed pulled on her shoulder.

'There,' she said. 'All done. No need to thank me.'

She winked at Olivia, while handing the phone back to Ed with a bow. He stared, wide-mouthed, down at the message.

Ed: I know this might sound weird, but do you want to come
    to a party with me next weekend? It's at a friend's house
    and I thought you might like to go with me
Ed: glyewbpg iurbijgnorgjn[oqrbegeubgrw'or

'Cassie! What the hell!!'

'You would have taken five years to build up to doing that.' Cassie raised an eyebrow. 'Am I wrong?'

He sat back down in the chair and put his head in his hands. 'Yes, you are! You're very wrong! I can't believe you! I did not give you permission to do that! Oh god, what if you've ruined everything? She'll hate me. Cassie, she'll hate me! She'll never speak to me again!'

Cassie threw her arms in the air. 'Jeez, sorry, I was just trying to help. A "thanks" would be nice!'

'Maybe you should have waited,' Henry chastised. 'There was no need to message her without Ed's go-ahead.'

Ed: Sorry, I sat on my phone please ignore me
Hannah: Ignore which message?
Ed: Um the second one? Or both? If you want to that is?
Hannah: Well I was going to say yes to the first message
    but if you want me to ignore it then I can
Ed: NO! No ignoring then. That would be great! So you'll come?!
Hannah: Yes, I'll come. But it would be good to have some
    details so I can get everything straight in my head?

'See,' Cassie said, 'I did you a favour.'

'Stop reading over my shoulder!'

'But, Ed!' Olivia said. 'It's so exciting! You've got to let us live vicariously through you; that's what best friends do!'

He felt exhausted. Cassie had no right to do what she'd done; what if Hannah had been freaked out by it? But she had said yes, which was confusing. Now he was starting to panic – did this count as a date?! He couldn't just come out with it and admit he liked her. *How will I deal with the rejection if she doesn't feel the same? How on earth will we be able to work with each other again?*

'You guys have ruined my life,' Ed mumbled. And then, louder, he said, 'Please tell me what I need to do next.'

'Just trust in your abilities,' Tabby said. 'You've got this, Ed. You must be capable of something because you're friends with us and we haven't run away. It's just like that, except please don't start getting all lovey-dovey with us. Now she's coming to the party, just take her off somewhere quiet and explain how you feel. It's as easy as that.'

'Oh god! Don't say that! I hadn't even thought about . . . I am no good at this! I've never been romantic before! I've barely had any crushes! I've been fine just doing my own thing, but now this has to come along and made me feel all these weird emotions that I've never felt before, and I'm scared I'm going to mess it up!'

Cassie snorted. 'You'll be fine, Ed. We'll just have to give you an earpiece for us to dictate all your words into.'

Ed beamed. 'Can you really do that?' he said optimistically.

'No!' they all cried in unison.

Olivia added, 'We won't interfere any more, we promise.'

'So when I want you to interfere, you won't; but when I don't want you to, you do. You lot don't make any sense.'

'But you love us,' Tabby said with a wink.

'Yep,' he begrudgingly admitted. 'I really do.'

Although ... *CURSE YOU, CASSIE. How on earth will I pull this off?!*

Ed sent a photo.

Ed: Here is the location of the party for the weekend! It's quite far out of town. I can pick you up if you like?

Hannah: No, it's fine, thank you! It will be easier if I make my own way there – but thanks anyway!

Ed: We're aiming to arrive about half 7? Do you want to meet outside then?

Hannah: Actually could we meet about 8 instead? I'd end up worried that I'd turn up before you and would be on my own. Getting there a little later will just ease some of that anxiety, I know it sounds silly! You won't leave me alone, will you? I'm pretty nervous and parties tend to be the kind of loud and overwhelming that threatens to melt my brain.

Ed: Of course I won't!

Hannah: Thanks Ed, I really appreciate it. It was so kind of you to invite me!

Ed: Not at all, I'm glad you can make it!

Chapter Seventeen

Not bad, Ed thought as he smoothed a hand through his hair, preening in front of the mirror. *I don't scrub up too bad after all.*

He wasn't wearing anything fancy, just his favourite T-shirt with a quote from his very favourite Shakespeare play, *Much Ado About Nothing*, that nobody ever understood, matched with a pair of jeans. The familiarity was comforting, and he needed that to calm his rising nerves.

It wasn't long before he'd have to leave. Cassie would get impatient otherwise, and he couldn't deal with her grumpiness this evening. He was tense enough as it was – mixed with excitement, which made little sense to him. How could he be both, all at once?

Am I really going to tell Hannah I like her tonight? Can I DO that? Am I CAPABLE? What will she say?!

There was a knock on the half-open door behind him. 'You look smart,' Mum said, and for a second, he forgot he was annoyed with her. But only for a second. 'I hope you have a good time.'

She was blocking the doorway so he couldn't even storm past.

'Ed . . .'

'I don't want to do this now!' he said. 'You'll just make me more confused and I need to leave!'

He pushed past gently – maybe he was softening a little – and down the stairs, putting as much distance between them as he could muster. The doorbell rang. Luckily, Ed was already ready, otherwise he would have been even more annoyed. He pulled the front door open with an almighty force that took even him by surprise.

'Hey, Ed!' Olivia said, but her grin soon faded as she read the expression on his face. 'Are you all right?'

'Absolutely fine, all right, super, great, and every other word that explains that feeling,' he said. 'Let's go.'

'Have a nice time!' Mum called, sadness in her voice.

Good, he thought.

'Hi!' Olivia called through the open door.

'Let's *go*,' Ed insisted, and practically dragged her away as he slammed the door behind him. The sudden force took her by surprise and she wobbled on her small velvet green heels, righting herself just in time to prevent an accident.

Maybe he was being a little abrupt . . .

'You look lovely, Livs!' he said, hoping to make up for it as he opened the car and they got in. She did: her velvet green dress hung prettily, matching her shoes, and she'd styled her hair so it looked even glossier than usual.

'Thanks, Ed.' She adjusted the skirt of the dress slightly as she sat down, pulling it closer to her knees. 'So do you. Well – handsome!'

After that, Ed didn't fancy talking. He turned up the radio, louder than was necessary. If he was left alone with his thoughts, he'd just keep going over possible Hannah scenarios – and the more he thought of, the more devastating the result turned out. He was his own worst enemy!

Olivia silently turned the dial down but kept quiet until they got to the end of the road. 'Are you, maybe, a little nervous?' she said, and he could feel her eyes boring into him. He turned the music up again, and kept his eyes on the road as he headed towards Tabby's and Henry's.

Olivia started to laugh and turned the music off. 'Edward Eastfield, I've known you for years and I know what you're like when you're nervous! You can't hide anything from me. Nice try!'

Ed slowed at a roundabout and was able to find some words. 'Fine, I might be a bit nervous. But it's not a big deal, Livs. Nerves are normal.'

'Are you trying to convince me or are you trying to convince yourself here?'

He made a grunting noise in response. *This is the problem with having friends who know you better than you know yourself.*

'Are things still bad at home?' Olivia asked.

He nodded, then added, 'But I don't want to talk about it. We're going to have fun tonight and I don't want that dark cloud overhanging us.'

He took a deep breath in and exhaled in the hope of releasing some of the tension in his body. It felt as if a lot of it was gone by the time he pulled up in front of Tabby's house. She rushed out of the front door before Ed had a chance to honk the horn.

'Ed's a bit tense,' Olivia whispered to Tabby as she climbed into the back.

Tabby reached forward and patted him on the shoulder. 'You'll be fine,' she said. 'Let's just go and have a good time and not worry about anything else.'

They picked up Henry next, who squeezed next to Tabby, then swung by to pick Cassie up last before making their way on to the party.

'This party is going to be *great*,' Cassie said, applying her lipstick using her phone on selfie mode. 'Yaz was saying in art class that she's got a new sound system.'

Yaz's house was in the middle of nowhere. She was renowned for her parties, which were always as loud as she wanted, on account of there being no neighbours for miles around.

'I do love noise pollution,' Henry laughed. 'Sign of a good night!'

'Anyway, what have you arranged with Hannah?' Tabby asked, leaning forward in her seat so she could hear Ed easier.

Ed signalled and turned down a country road. 'I'm meeting her outside at eight,' he said. 'I tried to send her as much information as possible, so she'd know what to expect. I know I don't often like parties, but I don't have to contend with the music being extra loud or the worry of flashing lights or crowds or anything like that. I wanted to make it as approachable as possible.'

He was relieved when the turning came into view and the car rolled up the gravel drive; the energy inside suddenly heightened, the anticipation building to a crescendo. Ed could practically feel Olivia buzzing in her seat, and even Tabby didn't look as nervous as she once would have done. He knew it was a big thing for her to come here tonight; it wasn't the easiest thing for her anxiety.

'Ohmigod, this is so fancy,' Tabby said, her mouth hanging open slightly as she gazed in awe. 'I know you said it was impressive – but I didn't realise it was *this* impressive!'

Ed knew exactly what she meant: the house was extremely modern, like something out of *Grand Designs*, and swamped the surrounding landscape in its sheer size. The front was almost entirely made up of glass windows – Ed didn't envy the person who had to clean them – and there was even a balcony.

Bit different to where I live. But somehow, he would prefer to live in his much smaller house any day.

'Just pull up here,' Cassie said as Ed drew up to the house. She got out almost the second he turned off the ignition, grabbing her little bag and swinging it over her shoulder, where it nestled against her signature denim jacket. Olivia followed, grabbing Cassie's hand in hers.

Henry, Tabby and Ed hung back slightly, steeling themselves.

'Parties never go well for me,' Ed said, and Tabby put her arm around his middle and squeezed into his side. Her black sequin minidress tickled where it touched him, and then he felt Henry's arm reach around his shoulders, too, so that they formed their own little line. A defence barrier, Ed thought, but he couldn't quite decide what it was defending against.

While there were a few people milling about outside, they followed Cassie's and Olivia's lead into the house, where people stood like packed sardines in a can. It was impossible to walk through without brushing against bodies, especially as nobody seemed willing to move out of the way, too busy chatting to each other, drinks in hand. Everyone was doing their own thing, caught up in their own little world. Everything else was inconsequential. This really was unlike any of the small-scale parties Ed had hosted before. It made them look like tiny gatherings, even if at the time they'd felt overwhelming enough.

Relax, Ed told himself, and he managed to as he spotted familiar faces from college. He switched into dazzling Ed mode, raising his hand lazily and pasting on a chilled grin. He was the Ed that people expected him to be, the Ed he wanted to be all the time. The Ed that found all of this straightforward. He was playing the part.

'Where do you want to go?' Henry shouted over the music and general party buzz. Tabby was shrugging, and Ed grabbed Tabby's hand, who grabbed Henry's hand, as they moved into the enormous kitchen with marbled countertops and gold finishes.

'There's Livs and Cassie outside,' Henry said, pointing through the large glass windows that stretched from floor to ceiling, out to the sprawling garden, lit with various lights. 'It might be a bit cold, but I think I can also see some kind of firepit. Do you want to head out there?' He and Tabby were still holding hands tightly.

Suddenly, the last thing Ed wanted was to awkwardly hang in the middle between Henry and Tabby, and Olivia and Cassie. *No fifth-wheeling. This is time for me now.*

Ed released Tabby's hand and turned her around to face Henry. 'You two go on ahead!' he said. 'I think I'll grab a drink!'

'Sure?' Tabby said.

'Yeah!' Ed said, looking for a glass that wasn't already half filled with liquid. 'It won't be long until Hannah is here! I'll see you later!'

He waited until they were gone before leaning up against one of the kitchen counters, gazing down at his phone just in case Hannah messaged to cancel.

I'll have to keep checking. I don't want to miss anything from her if she needs to get hold of me.

He tried to act more naturally, rather than the awkward one at the party who spends the whole time on his phone. He eventually found a spare glass and filled it with the remaining lemonade from a bottle standing on the side.

'Hey, Ed!' It was Ruby from his English language class. She was always gossiping about the other girls in the class, and here she was leaning over to reach a can from the side next to him.

'Hey!' he said, switching on his charm button again. 'I didn't realise you'd be here!'

She pulled a face. 'Everyone's here, silly! Anyone who's anyone, anyway. It's nice to see you; you're not usually at these things!'

Ed put on his fakest, cheesiest grin. 'Well, I don't turn into a pumpkin until midnight so I thought, why not?'

She laughed, and looked as if she was going to say something, but Ed was relieved and distracted as he noticed Henry weaving his way back through from outside. Presumably seeing Ed's distraction, Ruby waved to a friend, and melted away to talk to her instead.

'You're not drinking, are you, Ed?' Henry asked, looking at Ed's fizzing glass. All his friends were careful when Ed was around alcohol; it tended to make him overemotional in situations where he didn't want to be overcome by emotion.

'No, course not,' he said breezily. He waved the red cup in his hand, liquid sloshing over the side and covering his fingers. 'I'm driving!'

Although he wasn't drinking alcohol, Ed did feel slightly drunk; it was something about being in an atmosphere like this, surrounded by so many people who had an expectation of you. It made him ramp up his entire personality, make it bolder and brighter. The more people spoke to him, the greater the sensation would become, threatening to overtake him completely.

'You can come outside, you know!?' Henry said, angling his body to look through the large glass doors that stretched from floor to ceiling. Outside Ed could see Cassie, Olivia and Tabby sat around the firepit chatting, their faces illuminated by the flames. 'I just came in to get drinks! It's not too cold out there actually.'

Ed looked down at his phone, checking the time. Five minutes to go. 'Nah, I'm fine, thanks, but I'll come and find you later! I'd better head out. I don't want to miss Hannah when she gets here!' He nodded his head in the direction of the door.

Henry clapped him on the back. 'Just remember, be yourself. Don't overthink it and start asking for her hand in betrothment or whatever. Just be true to yourself.'

'Thanks, pal,' Ed said, but he didn't feel as if much of what Henry was saying had gone in. He took a big, deep breath, perhaps the biggest breath he'd ever taken in his life – minus his first after being born – and mightily exhaled, but it didn't really help. If anything, it reminded him of one of those weird characters from books who released breaths they didn't realise they'd been holding. How did they not ever realise?

Concentrate. Now you're just thinking of anything to stall yourself.

'Yes, right, going right now,' Ed said, to Henry, who had already gone back outside so it looked as if he was talking to himself. *Great!* But he was true to his word: he put one foot in front of the other and headed back out the way they'd come in.

The fresh air tickled his cheeks. He was jittery with hope and anticipation and almost wished he were out the back with The Paper & Hearts Society, gathered around the warm fire.

He looked down at his phone to check the time once more and when he looked up again, Hannah was coming straight towards him. He had to stop his jaw from dropping open or he thought it might never close again. He blinked to check she was real.

'You look lovely,' Ed said as she got closer, his breath catching. He hadn't even realised he'd said it aloud until he saw her smile. She really did look lovely: the long dress she was wearing, a midnight blue, contrasted against her green eyes and brought out the natural highlights in her hair, which she'd lightly curled. She had more make-up on than usual, too.

'Would it be weird to admit that I spent all afternoon googling pictures of what people wear at parties, so I knew I wouldn't stick out like a sore thumb?' Hannah said. 'I still don't think I did a particularly good job – all the clothes I saw looked as if they'd be super uncomfortable and no party is worth that. No offence.' When she smiled at him, though, the tension seemed to disappear, if only for a second. He took comfort from that.

'None taken,' Ed said. 'I can perfectly understand.'

'And I had to check I wasn't covered in hay because apparently it's not the best idea to feed your guinea pigs before you go to a party. Who knew?'

Ed laughed. 'At least it would have helped if you'd got hungry,' he teased, and she laughed back.

'Did you know guinea pigs eat their own poo?' she said, with another laugh, as they walked on the gravel back to the house. 'They produce two types and while one is basically like, well, normal poo, the other is undigested stuff that they eat all over again so they can absorb the good nutrients in it.'

Ed smiled. 'No way! That's awesome.' He ushered her inside. 'I'm so glad you're here; there is nobody I would rather spend time with at a party, especially not anyone else telling me facts about guinea pig poo.'

'Wow, there's a lot of people here,' she said, in a tone that sounded like awe, though her face told him it was anything but.

'We can go somewhere quiet,' he said, 'and we'll head back outside to get fresh air again if it's too much.'

Hannah's shoulders relaxed. 'That sounds good,' she said. 'Thanks.'

'So tell me more about guinea pig poop,' he said. She did, more slowly this time, with interruptions whenever the bass in the music picked up. As they wended their way in and out of people, Ed reached his hand out in the hope that she'd grab it, just so they could stay closer together. She took it, her palm warm in his, their fingers intertwined in a strong grip. He had to remind himself to keep walking.

Ed led Hannah upstairs, searching for some peace, but it was just as crowded. He couldn't believe he was holding Hannah's hand, but he was, with just the right amount of pressure, as she'd mentioned before that she didn't like light touch.

His head spun as he thought of everything he wanted to say to her. *Hannah, I can't keep this to myself any longer. I have to tell you, or I think I may combust just as the microwave did. Hannah, I know we got off to a rocky start, but you were right when you said you taught me everything I know about being a bookseller, and I'm so grateful for all your support and encouragement.*

The thing is, as we've got to know each other better and spent time with your very cute guinea pigs and possibly the only dog who could ever convert me – a dedicated cat lover – into someone that loves dogs too, I've learnt that I see you not only as a friend, but I'm beginning to have feelings for you, too.

My favourite time of the day is when we're messaging back and forth, and you make me laugh and smile like nobody else . . . do you feel the same about me?

Sure, he might have been good at getting through monologues in drama class, but somehow this was worse – he knew he'd stumble over his lines when speaking to

Hannah; history would back him up on that one. But the moment was getting closer, he could feel it.

Tucked into a corner of a bedroom was a group of people he recognised instantly from his college drama class.

I hope Hannah doesn't get the wrong idea about me taking her into a bedroom, Ed thought, but he couldn't worry about it for long.

'Ed! Hey, mate! Over here!' said a gangly boy called Tom who liked nothing more than the sound of his own voice. Ed always tried to be cheerful, but Tom took it to another level, and tonight seemed no different. He was with a few other lads and some of the girls, all holding drinks.

'Just a sec, Hannah,' Ed said. He couldn't be rude, could he? He had to spend hours each week with them, and it would be awkward if he didn't at least say hi.

'We were just talking about you!' one of the girls, Katherine, said. 'We were saying – I bet your monologue is going to be great when you perform it next week. I still haven't worked out what I'm properly doing with mine.' She rolled her eyes. 'It's been a massive pain!'

'Well, I'm still figuring mine out, too,' Ed said, glancing back at Hannah, who was waiting uneasily behind him. He could see her awkwardness and felt awkward himself. *How can I extricate myself now?* 'But sometimes it's best just to wing these things, isn't it? Anyway, Tom, mate, you always pretend you're not bothered but we all know you spend every minute of every day preparing.'

'I do not!' Tom guffawed, punching Ed lightly on the arm. 'Hey, look, you've nearly finished your drink. We're just about to refill – come with us! The others are down there.'

One of the other boys put an arm loosely round Ed's shoulder. 'Yeah, come on, Ed.' He twisted him in the direction of the stairs.

'No. I'll catch up with you guys later,' he said, but too weakly.

'Nah, come on!' Katherine said, close behind him. 'Maddy's downstairs and she wanted to talk to you about that production of *The Taming of the Shrew* you recommended. She'll be upset otherwise!'

Ed felt himself be pushed to the first step of the staircase, the big group behind him. He just had time to call out, 'Hannah, I'll be right back! I'll just grab us a drink!' before he was swept away. Down, down he went, pushed by the force of the group in the direction of the kitchen.

'Ed! How nice to see you here!' another girl, Priya, from drama said, as the group came to a halt. She was standing with more people he recognised from English language.

'Hi!' he said, to nobody and everybody, turning on enthusiastic Ed mode.

'Ed, Maddy's over here! Maddy, tell Ed what you thought about that production – do I need to watch it?

You're the one who wants to be on the stage of the Globe one day, Ed!'

There was nothing Ed loved more than talking about his ambitions to be a Shakespearean actor, and it was good to distract himself from the butterflies in his stomach whenever he thought about revealing his feelings to Hannah. It made his heart burst to think that one day he could follow in the footsteps of his actor heroes, playing Hamlet or Macbeth or Benedick. He didn't mind whether it was in a comedy or tragedy or history; he just wanted the opportunity to be on stage and shine.

I'll get back to Hannah right now, he thought, but then someone else came over to join the conversation, and it was a heady mix of music thumping, and good discussions. When Ed next looked at the gold gilded clock, the centrepiece on one of the kitchen walls, he was confused. *It can't have been twenty minutes since I've been downstairs, can it?*

Oh no, Hannah!

As Ed made his excuses to the big group now gathered around him and left the kitchen, he pulled his phone out of his jeans pocket to find a list of messages, ranging from twenty minutes ago to ten.

Hannah: Hey, where did you go? I can't seem to find you and you said you'd be right back.

Hannah: Ed? Did you get my last message? Where are you?

Hannah: I'm not feeling so comfortable up here. I know absolutely no one and I'm starting to panic just a little bit. I didn't think you'd leave me!

Ed hoped she wasn't annoyed with him; he couldn't help it, could he, if people demanded his attention?

He took the stairs two at a time, feeling as if he was fighting his way through a thick rainforest of vines instead of a party full of people. But when he got back up to the top, Hannah wasn't in the bedroom. He looked at his phone again, but there weren't any clues in her messages.

Hmm, maybe she's in the bathroom. Oh no, what if she's left? I'm such an idiot. I can't believe I didn't come back sooner. I didn't even get the chance to talk to her properly. Now I don't know when I can. Work is not the place!

He poked his head into the other six bedrooms but she wasn't in any of them. It wasn't until he glanced out of one of the final bedroom windows overlooking the front drive that he spotted two figures leaning against the low stone wall. Relief coursed through him. It was too dark to make out who the other figure was, but he recognised Hannah's blue dress instantly.

Ed squeezed past the group of people who had gathered on the landing – *Who hangs out on the landing?* – and jogged down the stairs, to the rhythm of his heart. The cold air wrapped around him as he opened the front door, and he wished he'd thought of wearing something a little warmer than a T-shirt.

'Hannah!' he shouted as he approached the pair. 'I'm here now. I'm so glad you didn't leave.'

'Tabby,' he said, confused. *What's she doing out here?*

Ed had never seen Tabby look so disappointed. She shot Ed a cruel look. 'Ed. Where have you been?'

Her curt tone cut him to the core. 'What do you mean?'

'What do you think I mean? Where have you *been*, Ed? You can't just invite Hannah here and abandon her! The others are in there looking for you – we had no idea where you'd disappeared off to!'

'I was only gone for a bit!' he said, working hard to defend himself.

Hannah looked shaken. 'No, Ed. You weren't. I was waiting for twenty minutes for you in a room where I knew nobody else, with the music getting louder and louder, because you told me you'd be right back, and I believed you.'

She didn't raise her voice and somehow that made it worse. Hannah was icy calm. Unlike Tabby. 'This is ridiculous, Ed! What the hell were you thinking?! Parties are awful at the best of times. You know that as well as I do. You'd better think long and hard about your actions.' Tabby looked at Hannah. 'Will you be okay, or do you want me to stay?'

'Thanks,' Hannah said, smiling at Tabby gratefully, 'but you can go inside. Honestly, it's fine.'

With one last icy glare in Ed's direction, Tabby turned on her heel and went back into the house.

Ed gulped as he realised how serious this was. Tabby had always been on his side – his best friend, through thick and thin, until this very moment.

'Listen, Hannah. I'm sorry. I shouldn't have left you, but—'

'Please, I can't bear to hear excuses. I'm not angry, Ed. I'm just so upset and unbelievably disappointed. You did the one thing I asked you not to do: you left me in a loud, overwhelming house, where I knew no one. I came here for *you*, knowing full well it was my worst nightmare, and you've made that nightmare even worse!'

Ed reached for Hannah's hand, but she pulled hers out of reach. 'I didn't mean to,' he said. 'I didn't think! It just happened!'

Hannah rubbed her face, refusing to meet Ed's gaze, instead looking straight down at the floor. 'I had to search social media on my phone to find Tabby, who I recognised from your Instagram, and message her, because I felt so lost that I thought I was going to have a meltdown in the middle of the party. I trusted you, Ed. I thought ... I thought you cared.'

Ed felt a lump form in his throat. 'I'm so sorry, Hannah.'

'I stepped outside my comfort zone for you! I can't do this. I've ordered a taxi to take me home.'

His heart thudded in his chest. 'Don't go! I'm so, so sorry,' he said again, with more force. 'I'll make it up to you with a hundred pictures of Mrs Simpkins a day?' He hoped to get a glimmer of a smile with that one.

'No, Ed.' Hannah turned to face him, looking directly at Ed this time, her gaze piercing. 'You don't understand. I mean, I can't do any of this. It was a mistake coming here; I don't know what I was thinking.'

'What?'

She threw her hands up in the air. 'It was a huge thing for me coming here and I mistakenly thought . . . It doesn't matter what I thought. I can't do this, I'm not doing this – I just want to forget I ever came here. I'm going home and don't even bother to contact me.'

'But, Hannah!'

'No, Ed.' She shook her head. 'I'm too disappointed.'

As she got up and walked away, Ed sank down against the brick wall. He was in total shock, and it felt as if his whole world was crumbling around him.

Don't bother to contact me.

That was it. His chance was blown.

He kicked up a spray of gravel, slamming his palm against the stone wall beneath him. 'Dammit, Ed!' he cried, fighting back tears. 'Damn you, damn you, *damn you*!'

Ed: Cassie tell the others I've gone home. I was right, you meddling and texting Hannah has ruined EVERYTHING. THANKS FOR NOTHING.

Ed: Livs she's blocked my number. I don't know what to do! I can't even apologise! She's blocked me on Instagram too! Work is going to be awful.

Olivia: I know it's hard but if she's blocked you, it's best not to push it right now! You can't change what you did and you've got to give her space, Ed. It's for the best!

Ed: Why am I like this? Why do I mess everything up?

Cassie: um how is this my fault?

Ed: How ISN'T this your fault? None of this would have
happened if you hadn't invited Hannah! I hope you're
happy!! You and your STUPID idea and your AWFUL
party. I hate you for this

Olivia: Ed, why are you being so nasty to Cassie? She just
showed me the messages you sent her!

Olivia: Ed!!! I can see you're online!

Chapter Eighteen

To say that the atmosphere was awkward in Woolf and Wilde when Ed walked in on Wednesday morning would have been an understatement of epic proportions. Ed had been dreading seeing Hannah after no contact with her, just as she'd asked, and dreading having to make conversation if she was still upset with him, especially in front of the customers, and Dinah.

But it turned out he'd been dreading the wrong thing. It soon became clear that Hannah had no desire to make conversation with him at all.

As soon as Ed arrived, Hannah asked Dinah if she could work upstairs in the children's section, as well as create new book displays in the cafe to tie in with the catering team's winter menu. The only time Ed saw her was when she came through the entrance carrying a large Peter Rabbit stuffed toy, which she used to cover her face as she moved past him.

He tried not to let on to Dinah that anything was up, but even she seemed a little wary of Ed today, asking him to dust down the shelves, while she was in and out, up and down, checking everything else was running like clockwork.

Maybe she thinks all I'm good for is dusting. No actual selling of books for me today. I wonder if Hannah has told her how useless I am ...

I didn't think I'd ever feel so miserable coming to work. Parties are cursed; they never end well. I should have guessed this one would be no different. I wish Hannah would acknowledge me, so I can apologise properly.

The bell rang and an older customer came into the shop, wearing a pale complexion which matched her cold grey eyes. She was aggressively pulling a checked canvas shopping trolley behind her, the kind that Ed associated with older people.

'My order,' the woman snapped, coming straight up to the till. 'I want to collect my order.'

'Of course,' Ed said, switching into happy-go-lucky, customer-facing mode. The mode that didn't allow for one jot of misery. 'Can you tell me your name, please?'

'Lomax. Mrs Lomax. Do you have my book or not?'

Ah, so this was Mrs Lomax, the woman he'd had a run-in with over the phone on his first day. It all made sense.

He turned around and rummaged through the order stack, looking for the one with the 'Mrs Lomax' Post-it

Note attached to it. 'Would you like anything else while you're here?' he asked, turning on his best small-talk charm.

'I want it now. Hurry up with it, boy,' she said, tapping the counter. 'I've got more important places to be.'

Great, he was having a bad day as it was, and now Mrs Lomax was insinuating that he was an unimportant speck in the grander scheme of the universe. He scanned the book and pressed the buttons on the till, prepared the card reader and entered the sum of £7.99, the cost of the book.

While she touched her card on to the reader, he popped a bookmark in the Woolf and Wilde branded paper bag.

'There we go,' he said, tearing off the receipt and handing Mrs Lomax's card back to her, along with the paper bag. 'Have a great day!'

She snatched them from him, then stared at the receipt, bringing it as close to her face as possible. 'You're scamming me!' she spluttered.

Ed felt his eyes widen. 'Excuse me?'

She waved the receipt in his face, so quickly that it was just a blur of motion. 'You're scamming me!' she repeated. 'Look here, you're cheating me out of my money, young man!'

'If you could let me see it, I can check for you, madam. I assure you, I haven't intentionally scammed you, but if you let me look—'

'Don't try to hoodwink me, boy! I know how young men like you can be. You're all scammers, the lot of you!' She continued to wave the receipt, refusing to calm down.

There wasn't a lot Ed could say to that.

'Thief!' she cried. Other customers started to look uncomfortable, stopping browsing to look over in their direction. What could he do? It wasn't as if he could snatch the receipt out of her hand!

'Is there a problem here?' Dinah rushed in from the cafe, looking worried. 'Ed, is everything all right?'

Oh god, what if I really have scammed her? What if I added four zeroes to the payment amount? What if I have accidentally sucked all the money from her bank account? Will I be ARRESTED?!

'He's taken all of my money!'

Dinah looked as if she was trying not to expect the worst. 'Ed, what's happened here?'

Ed opened his mouth to speak, but he couldn't get a word in. 'He's taken seven thousand pounds of my money!' Mrs Lomax shouted. 'Seven thousand pounds!'

Dinah turned on her professional voice. 'If you'll let me look at the receipt, Mrs Lomax, I can check for you.'

'I want him sacked!' she replied, still not giving up the receipt. 'I'll call the police!'

Seven thousand pounds. Oh god, Ed, what have you done now? Why are you LIKE THIS? Am I a criminal?!

'Mrs Lomax, please let me see the receipt,' Dinah said, 'and we can get this sorted. I need to find out what's going on.'

Mrs Lomax finally surrendered the receipt. Dinah took one look at it, sighed and said, 'No, this says you've been charged the correct amount: £7.99.'

'It does not! It says seven thousand—' The old woman looked at the receipt Dinah was proffering and then paused. 'Oh.'

'I think you must have missed the decimal point and added a zero in your head,' Dinah said, ignoring the fact that the customer was always right. In this case, she was most definitely wrong.

Ohmigod. Ed breathed a huge sigh of relief, his heart resuming to a more natural rhythm. He wasn't a criminal after all! It was all going to be okay!

Mrs Lomax slammed the door on the way out, taking her trolley and book with her, safe in the knowledge that she still had money to her name.

At least amid the chaos Ed hadn't had time to worry about him and Hannah, until now, when Dinah said, 'Time for your break. After all that fuss I bet you could do with a breather. Will you take this box of old posters up with you to the staffroom? Hannah's there now but I forgot to ask her before she went. I keep tripping over them!'

Ed had been planning on hiding out on the top floor during his break, but he guessed he'd have to brave the staffroom now he'd been asked to go there by his boss. He picked up the box at the end of the counter and slowly made his way upstairs.

He paused outside the closed door and geared himself up for what was ahead.

She'll have forgiven you by now. She must have done! he told himself.

He found Hannah sitting on the sofa, nose in a book. She looked up, but then quickly back down, turning the page pointedly and crunching the spine. Ed tried not to wince. If this was any other time, he'd joke about how much his friend Olivia would hate that.

Instead he said, 'Hey,' and went over to stand by the small kitchen, to give Hannah enough space. He didn't know whether to play it cool or immediately jump into sincerity, so he settled on somewhere in between. 'You haven't been around much this morning. You'll never guess what just happened.'

She said nothing.

'Look, Han, I'm sorry—'

'I don't really feel like talking to you actually, Ed.' She turned away from him, so he could only see the side of her face. Her mouth was pinched together, and her fingers were flicking in a quick motion at her side.

'I know I made a HUGE mistake, but I am sorry. If I could go back, I would – take it all away, and start over.'

'You can't, so don't bother. I'm reading. Leave me alone.'

This time, Ed was the one who turned away. He felt bruised, pained, as if he'd suffered a great injury.

But he mustered all the enthusiasm left in his body to say, 'Can we talk about it? I don't want this to come between us.'

Hannah looked as if she was about to cry. *I want to reach for her!*

'Too late for that. It already has come between us. And I don't really know what I can say that I haven't already: you invited me to a party, which I said yes to because I genuinely wanted to spend more time with you, despite the fact that a party is my worst nightmare, and then you left me on my own, when I knew absolutely no one! Do you know how I felt?'

He half-shook his head. 'I . . .'

'Do you know what would have happened if I'd had a meltdown? I'm not just some side character in your heroic story; I'm a person, too, with my own life, my own story. I trusted you. I liked you, Ed!'

Does she mean she liked me as more than friends? Maybe this is my cue to tell her how I feel, but what if it makes the whole thing ten times worse?

'I promise I'll know better next time. I promise!'

'There won't be a next time. That's it. I'm done.'

'No, Hannah,' he said, *'please.'*

Hannah got up, stuffed her book into her locker and turned on her heel. 'I'm going back to work. See you, Ed.'

Ed slumped against the wall, the sound of Hannah's footsteps on the staircase the only thing he could hear. He couldn't bear the thought that he couldn't change what he'd done, that he couldn't go back in time and do things differently. One little decision, one little moment that he'd been swept up in, had changed everything. And even though he could pinpoint it almost exactly, there was no going back.

There had been a distinct finality to her words. *End of conversation. End of friendship. End of the promise of something more. End of everything.*

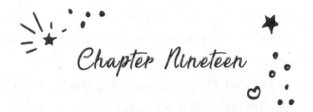

Chapter Nineteen

What a day! But there's not much that can't be made better by a good door-slamming. That was exactly what Ed did when he got home. He slammed the door once, then opened it again and slammed it harder the second time just to feel the satisfaction as the letterbox clanged.

And then, just for good measure, he tossed his keys into the pineapple dish and kicked the sideboard too.

'What on earth is going on out here?' Much to his irritation, Mum hurtled down the stairs in her dressing gown, fear and horror written in her features. She was the last person Ed wanted to see right now. The absolute last person on the planet.

'Like you care.' He felt very much like the stroppy teenager he was.

'Ed, what's happened, love?'

The anger was overtaken by a wave of laughter that rocked his shoulders. He wiped his eyes, finding tears there despite the fact it wasn't sadness he was feeling.

'Love!' he laughed. 'Love! What is that, Mum? You tell me. I didn't think you were capable of it.'

Mum cowered on the bottom step. 'What?' He liked how shocked she seemed. *Good*, he thought. *Good.*

'You heard me! How can you even think to call me "love"? Don't pretend as if you care.'

'Edward Eastfield. You're my son and I love you. You know that. What's all this really about?'

'Well, sometimes loving someone isn't good enough, is it?'

'Come on, Ed, what's going on? It's good you're here. You're never at home any more,' she said. 'If you're not at college, you're at work, and if you're not at work, you're out with friends. I never see you.'

'It's not my fault I can't stand to be in this house any more! Anyway, you won't have to worry for much longer – I doubt I'll have any friends left soon and I'll probably have to quit my job! Then you'll be happy!'

'What?'

'You heard me!' He could hear his voice rising, louder and louder, but he kept going, not caring if the neighbours heard him as long as he could get some of his rage out.

'Ed! Edward, what is this about? I told you, we can talk about this anytime.'

Ed scoffed. 'Why should I talk to you? You've made yourself very clear: you only care about yourself, not about me or my feelings! Does *anyone* care about me any more? Does anyone care how *I* feel? You spring a huge bombshell on me and think that everything's going to be okay, but it's not, Mum!'

He leant his head against the wall and curled his raised hands into fists. It was so difficult, *so* difficult to hold back the tears that threatened to overcome him. He groaned. 'I thought we had it all figured out! It was just you and me, against the world. Why does it have to change?'

'Ed, I love you, darling. I would never intentionally hurt you.'

Just like he'd never intentionally hurt Hannah or his friends, but he still had. He'd still disappointed them all. That was all he was: a huge disappointment.

'Well, you and Dad hurt me before and you're doing it to me all over again now!' He twisted around so he could look at her properly. 'I never got over it and I'll never get over this.'

Mum looked harrowed, as if he'd stabbed her in the heart. 'I'll put the kettle on. We can sort this out, love. We have every other time before, haven't we?'

'Forget it!'

Away. I have to get away. Run away as fast as I can.

'Ed!' she cried after him. 'Come back! Where are you going?!'

But he didn't know and he didn't really want to run – he didn't trust himself to drive anywhere safely. His only option was to flee up the stairs. He hurtled into his room and dived under his duvet, just as the tears came thick and fast.

He didn't think he'd ever cried so much in his life – years' worth of pain that he'd been bottling up all came pouring out: all the heartbreak left over from his parents' divorce, the rejection he felt from his dad, and the recent upset too, with his mum moving on, and losing Hannah. Losing the wonderful friendship between them.

Ed knew it hurt, but he hadn't realised it hurt this much. He couldn't help but cry and wail and claw at the duvet with his nails, so frustrated and angry and sad and scared. He was glad Mrs Simpkins wasn't in here to see him – the sight would have terrified her.

Why am I like this? WHY? *Why, why, why? Why isn't Mum following me upstairs? I've been so scared of losing her to her new boyfriend that I've pushed her away too.*

'Ed,' came Mum's voice, followed moments later by her warm arms wrapping around him in his duvet. 'Ed, I'm here. Shush, shush, it's okay, Ed. Let it all out. I'm here.'

At first, he tried to fight it, but it wasn't long before he gave in and succumbed to the security of his mum.

Now was the time to be honest. She was here and he was ready to talk. There would be no other opportunity like this one. He'd just feel worse if he pushed her away again now.

'I'm scared, Mum,' he confessed, feeling another wave

of tears and giving in to them. They fell freely down his pale cheeks.

'What are you scared of, my darling?' He was grateful for her soft voice. Even though he was still upset with her, he couldn't help but feel comforted by it.

It took him a while to find the words, but Mum waited until he was ready. 'That you're going to leave me. That you won't love me any more. That you'll love ... *him* more. That I just mess absolutely everything up and I don't know how to fix it and I make everyone upset or angry and I don't know how to stop! I ruin everything! I always do!'

'Of course I love you, Ed – and of course I'll always love you! You shouldn't get so down on yourself.'

'You have to love me! It's your job!'

Mum pulled back the duvet slightly and wiped one of the bigger tears from his face. The action, the sharp touch, made him pause. 'Ed, regardless of the fact that you're my son and as you say, I *have* to love you, I also admire you and I am so proud of who you are becoming.'

'You're ... proud of me?' he said, in a tiny voice.

'Of course I am! You can't imagine how I felt when I saw you head off to your first day at work – and how happy it makes me when you tell me about your shifts. You're beginning to bloom and it's wonderful to see.'

But that only made him hide under his duvet again, fighting back more tears.

'Ed, what is it? Has something happened at work?'

'I messed everything up, all right? I . . . Well, it's too embarrassing – but just trust me! I messed everything up!'

He could feel himself going red just at the thought of telling Mum about his feelings for Hannah. There was no way he could talk openly to her about it. No way!

'Is this about . . . a girl? A boy? At work?'

But she won't leave me alone until I tell her. And it did feel good to be talking to Mum once again, honestly, even if he did feel confused about where to go from here.

He lifted back the duvet but couldn't quite meet her gaze. 'A girl,' he admitted. 'We went to that party together that Cassie wanted to go to – and I stupidly left her on her own and did absolutely everything I shouldn't have done and now she hates me and I don't blame her.' His voice rose as he added, '*I* hate myself! Why can't I just think a little bit more before I do all these stupid things?'

'But that's what's lovely about you, Ed – and I'm sure all your friends would say the same. You throw yourself into life whole-heartedly, but sometimes our best features can also be the worst. It's not a bad thing to want to think more before you act; but these things come with time.'

'But now the one thing that was making me happy is gone! God, I'm such a disappointment. Listen to me, moping about. I need to get a grip.'

Mum looked confused. 'Why would you need to get a grip? There's nothing to be ashamed of.'

'Because I'm not a little boy any more! I'm an adult who needs to stop whingeing like a baby! I'm too sensitive.'

'Ed,' Mum said sternly. 'You are *not* too sensitive. Don't ever say that. Is this your father again? I wish he'd stop putting that rubbish into your head!'

He turned into his pillow so he couldn't see her face and mumbled, 'I feel so rejected. Even my own dad can't stand me. If I can just be better, maybe . . .'

'We can't choose our parents,' Mum said, 'and it's horrible to realise that they're real people who make mistakes, too. Sometimes they don't learn from those mistakes; but you should never have to change yourself to please your dad, not if you can help it. He does love you – but sometimes love can be disappointing, too. You just have to learn to listen to the people who matter – and listen to yourself in turn.'

Would Ed be able to switch off Dad's voice in his head? One day, maybe. He hadn't thought of it like that before.

'Look, why don't you go and wash your face, and I'll pop downstairs and make some tea. I may be able to rustle up a doughnut too, if you're lucky.' She patted him on the arm.

Once Mum had left, Ed got himself out of bed and lugged himself to the bathroom. He was shocked by his reflection in the mirror: pink, stained eyes and an even paler complexion than usual. He looked as tired as he felt.

But, somehow, he did feel a little bit better. It always helped to talk over the thoughts swirling around your head; they didn't seem so scary after that.

Back downstairs, freshened up, he sat on the sofa and picked up the doughnut that was awaiting him on the coffee table.

'Sorry, Mum,' he said. He'd thought it would be painful to admit it, but he knew he was speaking the truth. 'I shouldn't have tried to make you feel miserable. I mean – I wasn't *trying* to make you feel like that. I just felt so miserable about it myself, and scared, and I couldn't see past that.'

'It's understandable,' Mum said. 'I knew it wouldn't be easy for you – but I didn't think you'd find it this hard. I wasn't aware of how much you were still struggling after the divorce; you never said anything to me.'

He shrugged and wiped a tear from his face. 'What was there to say? I just had to get on with it, didn't I?'

'No, Ed,' she said. 'Just getting on with it and ignoring what's upsetting you is the worst thing to do; if you don't talk about it, the problem just gets bigger and bigger and bigger, and eventually it will all explode, just as it has done now.'

He shrugged again. He didn't know what to say.

'I wish you'd have spoken to me more,' Mum continued, 'instead of running off and not talking to me. I'm not asking anything of you, Ed, except for your support. This won't change our relationship.'

'Won't it?' he said through a mouthful of doughnut. A bittersweet doughnut.

'Of course not,' she said. 'If anything, our relationship will be even better. Because I'll be happier . . . I'm allowed to be happy too, Ed.'

He saw that now; how could he expect his mum to be happy about Hannah, when he couldn't even support his own mother's happiness?

'As long as I've still got you,' he said, 'and we've got each other – I guess that's all that matters.'

'Well, I do have to share you with Mrs Simpkins,' Mum pointed out.

He laughed. 'I cross the line at sharing Mrs Simpkins – she's all mine!'

'Love you, Ed.' Mum smiled, and he knew everything would be okay between them.

'Love you, Mum.'

Mum got up from her chair and came over to him, wrapping her arms around his shoulders and squeezing tight. 'It will be okay. I promise.'

'Thanks, Mum. I hope you're right.'

Later that night, emotionally exhausted, Ed found himself once again reading through Hannah's blog. Now that he and Mum had reached stable ground, he'd moved on to the next thing worrying him: how on earth to fix things with Hannah.

I have spent the majority of my life walking around with a mask on. No, not a medical one or one of those fancy ones that people wear to masked balls. A mask that looks and feels like my real face but is in fact not really me at all.

I didn't realise I did it until I was going through the process of diagnosis about two years ago now, but masking is a big part of the lives of autistic people – girls especially. Another way of thinking about it is that I'm a bit like a chameleon; I can change parts of my personality and mannerisms to fit the situation I'm in. It is EXHAUSTING.

As a kid, I would always try to mimic TV programmes I watched and would repeat sayings from books I read, especially in circumstances where I didn't know how to act. It doesn't mean I'm fake, although sometimes, when I've been masking a lot, I struggle to bring back the parts of myself that feel most like ME and I annoy myself terribly. It's just a way of coping that I never realised I was doing, until I thought about it more closely. I realised that there were so many moments in my life where I felt as if I was an actress playing a part, rather than Actually Me.

Think of it like this: in reality, I might be a bright pink chameleon, but when I'm around other people, I have to change so that I'm the same colour as all of them because it's easier to fit in rather than stand out too much; people aren't always understanding of neurodivergence. I've learnt that they don't always want to hear a five minute speech on baby guinea pigs or a book I've just read when I get enthusiastic, and they think there's something wrong if I don't make eye contact or start stimming ('stimming' means repetitive behaviours, for example I tap and flick my fingers a lot, especially when I'm in a stressful situation).

It's worse at big social occasions, especially with people my own age or people I don't know very well. I have to mask more, and then suppress things like stimming because people are very quick to judge, despite the fact I'd never judge the way they act or live their lives. The thing is, masking isn't always good. It takes a lot of effort and energy to hide a big part of yourself, even if you're not doing it intentionally. Masking is a bit like going into survival mode. You do it because you have to, rather than because you want to; and while everyone has the ability to mask to some degree, for autistic people, we can spend most of our lives doing it without even realising.

It's just something I've been thinking about a lot lately and wanted to share with you. I have to remind myself sometimes that I don't always have to hide – people will have to take me as they find me, and I have to hope that they won't judge.

Han x

And I took Hannah to a party, probably her worst nightmare, abandoned her and then expected everything to be okay. What was I thinking?

I always thought I was a kind, caring and considerate person, albeit a bit silly sometimes, but I'm turning into a monster who only thinks of himself. Look what I was like with Mum: I took it out on her, even though I knew it was wrong. I only did it to make myself feel better, but I made everyone else feel awful in the process.

There was only one thing for it: he'd have to sort it out.

Chapter Twenty

In the morning, as he headed to work, Ed found that his brain was just a little less cluttered than it had been this time yesterday. He'd made breakfast in bed for Mum as a peace offering, which she'd seemed pleased with. Things still weren't as they once had been, but they were looking up.

And today, fingers crossed, I'll be able to talk to Hannah properly. Sincerely, from the heart.

'Morning, Ed,' Dinah said as he pushed the door open. She looked as tired as he felt. 'Hannah's not in today, so I've called in Martha to cover, who's up in the staffroom now. You won't have met her because you're usually on different shifts, but she's really lovely.'

'Oh, cool,' he said. 'Is Hannah okay?'

'I think so,' she said. 'Maybe she's just feeling a bit under the weather, although she did mention something about swapping her shifts around. Hopefully she'll be up and running again soon.'

Swapping her shifts around?

'She didn't say anything about me, did she?'

Dinah shrugged. 'No, why would she?'

Quick, Ed. Think! 'Oh, I just said I'd lend her a book and for some reason, I thought she might have mentioned it. Don't worry, I'll go and take my stuff upstairs.'

He went up to the staffroom, overwhelmed by disappointment, worry and confusion. He'd been worried about having to quit – but maybe Hannah was thinking the same.

As Dinah had foreshadowed, he wasn't alone when he pushed the door open. But where Hannah once was, another girl stood by the lockers. She wasn't much older than him, and he recognised her from seeing her working at Woolf and Wilde before he'd got his job here.

'Hi. You must be Ed,' she said. 'I'm Martha. Nice to meet you.' She had red hair and her eye make-up – even though Ed knew very little about it – looked exquisite. Any other day, he might have been chattier and told her so, but today he was not in the mood.

'Nice to meet you too,' he said. He hoped Dinah hadn't said anything about how excitable he usually was – he'd be a severe anti-climax right now if so.

The staffroom, where he'd last spoken to Hannah, made him feel sadder than ever, like a ghostly shell of the fun they'd had together. He didn't want things to be left badly between them. But he was running out of things he could do.

'Well, I'd better be getting on,' he said, making his excuses. He didn't think he could stay there, making small talk, for much longer. 'Good luck with the readalong.'

'Thanks!' Martha said. Maybe he'd see her around another time and would be friendlier then. He didn't like feeling like this, not after he'd fixed things with Mum. One aspect of his life might be on the mend, but everything else was still super complicated.

Ed spent the morning under a haze, hoping he was doing everything right, but unsure of himself. He was happy to do the jobs that didn't involve him speaking to any customers, just stacking book after book and dealing with the returns of books that had sat around for ages without being sold. He kept hoping he'd see Hannah come around the corner and they could talk about pets, or books, or even Mrs Lomax, but she never did.

He was regularly reminded of his sadness: a kid coming in to buy a copy of *Guess How Much I Love You*, which his mum had read to him when he was younger; a little girl asking where Hannah was because she missed the special voice she put on at story time. The atmosphere no longer seemed magical.

Ed found himself looking out of the old paned-glass window upstairs, at the shoppers walking along the high street below, oblivious to him watching. They were like little ants, tiny yet busy, going on with their lives without a care in the world.

But that's not true – they'll have their own problems, their own concerns. I'm not the entire universe, even though sometimes it feels as if I am. Everyone feels as if they're the lead actor in their own play, but we forget that we're just the supporting cast, the ensemble, in everybody else's.

The haze continued all morning, headache-like, almost as if a very heavy cloud were sitting on top of his head.

It was a relief when he was able to go back down to Dinah at lunch.

'I didn't bring any food with me, so I'm going to head out and grab something and I'll be straight back,' Ed said, but his voice was flat. He was desperate to escape.

Dinah nodded. 'That's fine – see you in a bit!'

He felt like Ebenezer Scrooge in *A Christmas Carol*: he was miserable, making everyone else around him miserable too, and all he could say was, 'Bah Humbug!' *But Scrooge was able to change his ways. Yes, he was visited by a bunch of ghosts who showed him the way, but he did change. I don't think I need ghosts to help me; deep down, I know what I've got to do.*

Ed made sure to close the door gently behind him – he'd slammed enough doors to last a lifetime over the last few days – and treaded the cobbled street, off down the high street. He walked in the direction of the path that led over the town bridge and out to the river running along the bottom of the park.

It was part of the town's nature trail, with signs and boards put up along the way to point out the species of birds, plants and trees it was possible to spot. You could walk for miles along it, but Ed came to a stop at a bench a little way off that overlooked the riverbank. He had it entirely to himself, with just the twitter of the birds and the far-off sound of the park to keep him company.

I don't even have my friends to talk to.

But that wasn't true, was it? Maybe they were angry with him – but he hadn't bothered to message them after the party, and he had been rather rude to Cassie. Maybe they were just giving him space?

I can't expect them to make an effort with me if I don't do the same.

He pulled open The Paper & Hearts Society's group chat and stared at the dead conversations from last week, before the party. But as he looked back at his excited messages, it hit him: he hadn't even been happy then.

Just send the message, Ed. Then it's out of your hands how they choose to react – or if they respond at all.

Ed: Hey guys. Are you mad at me? I know I was awful to you Cassie and I'm sorry. I've been thinking about it and

I know I shouldn't have left Hannah all alone at the party
and I shouldn't have been such an idiot about it all. I
shouldn't have let you sort my mess out. Can we meet
up?

It was agonising waiting for a response. As they read the
message, one by one, and began to type responses, Ed
found himself putting his phone down, unable to bear
what they might say.

*It's the disappointment that's the worst. I can deal with
anger, but they're my best friends; when they're disappointed
in me, it makes me feel sick to my stomach.*

Tabby: Brain Freeze at 12 tomorrow? Just so you know,
    you're buying the ice cream x
Ed: Thank you, THANK YOU. Ice cream is on me!

He made his way back to Woolf and Wilde with a medium-
sized spark of hope inside him. With The Paper & Hearts
Society, things always felt possible.

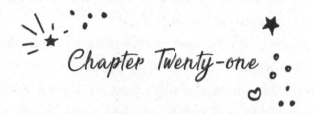

Chapter Twenty-one

There was no reason to be nervous exactly, but for some reason, Ed had butterflies. As he sat in one of the retro booths inside Brain Freeze, waiting for The Paper & Hearts Society to arrive, his hands felt shaky.

Maybe it was the coffee he was drinking – he'd been up all night looking at Hannah's blog posts, trying to work out how he could get back what they'd had. He'd made sure to get there earlier than the rest of them to grab a booth.

It wasn't long before the door tinkled and he looked up to find The Paper & Hearts Society walking in together. Tabby and Olivia were at the front, followed by Henry, and Cassie last.

They didn't look mad with him – not that he could tell, at least.

'Hey,' he said. *Don't be over the top today. Sincerity is the word.* 'Come and sit down.'

He slid out of the booth so they could fit in, and got out his phone, opening it to the notes app. 'What can I get you all? Ice cream? Sundaes? Coffee? Tea? Like Tabby said in our group chat, it's all on me!'

A glance passed between them, a moment's hesitation, and then everything was fine. They began to reel off their orders to him: mint chocolate chip for Cassie; cookie dough for Tabby; a chocolate caramel brownie sundae for Olivia.

'Okay, then.' Ed nodded to each of them. 'Coming right up!'

'I'll come with you,' Henry said. 'I haven't made up my mind yet.'

Henry and Ed went up to the counter, where a little queue had formed in front of them. Ed didn't know what to say, how to break the ice, so he settled for, 'Thanks for coming. I hoped you would but ... I didn't want to be sure. I know I've been an idiot.'

Henry clapped him on the back. 'It'll be okay, you know, Ed. We were more worried about you than anything else; Cassie was confused about why you were so mean, and Olivia ... Well, I'm sure they'll tell you. But we just want the best for you. You went quiet on us after the party!'

So I could have been talking to them all along?

Ed nodded, choking back tears. 'Thanks. Thanks, Henry. I appreciate it.'

He was saved from getting more emotional by suddenly finding himself at the front of the queue. He ordered and added a birthday cake and raspberry ripple combination for himself, with raspberry sauce. Henry asked for a strawberry shortcake sundae.

'Got it,' the lady behind the counter said. 'And you're over there in booth three? We'll be right over with your order . . . Next, please!'

Henry slid back into the booth beside Tabby and Ed followed on the other side. He was next to Olivia, who was next to Cassie

It's time. 'Right then . . .' he began. 'Well . . . Um . . .'

They all looked at him expectantly and he felt the weight of their attention.

'Look, I'm sorry. I've been a huge, huge idiot and I want to take it all back, but I know I can't, and I just want to say—'

'Chocolate caramel brownie sundae? And the mint chocolate chip ice cream?' Ed's grand speech was interrupted by the arrival of their order.

Great. Just as I was on a roll!

'Go on,' Olivia said softly and without her usual overenthusiasm, once they were all sorted and starting to tuck into their ice cream. 'We're listening.'

Ed nodded. 'I just want to say that I'm sorry I disappointed you so much. I've tried to apologise to Hannah, but she didn't want to hear it, and I really felt as if I'd burned all my bridges. I kept thinking that all parties were cursed and that it was always doomed to fail, but that's not true – it was my behaviour that caused everything to go wrong. I made those decisions; it wasn't fate. I could have changed things if I'd wanted to, but I didn't. Cassie, I shouldn't have said those things. It wasn't your fault that you invited Hannah; that wasn't the reason everything went wrong. I really regret sending that message now, so I am sorry. Really sorry.'

Cassie shrugged. 'As apologies go, I'm pretty happy with an ice cream sundae. I don't hold a grudge, you know me.'

Olivia snorted at that.

'What? I don't!'

'Sure,' Tabby said with a laugh. 'Sure you don't.'

Henry cut in, bringing them back on track. 'You've been acting a little strange for a while now though, Ed. You've been doing things that are like Ed pushed to the max. It hasn't gone unnoticed. First it was running away from home, then not telling me the truth when you came to see me about Hannah. I mean, why would you lie about writing a book? I'm your best mate! Then the party.'

Ed looked down at his ice cream, waving his spoon around the thick mixture. 'I've been so wrapped up in my own head. All that stuff with my mum ... I haven't dealt with it very well. My dad has decided he doesn't want to see me. I just feel so underappreciated. As if he doesn't care. So I tried to throw myself into work and I think I started to care too much – I just wanted a slice of happiness. But I forced it, I pushed it too hard. And now look what's happened.'

'I'm glad you've been honest with us,' Tabby said, 'and that you've apologised. But it's not us you have to say sorry to. It's Hannah. I was disappointed because I know I would have felt the same if I were in Hannah's situation and you'd abandoned me. Now you've come to your senses, maybe it's time to apologise to her again.'

He laughed. 'Yeah, right. No, what's done is done. There's no fixing it now. She doesn't want anything to do with me!'

'How did you form the apology?' Cassie asked, a spoonful of ice cream in mid-air. 'Like you've done with us now, or in that defensive way that you usually apologise?'

Ed scoffed. 'I do not . . .! Okay, maybe that was what it was like.'

'Nothing is unfixable,' Tabby said.

'Death,' Cassie pointed out. 'That usually is unfixable. I would know.'

Tabby looked a little guilty but continued. 'Well, in this instance, nobody has died. We're willing to forgive you and overlook your actions, and I'm sure if you're straight and heartfelt with Hannah, she'll understand. Honesty is the best policy.'

Henry said, 'Why don't we come up with something for you – something nice to say how sorry you are and make it up to her? A way to win back your friendship, if nothing else.'

'If you think it'll work . . .' Ed wasn't so sure.

'You won't know until you try,' Cassie said. 'It can't get much worse than it already is, let's be honest.'

'Thanks a lot!'

'Well, it's true,' she said with a shrug, going back to her ice cream. 'There's no harm in trying, but if you just give up, everyone will still be unhappy. You included.'

'Oh, good!' Olivia said. 'Something to organise!'

'Please don't go over the top, though,' Ed said, thinking of all the weird and wonderful ideas they might put together if they got carried away. He didn't want to scare Hannah further! 'It's got to be low-key. Okay?'

'Leave it to us,' Olivia said. 'We'll put our heads together and tell you everything you need to do. Got it? Ohmigod, I'm so excited now! Operation Paper & Hearts Society Saves the Day is a go!'

Once they'd finished their ice cream, Tabby, Henry and Olivia dashed off, leaving Ed with Cassie, who ordered a coffee. They didn't give an exact reason why they were going so soon, but Ed thought it was notable that he and Cassie were alone.

As she came back to the table, Ed took a deep breath. 'Do you really not hold a grudge against me?'

'I can if you want me to,' Cassie said, sitting down opposite him. She grinned. 'I could kick up a scene and start shouting at you in the middle of Brain Freeze; or even throw ice cream at your face if you'd like.'

Ed smiled back. 'I would like to see how the other customers react.'

Cassie wasn't the most openly affectionate of their friends, so it took Ed by surprise when she reached across the table and took his hand in hers.

She softened her voice as she said, 'I know what it's like to feel confused about family. When you see adverts on TV with parents and children sitting around, living a perfect life; when you watch people laugh and smile on the street, and wonder if they really have it that easy. I know what it's like, Ed.'

Ed gulped. How could he have been so selfish? 'Cass, I didn't think ... There's me going on about my dad and yours isn't even here any more. I'm sorry.' He squeezed Cassie's hand, encouraging her to go on.

'I managed to get Mum to come for a walk with me this morning. Just around the block, but she got out of the house and I saw her smiling. I caught her singing in the kitchen the other day. We might not have my dad any more and our lives have changed completely, but that doesn't mean there can't be happy moments in this new normal. It's hard, not gonna lie; I don't know how I've got through the last year or so, but I did and I wouldn't have changed looking after her for the world. She's my mum. I love her. If caring for her has taught me anything, though, it's that our parents are just plain old boring people with lives and problems of their own – and sometimes that affects us and it *sucks*. You're allowed to be disappointed in your dad and still love him at the same time. You're allowed to want more from him and feel sad when he lets you down. That doesn't make you a bad person, Ed.'

Mum had said something similar to him. Was he really not the bad one here? Did he really not have to change himself? The thought was freeing.

Ed shook his head, more to figure out what he was trying to say than anything else. 'I kept thinking that if I changed myself, Dad would be nicer towards me. But I can't change; I love acting, but I can't pretend to be someone else when it comes to real life. I've been worried that my mum will let me down, just like Dad does – that when things suddenly changed, I made sure she *would* let me down. I didn't listen to her, and I shut her out.'

'Maybe you should take some ice cream back for her,' Cassie suggested. 'I think I might do the same for Mum – even though she likes banana flavour and I do *not* understand it!'

Ed screwed his face up. 'That's a step too far, even for me – and I eat everything!' He let go of her hand. 'Thanks, Cassie. Don't tell anyone I said this – but you're the best.'

She flicked her hair over her shoulder with a laugh. 'Too right I am!'

They both went back up to the counter and got their takeaway ice cream, and then stood on the street corner, where Ed couldn't help himself – he shouted, 'GHOST HUG!' and wrapped his arms around her.

'Ed!' Cassie said but didn't struggle from his grasp. In fact, he felt her hug him back. 'The ice cream is cold on my neck! Get it off!'

From now on, Ed was going to give as many ghost hugs as he could possibly could. Minus the fake moustache like he'd had at the murder mystery party.

'Just leave the rest up to us,' Cassie said before heading off home. 'You can bet Olivia is already running wild with ideas.'

'I dread to think what she's going to come up with!'

But he didn't mean that; if anyone could help him, it was The Paper & Hearts Society.

Olivia: Okay, Ed! Here's the plan and TRUST US on this! Because Hannah has blocked you on social media one of us will send her a very nice message on your behalf to ask if she can go to the lake on Friday

Ed: I really don't think this is a good idea

Olivia: We have to try!! Don't give up before we've even begun!

Cassie: i am not wasting my time on this for you to say no now

Ed: FINE. And then what?

Tabby: Then on Friday afternoon you're going to pop around to mine and pick up the bits we've prepared for you, which you'll understand when you get here. Then, you head to the lake where Hannah will meet you

Ed: IF she says yes

Olivia: WHEN not IF! Believe in us!! Believe in our plan!

Tabby: Here's the message for Hannah, for your approval

Tabby: Hi Hannah, I hope you don't mind me messaging you. I know you don't really want to speak to Ed right now which is perfectly understandable, but he really has gone away and thought over his actions and would like to apologise again. If you feel comfortable, would you like to meet him on Friday at 2pm at the lake?

Ed: Okay okay okay SEND IT BEFORE I SAY NO

Tabby: Done! We'll just wait now to see if she replies. Hopefully she will!

Henry: It will be fine, Ed, just don't overthink it. That's what gets you in trouble.

Ed: Thanks guys, I hope it works. I don't want things to be left badly between us.

Tabby: Wow, that was super quick! I got a message back! It says 'Okay, yes, I'll be there on Friday. Thanks, Tabby. :)'

Olivia: AMAZING!!!!

Cassie: wow, i did not think this would work but fair play

Ed: Cassie!!!

Cassie: what?

Ed: You're not supposed to say that!!! ARGH, OKAY, IT'S REALLY HAPPENING

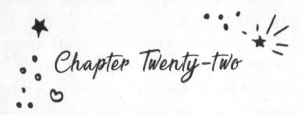

'Does this look okay?' Ed held out the phone camera as he FaceTimed The Paper & Hearts Society so they could judge his handiwork. 'I've stayed as far away from the lake as possible because I do not want to risk getting chased by a swan again. I was traumatised when we were here for my birthday!'

Ed had got to the lake on time, after picking up the items The Paper & Hearts Society had left for him at Tabby's gran's: a picnic basket and a plaid picnic rug. A handwritten note lay on top from Tabby: *Have a good time! Remember: honesty is the best policy! Just be your lovely self.* ×

The location Ed had scouted was on top of the hill on the western side of the lake, far away from the water and its frightening swans. From up here, it was possible to survey the entire expanse, with its bordering woods where Henry had once hid during their *Hunger Games* re-enactment.

It had been easy to set up the picnic, but he wanted it to be just right, which was why he'd called on his friends to give their seal of approval. He wouldn't have been able to do any of this without them.

'It looks great!' Olivia called out. 'Just turn to the left a little bit and let me see . . . Yes, you've done a good job!'

'Don't sound so surprised,' he replied.

'Frankly,' Cassie said, 'it is a surprise. But well done, you.'

He clutched his chest and stumbled back. 'Quick, help me! Cassie just complimented me and I can't take it! It's too much of a shock!'

'Oh, stop it,' she said. 'You know I can be nice when I want to be.'

'Good luck,' Henry said. 'We'll go now and leave you to it. But it will be fine, we promise.'

'I hope so,' Ed said with a sigh. 'I really hope so.'

He hung up and stood around, waiting for Hannah's arrival. Luckily they'd chosen a lovely day; spring felt just around the corner, the sun shining through faint clouds, and it was plenty warm enough if you were wearing a coat. Ed had made a sensible decision this time, and wore his duffle coat over a Shakespeare T-shirt.

Ed didn't feel as if he could sit down on the blanket – he didn't want to mess it up, and the nerves were making him jittery. The clock told him that it was already two o'clock, about time Hannah was here, but he couldn't spot her. *What if she doesn't turn up?* He turned around, running a hand through his hair with a groan. *I knew this would be a disaster! DISASTER. Can I just tell The Paper & Hearts Society to abort the mission?*

He was about to ring them when he spun back around and found Hannah heading straight towards him. *THIS IS EVEN WORSE. Now it's really happening!!! ARGH, SOMEONE HELP ME!*

Why hadn't he insisted his friends came with him?

Because I've got to do this all myself. JUST BELIEVE IT WILL BE FINE. ARGH, ARGH, ARGH!

Hannah was getting closer and closer and he had to force himself to breathe. He was sure he'd forgotten how. Closer and closer, closer and closer. And then she was there, practically in front of him.

Argh!

'Hi,' Hannah said, her hands knotted in the sleeves of her cream knitted jumper. She looked just as nervous as he felt. That was at least a consolation.

'Hi,' he returned. 'How are you?'

'Good, thanks. You?'

'Yeah, I'm okay.'

'Thanks for coming. I really appreciate it.'

He gestured to the picnic blanket and they sat down on opposite sides. He didn't want it to be so awkward between them, but he wasn't sure how to change it.

He reached to get the food from the basket: sandwiches tied up in brown paper, as well as little cakes and treats. He handed a paper plate to Hannah.

'I hope you like . . .'

'I do,' she said. 'Tabby asked me beforehand, so she wouldn't get anything I had an aversion to. She's a good friend.'

'They all are,' he said with a smile. The fact that he was having a civil conversation now with Hannah was testament to them. He'd been ready to give up all hope.

'So . . .' she said, but he wanted to begin first. This was his conversation to start, his responsibility.

Just say it. Don't beat around the bush. Open and honest, sincere. You can do this.

'Hannah, believe me, I would never have taken you to that party if I'd known you would hate it so much.'

'It's not entirely your fault,' she said, sipping at her water. 'The party was just the tipping point, I think. I made the mistake of assuming that I would be fine, that it would go okay. But, once we were there, I quickly realised that my neurodiverse brain really, *really* hates parties and I should never have pushed away the voice that told me so. I've been to parties in the past and it's always been a disastrous experience.'

He couldn't help himself; Ed found himself laughing.

'What?' she said.

'Parties have always been disastrous experiences for me, too. The last party I held I ended up sitting on the kerb outside, crying my eyes out and Tabby had to rescue me. Why did I think going to that one was a good idea?!' He groaned. 'I should have known!'

'Book parties are good; but *party* parties? Very bad.' She smiled. 'Let's not try to go to one again, hey?'

Ed shook his head. 'I've thought about it, I really have, and I was incredibly selfish. I don't want to beg for your forgiveness because I don't deserve it. I left you when you explicitly asked me not to, and you had to rely on my friends to bail you out of a situation that made you feel awful. There's no pressure on you to forgive me for that.'

Hannah thought about it, looking away from him and out at the lake. He looked, too, at both the thoughts flashing across her face and at the watery expanse, evil swans and all.

'I don't forgive you really,' she said quietly, and his heart dropped. Although he meant what he'd said, he'd kind of hoped she would. 'It wasn't a little thing to me; it was inconsiderate and uncaring and it hurt me, a lot. But' – she shrugged – 'I've missed you. I'm still upset, but I don't want it to come between us. I thought . . . Well, I like you, Ed. A lot. That's not easy for me to say, but I do.'

What? His head shot up, his eyes wide. What did she mean?

'I know it's silly, but I thought before the party that you might have liked me too. And now I just feel confused.'

Confusion was the word. What did she mean, she liked him? The same way he'd liked her? As friends? As . . . something else? He hadn't expected this, had no clue what to say. He had to force his mouth to shut because he was sure it was hanging open.

'I'm scared, Ed,' she went on. 'This is all new to me. I was so sure . . . Now, I don't know what to think.'

'Hannah,' he said. 'Hannah, I—'

'Please, just forget I said anything. Let's just eat our sandwiches and shut up.'

Usually Ed would have jumped at the chance of tucking into a magnificent picnic, but now he was completely distracted.

'No,' he said. 'I did, I *do*, like you. More than a lot. You weren't wrong. I was going to . . .' He felt himself blush but he kept going. 'I was going to tell you at the party, but, well, you know what happened.'

'Right . . .'

But he kept going. 'I didn't expect when I started working at Woolf and Wilde that I'd meet someone like you. God, you definitely didn't think highly of me at first! But then as we got to know each other and, let's be real, I got to know your guinea pigs and Indiana Bones, I found that we had lots in common, that I looked forward to seeing you, that I would brave even Mrs Lomax if it meant spending more time with you.'

'I knew it was all about the animals,' she joked.

'And you must know I'm speaking seriously because I am a cat person and you are a dog person – and this is a betrayal of all my instincts.'

'I'd never thought of it like that! Wow.'

'I like you, Hannah. I have the most embarrassing crush ever and it's made me a mess. I'm not asking anything of you but, if you feel the same then, maybe, just maybe . . . Well, maybe you feel the same?'

'This is a lot to take in,' she said. She bit her lip. 'I do, I do feel the same. I just . . . Can you give me some time to think about it? I feel anxious at the thought of being in a relationship. It involves all the things I hate most: close contact, touching, the expectation that you should know the other person like nobody else in the world does, despite the fact that I can barely decipher my own emotions most days. Then there's the fact that I'm used to doing things on my own. I don't have a lot of friends because I'm happy in my own company and I don't need other people for my hobbies. My grandad is my best friend. I don't know if I've got time for everything.'

'You don't have to give anything up for me. I would hate that. To be honest, I don't mind hanging out with you and your guinea pigs, or just sitting quietly and reading, as long as it's with you. Just knowing you're there makes me happy.'

Hannah smiled. 'That does make things easier.'

'I don't want to push you. I'm happy to be friends if that's what you would rather. The thought that we'd never be friends again was awful.'

'It was a bit, wasn't it?' she said, biting into a cupcake. 'I thought I hated all your annoying questions, but it turns out I really missed them. I was determined not to give in and contact you, but it was difficult.'

'I knew I was irresistible!'

She rolled her eyes. 'You are incredibly annoying! I swear, I have never met anyone more annoying and frustrating in my life! But yes ... I must admit, a little irresistible. God knows I've tried to resist.'

He laughed and stole another sandwich from the plate. 'Say that again so I can record it for posterity.'

Another roll of her eyes. 'Hey, stop digging for compliments! It's you who should be giving me them!'

'I'll give you a lift back after we've finished up,' he offered.

'Are you just saying that so I'll invite you in to see the guinea pigs?'

'Maybe just a little bit.'

But as it turned out he didn't see the guinea pigs after all; they decided waiting would be better.

'Give me time, Ed,' Hannah said softly, her parting words. 'Just while I figure things out. Maybe in the meantime I could, I don't know, meet your friends or something? Not at a party this time, though! But I want to get to know you better outside work, I really do.'

He beamed; he couldn't help it. Hannah at a Paper & Hearts Society meeting!

'I'd love that more than anything. And, Hannah? I'm not going anywhere. I'll be right here, if or when you're ready,' he said, and meant it.

Two Weeks Later . . .

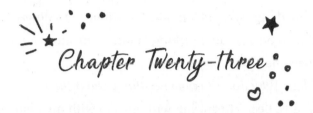

Chapter Twenty-three

'Answer, Livs! Dammit!' Ed growled at his phone, as if Olivia could hear him before she'd even answered. He'd tried to FaceTime her five times now and she wasn't answering. *Sixth time lucky, I hope.* Mrs Simpkins mewled at him from the end of his bed, but he ignored her in favour of staring down at his phone. Eventually, Olivia picked up.

'Finally!' he said instead of a greeting.

'Ed, what's going on? Are you okay? I have so many messages and missed calls from you.'

'I need to know about The Paper & Hearts Society meeting tomorrow. I'm getting concerned that you haven't told us anything about it and it's very important that I pass on the details to Hannah.'

'It will all be fine,' Olivia said, 'I promise. You don't need to worry about a thing.'

'But it's not me who's worrying,' Ed said. 'It's Hannah – I need to let her know what we're doing. It's not fair on her to leave her in the dark.'

'Trust me, you're the only one who will be in the dark. I've already spoken to Hannah. All you need to do is come to mine tomorrow after picking Hannah up and everything will become clear.'

What? Why don't I know anything about this?!

'You've been conspiring with my . . . with my Hannah! I can't believe this!' he spluttered.

'You can call her your girlfriend, you know, Ed. It's not a scary word.'

Ed felt himself blush and covered his cheeks with his hands. They burned to the touch. 'She's not my girlfriend! And, Olivia, don't change the subject! I can't believe you!'

'Trust me, Ed. It will be perfect. You'll love it.'

'I can't believe they've told you but they haven't told me,' Ed said to Hannah, who was giving absolutely nothing away. 'I'm a founding member! How could they go behind my back like this? It's outrageous!'

He'd driven to her house to pick her up and they were now driving back towards his house, where Olivia lived on the adjacent street. It felt disconcerting knowing that Hannah knew more about the meeting than he did.

That being said, he could not wait to spend time with all his favourite people. If only he'd been able to bring Mrs Simpkins, it really would have been the best day of his life!

'I just can't believe I'm allowed to attend a Paper & Hearts Society meeting,' Hannah said. She fiddled with the soft sleeve of her yellow vintage-style dress as she spoke. 'I've heard so much about the infamous meetings. Are you sure your friends are happy with me being there? Olivia seemed very enthusiastic on the phone, but I don't want to intrude on your book club. I can tell how much it means to all of you.'

'I'm more worried about what you'll think of them,' he admitted. 'We are a bit weird when we all get together.'

As Ed drove, the conversation turned to the recent customers they'd had at work, what they'd been reading recently and how cute Hannah's latest litter of baby guinea pigs was, photos of which she'd been posting on her Instagram page.

Usually, Ed liked to listen to the radio when he was in the car, but today the sound of Hannah's voice was all he needed.

They barely broke their conversation as he parked in his normal space outside his house and they walked to Olivia's.

'Ready?' he said, just before ringing the doorbell. He wanted to give her the chance to turn away if she needed to. It was no easy thing, meeting all his friends like this. He guessed she was terrified.

Hannah smiled up at him. 'As I'll ever be,' she replied.

And Ed took that as his cue to ring the bell. They didn't have to wait long before the door flung open and Olivia stood on the threshold.

'Hi!' she cried, ushering them in with, 'Come on in! Hannah – it's so lovely to meet you in person somewhere that's not a mad party. Welcome! Come on, don't let all the cold in, Ed!'

Ed didn't think it was that cold – or maybe he just hadn't noticed – but he did as he was told and stepped through with Hannah. He took Hannah's coat from her and hung it up, just as he knew Olivia liked to be done when anyone came over. He was about to push open the living room door when Olivia squeaked in horror.

'Not the living room! It's all set up and I will *not* have you spoiling the surprise, Edward! Cassie's waiting in the kitchen, so go and join her. No spoilers!!'

He'd do as he was told in front of Hannah; he didn't want to make himself look bad by teasing Olivia more than was necessary. They went through to the kitchen at the back of the house, just like Ed's was. In fact, the layout of their houses was almost identical; Ed would have been able to navigate it blindfolded.

'Cassie!' Ed said, spotting her seated on a barstool around the central island, looking at her phone. She put it down, to her credit, as they came in. 'What a joy!'

'Edward,' she said, then, 'Hi, Hannah.'

Ed hoped Cassie was on her best behaviour; she did have a tendency to rely on sarcasm.

Lizzie, who had previously been occupied by Cassie, immediately bounded over to Hannah, who crouched down on the kitchen tiles so Lizzie would cease jumping up. The little dog could leap surprisingly high!

'I always love it when people have animals,' Hannah said, with Lizzie sitting in the middle of her crossed legs, licking her cheek. 'I instantly feel so much more relaxed.'

'Wow, Ed, you really are made for each other,' Cassie said, looking faintly impressed. To Hannah, she said, 'Have you met Mrs Simpkins yet?'

'Not yet,' Hannah replied, still looking at Lizzie, stroking her behind the ears. 'But I've seen lots of pictures and it will certainly be an honour if I ever do get to meet her.'

Cassie laughed. 'It seems as if the honour will be all hers.'

It wasn't long before Tabby and Henry arrived, their cheeks rosy from being outside, both wearing almost matching jumpers.

'Total coincidence,' Tabby said, holding her hands up in defence, looking down at her red jumper and then across at Henry's.

'That's what you think,' Henry said with a wink, earning him a push to the shoulder.

While Hannah still had Lizzie sitting on her lap, she looked more than comfortable, as did Lizzie. Ed was pleased – as long as Hannah was happy, he was happy.

'Oh, you made a friend!' Olivia said once she'd finished bustling about doing last-minute preparation, coming into the kitchen and seeing Hannah with Lizzie. 'She won't leave you alone now, though. Good luck extricating yourself! Now, everyone: are you ready to see what I have in store for you? Follow me to the living room, please!'

While Tabby, Henry and Cassie made their way through, Ed hung back as Hannah tried to leave a clingy Lizzie behind.

'Everything okay?' Ed checked. 'Just let me know if it isn't; but it does look as if everyone is toning down the weirdness. They haven't even burst into unexpected song yet, which is a surprise, I've got to tell you!'

'All good!' Hannah replied as Lizzie finally clambered off her lap. She reached out a hand so Ed could pull her up, which he did, the warmth of her palm in his more than welcome.

'I'm so glad you're here,' he said just before letting go, pleased when the smile on her face mirrored his own.

'I can't wait to see your reaction when you find out what's going on.'

'Tell meeeeeeee!' Ed whined as they made their way to join the rest of The Paper & Hearts Society, but Hannah wouldn't give in.

'Be patient!' she laughed.

'You took your time,' Cassie said as they got to the shut living room door where everyone was waiting.

'Enough of that ... I can't wait any longer! Are you ready? Ta-da!' Olivia flung the living room door open and allowed them all to finally step in. The room was dark, apart from the strings of fairy lights hanging from the ceiling and most of the surfaces. The small table where the TV usually stood held a massive projector screen, and there were comfy cushions and soft beanbags laid out on the floor.

'Remember our last movie marathon, for one of our first meetings?' Olivia said. 'I *loved* that! I thought we could do the same today, except this time with a film that I – no, I should say *we*, because Hannah was more than helpful with the suggestion – think one Paper & Hearts Society member in particular is going to love. Just you wait and see!'

'Hannah! You've been conspiring against me!'

'Yes!' Hannah said. 'The pressure was unreal – but we got there in the end, didn't we?'

'We certainly did!' Olivia replied with a big smile. She fiddled around with the buttons on the projector, trying to get everything sorted.

The living room really did look cosy with all the fairy lights. There was space on the sofa for Hannah and Ed to sit next to each other, while the others occupied the beanbags. They looked a little *too* cosy for his liking, but Ed reminded himself that he wasn't the awkward fifth wheel any more. Now, there were six of them.

'Hannah, would you like to do the honours and reveal to Ed what's going on?' Olivia handed her what looked like pieces of card; Ed was intrigued.

'I'd be delighted,' she said, taking them from Olivia and turning to face Ed.

'We are going to be watching *Much Ado About Nothing*—'

'We're going to do what?!' Ed said. It was his favourite film! This was AWESOME. 'The one with Kenneth Branagh and Emma Thompson?'

Hannah was laughing, as was everyone else, as she said, 'Let me finish! I didn't even get to the good bit! We're going to have an interactive watchalong – which is why I've got these cards. Each of us will have a character and at specific points in the film, Olivia will pause it and we'll act it out before watching the scene for real.'

'OH MY ... SHAKESPEARE!' Ed cried. He thought he might actually cry from the excitement. 'Are you serious? This is the best thing ever! Shakespeare, my love! I think I might die like poor Yorick from all the shock!'

'I think he's happy,' Cassie murmured to Tabby, who looked delighted at Ed's joy.

Hannah handed out the cards that had all their lines on – and Ed thought he might burst when he saw he'd been given his two favourite parts: Dogberry, the fool of the play, as well as Benedick, the male lead.

Starring opposite him was Cassie as Beatrice, which was perfect for her sarcastic character, while Henry was Leonato, the fatherly figure, as well as the Messenger; Hannah was Verges, Dogberry's companion; Tabby's part was Don Pedro; and Olivia was Claudio. Between them, they also shared out some of the smaller roles.

'I am going to have the time of my life!'

But before they started on their Shakespeare re-enactment, they settled into watching the film; Ed had to be careful that he didn't spend the entire time jumping up and down in his seat, so extreme was his eagerness.

The premise of the play – and, therefore this film version – was that Beatrice and Benedick vehemently hated each other and made a point of letting everyone know, especially through their witty banter. But then they got tricked into believing they were in love; meanwhile, Benedick's friend Claudio was tricked into believing that Beatrice's cousin, and his love, Hero, had been unfaithful to him.

'Is the volume okay for you, Hannah?' Olivia asked during the opening scene. 'I can turn it down if it's too loud.'

Hannah smiled. 'It's great, thanks.'

Ed was proud of his friends for being so welcoming and considerate towards Hannah. He knew they wouldn't have let him down; they always treated people as they would wish to be treated.

Soon enough, just as the second act would be beginning in the play, Olivia paused the film for them to perform their first piece. First up: Henry and Cassie. They stood, Henry giving a little bow just before he spoke.

'"Well, niece, I hope to see you one day fitted with a husband,"' Henry read, testing the line out in his mouth. He was a terrible actor, Ed thought – he gave a nod of satisfaction after his line, breaking character, as if he was pleased with his performance.

Cassie had clearly decided that if she was going to do this, she was going to go all in. She was a fierce sight to behold – one hand on her hip as the other tightly gripped her script. '"Not till God make men of some other metal than earth. Would it not grieve a woman to be overmastered with a pierce of valiant dust? To make an account of her life to a clod of wayward marl?"' She gave a dramatic pause before saying, 'I like this girl. I think we'd be great friends.' Cassie cleared her throat, reading the rest of Beatrice's lines out and delivering a curtsy once she was finished.

The others clapped.

'Shakespeare is almost understandable when you read it,' Tabby said. '*Almost.*'

'No Shakespeare slander!' Ed cried. 'He was a genius! I will not hear a bad word spoken against him!'

But Tabby still seemed unsure even as Cassie and Ed stood up at the next pause in the film to act opposite each other as Beatrice and Benedick. Even though there was no romantic love between them, they were used to banter, and it only enlivened their performance.

Olivia giggled the entire way through, and Ed was proud of himself for keeping a straight face, even though he too was desperate to burst into laughter.

'Encore?' he said, as soon as their final lines had been read. 'Because I'm happy to do that all over again!'

But Cassie said, 'Actually, my performance was so perfect that there's no need to go again. But if you want to improve yours, be my guest . . .'

Hannah laughed at Ed's withering look, which made him protest, 'You're supposed to be on my side, Hannah!'

'In this one, I think I'd rather be Team Cassie,' she said, laughing even more when Ed started to pout.

It wasn't long before it was time for the appearance of his other character, Dogberry, whose chief role in the play was to mess everything up. The irony wasn't lost on Ed; he could rather relate to that himself.

'"Are you good men and true?"' He only needed to briefly glance at his card to know his lines – it meant he was able to put his everything into his performance, treating it as if he really was on stage at the Globe Theatre in front of a crowd of people. If anything, he didn't think he'd ever perform to a crowd as tough as this one; as his friends, they weren't afraid to tell him if he'd made a mistake, or laugh in the wrong places. Luckily, though, this time they did neither.

Hannah, as Dogberry's accomplice, came on stage – or the living room carpet, to be accurate and somewhat less glamorous – and Ed almost broke character for a second as he realised he was getting to perform Shakespeare with her. *I never would have foreseen this!*

There was a pause and he noticed how nervous Hannah looked. She fumbled with her card but she seemed to shake off the nerves as soon as they'd arrived. '"You have been always called a merciful man, partner."' Hannah read, and from then on, all ran smoothly.

Shakespeare wasn't the easiest to read, he had to admit, but it was about more than the actual words: it was about the connection between characters, the intonation, the atmosphere. When Shakespeare was performed properly, it felt like magic, and Ed felt a glimmer of such magic now, in this room with them.

Yes, he may have been over the top and didn't read all of the lines as he would have done in his drama class, but it didn't matter – it wasn't about a perfect performance, it was about living in the moment and enjoying every second of it.

'I can't believe I did that!' Hannah exclaimed, throwing her hair back as she practically crumbled with relief.

'Amazing!' Olivia stood up to give them a standing ovation, and the others joined her. 'That was fabulous! This is what The Paper & Hearts Society is all about – living your best bookish life!'

Hannah grinned. 'I certainly feel as if that's what I've just done!'

'Next time, we're performing Shakespeare with guinea pigs,' Ed suggested.

'Ohmigod, can we actually do that?!' Tabby said. 'Can you imagine how cool that would be?'

'As long as it's not a tragedy,' Henry said. 'I don't think I could bear seeing the guinea pig version of *Romeo and Juliet*.'

'But guinea pig witches in *Macbeth* could be interesting,' Hannah offered.

'Maybe we could do a medley of plays,' Tabby said. 'Hey, Cassie, could you make little costumes? Ah, now I want to do this!'

'I'm going to get a drink,' Ed said. 'Does anyone want anything from the kitchen?' He felt the sudden urge to get out of there; it was all so perfect, so *happy*, that he couldn't bear it, like the brightest ray of light shining directly in his eyes. He had to step away for a few seconds to be able to take it all in.

'No thanks!' they all called, turning back to the screen.

As Ed went out to the kitchen, Lizzie jumped up at his legs, but not with half as much enthusiasm as she'd shown Hannah; she really was gifted with animals. The calm of the kitchen slowed his excitable brain and for the first time all afternoon, he felt as if he was remembering to breathe properly. He got a glass of water from the tap and leant against the island, secretly smiling to himself.

What a day. What a beautiful day, filled with wonderful moments, he thought. Surrounded by his best friends, acting his heart out . . . Shakespeare! What could be better than that?

He stood up straighter as he heard the living room door creak and watched as Cassie strolled leisurely down the hall towards him.

'There you are,' she said. She went over to kettle and flicked the switch. 'You all right?'

'Yeah,' he said, and really, truly meant it. 'I mean . . . I know it sounds weird, but I just needed to take a breather because I felt so happy and didn't know what to do with all the emotion.'

Cassie nodded. 'I get that. Hannah's nice,' she said, 'in fact, more than nice. You seem very well suited. I'm glad you invited her.'

'Where's the real Cassie and what have you done with her?' Ed teased, but then smiled. 'Thanks. That means a lot.'

Cassie patted him on the shoulder with a flicker of humour in her eyes. 'Just don't go ruining it by blowing up any more microwaves. Promise me?'

He laughed. 'I *promise*, with all my heart.'

'You're nearly up again, by the way. Get back in there!'

'Yes, boss!' he cried, taking a running leap back to the living room. 'Time to shut up and Shakespeare!'

'Thanks for inviting me,' Hannah said as Ed dropped her back at home. They lingered in the car, and Ed got the sense that Hannah didn't want to leave this bubble of theirs just yet. 'I had more fun than I even thought was possible – so thank you. You're so lucky to have friends like you do.'

'I know,' he said with a smile. 'Right now, I couldn't feel any luckier if I tried.'

And he meant every word; as he watched Hannah get out and turn around to wave on the way up her driveway, he counted his blessings. And he'd keep counting them, keep remembering how lucky he was, for as long as it lasted.

And long may it last!

Hannah: Do you feel like meeting at Woolf and Wilde for a
non-work hot chocolate tomorrow? Just wondered!
Ed: Do you really think I'd ever say no to hot chocolate?
Hannah: Good point

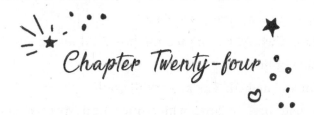

Chapter Twenty-four

It was strange entering Woolf and Wilde without the expectation of working that day, but Ed was looking forward to spending time in his favourite bookshop when he didn't have to worry about running around after customers or searching high and low for books that had decided to go missing.

And most of all, he was looking forward to hot chocolate. And seeing Hannah. But hot chocolate was also a very good thing.

'Hey, Ed! What are you doing here? It's not your shift today. You haven't got the wrong day, have you?'

He shut the door behind him and turned to find Dinah, behind the till, looking back at him brightly.

'I've just come to spend some of my hard-earnt money,' he said. 'Hot chocolate and book shopping is called for!'

'Well, have a good time, won't you? And tell the cafe team to let you try one of their new mini Hungry Caterpillar cakes. They're divine! I must admit to stealing one or two to take home with me of a night.'

'Don't worry, I won't tell the boss,' Ed joked, tapping the side of his nose.

Dinah laughed. 'Get away with you!'

It had been a long while since he'd spent a good amount of time in the glorious Woolf and Wilde cafe; now he worked here, he didn't feel the same pull to spend so much of his leisure time among the shelves or in the cafe. Saying that, he couldn't think of a better place to meet up with Hannah.

Not only was Woolf and Wilde full of bookshop magic, it was also the place they'd first met. Ed felt as if he'd come full circle.

The cafe entrance was an oval archway by the side of the bookshop counter, heavily decorated with mismatched, brightly coloured furniture, representations of famous book characters and even a giant teapot, which Dinah had once told him she'd jumped out of as a dare.

He glanced around for Hannah but it didn't look as if she was there yet, so he took a quiet table in a cosy corner, where Dinah couldn't easily watch them if she happened to pass by. He got himself settled, taking one of the book proofs he had to read out of his bag and scanning the pages.

It wasn't long before he heard footsteps approach and there was Hannah, her chestnut hair covered slightly by a green beret. She was wearing a black skater skirt and vintage-style Fair Isle jumper.

'Hello,' she said with the warm smile he'd come to know and love. She pulled out the chair opposite his and sat down, putting her black faux-leather rucksack down on the floor. 'Good book?'

'Yes, actually,' he said. He put his bookmark back in and shut the pages. 'I'm going to suggest to Dinah we do a display around it in the teen section; I think it would look great.'

'Speaking of Dinah . . . she did look a little suspicious when she saw me come in,' Hannah said, adding a smug giggle. 'She raised one eyebrow and said, "Did you know that Ed is here, too?" I had to act very innocent!'

'She did seem surprised to see me on a non-work day,' he said, 'but I think if we buy a book or two on our way out she'll forget all about it.'

Though somehow, he thought her forgetting might not last too long. Things might get a bit more difficult if this became a recurring event.

Hannah bent down and pulled her purse from her bag. 'How does hot chocolate and cake sound? Let me get it – you provided the picnic last time, so now it's my treat.'

'Are you sure?' She didn't need to do that!

'Of course!'

'Well, as I said in my message, I've never said no to hot chocolate before – and Dinah said we could ask the cafe team for their new mini Hungry Caterpillar cakes.'

'Be right back then,' she said, 'with hot chocolate hopefully in tow.'

It wasn't until she'd gone up to the counter to order that Ed realised his face was hurting from all the smiling. And she hadn't even been here for five minutes! How was he going to survive longer? His facial muscles might end up exploding.

He could see Hannah pointing at the different cakes in the sweet treat display with the girl behind the counter. Then she turned around and waved over at Ed; he waved back, not entirely sure what he was waving at, but going along with it.

Hannah waited, her foot tapping on the wooden floor, as the girl began making the hot chocolates. The machine whirred into life, drowning out some of the background conversation from other customers, the tinkling of cups and the barks of laughter; there was always one customer who spoke way, *way* too loudly. Always.

As soon as the machine stopped, the barista pulled out the mugs and sprayed on the cream, adding a flake and coloured sprinkles. And then Hannah was picking them up from the counter and making her way back.

'How great do these look?' Hannah said, walking so slowly and carefully that Ed jumped up to grab one of them from her. 'Thanks – I'm so clumsy and my co-ordination is so terrible that I never would have got both of them back in one piece.'

They got comfy at their little table, laughing and joking, but also enjoying a companionable silence at times. Ed didn't know why he was so surprised at how easy it was between them; it always had been, after they'd got over their initial problems. The main initial problem being his annoying habit of talking too much.

'So . . . is this a date?' Hannah asked over her mug of hot chocolate.

'You're the one who invited me,' Ed pointed out.

'Oh yes, I suppose I did. Well, then. Maybe it is.'

Ed couldn't stop himself from grinning. 'Really?'

'Really,' she said. Now, she was grinning. 'I've been thinking – *very* carefully! – and maybe we should give this' – she pointed between them – 'a go. I mean, if you still want to, that is. Spending time with you and your friends the other day made me realise that I couldn't imagine you not being a huge part of my life. I love what we have between us.'

'Serious?'

'Serious!' She looked into his face and must have found what she saw amusing because she began to laugh. 'I'm serious! I swear. I'd like it a lot.'

'Is this why you lured me here?' he teased. A joke to hide from the immense happiness he suddenly felt. *Pinch me – this can't actually be happening!*

'Oh, totally. I pretended it was all about the hot chocolate but really it was to offer you a proposal.' She blushed and waved her hands in the air. 'No, not like that!'

'Just so you know,' Ed said, 'when you actually propose, guinea pigs must be involved. It's got to be very outlandish.'

He noticed a dart of fear or overwhelm cross her face.

'We'll take things slow,' he said earnestly, 'one step at a time. Whatever you're most comfortable with. If you're happy, I'm happy. And no more talk of proposals.'

'As long as you don't abandon me anywhere again,' she warned. 'Or that'll be it.'

'I swear,' he said, putting a hand to his heart. 'I *swear*, Hannah, it was a one-off.'

'I believe you,' she said, and he hoped she knew he meant it. He wouldn't make a mistake like that again. There would be challenges, he was sure, mainly because of his inability to think before he acted, but he'd do his absolute best to put her happiness first.

It couldn't get much better than this – Hannah, hot chocolate and perfect cake, in the comfort and warmth of Woolf and Wilde.

It's funny how things work out. They don't always, but on the whole they find a way in the end. You've just got to keep that spark of hope alive. And he couldn't have done it without his best friends by his side.

'Are you glad you started working here?' she asked, wiping the cream from her top lip with a shy smile.

He didn't need to think carefully about his answer. 'Without a doubt,' he said. 'It's life-changing; it's tested me, it's pushed me to my limits at points, but I've learnt so much. I feel as if I could do this for ever. In between acting at the Globe, obviously.'

'Obviously.'

'What about you?'

'Am I glad I started working here?'

'Are you glad *I* started working here?'

She rolled her eyes at him. 'I was until you started digging for compliments! Things were far more uneventful before you arrived. I actually got some peace, for once!'

'Bookselling's pretty awesome, isn't it?' Ed said. 'Working in a bookshop like this – it's tough and it's easy to romanticise it, but we are lucky to get to work here.' He certainly felt very lucky. 'We get to put books into the hands of budding readers; we can really influence how people feel about what they're reading. Bookshops like this one make readers. I can't think of anything more awesome.'

'Guinea pigs,' Hannah pointed out, quite literally with her cake fork. 'Guinea pigs are also awesome. Just in a different way.'

'Too right!'

They finished off their cakes and drained the last of their hot chocolates, and then it was time to make a move. They could have stayed there all day, but Ed thought the cafe might get upset with him if he drank them out of the rest of their hot chocolate.

They tried to sneak through the bookshop quickly, but it was as if Dinah had been lying in wait for them. 'Oh, there you two are! I was wondering where you'd got to. Comparing notes about the latest shelving techniques, were you?'

'Of course,' Ed said. 'We're very devoted to our jobs, as you know, Dinah.'

'I'll believe you,' she said with a cheeky smile. Ed was grateful she didn't add anything else, except, 'Have a nice time, won't you?' as they left with the tinkle of the shop bell and a wave.

'She's totally on to us,' Hannah said, slightly breathless.

'Oh, totally,' Ed agreed. 'Want to go somewhere else? I don't really feel like bringing the afternoon to a close just yet.'

Hannah linked her arm in his and he smiled down at her. 'Let's do this.'

Thank you, universe. THANK YOU.

It was in that moment that he felt the page turn and a new chapter in the story of his life begin. Ed knew that the best was yet to come.

Epilogue

The Paper & Hearts Society

Summer

Tabitha Brown smoothed over her blue and white striped dress one final time as she looked in the mirror. She took a deep breath in, but she wasn't nervous today, not like she had been for her first Paper & Hearts Society meeting. Then, all had been stress and worry and insecurity; now, all was happiness and promise and joy.

A lot can happen in a year, she thought. *Moving to a new town, making new friends, being in a relationship for the first time, dealing with my anxiety and finally finding out what contentment feels like. Who would have thought I'd end up here?*

It was the one year anniversary of The Paper & Hearts Society – the day they'd all met for their first meeting – and they'd agreed to do something special. All chipping in to do their bit, they'd organised a trip to the Dorset coast, where they were going to spend all day on the beach, and then camp out tonight.

I really hope Ed remembers the tent pegs. She did not want to be blown off a cliff in the middle of the night; she wouldn't put it past him to forget something so important.

She'd packed her bag full of home comforts and sweet treats to share with the others. All she had to do now was collect the picnic that Gran had made up in the kitchen – sandwiches and little cakes and homemade sausage rolls and containers of fruit.

'I want to do something for your anniversary,' she'd said, even though Tabby had insisted she didn't need to go to any effort. 'It makes me happy to see you so happy.'

Tabby put the last few bits into her backpack and made her way into the kitchen, where Gran was closing the lid of a wicker picnic basket. She'd folded a red and white checked blanket on top, and tied a ribbon around the handle to make it extra special.

'Are you sure you'll be okay on your own tonight?' Tabby said. She hated leaving Gran on her own, but she also knew that she liked time to herself. 'Because I can . . .'

'Why, are you going to take me with you?' Gran interrupted. 'Oh, I'd love to camp out under the stars, just like in my youth! I did get up to some mischief.'

'I bet you did! It's obviously where I get my rebellious streak from.'

Gran laughed. 'You aren't a patch on me, my dear. My

poor parents were always worried sick about me. I was certainly no angel!'

There was a honking noise outside, and Tabby looked out of the window to see Ed's big red campervan out there, parked up on the pavement.

I didn't realise time was so tight!

While she was looking forward to heading to the coast today, she wasn't feeling too enthusiastic about the trip in the van, which somehow had got even messier and dirtier since they'd gone on their road trip last year. Tabby had to ignore her fears that she'd be bitten by fleas or catch a horrifying disease.

Gran lifted the picnic basket down and Tabby looped it into the crook of her arm. She couldn't wait to unload all of it; with her backpack and the basket, she felt completely weighed down.

They'd better eat all of this food because I am not bringing it back with me. Not that that would likely be a problem! Food didn't last very long with five teenagers around.

'Have a nice time, then,' Gran said, leading the way to the front door. 'Send a big hug to the others!'

'Will do!' Tabby kissed her papery thin cheek. 'Love you, Gran.'

'Love you too, Tabby dear. Now off with you! Don't keep my friend Edward waiting too long.'

As she headed out and down the garden path, she

turned back to wave and blow Gran a last kiss. She blew one right back, and stood in the open doorway, waving to The Paper & Hearts Society in the van.

It was the best decision I ever made to stay living with Gran rather than move in with my parents, she thought. *I love them too, but getting to spend as much time with Gran as possible is more important right now.*

Ed jumped out and gallantly opened the door for Tabby, with a bow and a flourish.

'I didn't realise I was last!' she said, climbing up into the back. She wrinkled her nose as the stale smell hit her – did Ed ever clean this thing? – but ignored it in favour of saying hello to Henry and Olivia, who were already in the back. Cassie was in the passenger seat today, her feet pressed up against the glove compartment, her knees pressed into her body.

'Are we all ready, kids?' Ed said, getting back in and starting the engine.

'Let's do this!' Olivia replied. 'I cannot *wait* to see the sea! Considering we live in a county with its own coastline, I really feel as if we should visit it more. Don't you?'

As they began to move, Ed honked the horn and Tabby saw Gran wave one final time before going back into the bungalow. She hoped she wouldn't find out when she got back that Gran had been entertaining Mr Helstone from over the road again; they were inseparable these days and Gran really did need to rest.

'I'd love to live by the sea one day,' Cassie said. 'Imagine always waking up to the sound of the ocean.'

'Imagine all the ice cream you could eat,' Ed said, concentrating on getting out of the housing estate and on to the main road. 'There's always lots of ice cream for sale near the beach. That would be the life!'

He reached out and switched on the van's music system, shouting, 'I hope you're ready for some awesome tunes, my friends!'

They waited in anticipation as the player woke itself up. Tabby dreaded to think what he'd decided on this time; they were used to a strange combination of songs, but lately Ed was really outdoing himself.

'Really?' Henry chuckled as the first beats began to play. And then Tabby got what he was laughing at – a childish voice began to sing 'The Wheels on the Bus'. Trust Ed to choose nursery rhymes! This was his idea of a hilarious joke, and Tabby loved him for it.

'All sing along now! I want to hear your voices loud and clear!' he said, grinning like a fool.

Cassie groaned, clawing her hands in her hair and turning around to stare at the others in despair. 'Ugh, somebody save me please from this horror.'

Olivia winked across at her. 'Don't tell me you don't

love it really. And just think: we've still got at least forty-five minutes to go! You heard Ed – voices loud and clear, everyone!'

Even though he wasn't always quick to show it, Henry was more than happy to be by the sea. Despite the fact they were in a warm spell at the height of summer, the salty breeze offered enough of a respite that it made everything seem pleasant. Henry watched through his sunglasses, a lazy grin on his lips, as his friends lounged around on the pebble beach, soaking up the sun's rays.

Once they'd arrived, got parked and scouted out their camping location, it hadn't taken them long to walk the winding road down to the ocean, past shops and houses that perched high up on the clifftops, children clattering their buckets and spades and fellow tourists wafting the smell of fresh fish and chips. The horseshoe-shaped beach was busy, but they didn't mind; they were just glad to be here, all together, with the aim of having the best anniversary week possible.

The Paper & Hearts Society had well and truly changed Henry's life. He'd been friends with them all before, of course, minus Tabby, but he loved how it had brought them closer together in unexpected ways: it had given them excuses to meet up and made them do things they never would have done before, when they would have just sat around doing not a lot at all. They had a purpose now, a shared goal and passion, and he would for ever be grateful to Olivia for suggesting a book club in the first place.

Tabby had called Henry mysterious when they'd first met, and he'd often questioned what role he played in the group, but he was beginning to realise that he was the glue that kept them all together, and that stuck them back again when they clashed or fought or got upset.

That was the thing about The Paper & Hearts Society: if you removed just one of them, it didn't quite work the same. They were a unit, a group, inseparable. The best of friends, through thick and through thin.

'Can we go rock-pooling now?' Ed asked, sitting up on his elbow. '*Please?*'

He's only asking that because we promised him he could have ice cream afterwards, Cassie thought. But she was also partial to a good ice cream so she couldn't exactly blame him, although she hoped he wouldn't get too wet or make mischief. The last thing they needed was a trip to A & E because Ed had broken his ankle in a rock pool.

'Ooh, yes!' Olivia said. She shot up and grabbed a small pink net that lay at her side, close to the bucket and spade she'd also insisted on bringing. 'Let's see what we can find!'

That means I'm in, too, then. Cassie loved seeing Olivia's enthusiasm; it was infectious. She'd always loved it – in the moments when she felt negative about everything or unsure of herself or the world, Olivia was guaranteed to pull her back around and show her just how wonderful life could be.

'Come on, then,' Cassie said, stretching out before standing up. 'But if you annoy me, Ed, I won't hesitate to push you in. Be warned.'

'I'm so scared!' Ed teased, rolling his eyes.

Cassie and Olivia let Ed run off ahead, picking his way over the pebbles to the far side of the beach, where he'd already scouted out the best rock pools.

'I don't know where he gets all that energy from,' Cassie said. Olivia's hand brushed against hers and she picked it up, squeezing it tightly. 'I swear, he just gets worse and worse.'

'He's not hurting anyone,' Olivia said.

'Yet.'

Maybe that's my problem, Cassie thought. *I worry too much. About all of them.*

'Can you believe you once told me that The Paper & Hearts Society would never work and that I would just end up disappointed?' Olivia said.

Cassie rolled her eyes with as much force as she could muster. 'You'll never let me live that down, will you?'

'Nope, not for as long as we live. You were most *certainly* wrong about that one. Imagine if I'd listened to you and cancelled the entire thing. We wouldn't be doing this now! We'd all be sat at home, miserable, pining away for something we never knew existed. Imagine!'

Cassie really would never live it down. She'd been so adamant that she didn't want to be part of Olivia's new book club, thinking it was a dreadful idea that would just end in failure and Olivia would only get upset.

That'll teach me. I need to remember that Olivia is mostly always right.

Olivia knew, of course, that she was always right and was delighted that she had a good excuse to remind Cassie about it. She looked over at her girlfriend and smiled. Cassie looked so relaxed these days; the last few months had been so positive with her mum, who had turned a really big corner. She didn't seem constantly worried any more. She could go out without rushing back – was looking forward to the future for once. And Olivia was looking forward to the future with her.

'Come on, slow coaches!' Ed called out. 'Stop ambling and get a move on! The tide might come in!'

'The tide is out, Ed. You've got hours yet before it comes in.'

'It might change its mind today,' he said, as if it were the most obvious idea in the world.

They had the rock pools to themselves. They kicked off their shoes to get a better grip and trod carefully on the slippery surfaces of the rocks, mindful of seaweed and hidden hazards.

'Look at the limpets,' Olivia said, the shells clinging to the wet stone, stuck as solid as cement. Cassie took out her phone from her back pocket and started snapping pictures. Olivia couldn't wait to watch her draw her finds in her sketchbook later, curled up in the tent.

'Ooh, take a picture of me!' Ed said, throwing his arms out wide. 'I said I'd send as many as I could to Hannah.'

'Ew, don't make me sick,' Cassie said.

He pulled a face. 'I've spent enough time around you and Olivia making kissing faces at each other! Now it's time for me to get my own back!'

'Yes, we know all about your kissing faces,' Olivia giggled. 'We bumped into you the other day, didn't we?'

Ed blushed but threw his arms back out. 'Just take the picture already!'

Pictures taken – with Ed reciprocating by taking his own of Olivia and Cassie – they set to work to look for tiny fish and other sea creatures in the pools. Olivia tried to tone down her competitive nature – she was here to enjoy herself more than anything – but she did enjoy teasing Ed about finding more than he had.

'We'll be here for ever now,' Cassie said, 'because he'll be trying to outdo you.'

'Oops!'

'I think I might do a page in my sketchbook all about different types of shells,' Cassie said. 'The different patterns and textures and colours. I could look at them all day.'

'I found a crab!' Ed called, looking immensely pleased with himself, as if he'd never before achieved anything so amazing. 'I really found one! Look at it! I'm going to call it Kylie – no, Carlos!'

Olivia giggled. 'Very nice!'

'Do you think I could take it home with me? It would make an awesome pet!'

'Not likely,' Cassie said. 'Where are you going to get seawater from? It will die.'

'I can pour salt into water from the tap. Sorted. See, I can be practical when I need to be.'

'That's very shell-fish of you,' Olivia joked.

'OUCH! It pinched me!' Ed dropped it back into the water with a splash, shaking his injured finger.

'Serves you right,' Cassie said. 'Carlos didn't want to be messed with. Imagine if you picked me up like that. I'd pinch you, too.'

Ed grinned. 'I'd like to see you try!'

'We'd better get back to the others,' Tabby said. 'They'll be wondering where we are.'

But she didn't want to leave Henry's side, where she was curled up while both of them watched the sun set over the sea. The sky was a brilliant orange, with streaks of red, pink and purple, the horizon line looking as though it was on fire. With the absence of the sun, Tabby felt goose pimples begin to appear on her arms as the day succumbed to night.

'Just a few more minutes won't hurt,' Henry said quietly.

She twisted her head so she could look up into his face, and found a picture of calm looking back at her. 'It's one year since we met,' Tabby said. 'I keep having to remind myself that I'm awake and not dreaming that all of this happened.'

'It's real all right,' Henry said. 'But I get it; I do the same, too. I always try to remind myself of how lucky I am – to have friends as special as this, to have *you*. Maybe I should have got the crab that pinched Ed to pinch me, just in case.'

'He did seem very upset about Carlos's betrayal.' Ed had been quick to run back and tell them all about it, before returning to the rock pools to see if he could find another, friendlier, crab. He hadn't succeeded.

'When I think about how sad and anxious I felt this time last year,' Tabby said, 'when The Paper & Hearts Society began, I can't believe how happy I feel now. It doesn't feel possible. I had no friends and I felt so helpless, it felt as if somebody had taken the colour out of the world. And now I'm surrounded by so much love. More love than a person could ever need. I don't feel deserving enough.'

'We all deserve love, Tabby,' he said. 'All of us. And you give so much love back; nobody could accuse you of not caring.'

'True,' she said. 'It just reminds you, doesn't it, on a day like today? My whole life has flipped upside down in the space of twelve months.'

She got up and Henry followed, but before she could make a move to head back to the campsite, he wrapped his arms around her shoulders and planted a kiss on her forehead.

'What's that for?' she said, catching him before he pulled away and reciprocating, but on his lips.

'For the past year,' he said. 'For everything, Tabby. For love.'

They held hands tightly as they took their time walking back, laughing and chatting and joking about – being whole-heartedly themselves, without a worry as to what anyone else would think.

'Oi, you two!' Ed called out as they approached the red van. 'We were just about to send out a search party!'

'Ha ha,' Tabby said. 'We weren't gone that long.'

'Well, you didn't clean up after dinner,' Ed said, 'and I'd just like to point out that you two aren't pulling your weight around here. We need to know we can rely on you, just in case we're ever in a life or death situation.'

'I'll remind you of that,' Cassie said. She, Olivia and Ed were sitting around a smoking camping stove, with two empty seats waiting for Henry and Tabby, which they took.

'Now you're back, it's time for the meeting!' Olivia said, clapping her hands together. She had The Paper & Hearts Society scrapbook on her lap, open to the very first page where they'd documented their very first meeting. The book looked far fuller than it had done back then.

One year of adventures, Tabby proudly thought.

'Thanks for coming, everyone!' Olivia began. 'A year ago today, The Paper & Hearts Society met as a book club for the first time. Even though some of us – yes, Cassie, I'm looking at you – doomed us to failure, we proved them – ahem, Cassie – wrong. We succeeded! We've had dance parties, movie marathons, travelled the country; we've had our very own Book Olympics and Ed even turned into a ghost and we solved his murder. What a year it's been!'

From underneath the scrapbook, Olivia pulled out five thin bars of milk chocolate and threw one to each member. 'A toast, please!' she said, unwrapping hers and holding it up to the sky. 'To The Paper & Hearts Society!'

'To The Paper & Hearts Society!' they all echoed.

'Wow, I'm beginning to feel quite emotional,' she said, fanning her face. 'I hoped we would get this far, but there were points when I wasn't quite sure. You're all pretty impossible to work with, you know, but I still love you. So thank you for making my dreams come true. I always wanted to be a part of my own exciting book club.'

With that, she stuffed the chocolate bar into her mouth. Tabby could tell Olivia was forcing herself to chew to distract from the tears that had entered her eyes.

Time to take over.

'I hope you don't mind,' Tabby said, pulling her notebook out of her bag and standing up, 'but I prepared a little speech to read to all of you.'

'Nerd,' Ed joked.

'We're all nerds, Ed,' Henry was quick to acknowledge. 'That's why we're here, isn't it?'

'True, very true, Henry. Good point, well made. Carry on, Tabby cat.'

Tabby found the right page and cleared her throat. She'd spent the past few days perfecting what she wanted to say, and she just hoped she could pull it off. Nobody else had known until now that she was going to do this; she'd wanted to surprise them.

'And no interruptions, please, Ed,' she insisted. And with a deep breath, she began.

'One day, just over a year ago, I found a poster. I was in the library, looking for a copy of my favourite book, and I had no idea then how that one moment – finding that poster – would change my life. I took a chance that day, when I messaged Olivia to ask her if I could come along to the first meeting. I was so nervous I thought I might be sick and I had no idea if I'd be accepted; I was scared to death that I wouldn't fit in. I was a very anxious person, then, and I didn't think it would ever go away. I thought I was stuck like that for ever. And then I turned up at the park and met Olivia, who was the most excitable, enthusiastic person I'd ever come across, and Henry, who made me feel instantly comfortable, and for the first time I had hope. And then I met Ed, and that all disappeared . . .'

'Hey!'

'I said no interruptions!' Tabby laughed. 'And I want to say something nice, Cassie, but we both know that things weren't fantastic between us at first. No hard feelings, though. I could see how much you cared about your friends, and I hope now you're just as protective of me as you were with them back then.'

'Of course,' Cassie said with a smile.

'I wouldn't be who I am now without The Paper & Hearts Society: confident, happy, free. I could go on and on and recount every moment from every meeting that has made me laugh and smile, but we'd be here until the second anniversary and Ed wouldn't be able to last that long without doughnuts. I just want to say thank you; thank you for accepting me for who I am, for allowing me to come on this bookish journey with you, for being there for me through thick and thin. You've changed my life and I love you all.'

She reached up to her face and found it was wet with tears. Tears of happiness. And when she looked around, everyone else was the same.

'Oh, Tabby!' Olivia said, jumping up and squeezing her into a hug. 'That was so beautiful! We love you, too!'

'You're not having a hug without me!' Ed said, joining the squash and pulling Cassie and Henry in with him. 'I didn't know it was possible to feel this much love!'

'What's been your favourite bit?' Henry asked, once they were all back in their seats. He stoked the campfire so it spat out warmth and smoke once again.

'Impossible!' Ed said. 'How could we choose just one moment?'

'We have achieved quite a lot,' Olivia said. 'Just think about it: we travelled around the country visiting literary locations, brought about change with the Read with Pride campaign, and Ed is inspiring the next generation of readers at Woolf and Wilde. Not bad for a year.'

'Do you think we'll still be having Paper & Hearts Society meetings when we're eighty?' Tabby asked, staring across at the horizon line, far out to sea.

'Oh, undoubtedly,' Ed said, not able to bear the thought of this one day ending. 'There are enough books to read and base meetings on, aren't there?'

'I'm not stopping anytime soon,' Olivia said. 'There's still so much more to be done! I won't rest until we inspire bookworms all over the world.'

She had to rein in the ideas for world domination that quickly entered her head; she'd learnt at the end of last year that they weren't always a good thing.

'Maybe,' Henry said, 'one of us will write a book about The Paper & Hearts Society one day.'

Cassie scoffed. 'No way. Our lives are way too boring for that. Nobody would read it!'

'Excuse me,' Ed said, 'but I am *extremely* entertaining. I think I'd be everyone's favourite character. In fact, I think the book should be called *Ed and Mrs Simpkins Take on the World*. Instant bestseller.'

'That was a stupid question, wasn't it?' Tabby said. 'I didn't really need to ask it because I already know the answer: The Paper & Hearts Society is for ever. It will always be with us, even when we're not together. For ever and always.'

And they all lived bookishly ever after.

THE END

Dear Reader . . .

I was sixteen and in the middle of my GCSE exams when I wrote the first words of the book that would become The Paper & Hearts Society. I felt all alone in the world back then – I've always joked that the reason I started writing the series in the first place was because I needed some friends – and fictional friends seemed far less complicated than real life ones. I dreamed of one day becoming an author, but that felt far off, something I might do when I was older, not while I was still at school.

But those first words multiplied, and I kept writing as if my life depended on it, determined that I'd one day have a finished story. Eventually, I did. It wasn't always easy and there were times when I doubted myself beyond belief, but now I'm able to hold in my hands three books I've written, knowing other people are reading and finding solace in them – and there's no other feeling like it.

If you're a young person reading this who one day dreams of becoming an author, my advice to you is this:

don't ever think you're not good enough, or too young, or that people like you don't become authors. Write about what you're most passionate about. Keep going, even when it feels tough. You can do this. The world deserves to hear your stories.

While my original purpose was to write myself some friends, what I hadn't counted on was the non-fictional people The Paper & Hearts Society would bring into my life. My biggest thanks have to go to my agent, Lauren Gardner, for being the brightest star in the publishing industry; my editor, Polly Lyall Grant, to whom this book is dedicated, for loving The Paper & Hearts Society just as much (maybe even more!) than I do; and to the rest of the teams at Bell Lomax Moreton and Hachette Children's Group.

By the time *Bookishly Ever After* is published, I will have been living with The Paper & Hearts Society for five years. I'm a very different person to the one I was when I first came up with Tabby, Olivia, Cassie, Henry and Ed – but just as I've grown, they've grown with me.

I hope you've enjoyed your time with The Paper & Hearts Society as much as I have. While I feel sad to leave my favourite book club behind, what they've taught me will stay with me for ever: the true meaning of friendship, on and off the page; the importance of fighting for what you believe in; and just how special it is to see yourself reflected in stories. And, of course, the pleasure you can get from a good doughnut or an ice cream sundae. Those scenes were always my favourite to write.

Thank you, reader, for supporting a young author on her journey to finding herself – one sentence at a time. This has been one of the most rewarding, surreal experiences of my life so far, and I wouldn't change it for the world.

Don't forget to live your best bookish life!

Lucy Powrie

LUCY P⏚WRIE

Lucy Powrie is an award-winning author,
blogger and BookTuber from the UK, and started
writing the first book in *The Paper & Hearts Society*
series while she was still at school.
To date, her YouTube channel has attracted over
40,000 subscribers and close to two million views.
When she's not reading, Lucy enjoys cuddling her
herd of guinea pigs and her three dogs,
but let's be real: she's almost always reading.

YOU CAN FIND LUCY AT:

▶ LUCYTHEREADER   🐦 @LUCYTHEREADER   📷 @LUCYTHEREADER
LUCYTHEREADER.COM